THE
PASSENGERS

THE
PASSENGERS

JOHN MARRS

BERKLEY

NEW YORK

BERKLEY
An imprint of Penguin Random House LLC
1745 Broadway, New York, NY 10019

Copyright © 2019 by John Marrs
Penguin Random House supports copyright. Copyright fuels creativity, encourages
diverse voices, promotes free speech, and creates a vibrant culture. Thank you for buying
an authorized edition of this book and for complying with copyright laws by not reproducing, scanning,
or distributing any part of it in any form without permission. You are supporting writers and
allowing Penguin Random House to continue to publish books for every reader.

First published in Great Britain in 2019 by Ebury Press,
an imprint of Penguin Random House UK.

BERKLEY and the BERKLEY & B colophon are registered trademarks of
Penguin Random House LLC.

Library of Congress Cataloging-in-Publication Data

Names: Marrs, John (Freelance journalist), author.
Title: The passengers / John Marrs.
Description: New York: Berkley, 2019.
Identifiers: LCCN 2019013185 | ISBN 9781984806970 (hardback) |
ISBN 9781984806987 (ebook)
Subjects: | BISAC: FICTION / Technological. | FICTION / Suspense. |
FICTION / Science Fiction / Adventure. | GSAFD: Suspense fiction.
Classification: LCC PR6113.A768 P37 2019 | DDC 823/.92—dc23
LC record available at https://lccn.loc.gov/2019013185

First Ebury Press (UK) edition: April 2019
First Berkley edition: August 2019

Printed in the United States of America
1   3   5   7   9   10   8   6   4   2

Cover design by Richard Ljoenes
Cover photo of blurred car by Pozdeyev Vitaly / Shutterstock
Interior graphics by Laura K. Corless
Book design by Elke Sigal

For Bridget Driscoll, 1851–1896

THE
PASSENGERS

||| UK NEWS

UK
NEWS

House of Lords votes unanimously in favour of driverless vehicles on British roads within five years. Ban on non-autonomous vehicles expected within a decade.

PART ONE

1. Programme car for Ben's office.
2. Use Uber app for car under "guest" account. Don't use real name.
3. Get picked up from Ben's car park, go to work.
4. Start texting Ben midmorning.
5. Call his boss around midday.

CLAIRE ARDEN

By the time the front door closed, the car was parked outside Claire Arden's home, waiting for her.

She lingered inside the porch, re-reading the notes she had made on her phone until she heard the faint beep-beep-beep of the alarm as the house secured itself. She gave a furtive glance across the suburban estate, one of many just like it in Peterborough. Sundraj from number twenty-seven was the only other neighbour outside, guiding his noisy young family of four into a people carrier like a farmer trying to herd sheep from one field to another. When he spotted her, he gave her a half-smile and an equally half-hearted wave. She reciprocated with the same.

Claire recalled the fifteenth anniversary party Sundraj and his wife, Siobhan, had thrown last spring. They'd celebrated with a barbecue and most of the street in attendance. He found time to drunkenly corner Claire in the downstairs bathroom and suggested that if she and her husband, Ben, were ever inclined to invite a third person into their bedroom, he was open to offers. Claire politely declined and he panicked, begging her not to tell Siobhan. She promised she wouldn't, and she meant it. She hadn't even told Ben. Claire

5

wagered every person in that street had at least one secret they kept hidden from the rest of the world, including her. *Especially* her.

As Sundraj's vehicle eased out of the cul-de-sac, Claire took a handful of deep, calming breaths and stared uneasily at her own car. It had been three weeks since Ben had signed the lease, and she was still struggling to acclimatise herself to its many new functions. The biggest contrast between it and their last vehicle was that this one no longer contained a steering wheel, pedals, or a manual override option. It was completely driverless and it scared her.

They had watched in fascination at the car's arrival as it delivered itself to their home and parked on the driveway. Sensing both Claire's unease and her reluctance, Ben assured her that anyone could operate it, even her, and that it was "idiot proof." As they personalised their settings from an app, she responded with narrowed eyes and a jab to his arm. He protested, claiming he hadn't meant she was the idiot in question.

"I don't like not being in control," she'd told him on their maiden voyage to the doctor's office. She gripped the seat when the car indicated and overtook another one of its own accord.

"That's because you're a control freak," he'd replied. "You need to learn to start putting your trust in things you're not in charge of. Besides, the insurance is next to nothing and we need to start saving some money, don't we?"

Claire gave a reluctant nod. As a man who thrived in the detail, Ben had spent considerable time and effort researching the right vehicle to suit their changing circumstances. And after a hellish few months, she was glad to see him returning to his old self. He had attempted to involve her in the process by suggesting she pick the paintwork colour and seating fabric. But she'd dismissed him as a misogynist for suggesting that buying a car was "man's work" and that the aesthetics were all she was capable of understanding. In the last few days, Claire found herself snapping at him frequently. It was never his fault and she'd immediately regretted it. But it hadn't prevented her from repeating it, and she feared her quiet resentment towards him was rising ever closer to the surface.

The rear of the car momentarily held Claire's gaze before a dull kick to her kidney snapped her from her thoughts. "Good morning," she whispered, and rubbed her swollen, rounded abdomen. It was the first time baby Tate had made his presence felt that morning. They had given him the nickname after the midwife informed them he weighed about a pound, the same size as a Tate & Lyle bag of sugar. However, what started as a joke had stuck, and they were giving it serious consideration.

Provided all went according to plan, in two months' time, Claire would be a first-time mother. Dr. Barraclough had warned her that with her high blood pressure, it was essential she kept life stress-free. It was easier said than done. And in the last few hours, it had become impossible.

"You can do this," she said aloud, and opened the car door. Claire placed her handbag on the front right-hand seat and lowered herself into the vehicle, bum first. Her expectant belly had begun to protrude much earlier than her friends' when they were pregnant, and sometimes it felt as if she were carrying a baby elephant. Her body was constantly contradicting itself—some parts sagged while others looked fit to burst.

She pressed a button to close the car door and faced the retinal scan. Taking a quick glance at her appearance, Claire noted her blue eyes were surrounded by a pinkish-white hue and the dark circles around them were still visible under her foundation. She'd not straightened her blond fringe that morning, so it hung loosely, resting on her eyebrows.

Once the scan confirmed Claire was a registered Passenger, the electric motor silently came to life and the dashboard's centre console and operating system illuminated in whites and blues. "Ben's work," she spoke, and a three-dimensional map appeared on the screen from her home to his office several miles outside of town.

As the car began to move, she jumped when a playlist of 1990s rock anthems blared from the speakers without warning. She hated Ben's appalling taste in music and the volume at which he played it. But she had yet to figure out how to turn off his streaming system and create playlists of her own. Then, as the opening bars began of an old Arctic Monkeys song Ben favoured, she failed to choke back her tears. He knew every word of it off by heart.

"Why did you do this to us?" she wept. "Why now?"

Claire wiped her eyes and cheeks with her palms, turned the music off, and remained in an apprehensive silence as the car continued its journey. She ran through the to-do list again; there was so much she needed to complete by the afternoon for this to work. She kept reminding herself that everything she was doing was for the right reasons; it was all for Tate. And as much as she longed to meet him, a tiny part of her wanted him to remain safe inside her forever, where she could continue to protect him from the cruelty of the world.

She glanced out from the windscreen just as the vehicle turned an unexpected right instead of left, the opposite direction to Ben's office on the outskirts of Peterborough. Claire squinted at the route map on the navigation system, sure that she had programmed it correctly. Then she remembered Ben telling her that sometimes, driverless cars take alternative routes if they learn of delays ahead. She hoped it wouldn't add much more time to the journey. The sooner she could get out of that car, the better.

Suddenly the console went blank. Claire hesitated, then poked at it, searching for a way to reboot it. It made no difference.

"Damn it," she muttered. Of all the days, this was not the one to be inside a faulty vehicle. The car chose another route, this time travelling along an on-ramp and onto a dual carriageway that she knew would take her even farther from her destination.

She began to feel uneasy. "What's going on?" she asked, and cursed Ben's decision to talk her into a car with no manual override. She poked more buttons in the hope something might happen to allow her to regain control and order the car to pull over.

"Alternative destination being programmed," came a softly spoken female voice that Claire recognised as the vehicle's operating system. "Route being recalculated. Two hours and thirty minutes until chosen destination reached."

"What?" Claire responded. "No! Where are we going?"

As the car pulled up at traffic lights, she spotted her chance to leave. Quickly, she unclipped her seat belt and hit the door release button. Once outside, she would compose herself and rethink her plan. She knew that whatever alternative she came up with, she could not leave the car unattended, not under any circumstances. However, the door held firm. Over and over again she pushed it, harder and harder, but it wouldn't budge. Her baby kicked again.

"It'll be okay, it'll be okay," she repeated, trying to convince them both she could find a way out.

Claire's head turned towards the car next to hers at the traffic lights, and she waved her hands to catch the driver's attention. But he was too distracted by a film playing on his smart windscreen. Her wave became more and more frantic until finally, she caught his eye. He turned his head towards her, but within the speed of a heartbeat, her windows switched from transparent to opaque. The privacy control had been set remotely so that no one could witness her desperation.

Terror overtook her when she finally realised what was happening— someone else was controlling her car.

"Good morning, Claire," a male voice began through the speakers.

She let out an involuntary scream. The voice was calm and relaxed, friendly almost, but most definitely unwelcome. "It may have come to your attention that your vehicle is no longer under your management," it continued. "From here on in, I am in charge of your destination."

"Who are you?" Claire asked. "What do you want?"

"Neither of those things matter right now," the voice replied. "The only thing you need to know at this point is that two hours and thirty minutes from now, it is highly likely that you will be dead."

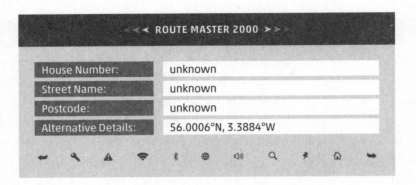

CHAPTER 2

JUDE HARRISON

Jude Harrison's eyes were fixed on the charger leading from the wall and plugged into the grille of his car.

He couldn't be sure for how long he had been sitting in the vehicle, staring at the charging point, or why it had captured his attention. Realising he'd lost all track of time, he checked the clock on his dashboard. To remain on schedule, he would need to start moving soon. His eyes flicked towards the battery cell light—ten minutes remained before it reached its capacity. The distance he was to travel wouldn't require a complete charge, but anything less than at least three-quarters full made him jittery.

Most other vehicles in the supermarket car park charged in smarter ways than his. They topped up using on-the-go overchargers embedded in the asphalt of traffic lights, roundabouts, parking spaces, or even drive-thru fast-food outlets. Jude had purchased his driverless car at the beginning of the government's much hyped "road revolution." Overnight, he went from a driver to a Passenger—someone whose vehicle contained no manual override. The car made all the decisions itself. Compared to many, his model was now outdated, and soon it would cease to automatically download the software that operated it, thus forcing him to upgrade. He'd been offered financial incentives to purchase a more advanced, high-tech model, but he refused. It was pointless spending money on something he would not need for much longer.

Jude's belly made a deep, guttural rumbling, reminding him it wanted to be fed. He knew that he must eat to keep his energy levels up and get him through the morning. But he had little appetite, not even for the chocolatey snacks he kept in the side pouches of the luggage on the seats behind him. Exiting the car, he made his way into the supermarket, but towards the bathroom, not the food aisles. There, he emptied his bowels in the toilet, washed his hands and face, and dried them under the wall-mounted machine. He removed from his pocket a disposable toothbrush containing paste that foamed up once it mixed with his saliva, and began to clean his teeth.

Harsh lighting above the mirror reflected from his scalp and emphasised how thin the hair was becoming around his temples. He'd recently begun keeping it cropped rather than trying to style and hide it. He remembered his father warning him and his brother that he had begun receding by his thirtieth birthday, and Jude was following suit. His friends took medication to keep their hair in place; Jude rejected it along with all other popular cosmetic alterations. He hadn't even fixed the two bottom teeth that leaned against each other, which meant he always smiled with closed lips.

It had been the best part of a week since he'd last run a razor across his face, and it made his olive complexion appear darker. Despite his fatigue, the whites of his eyes remained bright and made his green irises resemble the colour of ripe apples. He placed the palms of his hands on his T-shirt and traced the outline of his stomach and ribs with his fingers. He was aware of the weight he'd lost over the last month and blamed the pressure on all that needed to be organised for this day to be a success.

He looked to his wrist for the time, forgetting he had long discarded his watch. It had gathered details from his pulse and temperature to reveal his metabolism, blood pressure, and many other metrics he didn't care to be informed about. He didn't need to read the digits on a display to know his stress levels were soaring.

Jude returned to his car, and once satisfied the battery was now full, he unplugged the charger and took the first of a handful of deep breaths before climbing inside and informing the vehicle's voice-activated operating system of his next destination.

The car began cruising the suburban roads at no more than twenty-five miles an hour as Jude recalled how much he used to enjoy being in sole control of a vehicle. He passed his driving test on his seventeenth birthday, and at the time, it had felt like the greatest achievement in the world, giving him the freedom he craved. He could leave at will the confines of the village in which he was born and raised. He was no longer reliant on irregular bus timetables, or his parents or older brother, to give him glimpses of the outside world. It didn't sit comfortably with him that nowadays, children of fourteen were Passengers in fully autonomous vehicles. It was as if they were cheating.

Jude also remembered a time when roads like these were to be avoided at that time of the morning. They used to be gridlocked with rush hour, bumper-to-bumper traffic. Now, cars glided smoothly through the streets, conversing with one another through a network of internal communication systems to reduce bottlenecks and congestion. As much as he resented these cars, there were some benefits to having one.

Much of his dashboard was taken up by a soundbar and large interactive OLED screen in which he could control everything from his choice of television viewing to emails, social media, and reading material. He scrolled downwards until he located a blue folder labelled "Family Holidays." Inside, he checked a subfolder which read "Greece," and a selection of videos appeared. He opted for the one titled "Restaurant" and clicked play.

The super-high-definition picture was so crystal clear it was like he was there, relaxing on a restaurant terrace's lounger, lying by Stephenie's side and wrapped in a warm jumper as they enjoyed the setting sun over the vast vista. The camera panned slowly from left to right, zooming over the crescent bay and uninhabited islands ahead. The few clouds above them were illuminated with blues and oranges but cast the islands in shadows.

"Can you see the boat in the distance?" he heard her ask. "Over there, behind the island. The stern is just poking out."

"Ah yes, I see it now," Jude repeated aloud and over the recorded voice. He knew it off by heart and silently mouthed her reply too.

"One day we should book a trip on a round-the-world cruise ship," she said, "then we can spend our retirement seeing the sun set from every ocean and every continent. How does that sound?"

"Perfect," Jude replied. "Just perfect." It was only in recent years that he understood perfect was an impossible concept.

He closed the folder and used the screen to turn down the car's temperature. The spring morning was proving warmer than weather forecasters predicted. However, the display remained at a stubborn twenty-seven degrees.

"Car," he began, not having personalised his operating system by giving it a name like most owners. "Turn on the air con."

Nothing happened. The vehicle typically obeyed each task asked of it, and his was the only voice it was programmed to recognise. "Car," he repeated more firmly. "Acknowledge my request." Again there was nothing.

He cursed the software glitch and rolled up his shirtsleeves instead. Then, removing a wireless keyboard from the side pocket of the door, he logged on and began to compose an email. He chose to type it, preferring the old-fashioned means rather than dictating it or sending it via a videogram.

"Dear all," he began. "Apologies for the impersonal nature of this email but . . ."

"Good morning, Jude."

"Shit!" Jude blurted out loud, and dropped his keyboard into the footwell. He looked around his vehicle as if he were expecting to find a second Passenger hiding.

"How are you today?" the voice continued.

"Good . . . thanks," Jude replied. "Who is this and how did you get my number?" He examined the phone icon on the screen but it was switched off.

"I need you to listen carefully, Jude," the voice continued calmly. "In approximately two and half hours' time, you are going to die."

Jude blinked quickly. "What did you say?"

"The destination you programmed into your GPS is about to be replaced with an alternative location of my choosing."

His eyes darted towards his dashboard, where new coordinates appeared on-screen. "Seriously, what is going on?" asked Jude. "Who are you?"

"More details will follow soon, but for now, please sit back and make the most of this beautiful spring morning, as it will likely be your last."

Suddenly, the car's privacy windows switched from clear to opaque, meaning no one outside could see he was trapped inside.

||| ESSEX HERALD & POST ONLINE

One of Britain's best-loved actresses is set to visit young cancer patients at an Essex hospital today.

Sofia Bradbury, 78, will be visiting the recently opened wing of Princess Charlotte Hospital that she has helped to raise millions of pounds for during a three-year fundraising campaign.

SOFIA BRADBURY

Tell me where I'm supposed to be going because I can't bloody remember," Sofia Bradbury snapped.

"Again?" Rupert replied, exasperated.

Sofia was in no mood to be patronised. The painkillers and anti-inflammatory tablets she'd swallowed at breakfast along with a tumbler of brandy were doing little to ease the discomfort of the spinal osteoarthritis in her lower back. It also didn't help that her hearing aids were malfunctioning, making some words hard to hear.

"The hospital, remember?" he continued with a note of weariness. "Please assure me you're in the car now?"

"No, I'm in a bloody spaceship. Where do you think I am?"

"I'll send the address to your GPS."

"My what?"

"Oh Jesus. The map on your screen."

Sofia watched as coordinates appeared on the centre console and calculated the route her vehicle was to take from her home in Richmond,

London. The car's gull-wing doors automatically locked, and the vehicle began its journey, the only sound coming from the gravel of her lengthy driveway crunching under the thick tread of the tyres.

"And why am I going there again?" Sofia asked.

"I've already told her once this morning," she could just about hear Rupert saying. She assumed he was addressing the boy with the effeminate mannerisms interning in his office. Rupert went through assistants with alarming regularity, she thought, and they always shared a similar appearance—skinny T-shirts, skinny jeans, and skinny torsos.

"Rupert, you're my agent and my PR; if I ask you a question, I expect an answer."

"It's the meet and greet with the young cancer patients."

"Oh yes." A concern sprang to mind, causing her brow to furrow. However, her facial muscles were still too paralysed from last week's visit to the dermatologist to feel anything move above her mouth. "This is not going to be one of these events where nobody knows who the hell I am, is it?"

"No, of course it's not."

"Don't 'of course it's not' me like it's never happened before. Remember when I went to that school in Coventry and they were all too young to recognise me? It was humiliating. They thought I was Father Christmas's wife."

"No, as I explained to you earlier, this group are patients in their early teens, and I've been assured they are all huge fans of *Space & Time*."

"I finished filming that a decade ago," Sofia dismissed.

"No, it hasn't been that long, has it?"

"I may be seventy-eight, but I'm not bloody senile yet. I remember it as clear as day because it was the last time you got me an acting job on prime-time television. I'm hardly likely to forget it, am I?"

Despite reading the script a dozen times, even while filming, Sofia had no idea what the storyline was to the popular sci-fi show. All she grasped while acting against a green screen—and running away from an off-camera man with a tennis ball attached to a stick—was that an alien's head would be added to the shot in post-production. Not that Sofia had ever watched the finished version. She rarely viewed her own work, especially in her advancing years. She didn't take any satisfaction in seeing herself age.

Lately, her acting work had become sporadic and the parts offered, stale. Sofia had tried to remain relevant by waiving her fee for a handful of film student projects, and she'd toured the country in acclaimed regional productions of *Macbeth* and *The Tempest*. She had also been offered huge sums of money to join the casts of two long-running soap operas. But she didn't relish playing grandmothers clad in charity shop costumes and little make-up, and turned down both parts without hesitation.

Instead, she lifted her spirits by lifting her chin and her breasts with the help of a Harley Street surgeon's knife. Now, the wrinkles and creases on the backs of her hands were the only telltale signs of her true age.

"Oh, Oscar, what have you eaten?" she scolded the sleeping white Pomeranian lapdog lying by her side, and tried to waft away the toxic smell he omitted with her hands. He briefly opened one brown eye, shuffled his body further towards her thigh, then closed it again.

Sofia unhooked the clasp of her vintage Chanel handbag and removed a compact mirror. She applied another coat of her trademark crimson colour to her lips and watched, displeased, as it bled into vertical lines under her nose. She squinted at how pale her grey eyes had become, and made a mental note to ask Rupert's assistant to research medical procedures that might reduce their milky hue. With her veneers, enhanced cheekbones, hairpieces, and breast augmentations, she momentarily wondered if all that was left of the original Sofia Bradbury was her ambition.

"Do you have any new scripts for me to read?" she asked Rupert.

"A couple have appeared but I don't think they're right for you."

"Surely I should be the judge of that?"

"Well, one is playing an aging prostitute with terminal cancer in a long–running hospital drama, and the other is in a music video for a girl group. You would be . . . playing a ghost."

"Oh, for the love of God," Sofia sighed. "So they want me either on my deathbed with my legs apart or returning from beyond the grave. Sometimes I wonder what the bloody point of it all is."

"I'll send the treatments to the car now, and you can read them en route."

By the time Sofia had rolled her eyes, the characters' outlines were available to view on her windscreen, which at the flick of a switch became a panoramic monitor and television. She only needed to read the first couple of lines of each character description before dismissing them.

It wasn't a wage that she needed; it was recognition and appreciation. And annual appearances at sci-fi conventions or TV chat shows would not suffice. It riled her that the British Academy of Film and Television Arts had yet to offer her a lifetime membership despite her having first trod the boards at the age of seven.

Do they know? she asked herself suddenly. *Have there been rumours? Does BAFTA know what you've done so they're punishing you?* She hated that voice. It had haunted her for almost four decades. She shook it from her head as quickly as it had appeared.

Sofia sank her aching back into the seats and pressed a button to massage it with deep, penetrating vibrations. She poured herself another brandy from the refrigerated armrest. She decided the best thing about driverless cars was being able to drink and drive legally. She ran her manicured fingernails across the plush calfskin. Then she tapped the Macassar ebony panelling and dipped her bare feet into the thick vicuña-wool carpeting. By dispensing with her driver, she could afford a top-of-the-range Imperial GX70, the most expensive autonomous vehicle in production. She had no idea how a driverless car operated and she didn't care—as long as Rupert ensured she got from A to B remotely and on time, that was all that mattered.

"Rupert?" she asked tentatively. "Are you still there?"

"Of course. How can I help?"

"Will my . . . will . . . *Patrick* . . . be joining me today?"

"Yes, his account is still linked to your diary. He expressed an interest in attending, so I've a car booked to pick him up from the golf course. He'll meet you at the hospital."

Sofia let Rupert's response hang in the air, knowing the complications her husband's appearance might bring. "I'll speak to you later," she said quietly, not waiting for his reply before hanging up. Her nails were embedded in the palm of her hand before she realised she was close to drawing blood.

"Good morning, Sofia," a male voice she didn't recognise began.

She glared at the console, assuming she had touched something accidentally and answered a phone call. "Rupert? Why are you putting on a silly voice?"

"It's not Rupert," the voice replied. "And it might surprise you to learn that your vehicle is no longer under your control."

Sofia laughed. "It's never under my control, darling. That's why I have *people*. To make sure things are controlled for me."

"Alas, I am not one of your people. However, I am in charge of your destination."

"Good for you. Now can you stop playing silly beggars and put Rupert on, please."

"Rupert has nothing to do with this, Sofia. I have programmed your car to take you on an alternative route this morning. And in two hours and thirty minutes, it is likely that you will be dead."

Sofia sighed. "I've read the script, darling, I'm not playing a bloody dying whore on a Saturday-night hospital drama. I am Sofia Bradbury, and I think Sofia Bradbury is worth a little more than that."

"You will hear from me again soon."

The car fell silent again.

"Hello? Hello?"

Sofia glanced at the map on her windscreen, and it was only when she saw icons for the M25 and M1 that she realised she was leaving London and heading north, and not towards a hospital in Essex.

"Rupert?" she said. "Rupert? What in God's name is going on?"

Suddenly, Sofia narrowed her eyes and cocked her head to one side like a penny had dropped. A broad smile spread across her face. "Rupert, you sneaky little devil, you did it, didn't you? You got me on that programme."

She felt a twinge in her back when she moved to the edge of her seat. She winced as she looked around. "Where have they hidden the cameras, or are they just using the one in the dashboard?"

There were just three television reality shows that Sofia had ever considered participating in. However, Rupert's attempts to organise meetings with producers had been repeatedly rebuffed. Sofia had been judged too unfit to dance and too old to stay in a Peruvian jungle for a month. But *Celebs Against the Odds* was the new water-cooler show that everyone was talking about and which every entertainer whose career had stalled was desperate to appear on.

In the opening episode of each series, ten famous faces were snatched without warning from their day-to-day routine. They were whisked away to an unknown destination to compete in a series of physical and mental tasks. Cameras recorded their every move for a week. A year earlier, Sofia had watched in envy as Tracy Fenton, her acting rival for more than four decades, had been one of the chosen few. She too had been taken while in her car, and her popularity resurgence led to her being cast in two high-profile network dramas. Now it appeared the *Celebs Against the Odds* producers wanted Sofia.

She balled her fists to contain her excitement—her comeback was imminent; she could feel it. It wasn't going to be by playing aging grandmothers in soaps. It was by being herself, beamed into homes, vehicles, and telephones and onto tablets every night of the week.

Sofia removed the mirror from her handbag again and checked her make-up from all angles, dabbing, smoothing, and contouring where necessary. Then she took another painkiller and washed it down with a swig of brandy.

"This is it, Oscar," she said proudly as she petted his head. "Mummy's on her way back to the top. Just you wait and see."

She held her smile firm and looked directly into the camera, and for the first time in years, she wasn't afraid to stare at her own image as it appeared on the screen before her.

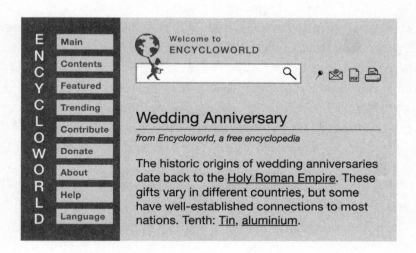

CHAPTER 4

ENCYCLOWORLD

Main
Contents
Featured
Trending
Contribute
Donate
About
Help
Language

Welcome to
ENCYCLOWORLD

Wedding Anniversary

from Encycloworld, a free encyclopedia

The historic origins of wedding anniversaries date back to the Holy Roman Empire. These gifts vary in different countries, but some have well-established connections to most nations. Tenth: Tin, aluminium.

SAM & HEIDI COLE

A re you sure your parents have kept the date free?" asked Sam. "Your mum's hopeless when it comes to remembering she's volunteered to babysit."

"Yes, I'm sure," Heidi replied. "I've already put the date into the family calendar so she'll get a text alert every day in the run-up to it. What about you? You'll definitely be back in Luton by then?"

"Uh-huh. Should be."

"So when are you going to tell me what you've organised?"

"I'm not. Like I keep saying, it's a surprise."

"You know I hate surprises."

"Most women love them."

"Most women aren't police officers, and in my job, surprises are rarely a good thing."

"Then let this be the exception. For once, have some faith in your husband."

Heidi wanted to laugh but she held herself back. Instead, she finished filing her fingernails and recalled last year's effort—a fish supper at their local pub. Money had been tight so she hadn't vocalised her disappointment. Many months later, she had stumbled across the real reason why they were struggling financially. But she had chosen to keep it to herself.

She checked the destination time on the car's dashboard—it would take another twenty minutes before she reached it. She needed something to distract her from her anxiousness about what was to come next. So she decided to paint her fingernails. She opened her handbag and removed three shades of white polish.

"Which one should I use?" she asked, holding them up to the dashboard camera.

From the console in his own car, she watched as Sam looked carefully at each of them. "The white one," he replied, and heaped another spoonful of warm porridge from a Tupperware pot into his mouth. Heidi hated it whenever she was a morning Passenger in his vehicle—it reeked of either milky oats or well-cooked bacon.

"Which white one?" she pressed, and watched Sam hesitate, as if his instinct was warning him this was a test. "The one on the left."

"Well remembered. That's the one I chose for our wedding day."

"I could never forget."

Heidi knew her husband was lying because so was she. She had worn a baby-pink polish that day. Recently, she had found herself testing him more and more frequently over the most minute and innocuous of topics, just to see how much he was prepared to fabricate.

"This colour always reminds me of sitting with Kim and Lisa in the nail bar," she continued, making it up as she went along. "We drove the owner mad trying to decide which shade to pick. Kim kept telling me to go with the ivory to match my dress, but I wanted something with a little more sparkle."

"You made the right choice. You looked amazing."

Heidi tried to read his smile, quietly hoping it was genuine. She remembered him waiting at the church altar, turning his head when the organist began to play the opening bars of Wagner's "Bridal Chorus" and how he dabbed at his eyes when he caught sight of her. Even now, after everything, she would do anything to relive those early, fairy-tale moments from their relationship again, even just for a moment.

"Do you remember where our first date was?" Heidi asked.

"Of course, in that fish restaurant in Aldeburgh high street."

"No, that was the second night."

"I don't count the first night because that's when we met."

"That's right, you were on the stag weekend from hell."

"Bob's best man had booked us all two static caravans in a park populated by pensioners, and the only club in town closed at eleven. Then I saw you and your friends walking back to the campsite, and the next thing I know, we'd spent the night swigging from a bottle of Prosecco and watching the sun rise over the beach."

Heidi felt a warmth spread across the surface of her skin, mirroring how she felt when Sam had leaned in to kiss her for the first time. Back then, and following the collapse of her parents' marriage, she hadn't believed in happy-ever-afters. And not for a moment had she assumed she could fall in love so hard and so fast. The warm feeling dissolved as quickly as it appeared. She blew gently on the fingernails of one hand as she began painting the other.

"Who'd have thought back then that one day we'd be celebrating our tenth anniversary?" she asked.

"I did because I'd never met anyone so on my wavelength like you were. There's no way I was letting you go. And while I remember, aside from a hacksaw to remove the ball and chain, what are we supposed to buy one another to celebrate?"

"Something made of tin."

"So if I wrapped up a tin of spaghetti hoops you'd be happy?"

"Give it a try and see how long the proctologist takes to surgically remove it."

"What was on that modern list of anniversary presents you googled?"

"Diamonds. Apparently, they're still a girl's best friend."

"I thought I was your best friend?"

You were, Heidi said to herself. *Once upon a time you were everything to me.*

She watched as Sam used his tie to clean his glasses. He hadn't worn them when they first met, but then his hair and beard hadn't been flecked with grey either, and the skin around his eyes didn't crease when he laughed. She wondered if he had watched her aging like she had him. Perhaps that's how this had all started. Her genetics had been to blame. Her body was no longer as attractive to him as it once was when they were in the first flush of love. But wasn't that what marriage was about? Not the ceremony or the grand gestures or the anniversaries, but standing by the side of someone come what may, growing older with each other and loving them regardless of all their faults. *Till death do us part*, she said to herself.

Heidi wondered what others saw when they looked at her. In her imagination, she was still a twenty-year-old girl with her whole life ahead of her. In reality, she was a forty-year-old mum of two whose once-thick head of blond hair was losing its lustre. Her teeth needed whitening and her jaw-line was fast losing its elasticity. As gravity pulled it south, it took with it her freckles. Nowadays they were less like cute brown dots and more like fat ink-blots. It wasn't just her looks that had toughened over the years; so had her personality. Her job had made it harder for her to see the good in people. And she had forgotten how to cry either happy or sad tears. Sometimes she felt as if she were made of rock; break her exterior and she was just as solid inside.

"Do you ever miss those days?" Heidi asked suddenly.

"Which days?"

"The ones when we could drink and smoke and go out whenever we wanted to or bugger off around Europe on a city break without having to worry about the kids?"

"Sometimes, like when they caught that stomach bug before Christmas and the house stank like a Roman vomitorium. But on the whole, no. The adventure we're on is much more fun with them in it."

"If we can get a late cheap deal, we should take them to the South of

France for a few days in August. Just pack up the essentials, programme the address, set off at night, and sleep in the car while it drives us there. We could be in Lyon by the morning."

Heidi knew what Sam's response would be before he gave it. "We'll see," he replied. When it came to trips abroad, he'd been "we'll see–ing" her for most of their married life. Every other Christmas he'd visit his mother at her flat in the Algarve. However, he always went alone.

"So remind me, where are you taking me for our anniversary?" she asked.

"Oh for God's sake, if you really want to know, then I'll tell you. But don't start moaning later that I've ruined the surprise."

"Come on then. Spill."

"Okay, well, I've hired us a caravan in Aldeburgh for the weekend and I was planning to take an early-morning breakfast picnic with us so we can start the day where it all began—under the rising sun."

"Aww, that's lovely," Heidi replied, not meaning a word of it. Sam clearly assumed it to be a thoughtful, romantic gesture though. "It's a really nice idea."

"That's what I thought," he replied. "But then I remembered how my wife's face tripped her up last year when I took her to the pub, so instead, I bought us tickets to a musical in London's West End, followed by a slap-up dinner at a posh restaurant and a room in a Covent Garden hotel."

Heidi knew it was never going to happen but she played along regardless. "Are you serious? Can we afford it? We've got James's school ski trip coming up . . ."

"Yes, we can afford it," Sam replied, and she recognised a hint of irritation in his voice for questioning him. "I've been putting some money aside for a while to pay for it."

Heidi opened her mouth to say something else, then changed her mind. Instead, she held her newly painted white fingernails to the camera. "What do you think?" she asked, but before Sam could reply, the picture went blank. "Sam? Have we been cut off?"

Meanwhile, inside her husband's car several miles behind, Sam slapped the dashboard to encourage the screen to function again. He was paying the price for ignoring the car's automatic reminders for its six-month mainte-nance check and software update. He hadn't booked Heidi's in yet either, but she didn't need to know that. There was a lot she didn't need to know.

"I can still hear you," he replied.

"What happened there?"

"We must have fallen into a Wi-Fi black hole."

"Then why is my GPS reprogramming itself with a different route?"

Sam placed his now-empty bowl of porridge on the seat next to him. "It does that sometimes, doesn't it? You know, if there's been an accident or problems ahead." Sam glanced at his own screen. "Hold on, mine is doing the same. What . . . Where the hell is it taking . . ."

He didn't get the opportunity to finish his sentence. The next voice to come from their speakers did not belong to either of them.

CHAPTER 5

TV News.co.uk

NEWS REPORT   *7:05 a.m.*

Leicestershire Police say they have arrested twelve people in connection with human trafficking, labour exploitation, and modern-day slavery.

Officers carried out early-morning raids on two business premises in Leicester and three homes in Rugby. Two men and a woman will appear in court later today while police are questioning nine others.

SHABANA KHARTRI

can do it, I can do it, I can do it . . ."

Shabana repeated the mantra under her breath over and over again as the car drove, leaving behind the only home she'd known for twenty years. *This is really it*, she thought. The unimaginable was becoming a reality.

Just thirty minutes had passed since her son, Reyansh, appeared at the front door of the family home begging for her to listen to him. Although overjoyed to see him, her first concern was for his safety.

"What are you doing here?" she replied, cupping his cheeks, her eyes flitting between her firstborn and the neighbours' houses to check if anyone had clocked his return. He was breathless. "You know you cannot come here," Shabana continued. "It's not safe for you."

"It doesn't matter anymore," he replied. "Please, Mum, you have to listen to me. This is the chance you've been waiting for—to get out of here."

"What are you talking about, son? What has happened?"

"It's Dad. He's been arrested."

Shabana took a step back into the porch and shook her head as if she had misunderstood him. "What do you mean he has been arrested? What for?"

"I don't know all the details; all I know is that his lawyer called, asking you to post bail for Dad. Because you don't speak English, he phoned me. All his solicitor would say was that his arrest involved people trafficking."

Shabana had heard the phrase before but hadn't thought to ask its meaning.

"It's where people are illegally smuggled out of one country and into another," Reyansh continued. "The men are often sold on for slave labour and the women forced into prostitution."

She covered her mouth with her hands. "And they are saying your father has been doing this?"

"It's what they're accusing him of, yes. Rohit and Sanjay were also arrested in the restaurant last night along with a bunch of other men at different addresses. The police say they're part of a gang shipping children and beggars over from the Assam slums before selling them."

Shabana recognised the other men's names but couldn't put faces to them. Whenever her husband, Vihaan, brought friends back to the house, she had been ordered upstairs and out of sight until they left. Often, they had remained in the dining room getting drunk on Sekmai until the early hours of the morning. It was also not uncommon for him to stay out for days at a time, so she hadn't missed him last night.

"Mum, this is your chance to leave him," Reyansh continued. "You are never going to get an opportunity like this again."

Shabana knew that if what her son was saying was accurate, everything she had once dreamed of might be about to come true. But still she hesitated. "I'm not ready," she whispered, her heart racing. "I would need to pack clothes, get the girls ready . . . What would I tell them? I have no money saved—how will we afford to eat? How will we live? Where will we go?"

"I have two taxis waiting," said Reyansh, and turned to point to them behind him. "One to take you to a solicitor and the other to drive the girls to a shelter. Dad's brief said there's money hidden in the shed, thousands of pounds that'll pay for his bail. There's nothing to stop you from taking it."

"But that's theft."

"He has stolen two decades of your life."

"What kind of shelter?"

"It's for families like us and women like you, wives from the Indian community who've spent their whole lives being controlled by their husbands, women who are sick of being beaten and bullied and treated like dogs, and who need help in starting afresh."

"But . . . but . . ." Shabana didn't know how to respond. For so many years, she had fantasised about escaping Vihaan. Nine years had passed since her last proper attempt, when she had made plans to travel from their home in Leicester to Newcastle, where a distant cousin lived. Mrs. Patel, who ran the local supermarket, was aiding her. Only when Mrs. Patel's husband discovered the National Express coach tickets his wife had been hiding for Shabana and her children, he'd felt duty bound to tell Vihaan of her plans. Her punishment was a beating so severe, she still couldn't place her full weight on her right ankle.

Since that day, her only hope was that an early death might rid the world of Vihaan. He smoked a pack of high-tar cigarettes a day, and his fatty diet meant he was at least twenty kilos overweight. It could only be a matter of time before his heart gave out. Sometimes she fantasised about watching him collapse on the kitchen floor, clutching his arm and chest and begging her to get help. "I can't," she would tell him. "I only speak Bengali. You wouldn't allow me to learn English, remember?"

"Mum," said Reyansh, bringing her back to the present. He took his mother's hands within his own. "This is what you want, isn't it? The opportunity to get you all away from him? Because it's actually happening now."

"When he gets home, he will come after us and find us and he will kill us. I know how vindictive your father is when he is pushed."

"No, he won't because he can't. I met with the women who run the shelter and explained your situation, and they told me that when you were ready, you are welcome there. It's completely anonymous; no one will ever know where you are. I spoke to them again on my way here—they can take all of you in this morning. There are beds waiting for you. And they've put me in touch with a solicitor who works closely with them. She will see you now to organise a restraining order against Dad. Everything is in place and ready. All we need is you and the girls."

"But what about you? Where will you go?"

"I've only got a few months until I start uni. I can sofa surf until then. I've been lucky—being kicked out because my dad thinks being gay is worse than being dead was the best thing he could've done for me. Mum, the world is beautiful beyond these walls if you give it a chance."

"Your lawyer friend, does she know I don't speak English?"

"Yes, and she says for you not to worry; she's seen it many times before. She wants to help you."

"And you promise to look after the girls while I sit with her?"

"Yes, of course I will."

Without warning, a warmth travelled quickly through Shabana's veins, infecting every part of her. Her nods were barely perceptible until she pictured how different the future could be if she trusted her son and the people he had engaged to assist her. That they could want to help someone they didn't know humbled her. She looked Reyansh directly in the eye. "Help me get your sisters ready," she said with growing confidence.

Shabana packed anything she might need for the next few days into two shopping bags, like clothes, underwear, and toiletries. From her bedroom, she listened as Reyansh organised his four sisters in the adjoining bedrooms. She was so proud of her only son; despite all he had learned about men by watching his father, he had still known it to be wrong. Instead, he had remained a kind, gentle, and considerate soul. The name she had given him translated to "first ray of sunlight," and now that was the gift he was giving to her—the chance to see a new day in a new light. She was ready to leave the shadows and join a world illuminated in a way she could barely remember.

As she heard the girls make their way downstairs, she said a small prayer for them. She had begun motherhood with the best of intentions and had wanted to teach them to be independent and not to allow anyone to control them. But aged fourteen and under, they had known her only as a subservient, frightened woman. After they had grown up under that roof, she hoped it wasn't too late for them to change their expectations of what a marriage could be. If they repeated her mistakes, it would not be their fault; it would be hers. And for that, she would never forgive herself.

With her bag packed, Shabana hurried into the kitchen to grab a key,

then made her way to the padlocked shed where she had never been allowed. She yanked containers from shelves and rifled through boxes and
bags until she pulled out wad after wad of cash. She was stunned by the
sum. While she had been forced to micromanage a paltry food and clothing
budget for a growing family, Vihaan had been sitting on thousands upon
thousands of pounds. It compounded her hatred for him.

After scooping the money into her pockets, she joined the rest of her
family in the lounge Vihaan had taken as his own and banned them from.
She began to feel a strength she hadn't realised was still inside her when she
saw the girls with their school bags hanging from their shoulders, crammed
with clothes, books, and toys. Meanwhile, Reyansh hovered nervously behind the thick net curtain, checking that all was well outside, ready for their
escape. For so long that curtain had hidden what had become of Shabana
from the rest of the world. But not any longer. She yanked it from the run-
ner until it fell into a heap on the floor. Finally, she was able to see from the
window with clarity. "Let them look at me," she said defiantly.

As she kissed each one of her children's cheeks in turn, the youngest
two, Aditya and Krish, began to cry. Their mother responded by giving
them the tightest of embraces. "I will show you what it means to be happy,"
she whispered, before letting them go. Reyansh escorted them from the
front door and into one of the two driverless taxis parked outside. Then he
assisted Shabana in placing her bags into the second vehicle parked behind
it, programming the solicitor's address into the GPS.

"We'll see you this afternoon," he replied, and handed her a mobile
phone before remembering she had never operated one before. "I'll call you
on this—press the green button to answer—then I'll order your car to bring
you to us."

Shabana wrapped her arms around her son and held him. "Thank you,"
she whispered before allowing him to leave.

It was the first time she had ever travelled inside a vehicle with no
driver. But she trusted Reyansh when he assured her it would get her to
where she needed to be of its own volition. Her only boy had not yet turned
eighteen, but he was the only man she trusted—not her father, who had arranged her marriage to a man he knew to be violent, or the brothers who

almost beat to death a boyfriend she had from a lower caste back in India as a teenager.

Shabana began to allow herself to imagine where she might go now that she was free. A small council-owned flat would suffice, one with a radio and a television so she could watch films when the girls had gone to bed. Over the years, movies had become her only means of escape. Sometimes, when Vihaan was out and had forgotten to hide the television remote control, she'd watch an Indian channel and live vicariously through Bollywood's greatest love stories. She'd become hypnotised by the beautiful girls with their flawless hair and bright, colourful clothing, dancing with a joy she had rarely known. It was as if they'd been blessed by a different god to the one she worshipped.

Shabana looked at the map on the dashboard monitor as the car drove along roads she had only ever walked. She had grown used to the muscles in her arms burning as she made her way home laden down by the weight of heavy food bags.

Never again. Soon she could take a bus or a taxi or perhaps make a friend and go shopping with them. Thanks to Reyansh's tenacity, a huge world of possibilities now lay ahead for her and her family. The four words that Vihaan had beaten out of her slowly began to creep back into her vocabulary.

I can do it, she told herself. *I can do it.*

Her inner voice was the last one Shabana heard before an English one appeared out of nowhere through the car's speakers. It arrived so suddenly, it startled her. "What is happening?" she asked aloud in her native tongue. Her eyes darted around the car's interior. The voice continued to talk, but there were only a few words here and there that she could understand. One of them sounded like "die."

Suddenly the monitor switched on. The main screen was filled with much smaller screens and by other people in cars. None of them were smiling—they all looked afraid. She moved her head closer to it in the hope of seeing her son. But hers was the only familiar face.

Panic rose inside Shabana in the same way it did when she heard Vihaan slamming the front door after a night out. If he was drunk, he was angry. And if he was angry, he was going to release his aggression upon his wife by doing what he wanted to her while she lay still, eyes closed and fists balled, dreaming of a better life.

Other voices began to fill her car, more words and languages that she didn't understand, along with haunting cries, shouting, and people in distress.

"What is happening?" she pleaded aloud. "I don't like this, please, can you make the car stop? I would like to get out."

She pushed a button on the door, hoping it would open, but nothing happened. She looked at the phone Reyansh had given her and pressed the green button, holding it to her ear. "Reyansh?" she asked. "Reyansh, son, can you hear me? Are you there? Please?"

But there was no reply. Shabana had a feeling the new life she dared to dream of was already slipping from her grasp.

PART TWO

Why do we want driverless cars?
Back in 2019, one million people died in car accidents worldwide. Driverless cars aim to cut that number by at least 95 per cent. Other benefits include less pollution, fewer traffic delays, and more spare time. They are also less expensive to run.

How do they work?
Each vehicle is powered by rechargeable batteries and is operated by a bank of computers. Attached to the car are digital video cameras, ultrasonic sensors, radar, sonar, infrared systems, and lidar. Together, they build up a 360-degree picture of the vehicle's surroundings and are updated hundreds of times per second. In the event of a potential accident, onboard computers use artificial intelligence to make decisions on how to minimise fatalities. Those details are stored in an onboard black box device.

When will these vehicles be mandatory?
Following legislation passed by both the House of Commons and the House of Lords, the government has pledged England's roads will become the world's first completely autonomous network, with plans to ban all manual vehicles within a decade.

L ibby Dixon didn't need to check her reflection in the bathroom mirror to know she was still scowling.

Her expression was already fixed in place by the time her alarm clock sounded at 6:45 a.m. and she remembered where she would be spending her day. Her neck ached from sleeping at an awkward angle, so she pressed her fingertips into muscles on either side to try to loosen them up. Her scowl remained as she trudged across the landing, showered, and then put minimal effort into applying her make-up. She scowled as she covered a spot on her chin, tied her naturally wavy brown hair into a ponytail, and sifted through her wardrobe. She settled on a conservative outfit incorporating a simple cream blouse, navy A-line skirt, and matching jacket. She had no one to impress.

And now, as she stood in the kitchen, even her house rabbits, Michael and Jackson, couldn't bring a smile to her face as they chased each other around her feet. She poured herself a second cup of coffee in the hope that an extra caffeine hit might lift her spirits. It didn't, so still she scowled.

A sulky, grumpy mindset wasn't a natural fit for Libby. She invariably found a positive in the bleakest of moments. But today was an exception. And if the next twelve hours were anything like yesterday, she wasn't going to smile again until the end of the week when it was all over. And that meant four more days of scowling.

She fed the rabbits fresh hay and pellets, slipped on an old pair of scuffed mules, threw her handbag over her shoulder, and made her way towards the front door. She paused to remove a mobile phone from her pocket and checked her emails, texts, and social media. She let out a silent sigh when, once again, there were no updates in her search for him.

Maybe it's time to give up on you? she asked herself, and dropped the phone into her bag.

Libby's mood was at rock bottom and a stark contrast to twenty-four hours earlier, when she'd awoken with nervous excitement. She had set her alarm for earlier than usual to allow time for a run along Birmingham's canal towpaths that looped around regenerated factories before returning home for a breakfast of organic fruit and a low-fat yoghurt. Then once she washed and conditioned her hair, she had used her most expensive brand-name cosmetics and removed the plastic cover from one of five freshly dry-cleaned suits, one for each day of the week.

Libby had been keen to make a good first impression on the strangers she was to spend a week in close confines with. However, her fervour had sunk like a lead balloon within minutes of her arrival. By the strangers' unwelcoming looks, her presence was a formality they'd had no say in. Their disdain quickly became mutual.

The front door locked behind her, and once outside, she felt the glow of the early-morning sun on her face. At least the warm April morning was something to be thankful for, she thought, and she rolled up the sleeves of her jacket and began her journey.

She walked through the shared gardens of the gated community in which she lived, out through the towering black wrought iron gates, along the towpath, and towards Birmingham's city centre, which loomed in the distance. The skyscrapers that peppered the horizon hadn't been there when she had first moved to the city from Northampton nine years earlier. Her adopted home was changing with the times and at such a rapid pace that she often felt the modern world was leaving her behind.

It was the same with relationships. Many of her friends were now cohabiting or married and starting families. Libby had lost count of the amount of baby showers she'd attended, or the number of times friends asked if she'd found someone to replace her ex-fiancé, William, yet. She hadn't.

At the time, she had forgiven him for a drunken kiss with an attractive intern at work, until seven months later, when the teenager turned up on their doorstep, clearly pregnant. Libby kicked William out of their house and had refused to engage with him in any way since. But hating him hadn't prevented her from spending a whole weekend in tears when mutual friends informed her he was now engaged and the father to a baby girl.

He was the love of her life and no one could understand why, after splitting up almost two and a half years earlier, Libby remained single. But she had made a vow to herself that rather than worrying about finding Mr. Right or comparing her life to those of her peers, she would embrace being a single, independent woman. But on the nights with just her pets and a bottle of Pinot Grigio for company, she'd log on to dating websites to see who else had been left on the shelf. Sometimes she'd just look at their photographs; other times she'd hover over their profiles, finding reasons not to talk to them. She might make polite conversation with those who made the first move, but once they became too persistent or interested, she would either ghost or block them.

Then *he* came into her world. But within the blink of an eye, he vanished as quickly as he appeared. Even now, after six months, he crossed her mind on a daily basis. She wondered if he'd given her as much thought as she had given him.

Libby passed a handful of council workmen on a trawler barge lowering dredges into the water, scraping them along the bottom of the canal to collect submerged objects. More often than not, they were the ride-and-go dockless bikes that blighted the city like a plague of large metal rats. They were supposed to be the solution for those in lower wage brackets who could not afford escalating insurance costs for regular vehicles or to replace their soon-to-be-outdated cars with the next generation of electric driverless cars.

However, little regulation meant manufacturers were undercutting one another, and the bikes had flooded the market. And as some went out of business, they became free to use and abuse. Libby shook her head as the steel-rimmed net rose above the water's surface and she counted six more brightly coloured cycles. The environment was fast becoming another casualty of the race for driverless cars that Libby had grown to hate.

She left the quiet of the canals and made her way up a set of steep brick steps to street level. She passed one of the Birmingham City University campuses where, after casting aside a less than rewarding career as a bank's mortgage advisor, she'd spent most of three years retraining to become a mental health nurse. Her new career was a good fit, and she longed to return to it once this week was out of the way.

As Libby passed Monroe Street, a long, curved road surrounded on either side by cafés, bistros, independent retailers, and boutiques, she refused to allow her eyes to rest on it. Once, it was a neighbourhood she regularly frequented. But two years had passed since she last ventured along it. She remembered every second of the sequence of events like it was yesterday.

There were three moments in Libby's life that she had no desire to revisit. And that was one of them.

CHAPTER 7

BLABBERBOX)) **Welcome to Blabberbox**
Trending posts: 534

What's Happened 2 My News Feed? Submitted 2 minutes ago

BeastWithin: Anyone know why Facebook keeps showing me live images from inside some bloke's car? Looks like he's freaking out.
MySoreSmile: I keep getting him too plus a pregnant woman. Is it an advert?
Wonderland: Don't think so. It's been going on for about ten minutes.

C ome rain or shine, Libby chose to complete her twenty-five-minute walk to work on foot. Only rarely, such as when forecasters predicted a particularly nasty weather front, might she book a taxi. And even then, she only chose a firm that provided a driver. But as cheaper, fully autonomous vehicles became the norm, manned cabs were proving costly to operate and were becoming few and far between.

Much to her annoyance, the driverless-car propaganda was at an all-time high. Tax breaks, free battery charging, and drastically reduced insurance rates encouraged 80 per cent of drivers to switch to autonomous vehicles within the first year, a target reached more rapidly than predicted. Libby couldn't be persuaded. She would not put her life in the hands of a robot, because she knew the damage they were capable of. She cursed under her breath as a fleet of empty autonomous cars emblazoned with garish, illuminated advertising passed her. The sooner robot car spam was regulated, the better, she thought.

She was maintaining a steady pace towards Birmingham city centre when she heard a woman's voice cut through the air. "Hey, Libs!" Nia bellowed, her Caribbean-edged Midlands accent making her instantly identifiable. Libby turned to greet her friend and colleague. "If your face was any more miserable, you'd be picking it up off the floor." Nia laughed. "What's wrong with you? Is the training course so bad?"

"It's not great," Libby replied, but chose not to elaborate.

"What's it for again? I forget."

"Patient confidentiality and data protection."

"Ah, that's why. Sounds as boring as hell."

Libby loathed lying to anyone about her absence from work, especially a friend. But legally—and reiterated by the forty pages of detailed forms she'd been made to sign yesterday—she had no choice. Only Libby and the human resources department at the hospital where she and Nia were based could know what she was actually doing.

"Tell me all about it on the bus."

Libby glared at the long white vehicle parked on the other side of the road, emblazoned with video advertisements across both sides. It would drop them off at the hospital's front entrance. But Libby was headed elsewhere, so she made up an excuse.

"I haven't been on public transport since they replaced the drivers with computers," she said. "Putting the lives of dozens of people in the hands of artificial intelligence is asking for trouble."

"You sound like a dinosaur from the Dark Ages."

Libby stopped herself from pointing out that dinosaurs didn't live in the Dark Ages, and agreed instead. "Yep, and the only time you'll see me in something that drives itself is when I'm in the back of a hearse."

"If it's cheap and gets me to where I need to be, it could be pulled by unicorns on roller skates as far as I care." Nia threw her head back and gave a hearty laugh. "Anyway, I'm going to be late if I don't get a move on. Are we still on for lunch on Monday? You'll be finished by then?"

"Definitely."

"Good, because it's your turn to pay," Nia added as she moved into the road.

"Careful!" Libby yelled, grabbing Nia's arm and yanking her from the path of an oncoming car.

"Those electric things are so damn quiet, aren't they? They'll be the death of me."

"They'll be the death of all of us," Libby replied as Nia crossed the road, safely this time.

She waited until her friend's bus made its way along the road before she continued to walk in a different direction. She checked her phone one more time to see if there were any updates about *him*. Again there was nothing.

Libby had been with Nia and a group of friends on a weekend away in Manchester the night he and Libby met. They had gravitated towards the karaoke room at the back of a pub when she first set eyes on him. They got onstage as a group and huddled around two mics to sing Libby's choice, Michael Jackson's "Man in the Mirror." But the song was more than five minutes long, and they lost interest, leaving Libby to finish it by herself.

It was then that she saw him. Their eyes had connected across a noisy pub when he gave her a cheeky, almost lopsided grin. He wasn't the most handsome of the group of young men he was standing with; his shoulders weren't the broadest, and he wasn't the tallest. And he hovered behind them almost as if he was embarrassed by their laddish behaviour. Like her, he was obviously a Michael Jackson fan and mimed along with her. He also knew every whoop, holler, and hee-hee in the song.

"That boy can't take his eyes off you," Nia had encouraged when Libby finally left the stage. "Go talk to him."

Libby opened her mouth to protest like she always did when her friends encouraged her to flirt. The memory of William's betrayal was never far from the surface. However, this time, she pushed him back into the room from where he came and locked the door. This time, she was interested. After knocking back her gin and tonic for Dutch courage, she approached him.

"Hi," she began nervously. She thrust her hand out to shake his.

"That's very formal," he teased, but shook it regardless. "What's your name?"

"Libby."

"I'm . . ." But she couldn't hear his response through the feedback of a DJ's microphone. She was about to ask him to repeat it when he spoke. "So you're a Michael Jackson fan?"

"My brother and I were raised on his music. My mum would play him all the time."

"My dad was the fan in our house. When I was a kid, he bought us tickets to see him play in London, but then Jacko died so we never got the chance to go."

"My mum did the same! She still has the tickets in a frame on the bathroom wall."

Libby smiled at him and already felt a tingle inside her stomach.

"Are you from around here?" he asked.

"No, we've come up from Birmingham for a girlie weekend." She pointed towards her six friends, then immediately wished she hadn't when they blew exaggerated air kisses in his direction. He responded by doing exactly the same. Libby liked that.

"Can I buy you a drink?" she asked, and he agreed.

As the two made their way towards the bar, it was as if the pub had emptied around them because all they saw and heard was each other; not the dancing, drunken bodies and voices filling the room or the thumping beat of the dance music. Libby chatted about her job in nursing while he explained how he'd worked in the automotive industry until the driverless-car revolution made his role redundant. Their dislike of the vehicles appeared mutual, but Libby didn't want to put a damper on the evening by explaining why.

She appreciated that he asked her as many questions as she asked him, and there was a warmth to his eyes that made her want to dive in and learn everything about him. When he laughed, the dimples in his cheeks appeared. The walls she had spent two years constructing since William left were falling quickly. She had never experienced anything so intense as her desire to kiss him there and then. However, she held back.

"Shall we go outside where it's quieter?" he asked, and she agreed.

The beer garden was illuminated by lines of cables and electric lanterns offering the night sky a creamy white glow, stretching the length and breadth of the outside space. Fairy lights were wrapped around the branches of three trees, and a fitting playlist of laid-back Balearic beats music came through speakers. A table emptied of drinkers as they arrived so they took it, while a waitress placed a lit candle inside a terra-cotta pot between them.

For the first minute they just sat, looking at each other, both comfortable with the silence. "It's probably the alcohol making me say this," Libby began eventually, "but I feel like I've known you for ages and not two hours."

"Ditto," he replied. "And no, I don't think it's the alcohol talking."

He moved his hand to reach for his glass. His little finger brushed against hers before he moved it away again. Libby slid hers back so they were touching.

Another hour passed as they talked until Libby couldn't hold back any longer. She leaned across the wooden table, placed her hand on his arm, and moved her lips towards his until they connected. It was a first kiss, a kiss between lovers, and the kiss of two people who knew each other inside out, all rolled into one. She didn't want it to end.

Suddenly she felt a tugging at her sleeve. "Libs, I'm so sorry but we need you," Nia said urgently.

"What?" Libby snapped.

"I'm so sorry," she mouthed towards Libby's new friend. "Cerys has fallen off the toilet cistern."

"Fallen off it? What was she doing on it?"

"She's had too many vodka and oranges and was dancing on it when she slipped and smashed her face on the floor. She's out cold. We've called for an ambulance."

"Shit," cursed Libby, and turned to face the man whose name she still didn't know. "I'm coming back," she said, and smiled hopefully at him as she rose from the bench. "Please, just wait here."

In the ladies' bathroom, it was clear Cerys's injury was more than just a superficial wound. Then, as she walked alongside the gurney carrying her friend to the ambulance, she turned her head to see *him* one last time, only drinkers blocked the doorway to the rear and she couldn't make him out.

Six long months had passed and Libby still hadn't put the stranger out of her mind. Once, she even caught herself wandering between the fragrance counters of the department store John Lewis, spraying colognes onto pieces of card and trying to match them with the scent she remembered him wearing.

She cursed herself for not asking him to repeat his name, because without it, her online search for him became a Herculean task. Hours were spent trawling the internet and placing his description on social media, leaving her email address as a contact if anyone recognised him. With the exception of a handful of prankster replies, she drew a blank.

Twice she had made the ninety-mile journey to revisit that Manchester bar on the off chance he might be a regular patron. But despite hours spent sitting alone in a booth and people watching, he was nowhere to be seen. The bar staff didn't recognise him from his description and he had not "liked" the pub's Facebook page. Taxi operators refused to search their records without a name; a LinkedIn trawl of former car manufacturers didn't throw up any recognisable pictures. Her last resort, a psychic, was of predictably little use.

In her heart of hearts, Libby knew that it was time to admit defeat. The man with no name would never be found. She wondered if, deep down, she was using her search as an excuse not to return to the dating scene. Perhaps it was the perfect relationship for her—if she couldn't locate him, she could never truly know him and he couldn't let her down. He could never be another William.

Without realising it, Libby had reached her destination. She hesitated, staring across the busy road and towards a two-hundred-year-old building. Birmingham's former town hall stood out from its more modern surroundings. Its Roman-influenced architecture was made up of limestone and whitish-grey bricks and featured dozens of pillars supporting its pitched roof. It was an impressive construction, but one she dreaded spending the rest of the day inside.

CHAPTER 8

HowThingsOperate.com

What are the five levels of driverless cars?

Level 0: The driver performs all tasks.

Level 1: The car can help keep itself in lane and use auto cruise control and braking.

Level 2: The vehicle now has added self-parking and self-acceleration.

Level 3: Technology means it can drive itself under certain circumstances.

Level 4: A car can steer, brake, accelerate, change lanes, turn, use signals, and respond to events by itself in geofenced areas. Drivers can still take control.

Level 5: The vehicle is completely autonomous. It does everything and requires no human attention. There are no manual brakes or a steering wheel.

L ibby dragged her feet along the flagstones, through the glass sliding doors, and into the foyer. The aroma of pastries and coffees caught her attention, so she bought a pain au chocolat and a banana from a café.

She avoided the elevator and chose to delay the inevitable by climbing five flights of stone stairs. At a set of solid oak doors with hinges as wide as boat paddles, she patted out any creases from her outfit and pressed the buzzer. A bright blue LED panel illuminated.

"Fingerprint scan required," an automated female voice began, and Libby held her right hand towards a camera lens. "Verified," it continued, and the doors opened.

Inside the room, she counted six formally dressed men and women. Some spoke into earbuds linked to mobile phones; others worked on computer screens, but Libby couldn't see what they displayed. Two male security operatives clad in black approached her. They each had one slightly discoloured iris that Libby recognised as smart lenses. *Why does everything these days have to be smart?* she wondered. Perhaps Nia was right and Libby would have been better suited to the Dark Ages, albeit without the dinosaurs. They escorted her towards a table.

"Put your belongings in this box," said one in a gruff tone, and Libby obliged, placing her handbag, watch, and mobile phone inside it.

"Haven't seen one of these for a while," said the second operative, who picked up Libby's device to show his colleague. He tried to flex its unbendable chassis and it threatened to crack.

"Careful," said Libby.

"I bet she still uses cash too," his colleague added.

Once her belongings were X-rayed, they returned her handbag, but her phone and watch were placed in a silver metal locker under the table. White discs strapped to the palms of the operative's hands were used to scan Libby from head to toe in search of recording or communication devices. Satisfied she possessed neither, the shorter of the two men removed a swab from a sealed packet.

"Mouth," he said, and on her tongue placed the cotton end, which was then inserted into a cylindrical case the size of a pen lid. With his face up close to hers, Libby noticed that reflected on the inside of his smart lens was a tiny image of herself, likely taken from her National Identity Card along with information only he could read.

"Speak into this," he continued, and held a tablet towards her mouth. "Name."

"Libby Dixon," she said, and a green tick appeared on the voiceprint recognition screen.

"Will I have to do this every day?" she asked. "I don't see my DNA or voice changing much over the next twenty-four hours."

"Rules are rules," he replied, and escorted her towards another hefty set of doors. He typed in a code and scanned his own eye before they opened into a generous-sized, square chamber. Inside, two men and two women were gathered in a corner under arched opaque windows that could not be seen into or out of. With their backs towards Libby, they turned only their heads at the sound of the moving hinges.

"Hello again," she began, and offered a nervous smile to no one in particular. They replied with nods instead of words and continued their conversation.

It was exactly the same unfriendly, sterile environment as it had been yesterday. Four broad wooden desks were set out in a semicircle formation in the centre of the room. They faced a triple aspect wall on which Libby could just about make out the faint outlines of twelve television screens, one much larger than the others. In the corner of each was the word "offline." Shoulder-high mahogany wall panelling ran all the way around the room.

To Libby's left were three more tables where two men sat quietly, each wearing smart glasses and with only tablets laid out in front of them and virtual keyboards projected onto smoked glass surfaces. Now that phones and tablets had the same capabilities as desktop computers or laptops, Libby couldn't recall the last time she'd come across either.

One of the men was a stenographer, there to digitally record and type notes of everything discussed once proceedings were called to order. The other was responsible for projecting visuals onto the wall. Neither had spoken more than a handful of words yesterday.

Unsure of what to do with herself until the clock struck nine, Libby removed her pastry from a paper bag and pulled off a piece to nibble on.

"There is no food to be consumed in here," sniffed a woman with a Scottish accent. She wore a dark blue plaid skirt and matching jacket. Libby felt her face redden like she'd been told off by a teacher, and she dropped the snack into a metal bin. "That's for paper only," the woman added.

Libby searched for another dustbin to no avail, so she reached in to grab it, then slipped the pastry back into her handbag instead. Suddenly, a green light on the wall flashed.

"Right, shall we begin?" a voice began, and a man turned. He eyed Libby up and down distrustfully but tried to disguise it with a disingenuous smile. Jack Larsson was a member of Parliament, cabinet minister, and the only face she recognised from outside the room from his occasional television appearances. As he moved towards the tables, he whistled the opening bars of an old song she recognised called "Feeling Good." Considering the serious nature of what they were about to discuss, it wasn't the most appropriate of choices.

As each of his colleagues made their way towards the desks, she hesitated, waiting until they were all seated before pulling out a chair. Yesterday she'd received short shrift from the woman in plaid for choosing a seat not apparently allocated to her. Libby's chair was the farthest from the exit she'd have to wait the entire day to use again.

Aside from Jack Larsson, she had no idea of the other people's names. She had been warned by one of the security operatives that asking any personal details, even a Christian name, was strictly prohibited. However, she had been made to wear a silver badge with "Miss Dixon" etched in black capital letters.

The person controlling the footage placed a black, metallic briefcase in front of Jack, then typed a combination into an electronic keypad before the catches clicked open. He removed its only contents—five electronic tablet-like devices—and handed one to each person. Libby was the last.

"Begin recording," Jack ordered.

"System recording," the stenographer replied, and Libby could just about hear his fingers gently tapping on the glass keyboard.

"Well, ladies and gentlemen, we all know the routine by now," Jack continued. "But in accordance with the Road Traffic Act Autonomous Car Provisions, I'm obliged to remind you that I am calling a start to meeting number 3121 of the Vehicle Inquest Jury. Our purpose is to hear what each car's 'black box' has to say about an accident and thus apportion liability. Today, the burden of responsibility will be upon you to decide whether people involved in fatal collisions with driverless vehicles were killed either lawfully or unlawfully. Either man or machine is to blame, and you will decide."

Libby knew what was to come next, and she hated that she had been forced to be a part of it.

CHAPTER 9

InquestJD.co.uk

Home > Justice and the Law > Courts

IF YOU HAVE BEEN SELECTED FOR VEHICLE INQUEST JURY DUTY, HERE IS WHAT YOU NEED TO KNOW:

1. The jury is made up of four government-appointed individuals, including a member of Parliament and representatives of the General Medical Council, Legal Services Board, and Religious Pluralists—the organisation assembled by religious leaders to ensure all major faiths practised in Britain have their voices heard by one body.

2. A fifth member randomly selected from the public will complete the line-up and serve a five-day term. Service is mandatory, and inclusion may not be shared with anyone due to the sensitive nature of an inquest.

3. The jury meets for one week a month in different UK locations and decides upon the cause of a fatal vehicular accident.

4. The identities of all jurors and associated staff are protected from records so as to remain impartial and free from the risk of repercussions following the decision-making process.

L ibby ran her eyes across her fellow jury members as foreman Jack Larsson continued to read aloud a mandatory list of rules and guidelines.

As Jack was the head of the government's Ministry for Transport, his appearance yesterday came as a surprise to her. Initially she found him an affable man and the only one of the four to introduce himself to her, shake her hand, and offer her a coffee. Despite landing somewhere in his sixties, Jack had a stocky physique and shaven head which made him a physically dominating presence. His nose and thick lips were pronounced, and his hazel eyes bored straight through anyone who challenged him with the ease of a drill going through water. His perma-tan suggested a man who frequently holidayed abroad.

Libby had been too self-conscious to regard any of the jurors properly yesterday. But now, as Jack spoke, she took the opportunity to assess them all.

She placed the Scottish woman in plaid sitting next to Jack as in her forties. She wasn't listening to the speech she must have heard a hundred times before, and surfed her tablet instead. Libby noted that each time she dropped her head to something, her frameless glasses slipped to the end of her nose before she pushed them up again.

Adjacent to her was a handsome younger man who represented the General Medical Council and wore an olive-green tailored tweed jacket over a crisp white shirt with silver cufflinks in the shape of pills. His eyes were as rich and chocolatey as the colour of his hair and the stubble growing from his cheeks and chin. He had paid her no attention and Libby had yet to witness him smile. Outside of those four walls, she might well have been attracted to him.

At the end of the row of desks sat a plump woman with thick red hair and little to no make-up, clad in dull, shapeless clothing and a chunky black wristwatch. Her face was softer than the woman in plaid's. A solitary hair poked out from a nostril and it was all Libby could do to stop herself from leaning over and plucking it. On the lapel of the woman's jacket were the red embroidered letters "RP," an acronym for Religious Pluralist.

And then there was Libby. Her mandatory participation began when a young courier in a fluorescent top thrust a padded envelope into her hands as she left for work one morning. He'd mounted his bike and hurriedly pedalled out of sight before she had the chance to tear it open, read the instructions, and throw it back at him.

Libby thought it was a prank that she of all people—someone with a profound hatred for all things driverless—had been chosen. Once she had been part of a twenty-thousand-strong protest, marching to Downing Street to voice their fears against Level Five cars. So she assumed that if challenged and warned of her bias, the jury request would be hastily rescinded. It wasn't. And with no friends who had been similarly sequestered—at least as far as she was aware—Libby had gone online to search for recollections of former participants. However, information was scarce.

Each of the major internet service providers had been legally ordered to remove and block inflammatory comments that contained any accounts or speculation of what Vehicle Inquest Jury Duty involved.

Her last resort was the official VIJD website, which comprised a five-minute film churning out nothing but government propaganda. Under pressure from those in opposition to artificial intelligence having so much control of cars, the government created the Vehicle Inquest Jury. Using cameras and a vehicle's black box data, the jury decided if a fatality was the fault of a vehicle's AI or the Passenger. If it was the former, manufacturers and insurers jointly faced compensation claims. Adequate and costly software reprogramming would also be necessary to ensure the error was not repeated.

But Libby knew how rarely the inquests blamed AI, a system seen as virtually infallible. She had read about angry, bereaved families protesting the jury's unjust verdicts placing the cause of a fatal accident squarely upon their loved ones. Those related to the dead had no right to appeal, and as a result, some next of kin who had lost their main bread-winner went on to lose their homes too.

How the jury reached a verdict was also kept secret. It was self-governing and did not have to justify its decisions. As Libby was someone who believed in complete transparency, it was yet another part of the process that didn't sit comfortably with her.

As the day of her duty approached, she vowed to use her five days of service to provide a voice to the minority and challenge decisions where she saw fit.

But once inside that inquest room, it became apparent her best intentions would be thwarted. Each time she made her point of view known, the initially friendly Jack patronised, belittled, and encouraged her to back down in such a subtle, passive-aggressive way that she couldn't be sure if she was imagining it. Eventually, and to her shame, she sank into her chair, defeated. In the real world, she wouldn't hesitate to stand up for herself or her patients. But that room did not represent the real world. It was a private members' club and she had only been given a guest pass.

Suddenly, Libby became aware of all eyes upon her.

"Miss Dixon, have we lost your interest already?" Jack said with a smile. "Do you need me to repeat anything I've just said?"

"No, please go on," she whispered, her throat dry.

"How generous of you," the woman in plaid replied.

"Well, hopefully with no further lapses of attention from our guest, we can begin," Jack continued, and gave Libby a wink. "And please be advised, what you are about to witness contains particularly graphic evidence."

Libby thought she caught a glimmer of delight behind Jack's eyes as he ordered the footage to be shown.

CHAPTER 10

JUDE HARRISON

J ude remained paralysed inside his vehicle, his hands clasped on either side of his head and his mouth open. He watched helplessly as the GPS map on his monitor calculated a destination he had no control over. The arrival time for an address in Birmingham was in two hours and twenty-five minutes' time.

In his head, he replayed the voice that moments ago had come through his speakers and informed him someone else was controlling his car. And if it were to be believed, he soon would be dead. He reached for the door release button but it didn't work. He leaned over and tried the same with the other door, but again, nothing.

"Okay, you've got me," he said aloud. "Whoever is doing this, you've had your fun. Can I have my car back, please?" He awaited a response, but none came. Instead, the car continued driving in a direction he had not chosen for it.

"Think, think," he muttered, before jabbing icon after icon on the screen of his dashboard, attempting to regain control of both the vehicle and the programmed destination. But nothing he pressed made any difference.

"Car, go online," he ordered, trusting that the vehicle's operating system would allow him to open its user manual and override the navigational system.

"Vehicle offline," it replied.

"No," Jude commanded. "I need you to go online."

"Vehicle offline," the car repeated.

He ran through a list of alternative phrases, hoping one might work. "System override," he said. "Pull vehicle over. Let the driver take control. Open owner manual." The car failed to respond to any. "Car, do as I fucking tell you!" he yelled in frustration. After a pause, the OS responded.

"No."

Jude hesitated. He had never heard the car use that word before. Typically, if his vehicle was unable to carry out an order, it was programmed to politely reply with an "I apologise, your request is not possible at this time," followed by an explanation. It had never been a point-blank refusal.

He grabbed an earpiece from his pocket and affixed it to make a telephone call. "Dial emergency services," he said.

"No," the OS repeated.

Jude remembered that each time he entered the car, his phone automatically logged on to the vehicle's Wi-Fi. He scrambled around until he found the accompanying handset in the glove box. He devised a way to turn off the Wi-Fi and reroute the phone to find a 5G signal. But the symbol to confirm it was connected vanished as soon as it appeared. "Signal jammed," it read. He took a deep breath and tried to look outside for help, but the frosted glass windows remained.

Suddenly, his speakers came to life, startling him. This time the voice belonged to a woman. "Please, let us go," he heard her sob. "I haven't done anything to you."

Jude spoke tentatively. "Hello? Who is this?"

"Who . . . who are you?" she replied, with equal uncertainty.

"Jude . . . Jude Harrison," he replied. "Something's happening to my car."

"My name is Claire Arden and I'm inside a Skepter AR5, registration number FGY778. I was on my way to work when my car started driving in a different direction and a voice told me I was going to die. My phone won't work—can you send someone to help me?"

"I wish I could but I'm in the same boat as you," Jude replied. "I'm locked in my car and I can't get out."

"I don't understand?" she replied. "Ben told me he'd taken out the full service and emergency plan. Aren't you an operator?"

"No, I'm sorry," said Jude. "I've tried everything I can think of but I can't get my car to stop either."

"Why . . . why is this happening?" she stammered. "What do they want from me? Do they want money? I haven't got much but I can try and find some?"

"Did someone tell you that your car had been hacked?" he asked.

"Yes."

"And did they ask you for money?"

"No. All they said was that in two and a half hours, I was going to die." Her voice broke and Jude heard her crying again. "They said the same to me," he replied.

"Who's going to help us?"

"I have no idea. I think we just have to wait until they tell us—"

"Sam, what's going on?" A second distressed voice, a female one, came from nowhere and filled Jude's car.

"I don't know, but please try and stay calm," came a third, this time male.

"Hello!" yelled both Claire and Jude together.

How many more of us are there? Jude thought. "Can you hear us?" he asked.

"Yes, who's that?" the man replied.

"We are trapped in our cars and can't get out—can you help us? Do you have access to a phone signal or Wi-Fi?"

"No, my wife and I . . . someone has us locked inside . . ."

But before the male voice could continue, the dashboard in Jude's vehicle turned on and he saw himself on the television monitor. He was being filmed face-on, from a camera embedded in his dashboard. Then smaller screens appeared with strangers' faces inside. Jude counted five in total.

His heart was beating twenty to the dozen as he listened to the terror-stricken confusion of the others as they begged to be told what was happening to them.

Then, as quickly as they arrived, they were muted, leaving him in an ominous silence again.

Jack Larsson raised his right hand into the air and lowered his index finger to signal to one of his two assistants.

"Case number 322," he began, and footage from a moving vehicle appeared on the jurors' tablets. A street was also projected as a three-dimensional moving hologram, coming from wall-attached lasers that were directed towards a table in the centre of the room. Moving vehicles could be seen from every angle.

On her tablet, Libby assumed that from the positioning and close proximity to the road, footage had been taken from high-definition cameras integrated into the front grille of a vehicle. The corner of the screen displayed various statistics, including its speed, and the weather conditions, road gradient, and geographical coordinates.

"The location of this incident was a new town development just outside Hemel Hempstead," continued Jack. "The car is a Howley ET, a Level Five autonomous vehicle manufactured like most, from graphene and carbon-reinforced plastic. One owner, no previous incidents recorded, the road tax and insurance details are up to date and the latest software had been down-loaded."

Libby watched her tablet's screen as the car maintained a steady pace, travelling at twenty-five miles per hour. The footage switched to a dashboard lens.

"The temperature outside was a steady twenty-two degrees," continued Jack. "There was no precipitation, the vehicle was journeying five miles under the speed limit on a dry asphalt dual carriageway, which had seen resurfacing work three months prior. There is one Passenger inside and the vehicle has been on the road in moderate two-way traffic for twenty-two consecutive minutes."

Out of nowhere, a white moped appeared and attempted to overtake the car. Libby pushed back in her seat, anxious at what was to come. Her eyes moved towards the hologram images and watched as the moped weaved its way into the gap between the Howley and the truck ahead, clipping the car's front right bumper. Suddenly, the moped lurched to its left and as the motorcyclist attempted to take control of it, it spun around in a half-circle. Behind it, the autonomous car braked sharply but failed to swerve to avoid it. Then, as quickly as the moped appeared, it toppled to one side, and both it and the rider slipped out of view and under the car.

Jack lifted his hand again to give a second signal. Without warning, the camera was replaced by another affixed to the car's chassis. On the jurors' tablets and the largest of the wall screens, a young woman lay motionless on the road, her limbs protruding at awkward angles and the left-hand side of her skull crushed. Next to her was her helmet. Libby looked away from her tablet, only to be confronted by the same, much larger image, frozen on the wall.

She became overwhelmed by a feeling of nausea when, for a moment, she was transported back two years ago to Birmingham's Monroe Street. She could see herself standing in the road, utterly helpless, inhaling the odour of rubber tyres, recalling the crunch of broken glass under the soles of her trainers and staring at her hands, wrists, and shirt cuffs, all stained by blood. She blinked the memory away.

Of the six cases presented to the inquest yesterday, none had been as graphic as what she had just witnessed. She turned her head to look at her colleagues, but their faces showed no flickers of emotion. They had been doing this for so long, they were immune to death. Libby was not. Especially as it had followed her all her life.

The dark-haired, dark-eyed man representing the General Medical Council rose to his feet and pointed a laser pen towards the wall. A red dot appeared as the clip was repeated in slow motion. Libby held her eyelids shut.

"As you can see," he began, "when the motorcyclist appears, there is very little the vehicle can do to avoid it. It does as it is programmed to do and brakes sharply, but a collision is inevitable."

"What was the cause of death?" Jack asked.

"The autopsy revealed it was a result of severe cranial injuries to the brain stem, limbic cortex, and skull. It's likely her death would have been instant."

"What happened to her crash helmet?" asked the woman in plaid. "Did the impact knock it off?"

"Yes, it wasn't fastened properly. It was independently tested and there were no hairline cracks in its shell, no issues with the chin strap or flaws in its manufacture."

Jack sniffed sharply. "Vanity. That will be the root cause of this, mark my words. A silly girl less concerned with her own safety than her appearance."

Libby opened her eyes and mouth to protest but quickly lost her nerve.

"What do we know about the Passenger?" asked the religion rep.

"Male, thirty-seven years old, works in the financial district of London, has no criminal record or convictions," Jack explained. "He has two children under five years of age and is the sole bread-winner in the house. Obviously, he was left very shaken by this and out of pocket following the repairs that needed to be carried out to his vehicle."

"And the victim?"

Jack shot her a warning glance. "You know very well that we don't *ever* refer to the deceased as 'victims,'" he said. "There are no victims here unless we judge they have been unlawfully killed." The religion rep's head fell like that of a scolded dog as Jack continued. "The motorcyclist was nineteen years old, with a similarly clean criminal record, a theatre studies student in her first year of university. No dependents of note."

Libby reflected upon her own late teenage years, specifically how her attitude towards her life changed the day her brother took his. Nothing had ever been the same again after she found Nicky's body hanging from a light fitting in his bedroom. The cracks in her family were instant, then grew longer and wider as the years progressed. It was her fault that he died, and she would never forgive herself for letting it happen. Failure to use her voice and speak of her concerns would always be Libby's biggest regret. She would not let it happen again.

Suddenly, the urge to defend the motorcyclist got the better of her. The girl's life was worth more than a case number.

"What was her name?" Libby asked gingerly.

"Does it matter?" the woman in plaid replied, tilting her head forward so her glasses slid down her nose again.

"Yes, because I'd like to know."

She rolled her eyes and looked to one of the assistants in the corner of the room. He swiped his screen, and something appeared on the plaid woman's tablet. She was about to answer, when Jack interrupted.

"That's classified," he replied.

"What were her grades?"

"Again, classified information, Miss Dixon."

Libby was reluctant to give up. "You said she had no dependents of note. Precisely what relatives did she have?"

"Classified."

This time he shrugged as if to apologise. But everyone in the room knew better than to believe him.

"What about the name of the Passenger whose vehicle killed her?"

Jack shook his head. "I appreciate you have a curious nature, somewhat like an excitable puppy, however, none of this is of any consequence to the outcome of our decision, I'm afraid." He looked to the woman in plaid. "Any faults reported within the vehicle?"

"The black box was given the standard examination along with a full diagnostic check, and there were no errors reported," she replied. "From a legal perspective, I have no doubt that this is human error caused by the motorcyclist."

"Why didn't the car try to avoid her?" Libby continued. "All it does is brake."

Jack looked at the others and rolled his eyes, offering another fake smile. "Are you not aware of how an autonomous vehicle makes a decision in a life-or-death scenario, Miss Dixon?"

"Yes, of course, but . . ." However, Jack had little interest in Libby's reply and spoke over her.

"Then you will know that if a vehicle, like the one we have just watched, brakes without swerving, it has calculated the risk cost and makes its choice for a very, very good reason."

"Look to the left- and right-hand sides of hologram," added the dark-haired man. He was less condescending than Jack but still had yet to make eye contact with her. "On one side are parked cars, and on the other there's a stream of moving vehicles. Swerving into the path of moving traffic could have caused more fatalities. Next to the parked vehicles is a pavement—from this angle you can see there are at least twelve pedestrians. Colliding with any of those cars could have pushed them into their path."

"*Could have*," Libby repeated. "That's by no means a certainty though, is it?"

The room fell silent and she became aware that even Jack's assistants were looking at each other nervously. But Libby wasn't prepared to back down now. "Do you have a projection of exactly which cars it could have hit, the materials they're made of, and the force required to push them onto the pavement?" she asked.

"I . . . I . . . don't believe we have . . ." said the woman in plaid.

"Shouldn't we have that kind of information before we can make a judgement?"

"Miss Dixon . . ." began Jack, and he walked towards Libby, stopping in front of her. She felt small and insignificant as he towered above her. "Would you have preferred it if the vehicle had calculated a course of action that sacrificed the life of the Passenger and pedestrians to save one foolish girl?

Should more people have been made to pay with their lives because of her idiocy?"

Libby bit the inside of her bottom lip to stop it from quivering. "I thought that's what these inquests were about, to discuss what happened and to make that decision together?" she said. "Today is turning out to be just like yesterday—you've already decided on a verdict and it's never the fault of the car."

Jack took a step back and pinched the bridge of his nose. "This is, what, your second day here? I don't expect someone like you to grasp the ins and outs of software development. I do, however, expect you to trust what your government has told you. The software used in AI has been embedded with human principles to help to guide the vehicle's decision-making process."

The more condescending Jack became, the more it spurred Libby's defiance. "Are you trying to make me believe AI has the same cognitive abilities as you or me? A car can't feel sympathy and empathy or operate with a moral code like we do."

"We have a lot to get through so perhaps it's best we move on," said Jack. "Unless anyone has anything else to add that is pertinent to this case, then shall we take a vote?" The others, with the exception of Libby, voiced their agreement.

"If you could please tick one of the two boxes in the corner of the screen—"

A ringing phone coming from the corner of the room interrupted him. One of his assistants answered, and Libby noticed the colour draining quickly from his face.

"Sir," he directed towards Jack. "We will need to suspend proceedings for the time being." The hologram disappeared and at a beeping sound, all heads turned towards the large double doors as they unlocked and opened wide. The two bulky security operatives who had searched Libby on her arrival hurried inside, followed by their colleagues.

"Will someone please explain to me what is happening?" Jack asked.

"I'm sorry to interrupt," the shorter of the two security men began sternly. "But a situation has arisen that requires your immediate attention."

With his own tablet he swiped the screen until a television news channel appeared. He projected it onto one of the television screens on the large wall. It showed a rolling news channel and what appeared to be a distressed woman inside her moving vehicle, scrambling from window to window, banging on the glass with her fists. Libby immediately noticed she was pregnant.

"Who is this?" asked the religious rep. Around the image of the distressed stranger, four smaller screens flickered to life. Each appeared to contain other Passengers inside more vehicles, and all were clearly scared and confused.

"Jack?" asked the woman in plaid, looking to him for answers. Libby assumed by his blank expression that he had no more knowledge than she did. "Turn the volume up," he said as a female news anchor spoke.

"For those viewers just joining us, we are still trying to verify the validity of this live feed. But if what we are being told is correct, then it appears that four driverless vehicles are no longer under the control of their Passengers. We are still awaiting an official statement, but there is speculation that the vehicles you are watching have been hacked."

"That's ridiculous," Jack said dismissively. "It's not possible."

"They're scaremongering," the woman in plaid replied. "How can they broadcast this? It's irresponsible."

Jack turned to the shorter of the security operatives. "Get me Westminster on a secure line now."

Libby's eyes moved from Passenger to Passenger, each of them responding to what was happening to them in contrasting ways. Suddenly, as a fifth screen appeared, her jaw dropped and she struggled to catch her breath.

CHAPTER 12

Global Headlines Foundation

EDITION—UNITED KINGDOM   *London, April 6*

SOFTWARE MALFUNCTION FOUND IN LEVEL 5 DRIVERLESS CARS

Passengers in some British autonomous cars have been reportedly experiencing problems when attempting to exit them.

Footage of distressed Passengers in different locations is being broadcast live on social media by an unknown source. Government transport secretary Harry Dowling has used Twitter to reassure Level Five Passengers there is "nothing to be alarmed about" and that they are investigating.

CLAIRE ARDEN

The voices of the other trapped Passengers offered Claire a tiny shred of comfort that it wasn't just her being held against her will. But when the sound from her stereo was switched off as quickly as it had begun, her solitude returned. Anxiety tasted like acid repeating on her, so she swallowed hard to hold it back rather than risk having it consume her.

Ben will know what to do, she thought, *Ben always knows what to do.* She stopped in her tracks—she had momentarily forgotten that she couldn't call him.

Claire ran through her options. She couldn't contact the police or her girlfriends for help—that would require too much explaining. It left only one person. *Andy. He's the only one.*

She hadn't seen her estranged brother in person for three Christmases, but they had stayed in touch through vague, sporadic voice notes. However, she couldn't be sure where he was staying since the parole board had granted him an early release. She could only hope that he wasn't living too far away. If he answered his phone and she told him the whole truth about what had happened earlier that morning, she was sure he wouldn't judge her. But knowing him as well as only family could, she had no doubt that he would expect to be financially compensated in return for his assistance and his silence.

"Roxanne," she said aloud, the name Ben had christened the car's operating system. He named it after an ex-girlfriend whom Claire had met once and taken an instant dislike to. Ben had thought it funny. "I need you to telephone Andy . . ." But she didn't get the opportunity to say anything else.

"Communication system offline," Roxanne replied. Claire made several attempts to repeat the command but with no success.

The realisation hit her hard—there was no way out of that car. She was completely alone. As if to remind her of his presence, she felt her baby kicking inside her again. Claire corrected herself: she wasn't on her own; she was with her son. And for his sake, she had to survive this ordeal. She would need to protect him like she had never protected anyone else before, even Ben. She could not give up on him.

When her baby wriggled and kicked again, Claire hoped the stress of what was happening that morning was not hurting him. All she could do was put into practice the breathing techniques she had learned in her Lamaze classes. She recalled how both she and Ben had giggled their way through the lessons and how the colour had drained from his face when he was forced to watch a childbirth video. Now, she began with a deep, slow, cleansing breath before continuing with gentle, shallow ones. After a few moments, it seemed to work, and her baby settled again.

"We are going to be okay," she whispered to him, her hands gently massaging the football-sized shape of her stomach. "Just stay calm and we'll find a way out of this. We have managed to get this far; we're not giving up now."

Claire gave a furtive glance towards the rear of the car and the fine hairs on the back of her neck stood up on end. "Mummy's going to do whatever it takes, no matter what."

CHAPTER 13

I t can't be!" Libby whispered, staring at an image on the screen and scarcely able to believe her eyes. She tilted her head as she gave him an unrelenting stare and tried to regain control of her breathlessness. She ignored the other Passengers and confusion in the inquest room to concentrate on just one face.

The person you've spent six months searching for is trapped inside a driverless car.

The rational side of Libby's brain took charge and questioned whether it was really the man she met in the bar six months earlier. Was her mind playing tricks on her? Or was it someone paying him a very close resemblance? She couldn't be sure.

Slowly, she took in his appearance. He was slimmer than she remembered him. His cheekbones were more pronounced and his eyes drained of the sparkle she so clearly recalled. But she was sure that if she were in his position, the shine would have left her eyes too.

The only way she could be sure she was staring at the right man was if she heard him speak. His lips were moving but no sound was being emitted from the speakers in the room. Libby considered sharing her news with the other jurors, but the confidence she had conjured up moments earlier to argue with Jack had vanished as quickly as it arrived and taken her voice with it. For now, she would hold her tongue.

Libby looked away from the screen, momentarily distracted by the operative responsible for beaming video footage onto the largest of the walls. He frantically swiped the screen of his tablet in all directions before reaching for the stenographer's device and repeating the action. "Nothing's happening," he said. "I don't understand it. I no longer have any control over what's being shown."

"Then who does?" his colleague asked. He shrugged.

Meanwhile one of the security men handed Jack a telephone. He strode towards the doorway and hovered under the architrave out of earshot as all eyes fell upon him, awaiting a logical explanation for what was being broadcast. It was clear from Jack's slowly reddening face and expanding veins on either side of his thick neck that he was losing his patience.

"Well, find someone who *can* tell me!" he barked, and hung up.

"Jack?" asked the only other male juror. "What's happening?"

Jack took a moment to gather his thoughts. "This has yet to be confirmed, but there's a possibility a handful of vehicles may have been . . . *temporarily* compromised."

"What do you mean by 'compromised'?" asked the religious rep.

"Are you saying they've been hacked?" her male colleague chipped in.

Jack said nothing, and Libby felt her stomach tighten into a fist-sized ball.

"I am not saying that *is* what has happened; I am saying that it is a *possibility* something along those lines may have occurred. I am awaiting further information from my colleagues in the Home Office and the Ministry for Transport."

"Hacked?" the woman in plaid repeated. "But that doesn't make any sense. These vehicles are *unhackable*. That's what we were told from the very start, isn't it?"

"It's how you persuaded the public to place their trust in driverless cars," added the dark-haired man. "Cast-iron guarantees were made that because vehicles only communicate with the outside world when they have to, there's no continuous line or cloud to be hacked. Are you telling us now they can be compromised?"

"I'm sure this is nothing more than speculation and rumour," Jack replied, but his thin smile disappeared quickly and he struggled to mask his concern.

Suddenly, another of the twelve television screens became filled with an image: this time of an elderly man with a handful of medals pinned to the left breast of his jacket. His body language contrasted with that of the others—he appeared relaxed as he stared from the windows of his moving vehicle.

"That makes six of them," the male juror commented just as the sound feed to the TV news channel returned.

"And we have just had government confirmation that the people you are watching have had their cars taken over by a third party, but by whom and for what purpose, we do not yet know. All we can tell you is that they all appear to be travelling from different parts of the country to the same destination. Police have also admitted each Passenger has also been warned they may end up dead by the end of the morning."

"Dead?" gasped the religious rep, and turned to Jack. "You just this minute said it was only a possibility those cars had been hacked! These people are now, what? *Hostages?* Do you even know what is going on out there?"

Jack could no longer hold back his frustration. "Why am I hearing this from a news channel and not from any of you?" he yelled at the nearest member of his team. "If cars on my roads are being hijacked, then why am I the last to hear about it?"

"We are trying to identify who is in each car and the makes and models being driven in the hope the manufacturers can find a way of bringing them to a halt remotely."

"*In the hope?*" said Jack. "Don't give me 'hope,' give me results. And why has nobody from my own office called me back? Get me the Government Communications Headquarters online now." Jack pinched his eyes and shook his head as the assistant scurried away.

"There's number seven," the dark-haired man noted as another petrified face filled a screen, this time a woman of Asian origin.

"When is it going to stop?" asked the religious rep. "Who are these people? How are they being chosen? Why are they being targeted?"

"Shouldn't you be praying for them instead of asking so many bloody questions?" snapped Jack, and stared at the phone in his hand.

"Number eight," the dark-haired man continued. A woman wearing a hijab appeared inside another screen. "How many more will there be?"

Libby spotted Jack's hands curling into tight fists, his eyes burning with rage. "For God's sake, I can see what is happening. I don't need a running fucking commentary! I need you all to shut up so that I can think."

"Isn't that Sofia Bradbury, the actress?" asked the woman in plaid.

"No, it can't be," the religious rep replied. She perched on the end of her chair to get a closer look. Meanwhile the news channel focused on Sofia and compared it to stock footage of her in an acting role. "You're right. Well, I'll be . . ."

She was interrupted by the news anchor. "The footage we are about to broadcast has been taken from social media sources. It contains the moment each of these people, who are now being referred to as the Passengers, was informed of what is happening to them."

Each pair of eyes in the room was directed towards the largest of the screens as Claire Arden climbed into her car before it pulled away. Soon after, a voice informed her of her hijack. More Passengers' stories followed, and all were similarly informed they were facing a death sentence. They reacted with a combination of disbelief, fear, and confusion. Libby felt for all of them, but one more above the others. *Him.*

She absent-mindedly twisted a silver ring around her finger over and over again until his clip finally began to play. The Hacker called him Jude and when he replied, she listened intently to his voice. "Who is this and how did you get my number?" he asked. It was the confirmation she needed and dreaded in equal measure.

It is you, she thought.

CHAPTER 14

L ibby didn't know how to react. She wanted to grin, cry, scream, and bang her fists on the table, yelling how unfair it was. But she knew she must keep a firm grip of her emotions. She had to process what she knew about Jude before she revealed her truth to a group of strangers she didn't much care for.

Jude, she repeated to herself—he now had a name. It was like the Beatles song her brother Nicky played often. She couldn't help but wonder if only she'd heard Jude's name the night they'd met, perhaps she might have located him sooner. Then he might not be on the screen ahead of her, locked inside a car, threatened with death. Each Passenger's name now appeared on their screens, and suddenly they became people and not anonymous faces.

"Updates, now!" Libby jumped as Jack bellowed across the room.

"The National Cyber Security Centre is trying to trace the servers where the live streaming is coming from," said one of his team. "But they could be located anywhere, re-routed through numerous countries. And even if they do find them, it's unlikely they'd be in an enforceable jurisdiction."

"Well, order the news channels to pull the plug on their coverage. The public doesn't need to know any more about what's happening than what's already been reported. It'll only make things worse."

"We have no influence over them."

"We do when it's an act of terror. Who do I need to talk to about an immediate news blackout?"

"But it's not just this channel, Mr. Larsson, it's every major news station on terrestrial, cable, and satellite. Even if they're all taken off-air, people will be able to watch it online as everything is also being broadcast as it happens on social media. Facebook Live, its own TV channel, Twitter, Snapchat, YouTube Live, Instagram Stories, IGTV, and Vevo . . . and they're only the major ones. There are countless other start-ups . . ."

He ceased talking at the sound of Jack's telephone ringing. Moments later, his employer's conversation ended abruptly and Jack emitted a long breath.

"I have been informed that this incident is now being treated as a critical attack on our country," he said.

"Who by?" asked the dark-haired man.

"No faction or political group has yet to step forward. I've been informed that everyone available at GCHQ is working on this as a priority. They're getting assistance from the US and Russia too."

"There must be a procedure in place in case something like this happens?" Libby asked. Jack narrowed his eyes but it didn't stop her questions. "Surely there's a plan B for everything?"

"Does it look like there's a bloody procedure?" Jack replied. "Do you not think that if we had, we'd be carrying it out right now?"

"I don't know anything about programming, but I do know that when a computer is involved, nothing is completely safe. Anything can be exploited with the right know-how and motivation."

Jack gave Libby a stare so aggressive it made her want to melt like snow. "Why are you still here, Miss Dixon?" he asked, his change of subject throwing her off course.

"Because . . . I . . ."

"None of what is happening here concerns you, does it? In case it's not clear to you, this is a national security incident; therefore you are no longer required to serve on my jury. Now get out."

Libby surveyed the room. With no one stepping up to defend her inclusion, she rose to her feet. But as she reached for her bag, she was overcome by concern for what might happen to Jude if she were not in that room. There was nothing she could do to help him, but circumstance and coincidence had made their paths cross for a second time, and she felt duty bound to remain until the threat was over. Not being present scared her much more than Jack ever could.

"No," she said, and dropped her bag back upon the table. "I didn't ask to be on this jury; in fact, I fought not to be a part of it. But the laws you created forced me here against my will, so this is where I'm staying. If there's no precedent for what's happening, there is no reason you can have me removed."

Libby placed her hands on her hips, more determined than she could remember. No one noticed that behind the desk her legs were trembling like a leaf.

"Miss Dixon!" Jack bellowed. "Kindly get the hell out of my inquest now before I throw you out myself."

He marched towards her as the dark-haired man leaped from his seat to come between them. "Stop it, Jack, Miss Dixon is not the problem here." He looked at Libby for the first time—almost bashfully—as if to apologise for his colleague's behaviour. "If she wants to stay, let her. We have more important things to worry about."

The moment the voice came from the speakers, a chill spread through the air. They recognised it from the clips when he warned each Passenger of their fate. It was deep and honeyed, oozing calm that undermined the severity of his words.

"You should listen to him, Jack," the Hacker began. "You have more crucial matters to deal with than trying to omit Miss Dixon from this process."

Jack turned his head sharply, looking towards his team for an explanation. "Who patched him through?"

"I let myself in," the Hacker replied. "If I can hijack eight random cars and broadcast them live for the world to see, then it stands to reason I can find my way under your roof, doesn't it?"

"Who the hell is he, and how does he know I am here?" continued Jack, his top lip curled, like a snarling dog backed into a corner. He turned to Libby and pointed his finger towards her. "Is this your doing? I trust the others, but you are the cuckoo in my nest."

"Of course not!" she replied.

"I'm well versed with you all," the Hacker continued. "There's Fiona Prentice, a Scottish-born barrister at Rogers and Freemouth Solicitors, mother to daughter Tabitha and married to husband George for twenty-five years. Then there's Muriel Davidson, Religious Pluralist, married to wife of six years Laura, expecting their first child together in July. To your right is Dr. Matthew Nelson, a pathologist and recent divorcé with no children, and finally, member of Parliament and transport minister Jack Larsson, twice married and twice divorced, with no children."

The jurors turned to one another and then to Jack, as if he might offer assurances that their identities didn't matter. He gave them nothing. Instead, he lifted his head skywards, his eyes facing the ceiling as if he were talking to God.

"What you are doing is an act of terror," he said. "You are attacking our country and threatening to murder our people."

"You misunderstand me. I'm not *threatening* to murder our people. I am giving you my word that I *will* murder our people before the morning is through. And there's not a thing you can do to stop me. So please, take a seat, so that we can discuss what is going to happen next. Miss Dixon, pull up a chair and make yourself at home."

Jack tried to remain defiant, remaining where he was standing, his chest puffed out and his deep nasal breaths rippling across the room. Eventually, and without looking at anyone, he backed down and returned to his seat.

| | | GLOBAL NEWS ONLINE

GLOBAL
◄NEWS►
ONLINE

CAR HACK:
14 COUNTRIES FEAR THEY ARE NEXT.

Spain, Japan, France, and 11 other countries that bought the
UK's driverless-car operating system fear they could be
targeted next by terrorists. They were scheduled to go live with
Level Five autonomous vehicles next year.

The silence in the inquest room among jurors, security operatives, and backroom staff was palpable as each person absorbed the enormity of the Hacker's threat.

"What do you want from us?" Jack asked. He clasped his hands together as if in prayer.

"Now, now, Jack, all in good time," said the Hacker. "Why hurry things? That's the trouble with men like you, isn't it? Always wanting to get somewhere faster, always reluctant to sit back and appreciate the now. What you're witnessing is history in the making, something the world has never seen the likes of before. Today is going to be a moment in time that people will remember for decades to come. And you and your team are at the heart of it. If I can turn your attention back towards the wall."

Jack hesitated before his gaze reluctantly followed everyone else's. There were bewildered gasps when they saw their own faces reflected on-screen. From somewhere in the classified room, a camera was pointed at them, and, specifically, Jack.

"You're a covert little group, aren't you?" the Hacker continued. "Shifting from location to location the one week a month you sit; the public don't know who you are; you aren't legally bound to offer an explanation as to the decisions you make; you threaten the token member of the public with prosecution if they refuse to participate, then when they do take part, you belittle them so much that they're too frightened to ask a question or offer an opinion. Quite the little autocracy. Well, that's all in the past now, Jack. It ends today. You are being broadcast globally. There is no corner of the world where your face does not have a presence."

The jurors watched as Jack's team sprang to life, fanning out across the room with photographic image locators to find the position of the camera. "Over here!" yelled one as his gadget beeped. "It's above the door!" Jack leaped from his seat and when he reached the doorframe, he grabbed a chair and climbed upon it. He balanced precariously, running his fingertips across the walls' uneven surfaces until he touched upon something slightly raised. The large screen suddenly darkened as Jack's fingers picked at the tiny lens, no more than half a centimetre in diameter, before he prised it from the plaster. He glowered at the object in the palm of his hand before dropping it to the floor and climbing off the chair. He raised his foot.

"I'd think twice before I did that," said the Hacker. "It wouldn't be the wisest decision you've ever made. For every one of your actions today, there will be a reaction."

"Jack," whispered Muriel anxiously, "perhaps you should listen . . ."

"They know what we look like and who we are," Jack replied stubbornly. "We must nip this in the bud. We cannot be seen to be kow-towing."

Jack offered a smile to the lens below before stamping upon on it and twisting the heel of his shoe for good measure. The screen went blank. However, the image was hastily replaced by another view of the room and its people, this time from a different angle. The smile slipped from Jack's face.

"Do you think I installed just one camera?" asked the Hacker. "I'm a little aggrieved if you think I'm that lazy. There are, in fact, dozens of lenses scattered around this room, some of which you might be able to reach, others that you won't. But they are the least of your problems right now. Do you understand?"

Jack gave an almost imperceptible nod.

"So on to the business of the day. I have taken over eight of your autonomous cars—the same vehicles your government promised were impossible to penetrate or corrupt—to operate as I see fit. These Passengers represent different walks of modern British life. Some are parents, others are childless. The youngest is in her twenties, the eldest are in their seventies. Some are employed, others are not. Some have been born and raised here, others have gravitated towards this once great, but alas now fractured, country. Six of them have been purposefully chosen, and the other two have unfortunately found themselves in the wrong place at the wrong time because they needed a cab and are just as much strangers to me as they are to you. However, the one thing that every face on this wall has in common is that I have programmed each of their vehicles with an identical location.

"In approximately two hours and ten minutes from now, they will come together and, travelling at speeds of approximately seventy miles an hour, these eight vehicles will collide with one another, head-on."

CHAPTER 16

T he sound feed from the Passengers' cars immediately returned; a chorus of shock, fear, and desperation at the Hacker's threat.

Libby wanted to slap her hands over her ears to try to block out their voices as they begged for their lives. Instead, they remained clasped tightly together on the tabletop. While her life was not in danger, she was as much a part of this as they were. And she owed it to them to hear and feel their pain, not to shy away from it.

It was the reaction of the pregnant woman that chilled her the most. Claire, as the caption on-screen named her, was inconsolable. "What about my baby?" she wept. "Please don't kill my son." Libby looked to another screen, where a dark-skinned woman wearing a colourful hijab had closed her eyes and was either chanting or praying in a different language. Then Libby's gaze returned to Jude. His chest slowly rose and fell, his expression blank. *Of the seventy million people in the country, why are you caught up in this?* she asked herself. *But then, why not him? Why not any of them?*

Without warning, one of the Passenger's voices rang out through the room. "Libby, is that you?"

All heads turned to face her as Jude stared directly into his dashboard camera. Libby gazed at him, her heart racing. She wanted to give him the same warm smile she had the moment their eyes locked across the pub. Instead, she chose a more fitting, sympathetic one. "Yes, it is." She raised her hand to wave at him, then thought better of it.

"Libby, oh my God!" he replied as if equally as grateful to see her as she was to see him. "What are you doing there?" he asked.

"I was picked for jury duty."

"How . . . how are you?"

"I'm good . . . well, I was until you appeared on the screen."

"You two know each other?" said Jack. His surprise quickly turned accusatory. "I told you she had something to do with this. I want her removed and held until the police—"

"Now, now, Jack," the Hacker interrupted. "Calm yourself and let them continue."

"Why didn't you mention you knew him?" asked Muriel. She sounded as suspicious of Libby as Jack.

"I couldn't be sure until I heard his voice. We only met once, a few months ago at a bar in Manchester."

"Do you know how hard I tried to find you after that night?" Jude asked.

Libby's heart fluttered. "I tried to find you too," she replied. "The music was too loud to hear your name, so it's been like trying to find a needle in a haystack."

Jude appeared about to reply when the Hacker interrupted. "There will be an opportunity for you sweethearts to catch up later. But time waits for no man and certainly not for you, Jack."

Jack redirected his eyes up towards the speakers.

"You can spend the rest of the morning playing I spy and searching for where in the room I've placed my beady little eyes, or I can draw your attention towards car number eight."

The largest of the screens switched from a shot of the jurors to the most elderly of Passengers. He sported a head of thick, white hair, had milky blue eyes, and wore a relaxed expression. Colourful medals were pinned above his jacket pocket. The inside trim of his vehicle was plastic, and Contra Vision advertisements were spread across the windows, suggesting he was inside a taxi. He spotted himself on the dashboard monitor and cleared his throat.

"Hello?" he asked.

"Good morning, sir," began the Hacker. "Can you tell us who you are?"

He sat up straight, leaned forwards, and stared directly into the lens. "My name is Victor Patterson," he said slowly and a little louder than necessary. "That's P-A-T-T-E-R-S-O-N."

"Can you tell us a little about yourself, Mr. Patterson?" said the Hacker.

"I'm seventy-five years old and a retired printer. I have three children and seven grandchildren. Who are you? Did my daughter give the car the wrong address?"

"I see by your medals that you've served in the armed forces?"

"Oh yes," Victor replied proudly. "Twenty-Nine Commando Regiment Royal Artillery in the Falklands War, then two tours of duty in Afghanistan before the landmine got me."

"I'm sorry to hear that. Can you tell me what happened?"

"What do you think happens when a landmine gets you, son?" He chuckled. "It blew my bloody arm and leg off." He tapped his right knee with his right hand, and both made hollow thumps. "But there's no use in complaining, is there? You just get on with it. And I enjoyed a good twenty years driving the buses before they got rid of us all."

"Who got rid of you all?"

"The council did when they brought in the driverless ones. There was no need for the likes of me, was there?"

"And where are you going today, Mr. Patterson?"

"Well, this taxi picked me up and was supposed to be taking me to a hospital appointment. And then I started hearing all these voices telling me about a car crash that hasn't happened yet. So I'm a bit confused."

"What are you attending hospital for, if you don't mind me asking?"

"Radiotherapy, son. I have prostate cancer. The doctors tell me the treatment will give me another eight to ten years. That'll be enough."

Victor reminded Libby of her late grandfather, a man she had rarely seen without a smile on his face until the death of her brother. Soon after, he too had died. She could still remember him as though he'd disappeared from her life only yesterday. It was the same for everyone she had loved and lost; it was as if she remembered the dead better than those they left behind. She pulled at the ring on her finger, this time revealing a tattoo underneath. "Nicky," it read in a five-point font. She had a larger one across her left collarbone written in a bigger font, and the words "Don't carry the world upon your shoulders" from the Beatles song he loved.

Suddenly, the camera left Victor's face and switched to one outside the taxi, which appeared to be following his car along a busy city centre street.

"Jack," said the Hacker calmly. "Do you remember earlier when I told you that for every one of your actions, there will be a reaction from me? Well, when I ask you not to do something, such as touch my cameras, it is best that you listen."

Without warning, Victor's car suddenly exploded into a giant fireball, with huge plumes of black smoke and bright orange flames shooting high up into the morning sky.

CHAPTER 17

FinancialHeadlines.com

Driverless cars to have massive impact on UK workforce when they become mandatory.

- New report reveals within the decade 320,000 jobs to be created in field of autonomous vehicles.

- However, 270,000 expected to be lost in trucking, driving schools, crash repairs, valet parking, parking wardens, and taxi drivers.

- Experts warn: "More needs to be done so we are future-ready."

SOFIA BRADBURY

'm quite impressed by the special effects," Sofia whispered to her dog, Oscar. "It looks like they've invested some money into this show."

She watched on her monitor with interest as Victor's car "exploded." She was relieved that one of her competitors in the reality TV programme she assumed she was a part of had exited so swiftly. She rolled her eyes as the other contestants reacted with loud screams and obscenities. "They're a bit over the top, aren't they?" Her dog rolled from his side and onto his back, kicking her arm with his paw until she rubbed his belly. "I wonder if they still pay the full fee even if you've been voted off after half an hour? Doesn't seem fair if they don't."

Oscar let out a noxious odour, which Sofia turned her nose up at. "Sometimes you are a disgusting little beast," she muttered, and went to press the button that wound the window down. Nothing happened. Then she remembered that the producers from *Celebs Against the Odds* were now in charge of everything. "It must be for the realism . . . Making us feel like we're trapped probably adds to the tension." She dipped into her handbag and removed an almost empty bottle of Chanel No. 5, spraying it around the car.

"What are they expecting of me now? Am I supposed to scream too, or do I sit here grinning to camera like a Cheshire cat until the car reaches the studio? This lighting is a little harsh, isn't it?"

In an age when appointment television was a thing of the past and viewers watched what they wanted, when they wanted, and how they wanted to, *Celebs Against the Odds* was a phenomenon. It wiped the floor with the competition as celebrities were put through their paces in activities as varied as Formula 1 racing to assisting a surgeon during an actual operation. None of it was faked. And most participants came out the other side with their reputations intact and their popularity soaring. Sofia was thrilled to be a part of it.

Her biggest adjustment would be growing acclimatised to being on-camera twenty-four hours a day for the next week. Just minutes into it, she was already slipping, so she switched from her regular resting face and into a broad smile. She speculated as to how she looked on-screen, as she no longer saw herself on the dashboard monitor. The only people to benefit from ultra-high-definition 8K television were viewers and plastic surgeons, certainly not actors over a certain age like her.

Her focus returned to her competition, the other celebrity contestants. Try as she might, she was unable to put names to their faces. She assumed they either worked on soaps she didn't watch or had been created on other reality TV shows—a genre whose bubble just wouldn't burst, no matter how sharp the pin.

Sofia listened intently as they begged to be set free from their cars, and shook her head. She doubted any of them had paid their dues like she had, or even knew their Pinters from their Pirandellos. "They're appalling," she whispered to Oscar. "I don't know where they were trained, but they should be asking for refunds on their term fees."

She glanced outside as her vehicle travelled along the motorway, unable to keep up with a high-speed supertrain on a track close to the road. She thought back to the last time she had journeyed by train herself, and settled on the 1970s, when she and her sister Peggy made their way to Newcastle to see a Richard Burton play. Sofia had maintained a huge crush on him since her teenage years, and he didn't disappoint when she met him backstage afterwards. She had not told another living soul what had happened in that dressing room, not even Peggy. Even now, the memory brought about a guilty smile.

Without her glasses, she struggled to make out the destination on her GPS map but could just about see it would take an estimated two more hours to reach. She wondered where the studios were located, and recalled how it was all so much easier when London was the centre of the British television industry. In the name of diversity, studios were now scattered around the country, making some areas harder to reach. She hoped that Oscar would last the car journey without needing a toilet break. Or her, for that matter.

Sofia felt her resting face had slipped back into place. She removed lip gloss from her handbag, applied another coat, looked into the camera once again, and gave it an actress's smile. Using her little finger, she pushed her hearing aids deeper into each ear in the hope that when she was given further instruction, she could pick up more of what was being said.

She also hoped that upon her arrival at the studio, she might find that her agent, Rupert, had acquired her a new wardrobe. He knew the designers she favoured, even if they no longer favoured her. Once upon a time, they'd be falling over themselves to clothe her for red carpet events. But as she fell from the pages of the newspapers in favour of prettier, slimmer, and younger versions of herself, they weren't as willing to part with their designs when she couldn't guarantee them coverage.

Sofia last attended a premiere with her husband, Patrick, in February. The film title escaped her, but Patrick's face lingered. She assumed that by now Rupert had informed him where she was going and that she was uncontactable. Or perhaps he'd been in on the secret since the beginning. She knew all too well just how practised he was at holding a secret, and as a result, so was she. For forty years, he had made her complicit.

Now she would gain a much-needed break from him while filming for *Celebs Against the Odds*. The downside was he was free to do what he wanted without her watching over him. She prayed he was being careful. Over the years his mistakes had cost her a lot of money.

CHAPTER 18

JUDE HARRISON

J esus Christ!" gasped Jude as Victor Patterson's death unfolded before him.
The terror felt by the other Passengers came through his car's speakers alongside the uproar from the inquest room. His stomach muscles clenched as a wave of nausea rushed through his body. Having failed to eat for the best part of twenty-four hours, there was little left inside him to make a reappearance.

Jude couldn't tear his eyes away from the screen. Live footage continued from an unidentified second vehicle behind Victor's burning taxi. It braked and attempted to swerve the fireball ahead. But of all the potential hazards it had been programmed to react to, a car bomb was not one. It smashed into the rear, its bonnet crumpling like a concertina. Jude could hear more screaming, this time from inside that second car, then the car doors opened and its Passengers scrambled to safety. Moments later, a second fireball engulfed that car too, and the footage came to a swift end.

He briefly forgot about Libby as his attention was drawn to the other Passengers, trapped like him, all with no means of escape. In particular, he was concerned about the visibly distressed Claire. Hers was the first voice he'd heard in his car after the Hacker's. He watched as she held one hand over her mouth, the other protecting her unborn child. When faced with death, her maternal instinct was to shield something she loved unconditionally. He admired her selflessness. Amongst the other terrified voices, he could just about make hers out. "Please . . . I'm begging you," she sobbed. "Please."

Jude was filled with a need to try to reassure her that help was imminent and that they mustn't give up hope. There was very little he could say to reassure her or anyone else held in their vehicles against their will. But he had to try.

"Claire," he began, attempting to make his voice heard above the others. "Claire. It's Jude Harrison." He waited for her to acknowledge his waving at her. "Are you okay?"

Her hand moved from her mouth to her eyes to brush away the tears. "I can't die," she said, her voice barely audible above the others. "I can't die now. Not like this."

"Please, try not to panic. I know it's easier said than done, but we can't give in, okay? My instinct rarely lets me down, and it's telling me that you're a strong woman. You need to hold on to that for both of your sakes. You hear me? Don't give up. None of us should give up. We will find a way out of this."

"How?" she asked. "That Hacker, he said we are all going to die like that poor old man. How can we stop that happening?"

"I don't know yet and it's going to be difficult, but try and keep faith until we've exhausted every avenue. Okay? Will you promise me that?"

Claire sniffed much of the snot running from her nostrils and wiped away the rest with the back of her hand. Jude watched as her response came in short, sharp nods.

His eyes returned to the screen and, in particular, to Libby. In an instant he noticed that something wasn't right with her.

CHAPTER 19

> **DigitalMailNews.co.uk**
>
> *BREAKING NEWS: TERROR attacks on our roads as FALKLANDS HERO is blown up by hacker WAGING WAR on BRITAIN.*
>
> - Millions watching live are left reeling as pensioner and DOUBLE AMPUTEE is killed when his car is detonated.
>
> - Hacker warns more will follow as all hijacked cars set to COLLIDE.
>
> - Lid blown on notoriously TOP SECRET inquest as jurors' FACES are BEAMED LIVE to the world.
>
> - Royal family and government officials warned to AVOID travelling until attack brought to an end.

Almost a year had passed since Libby last suffered a panic attack.

They'd plagued her through her early twenties before gradually tapering off as her thirties loomed. When they reappeared and limited her tasks as an in-patient mental health nurse, her ex-fiancé, William, insisted she tell Occupational Health, who matched her with a counsellor. Dr. Goodwin suggested what Libby already suspected, that they were a symptom of post-traumatic stress disorder. Now, witnessing Victor Patterson's murder brought to the surface memories of both Monroe Street and her brother Nicky's death.

The counselling sessions taught her mechanisms for when she sensed an attack looming. So soon after her heart palpitations began in the inquest room, she pushed her chair back from the table, ignoring the commotion surrounding her, and tried to keep herself steady despite the disorientation. Next came the dizziness and underarm and chest sweats. She picked a blank wall to stare at and clear her mind.

Ride it out, she told herself, *don't run away from it, confront it head-on, it's not going to kill you.*

Libby had been advised that having someone with her during an episode might help to reassure her. But there was no one she placed her trust in inside that room. The only person she had any faith in was just an image on a screen and was facing much more life-threatening problems than hers. Gradually, Libby's eyes left the blank wall and returned to Jude's screen until the anxiety slowly drained from her body and her escalated heart rate decreased.

Six of the remaining Passengers appeared afraid. If the Hacker could kill a disabled pensioner and war hero so casually, he could do the same to any of them.

There was so much shouting and talking over one another that Libby struggled to take in complete sentences and could only pick up on a few random words and phrases. Sam kept repeating to his wife Heidi that he loved her and that they would be okay, but neither looked convinced. Bilquis, the woman wearing the colourful hijab, wouldn't give up hope that her telephone might just work, and kept pushing at buttons and trying to summon her operating system. Meanwhile, Shabana didn't appear to understand much of what happening, only that it wasn't good. Only Sofia was taking it all in her stride and kept smiling to camera.

Jude was more concerned with putting someone else's well-being above his own. Libby watched Jude reassure Claire, who was clearly distressed. Listening to him trying to persuade her not to lose hope was proof her instinct about him the night they'd met was the right one. He was a good man, a man who cared for others. And in Libby's experience, they were few and far between.

The Hacker's voice cut through the chatter. "Now, Jack," he continued. "Do I have your attention?" But before he answered, Libby jumped in.

"You didn't have to do that," she began, and rose from her chair. She steadied herself against the rim of the table, her legs still weak from the panic attack. "Victor didn't deserve that; he was innocent."

"Well, someone has truly found their voice, haven't they?" the Hacker replied. "I have to disagree with you though. He wasn't innocent. None of us are innocent."

"Why did you kill him? He's done nothing to you."

"Miss Dixon, hush, please," snapped Jack, glaring at her. "You are only making this worse."

"Worse? I've just watched a man blown to bits because you wouldn't follow the Hacker's instructions when you were told to! How could this get any worse?"

"Let her speak. You're not in charge of your kangaroo court now, Jack," the Hacker continued. "What's on your mind, Libby?"

"Victor was a war hero and had terminal cancer. What you did to him was completely unjust."

"I think the families of those men and women he killed in combat would disagree with you on both the 'innocent' and 'unjust' parts of your argument."

"Is that your best defence?"

"I don't have to defend myself, Libby. May I call you Libby? Now we are getting to know one another, it feels much less formal than Miss Dixon. Victor died for precisely the reason you have said—because Jack didn't listen to me."

"Even if he had listened, you'd have found an excuse to kill one of them. You just wanted to prove a point."

"And what do you think that point is?"

"That you are in charge."

"And did I get that across to you in an effective and suitable manner?"

"Effective, yes. Suitable? You must be kidding."

"Will you please stop trying to goad him!" said Jack.

"This might be an opportune moment to mention there are many more details about you that I also know, Jack," continued the Hacker. "Such as your medical records, home address, your credit card numbers, the call girls you hire, passwords, bank statements, mortgage deficits, the emails you've sent, the texts you've received, and even where you invest the cash you don't want HM Revenue and Customs to find. When you scratch beneath the surface, it's interesting to see where some of your investments have been made. And the best part about being the gatekeeper of all this knowledge? I get to impart it to an audience of millions. If you look carefully at the centre screen on the wall, you will note that everything I know about you, I'm now making public."

On cue, Jack's private information filled the screen along with links to download it.

"Take that down!" shouted Jack at the technicians around him. All scrambled to their keyboards, hitting buttons and trying to input keystrokes and instructions. Libby noted Jack staring wide-eyed back at the screen as the links remained in place. An anxious half-minute passed before he turned his head again. Libby had never seen anyone so close to exploding as Jack.

"Well?" he growled. "Why is that link still up?"

"We can't access it," replied one of Jack's staff. "It's impossible to triangulate."

"Then get the police or the National Cyber Crime Unit to do it!"

"They're patched in and they are doing everything they can, but we can't find the source."

"Jesus Fucking Christ!" yelled Jack. "There must be someone who can help me?"

"He is in our system," a technician replied. "It'll take specialised programmers time to find him and recode it all. We don't have the training or the security clearance."

"You're all fucking useless!" he bellowed, and hurled his tablet towards them. It clipped one man's shoulder and then spiralled into the wall before landing on the floor, its screen shattering.

"Someone has quite the temper, don't they?" mocked the Hacker. "Don't forget, there are cameras watching your every move."

Jack turned to look up at the screens and hesitated, as if weighing the public's potential perception of him with his need to act out his fury. Reluctantly, he erred on the side of caution.

"My system tells me that my links have already been downloaded almost fifteen thousand times," the Hacker added. "Quite incredible the reach we have these days, isn't it? People as far away as Australia and Hong Kong are now using your credit cards to purchase goods."

An on-screen counter revealed the number of shares and reposts rising by dozens each second.

"It's not too late to make any of this stop," Jack said, his tone becoming desperate. "Set the remaining Passengers free and just disappear back to where you came from. If you're that clever, you'll have covered your tracks so no one will find you."

"I'm sorry but we've gone too far for that to happen. Besides, isn't there a little part of you that wants to see what I have planned next? I am sure that Libby is dying to know."

His sudden attention startled her, and she looked up towards Jude's screen. "No, I'm not," she replied.

"I understand. But unfortunately, if you thought witnessing Victor Patterson's death was difficult, Libby, then I doubt that you are going to like what I'm about to ask you to do next."

CHAPTER 20

HEIDI & SAM COLE

What the hell have I done to my wife?

For the last few minutes, Sam's guilty conscience had been drowning out the multitude of voices coming through his car's speakers. Suddenly, more than anything else in the world, he needed to hear her.

"Heidi, are you there?" he yelled. He paused but couldn't make her out. "Heidi, please, talk and tell me you're okay."

Without warning, he became distracted by his vehicle decelerating. It had been travelling at a steady fifty-seven miles per hour, and now it was approaching the twenty-five mark. Was their nightmare coming to an end? Had whomever he crossed taken this as far as it was going? It was only when he spotted the red traffic lights ahead that he realised why his car was slowing down. His ordeal wasn't over yet.

Sam desperately wanted to shout at the top of his voice, "I've got what you want, now let us go," but he refrained. Because there was something about this scenario that felt bigger than him or the lies he'd told.

When the footage on his screen alternated from Victor Patterson's burning car to all the other Passengers, he spotted her.

"Heidi," he bellowed, determined to be heard above the others. His eyes were locked on her image until, finally, she heard him and spoke. He moved his head towards a speaker to listen carefully until he could make out her voice.

"Sam!" she replied. "Why's this happening?"

He hesitated. He would exhaust all avenues before admitting to how he might have got them into such a mess. "I don't know, but we have to be strong," he said. "You and me, we're in this together."

"It doesn't make any sense. Why is he threatening to kill us?"

Heidi's despair matched his own. Sam couldn't recall a time he had last seen his wife so vulnerable—not after the sudden death of her father or the birth of their two children. She was the solid one in their partnership, the rational one, the clear thinker. Whatever was happening to them had knocked her for six. He would do anything to take her fear away.

"Did you see what he did to that man's car?" she continued. "He was just . . . blown up."

"We only have the Hacker's word that he did that. Computer programmes and special effects can make anything look real."

"It looked bloody real to me!"

"We're not going to die, I promise you."

"You can't promise me anything."

"This is someone's idea of a sick joke, and once your police colleagues become involved and see that one of their own is caught up in it, they'll get us out."

"Jesus, Sam, don't be so bloody naive! It doesn't matter whether I'm in the police or not. Look at what's happening. Our cars have been hacked and are being controlled by somebody else. If he's gone to all this effort, it's hardly likely a few harsh words from my sarge are going to make him have a change of heart, is it?"

Sam slumped in his seat and rubbed his hands against his scalp as if it might stimulate his brain into coming up with a way to free them. Locked doors meant he ruled out jumping from the moving car. He had seen one Passenger in her hijab try and fail to kick her way through the reinforced glass. The car's battery kept topping itself up as it drove over recharging points, so it was unlikely to drain before his arrival at their final destination. And with no operating system to obey his commands or allow him to communicate with anyone aside from other Passengers, he was stuck.

He kept repeating one word to himself over and over again—*why?* It was the question that had plagued him since the people blackmailing him first appeared in his life six weeks earlier. In some ways it made sense they were now behind the hijacking—after all, they had taken grim pleasure in tormenting and taunting him before revealing what they wanted. But in other ways, it was illogical. Twenty minutes before the Hacker's voice was heard, he had sent them an email informing them that he had what they wanted. He had also attached a videogram of it as proof. They had responded with the drop-off instructions—a shopping centre in Milton Keynes. If they kept their end of the bargain, Sam could have his old life back.

So why, before the handover, were they now involving Heidi? If she found out what he'd done, he wouldn't need to keep quiet. And if they were going to up the ante, they were in for a disappointment because there was nothing left.

The more thought he gave it, the more he realised too many other things about the scenario weren't making sense either, like the involvement of his fellow Passengers and the apparent murder of one of them. Was he part of a much wider scam, and were they in on it too? Or were they, like him, victims?

More and more he was considering whether he and Heidi had found themselves caught up in something much bigger that had nothing to do with the extortion. And that scared him more than being blackmailed, because at least he knew what they wanted.

There was one thing he could be certain about, however. He was not going to end up in a ball of flames like Victor Patterson. If it came down to the choice of husband or wife, they would kill her first.

Otherwise they would never get their hands on the £100,000 in cash that was sitting in a hold-all behind him.

CHAPTER 21

Libby couldn't be sure how many cameras the Hacker had installed to monitor the inquest room, only that one of them was trained on her face and was now filling the largest of the screens.

It was uncomfortable and disconcerting, and while she wasn't particularly self-conscious, the ultra-high-definition screen highlighted her every flaw, pore, and skin blemish. It made her want to suck in her cheeks, raise her head to hide her double chin, and adjust her posture so she didn't appear quite so round-shouldered. She looked to the other screens, and two news channels were using the same image, with her full name printed in large letters across the bottom and the word "live" emblazoned on the top.

Inevitably, her attention returned to Jude. She was desperate to speak to him again but of all the conversations she had rehearsed should she have found him, none fitted these circumstances. She also didn't know whether to believe the Hacker when he informed them they would have time to talk later. And only now was it registering that he had referred to them as "sweethearts." How had the Hacker known there had been something, albeit brief, between them? Had he been following her attempts to trace Jude? For how long had she been on his radar?

Libby realised that while she was lost in thought, the room had become muted. Even the blusterous Jack was reticent to speak now that he was aware he was on-camera. In fact all the jurors had become less vocal since they were publicly identified.

She assumed they were all waiting to hear the Hacker's instructions.

But he wasn't hurrying to impart his plan. Libby had an inkling he was waiting to be asked. To him, this was a game and he enjoyed the interaction with his players. So when no one else appeared willing, she stepped up to the plate.

"What do you want me to do next?" she said.

"I thought you'd never ask," the Hacker replied. "But first, a polite reminder. One of the many benefits of the electric motors and circuit boards that operate an autonomous car is that it's freed up room inside them, far more than diesel or petrol vehicles ever had. There's more legroom, the seats are larger, there is more space for storage for suitcases, shopping, and several kilos of explosives. So, if any of the remaining seven vehicles under my control are interfered with in any way whatsoever, I will not hesitate to detonate more. If any person, persons, emergency services, or armed forces personnel attempt to bring one to a standstill, I will detonate it. If anyone encourages it to stray from its programmed path or messes with signs or traffic signals, I will detonate it. If anyone tries to break a Passenger free, I will detonate it. If anyone slows it down, I will detonate it. I would not go to all this effort only to make empty threats. Have I made myself clear?"

"Yes," Libby replied.

"You'll forgive me for saying this, Libby, but your word carries little gravitas. I'm referring to you, Jack. What do you have to say? Will you adhere to my rules?"

Jack hesitated before he replied with a simple "Yes."

"I'm pleased to hear it. But as we all know, saying something and doing something are two very different things. I need to know that you're not just paying me lip service. I explained to you earlier that each of the Passengers would be dead by the end of the morning in a collision. In an effort to show you I'm not as heartless as you think I am, I'm willing to allow one of them to exit this process without hurting so much as a hair on their head. While the remaining six cars will still all collide with one another in two hours and five minutes from now, one lucky Passenger will walk away unscathed."

"Who?" Libby asked, her eyes drawn straight to Jude. Raised voices coming from the other side of the closed doors distracted her.

"First things first. To fully appreciate what it feels like to save a life, you must take one. Between you, you are to decide which Passenger to sacrifice to save the others."

"We can't do that!" Libby exclaimed. "You can't ask us to murder someone!"

The noise from the other side of the doors grew louder.

"We are not going to send anyone to their death," said Muriel adamantly, and folded her arms.

"What if I told you that if you didn't kill one person, then I would kill them all? In front of me I have a keyboard and four-figure command at my disposal. If I type in those numbers, each car will be detonated at exactly the same time."

They heard a gentle tapping sound as the Hacker made his first keystroke.

"He's bluffing," said Jack.

A second key was pressed.

"He could be hitting anything. We don't know."

The sound of a third keystroke followed.

"Do you really want to take the risk?" the Hacker asked. Nobody answered.

"Choosing someone, it's . . . it's impossible," said Libby.

"Not always," the Hacker replied. "Allow me to make a comparison. Say, for example, two of the cars contained almost identical Passengers, two men—they're the same age, are of the same appearance, work in the same careers, have similar dependents—which one would you choose to die?"

"I couldn't."

"What if I told you one of the men had a history of sexual violence against women? Would that make a difference?"

"That's hypothetical; what you're asking us to do is real," said Libby.

"You haven't answered me."

"The sex offender," interrupted Jack. "That's the answer he wants, just give it to him."

"I'd choose neither," said Libby. "I wouldn't make that decision."

"Then you'd be sending them both to their deaths," said the Hacker. "How would you feel being responsible for the murder of an innocent man?"

"I wouldn't be responsible because you're the one controlling their cars. You're the one killing them."

"Yet I'd be the one sleeping soundly of a night while you'd remain trying to convince yourself that taking the moral high ground was the right thing to do. But quietly, you'd know that you did the wrong thing."

Before Libby could answer, the increasing volume of voices in the other room became impossible to ignore. The two security operatives looked to each other and then moved towards it, removing electric stun gun–like devices from their jacket pockets.

"Would it help if I told you that the five of you won't have to make the decision alone, Libby?" the Hacker continued. "Because the rest of the world will have its say too."

Suddenly, the double doors opened and the security operatives jumped into position, ready to defend themselves against what was to come. However, ready to enter were six uniformed police offers, each holding semi-automatic rifles to their chest, flanking two men, two women, and trolleys packed with electronic devices.

"Who the hell are you?" Jack asked the officer with the most accolades pinned to his uniform.

"We've been ordered by the Home Office and National Counter Terrorism Office to escort these people inside this room to assist." He thrust a tablet into Jack's hands. "It'll all here."

"To assist in what?"

CHAPTER 22

@HijackerHacker
Which Passengers should die first?

POLL IT
✔ ✗

O Claire

O Sofia

O Jude

O Shabana

O Heidi

O Sam

O Bilquis

947,098 votes

At the beginning of the day, the inquest room felt vast, airless, and empty. Within the space of thirty minutes, there was disarray. Five jurors, a stenographer, and a clerk had expanded to include security operatives, backroom staff, police officers, and now a new group of unfamiliar faces.

A man with Southeast Asian features, peroxide-blond hair, thick-framed glasses, and unnaturally cobalt-blue eyes caught everyone's attention. He strode into the centre of the room, lifted his glasses, and gave the available space the once-over. "Put the tables here," he said, and directed with his finger to a position under the windows. His team moved swiftly, returning from the other room and sliding the tables across the flagstones with a piercing shriek, like fingernails being dragged down a blackboard.

"Will someone please tell me what is going on?" Jack asked the police officer in charge. An embroidered badge above his pocket gave his name as Commander Riley. He wore body armour and, like his colleagues, held a semi-automatic rifle in both hands against the lower portion of his chest.

"We have been escorting a specialist team here to help you," he replied.

"With what? And who told them to come here? I certainly didn't request them."

"The Home Office has given them special dispensation."

"But they need clearance, they need to be vetted—"

"Have no fear, we are no strangers to a crisis," interrupted the man with the peroxide hair. "And boy, do you have a crisis on your hands. We've worked with most of your government departments over the years."

"Then why haven't I seen you before?"

He eyed Jack up and down. "I could ask the same."

Jack turned to Commander Riley. "Get them out of here," he growled.

"You are not in charge of this room, sir. I am, and I have clear instructions they are to remain here."

"Get me the Home Office on the phone," Jack ordered to no one in particular.

Libby and the jurors watched with interest as the latest additions to the room busied themselves unpacking the trolley of electrical equipment and setting up phones, monitors, cables, Wi-Fi routers, keyboards, and tablets.

"Sorry, sir, the line is engaged," one of Jack's assistants said nervously.

"What, the red line?"

"Yes, all of the lines."

"Jesus!" he yelled in frustration, then forced himself to sound calmer. "Right, anyone who doesn't need to be in this room, please get out." He glared at the two security operatives and his staff who had entered with Commander Riley. To Jack's irritation, they turned to the commander and awaited his signal before shuffling out the door. Riley then nodded to his armed colleagues, who also left.

"I'll be outside if you require me," Commander Riley directed towards the blond-haired man before closing the door behind him. Jack waited until he heard the electronic beep of the door locking before he turned to confront the new arrivals.

"Now give me a straight answer—who are you people?"

"Straight is not a concept I'm overly familiar with," the peroxide-haired man replied, and gave Jack a wink that briefly amused Libby despite the circumstances. He removed his glasses and wiped them with the sleeve of his jumper. "Cadman," he continued without looking Jack in the eye.

"What the hell is a Cadman?" asked Jack blankly.

"A Cadman is what you're going to need for the duration of whatever *this* is and to translate to you what the world is saying about it."

"Why should I give a damn what the world has to say?"

"Because, collectively, they are the sixth juror."

"Are you kidding me?"

Cadman moved towards the other jurors. "I hate to showboat but if I don't, then no one else will. I'm the country's foremost expert in all things social media. If it's been on the web and I haven't seen it, then it's not worth talking about. My team and I are here to interpret whom the people beyond these four walls are talking about online. Nobody knows more about mass communication than I do. I know my machine learning from my micro-moments, my conversions from my clickbait, my organic reach from my omni-channels, and my big data from my business intelligence. I know the words that matter and the words that don't; I know what will trend because, frequently, I have made them trend; I have created algorithms that will collate the data we require quicker than Tim Berners-Lee can blink. I know this because *this is what I do*. You asked me what a Cadman was? You are looking at it. I am Cadman, and you are going to allow me to do the job I have been summoned here to do. Those using social media will be voting alongside you, and I am here to search and translate the results of who they want to live and who they want to die."

"Why would the rest of the world care?" Jack asked.

Cadman laughed. "Oh, you are such a kidder, aren't you?" He turned to the jurors. "He is kidding, isn't he?" Muriel shook her head. "Jack, five minutes after this all blew up, excuse the pun and RIP Victor, it's been the only thing anyone is talking about. Every country in the world with access to social media is watching you, they're watching the Passengers, and they're taking in everything as it happens live. Look." He turned his tablet to face Jack. "On average there are six thousand tweets sent every second of every day. That number has doubled today. Facebook has never seen so much traffic since its peak back in 2020, and this one event is bringing them millions of pounds of revenue every minute. It is pulling the world together."

Cadman flicked the page of his tablet to project against another wall. It featured news channels from around the world. The USA, Japan, Russia, Saudi Arabia, and New Zealand were all running live footage of the events on British roads.

"Who sent you?" asked Jack.

"Now that, I can't answer you. We were booked months ago through the usual government channels and paid in advance," he continued. "We were told we'd be informed of what would be required of us on the day. Taxis were sent to our hotel this morning, and on our way here I was sent profiles of six of the people trapped in these cars. Then we received an urgent call from Cabinet Office Briefing Room A, or COBRA to you and I, urging us to attend—they were taken aback to learn we'd already been booked. Commander Riley and his team escorted us up here and explained what we'd find behind closed doors."

If Cadman felt intimidated by Jack's piercing gaze, he didn't show it. He looked to the Passengers' screens. "So get me up to speed. Which one of this lot are you killing off first then?"

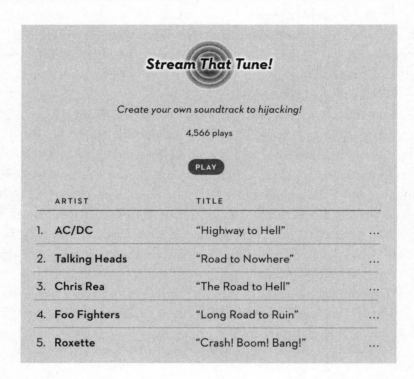

CHAPTER 23

Stream That Tune!

Create your own soundtrack to hijacking!

4,566 plays

PLAY

	ARTIST	TITLE	
1.	**AC/DC**	"Highway to Hell"	...
2.	**Talking Heads**	"Road to Nowhere"	...
3.	**Chris Rea**	"The Road to Hell"	...
4.	**Foo Fighters**	"Long Road to Ruin"	...
5.	**Roxette**	"Crash! Boom! Bang!"	...

L ibby did not appreciate the flippancy with which Cadman referred to the Passengers.

"We have yet to discuss it properly," she said. "And I wouldn't know where to start. It's impossible."

Cadman shrugged. "Bringing the dead back to life, travelling at the speed of light, standing at a supermarket checkout and not looking at what the person in front of you has put on the conveyer belt—they are impossible things. Voting for someone to die whom you've never met? Not so impossible. And the public is already lapping up the opportunity to have its say."

"Who in their right mind would want to send someone to their death?"

Cadman read the tablet he held. "Approximately two hundred thousand people so far—and that's based only on what's trending on Twitter."

"I don't understand. Two hundred thousand people are doing what so far?" asked Libby.

Cadman turned to his team. "Am I going to have to spell everything out to them?" He sighed. "Of the million Twitter mentions of the hijacking, at least two hundred thousand of them have hashtagged the name of a Passenger they'd most like to see dead."

"How can they be so quick to judge?" asked Muriel. "They know as much about the Passengers as we do. You can't make a decision based on so little."

"Wars have been started, fought, and won on less detail," Cadman replied.

"Muriel is correct," the Hacker began, and a hush befell the room. "People are voting purely on the basis of what they have seen and little else—much like how decisions are made in your inquests." Libby was the only juror not to look sheepish. "Your process is biased and unfair," the Hacker continued. "I would like to make my process fairer." He paused.

"Is he always this dramatic?" Cadman whispered.

"He's waiting for us to ask how," said Libby.

"Ooh, mind games. I'll bite. How, Mr. Hacker?"

"Let's find out a little bit more about our Passengers, shall we?" the Hacker replied. "Please turn your attention to the wall."

Libby watched as some screens blanked and others rotated so that just eight remained. Seven contained one Passenger, and the last showed footage of firefighters dampening the blaze of Victor Patterson's taxi. It was a stark reminder of what the Hacker was capable of.

"Let's begin with Passenger number one. Claire Arden is a twenty-six-year-old teaching assistant at a school for children with special needs. She is married to husband Benjamin and seven months pregnant with their first child." Libby's heart broke for the red-eyed woman, tears streaming down her face and clutching her stomach. And when #killclaire appeared in the corner of the screen, it nauseated Libby.

"In vehicle number two, we have Bilquis Hamila, forty-six, who arrived in this country two years ago from Somalia, claiming political asylum. She is widowed and has a daughter back home whom she hopes to bring to the UK. Her application to become a British citizen has already been refused by the Home Office, and she is currently midway through the appeals process."

In her nursing career, Libby had worked with refugees, foreign nationals, and asylum seekers. So she was no stranger to hearing the horrors inflicted on a person by war and torture and seeing how regularly it manifested itself with psychoses, depression, and PTSD. She wondered how much Bilquis had suffered to make her flee her country and leave her child behind.

"Our third Passenger, you might recognise. It's actress Sofia Bradbury, seventy-eight, a star of stage and screen for seven decades. She is married to husband Patrick, they are childless, and she has dedicated much of her spare time to raising millions of pounds for children's charities and hospitals." To everyone's surprise, Sofia gave the camera a smile and a wave.

When Passenger four's face filled the screen, Libby's heart raced again. "Jude Harrison is twenty-nine years old, a former computer programmer for a car manufacturing company. He has no partner, no dependents, and is currently unemployed. He is also presently homeless and living out of his car."

Libby drew in a long breath, the homeless part of his description having come out of the blue. She noted Jude's eyes shifting away from his camera, embarrassed. What had happened to him in their time apart that caused him to live in his vehicle? This time, she looked beyond him and spotted empty pizza boxes and fast-food cartons next to a rucksack, all spread out across the seats behind him. For the first time, she noticed a sadness in Jude that ran deeper than his current circumstances. She had seen the same look before in her brother Nicky's eyes.

"Passengers five and six are husband and wife Samuel and Heidi Cole, both forty years of age," the Hacker continued. "They are parents to children Beccy and James, aged nine and eight. They have been married for ten years. Sam runs a refurbishment and construction company, while Heidi is a police officer in the Bedfordshire constabulary." Libby's heart went out to their children, and she hoped they had been shielded from what was being broadcast. The couple appeared equally anxious. She couldn't decide if having your partner trapped in the same life-or-death situation as you would be a comfort or more stressful.

"And finally, Passenger number seven is Shabana Khartri, thirty-eight, a stay-at-home mother of five who is married to husband Vihaan, an alleged people trafficker. She moved to the UK when she married at eighteen and has lived here ever since. She has never worked and does not speak English."

How much does she understand about what's happening around her? Libby asked herself. By the way she wrung her hands and kept her eyes tightly shut, Libby assumed Shabana was only too aware that she was caught up in something awful.

"Now, jurors," the Hacker continued. "Without discussing your decision with your colleagues and based only upon the information I have presented to you, it is decision time. One by one, please tell me which Passenger you are choosing to send to their death."

ONLINE TRENDS FOR YOU	#EnglishBeforeImmigrants—251,098 tweets
	#WeHateThe8—167,918 tweets
	#KillThemAll—104,221 tweets
	#SaveThemAll—12,001 tweets
	#SendingPositiveVibes—2,566 tweets

Libby turned her head towards the rest of the jurors. By their blank expressions, nobody else appeared to know how to respond to the Hacker's request for the name of a Passenger to send to their death. She cleared her throat to speak first.

"You've only given us an outline of these people; that's not who they are," she began. "You can't expect us to decide who should die based on a pencil portrait."

"I think you'll find that I can and that I just have," the Hacker replied. "Now who would like to go first?"

Libby gave a dismissive wave of her hand. "No, I am not participating. You might have the Passengers under your control, but you don't have me."

"Do I really need to remind you of what happens when you don't do as I ask, Libby? Thanks to Jack, there are pieces of Victor Patterson still falling from the skies. I have no hesitation in re-enacting that moment with the aid of your friend Jude. So, I'll ask you again. Who would you like to pick first?"

"Number two—Bilquis," said Jack, taking the room by surprise. He folded his arms defiantly. "Well, someone had to get this charade moving," he added. He fixed his gaze on Muriel as if to cajole her into a decision.

"It is with a heavy heart that I choose Bilquis too," said Muriel quietly.

"Bilquis," repeated Matthew.

"Bilquis," said Fiona.

Libby watched the screen as a helpless Bilquis covered her mouth and wept.

"And you, Libby?" the Hacker asked.

She looked at each Passenger in turn, but there was not one candidate who deserved to live or die more than another. It didn't matter whom she picked as neither she nor the public vote would make up the majority. Bilquis had already been handed a death sentence, so she chose the person with the least number of years ahead of them.

"Sofia," she said, and like the other jurors, she couldn't bring herself to look up at the face of the person she'd picked.

"Thank you," said the Hacker. "It doesn't take a statistician to point out that it's an almost unanimous decision, but, Cadman, out of interest, could you reveal the results from social media, please?"

Cadman looked to one of his team, who mouthed the word "sent" before Cadman examined his tablet. "My algorithms tell me the Passenger the public would most like to die is the same as the jury's choice—Bilquis."

Libby and Matthew were the only jury members whose eyes returned to the wall where Bilquis was now the main image. Gradually, the volume grew louder and louder until her distress and pleas for mercy were impossible to ignore. Muriel clamped her hands over her ears.

"Please," Bilquis begged. "Please, change your minds . . . I am a good woman, I want to be with my daughter again, let me tell you what I do to help others and you might think diff—"

Before she was allowed to finish her sentence, Bilquis's car shook violently before a flash of light and flames could be seen racing from the rear and towards her. Within seconds, Bilquis became engulfed in an inferno. Libby was paralysed, unable to move her head or tear her eyes away from what was unfolding as Bilquis's clothes caught fire. She thrashed around, making agonising noises Libby had never heard another human make. Suddenly a figure appeared in front of Libby so that she could no longer see the screen. Without saying anything, Matthew placed his hands on her shoulders.

"Look at me," he said. "Look at me."

Libby's eyes met his. "Keep looking at me until this is over and I tell you to stop." More screaming followed, and then the sounds of flames and skin crackling before another explosion and a loss of picture. By the time Matthew let go of Libby, all that remained on the wall was a blank screen.

"I can't be here, I need to leave," she exclaimed, rising from her seat and hurrying on shaky legs towards the door. "I need air, I have to go home." She banged both hands on the door until it opened. Commander Riley and his colleague blocked the door, preventing her escape.

"Please, let me out," Libby begged. "I can't stay here any longer and watch more people die."

"I am sorry, ma'am, but I'm not allowed to let anyone leave the room until the process is complete," the commander replied. "I have my orders."

"I don't care!" Libby shouted, tears streaming down her face. Her breathing was rapid and, once again, she felt as if her skin was close to boiling point. Another panic attack, this time more full-blown than the last, was imminent. She needed cool, fresh air and to feel safe again.

She reached to grab the officer's broad arm and to pull it to one side. It wouldn't budge, and in her frustration, she lashed out, clipping him around the head and knocking his earpiece to the floor. In one swift manoeuvre, he grabbed both ends of his gun and used it to push her sharply backwards, where she lost her balance and fell, backside first. She yelped in pain as her coccyx connected with the flagstone floor.

"Social media is not going to like that," muttered Cadman.

"Do not treat her like that," snapped Matthew, and squared up to the commander.

"Sit down, please, sir," Commander Riley ordered. "This building is on complete lockdown. Every street within a one-mile radius has been evacuated, and this building is also being searched for explosive devices. Until either the Hacker is traced or we know how to disable those cars, you will all remain in here."

He pointed to a news channel that had reappeared on the wall. The jurors recognised the town hall where armed soldiers were redirecting members of the public from behind blue tape. Police cars, ambulances, fire engines, and army bomb disposal units could all be seen. Above the building a swarm of drones competed for airspace.

"We should have just held firm. We shouldn't have done what he told us to," said Libby. Matthew stretched out his arm to help her off the floor. She accepted it, and the doors closed behind her.

Once again, the Hacker's voice came from nowhere. "If that had been your course of action, I would have detonated all vehicles," he said.

"You're sick," Libby replied. "You don't blow people up to get attention. That's not how the world works."

"Have you read the news in the last century? Did Oppenheimer, the IRA, Al-Qaeda, ETA, Hamas, and ISIS pass you by?"

"You know what I mean. *Ordinary* members of society don't behave in this way. They don't kill for the sake of it."

"And neither do I. I kill for a purpose."

"Which is?"

The Hacker didn't reply.

"You knew that Bilquis was going to be chosen first—her or Shabana, didn't you?"

"Why might you assume that?"

"Because you didn't include anything positive about them. Instead, you emphasised that Shabana didn't work, she spoke no English, had five children, and her husband's been accused of people trafficking. And Bilquis was a failed asylum seeker wanting to bring another family member over here. You cherry-picked nuggets of information to encourage us and social media to vote in a particular way."

"Which is exactly how this jury operates. You make decisions based on the bare minimum of facts. Are you saying it might have made a difference if I'd mentioned her daughter in Somalia has been dead for two years and it's her ashes Bilquis wanted to bring to Britain? Or that before Bilquis escaped the civil war in her country, she was made to watch her five-year-old child being raped by rebel fighters? Should I have told you that she nursed her daughter as she bled to death in her arms? Perhaps I should have added that despite all this, Bilquis still found the strength to help and pay for fifteen orphaned children to flee Somalia on the same boat as her? If you had been given these facts, would you have allowed her to burn to death?"

Libby's expression hardened. "You told the people what they wanted to hear to make their decision easier."

"As with your inquests, the full disclosure can be an inconvenience when a decision needs to be made. Am I wrong, Jack?"

CHAPTER 25

#ShaantiSeAaraamKaren—401,301 tweets
#RIPBilquis—345,988 tweets
#EnglishBeforeImmigrants—253,098 tweets
#SaveThemAll—177,918 tweets
#SendingPositiveVibes—19,566 tweets

W hat does he mean?" Libby directed to Jack.

"With regards to what?" he replied.

"When he said the truth is an inconvenience. Why was he directing that towards you?"

"I have no idea. Perhaps you should ask him? You two appear to have developed quite the little rapport. A friendly word of advice though—you'd best be careful or people might come to the wrong conclusions."

His tone was far from friendly and Libby's eyebrows rose. "Why would you even think that?"

Jack straightened his tie, the corners of his mouth rising to indicate his amusement at having goaded her. "Centre stage suits you, Miss Dixon. When you came into this room, you were a shy little wallflower, and look at you now; you're like Japanese knotweed, spreading your roots into places they don't belong and proving quite impossible to restrain. Some might think you're beginning to enjoy your time in the spotlight." He looked to the cameras and smiled.

"I thought beneath that façade there just might lie a shred of decency. But you're empty, aren't you?"

Jack's response was to flick her away with his hand as though he were swatting a fly. "I think you'll find the many thousands of constituents I tirelessly serve may disagree."

Muriel interrupted, her expression concerned. "Why hasn't the Hacker told us where the collision point is?"

Matthew shook his head. "He only tells us what he wants us to know."

"Is it just me or does anyone else have a horrible feeling he plans to send the cars to this building?"

"That wouldn't happen because they won't be permitted access into Birmingham city centre, or any city centre for that matter," said Jack. "If each of these vehicles is packed with explosives like the Hacker claims, they are unlikely to reach a one-mile radius of an exclusion zone."

A new camera angle appeared on a screen. Footage came from high above a moving car. Framing the screen were numbers, graphics, and coordinates.

"Hmm," Cadman began, and rubbed at the stubble on his chin. "This is interesting. Apparently, we shouldn't have access to this."

"Isn't it a news channel's drone?" asked Libby.

"Not according to Reddit. Users say the graphics are military."

An ominous feeling swept through her. "What's social media saying about the purpose of these drones?"

"Bear with me," he replied as he and his team typed key words and phrases into their devices. "Okay, José . . . so, footage of one of the drones was recorded by a regular Passenger and uploaded onto Snapchat seven minutes ago. The consensus is that it's an unmanned combat aerial vehicle operated by the army . . . and now KnowHow users are claiming it's an RP 7876V. Said drones are apparently 'armed and capable of discharging many rounds of ammunition.'"

Libby faced Jack. "Are they going to shoot the Passengers off the roads?"

"Isn't it obvious? What else do you think they're going to do? Sit back and watch them blow up in the middle of our cities? You must remove the smallest number possible to save the most. It's standard warfare technique."

"But this isn't a war."

"But it is, you silly woman!" he mocked, then turned his eyes sharply to the camera, as if reminding himself of his audience. He adjusted his tone accordingly. "This Hacker is waging war on our country, on our roads, on our people, *on you and me.* Do you expect the government to just accept it? We cannot allow terror to prevail, even if it means some of our own suffering for the greater good."

As Libby looked towards Jude, her shoulders slumped. She had assumed the only threat to his life was from the Hacker, not from his own country.

"When will it happen?"

"I doubt very much that it will," the Hacker interrupted.

"Then you are fooling yourself," said Jack. "The will of one shall never prevail over the safety of the masses."

"Do you know how many schools, colleges, and academies there are in the UK, Jack?" the Hacker continued. He waited long enough for Jack to shake his head. "There are almost twenty-six thousand, containing nine point two million children."

"And why are you telling me this?"

"Do you not think I have planned for every eventuality? Ten of these twenty-six thousand schools contain a number of explosive devices inside them, which I am able to detonate at any given moment. The explosives could be located anywhere on each of the premises—classrooms, store cupboards, gymnasiums, lockers. Should an order be given to remove any Passengers from the road, then I will not hesitate to detonate my devices in all ten schools at once."

"They all need evacuating now . . ." Jack muttered, and removed his phone from his pocket.

"Attempting to move more than nine million children within the next eighty minutes is an impossibility. Contacting each parent, then having them leave their places of employment to pick their children up will see countrywide chaos and traffic jams of the like we have never witnessed before. And if our country is gridlocked and my vehicles do not reach their destination, both they and the schools will be detonated. Would you like that on your conscience?"

"Your threats aren't going to stop panicking parents making sure their kids are safe," said Libby.

"Perhaps I should add that each of those ten schools also has vehicles that contain nail bombs parked within close proximity to exits and entrances. Those pupils, parents, and teachers in the blast radius who are not immediately killed will certainly suffer life-changing injuries."

Libby's heart sank. Even Jack appeared unsure of his next approach, holding his phone in his hand but not using it. The news channels reappeared, each broadcasting live footage from the inquest room. "Breaking news— bombs in our schools," ran a news ticker along the bottom of a screen. Libby could only imagine the angst of parents up and down the land.

She noted Jude was the only Passenger staring calmly into his monitor, as if he were resigned to his fate. Once again, she recognised a sadness in his eyes that ran much deeper than his current circumstances. Was it the cause of why he was now living out of his car?

"Let us lighten the mood and see what our friends on social media have to say about this latest turn of events, shall we, Cadman?" continued the Hacker.

"There's a mass panic amongst parents, as you'd expect," he began. "And many are threatening to go against your warning and pull their kids out of school immediately." He removed his glasses and smiled. "You see, this is what I love about my fellow social media users. Despite threats to their kids' lives, they still prioritise sharing their fears with the world before they scuttle off to rescue their little ones. Share, then react. I love it."

"Is anything being said about us?" asked Muriel. She fiddled nervously with her wristwatch as Cadman and his team scanned their feeds.

"I'm generalising here, of course, but it appears they don't like the colour of Fiona's jacket, Matthew's name is trending with #hotdoc, thousands are calling for Jack to be deselected, they find Muriel's voice 'irritating' and 'whiny,' and they think Libby is a 'bleeding-heart snowflake with a terrible taste in shoes.'"

"Seriously?" asked Libby, and crossed her arms. She wasn't sure which criticism offended her more. "Two people have been murdered by car bombs, and the lives of thousands of children are at risk, yet they're tweeting about my shoes?"

"They have a point though," Cadman replied. "I assume they were a gift?"

"No, they were not."

Cadman appeared surprised. "I suggest you think of social media as a river. It begins in one place, but the farther it travels, the more it meanders in different directions. Some new routes dry up quickly; others take on directions all their own. Everyone has an opinion. You could personally travel to each one of those schools, deactivate every explosive device yourself, and then single-handedly save the lives of every Passenger. Yet some troll in a council flat in Hackney with split ends and badly spelled tattoos will still complain you've set woman's rights back a decade because you did it while wearing a skirt."

Libby was exasperated. All she wanted was to escape that room, return home, curl up under the duvet, and never think about a driverless car again. "Please," she directed to the Hacker. "Just bring this to an end. You've shown us driverless cars aren't infallible like we were told. So you don't have anything left to prove."

"I never said I had anything to prove, Libby."

"Then what's the point of all this?"

"On a daily basis we have allowed our lives to become dictated by the decisions artificial intelligence makes for us. That's what you believe, isn't it, Libby? That we have such little regard for our own existence, we've willingly surrendered ourselves to AI, something man-made yet incapable of empathy, sympathy, or moral judgement. You think we've taken the human out of humanity?"

"I don't want gadgets thinking for me."

"But you are just as much a slave to AI as every other person. How do I know about the protest march you attended in London against the Road Revolution bill two years ago?"

"I . . . I . . . don't know."

"Because AI and its associated technology have told me everything I need to know about who you are and what you believe in. The credit card transactional data on your watch told me where and when you purchased day-return train tickets and which train it told you to take. It also informed which eatery you asked your virtual assistant to recommend for lunch and the name of the bar where you went for drinks afterwards. Your fitness tracker revealed how long you were on your feet marching, how many steps and kilometres you covered, your adrenaline levels, and by how much your pulse rose when you reached your Downing Street destination. Your mobile phone gave up the names and numbers of the friends in your address book with whom you attended, the music you listened to on your way home, and how deeply you slept that night. Even now, I know that your cholesterol is at a steady 3.8 and that you will begin ovulating in three days. As this conversation has continued, your heart rate has risen to 133 beats per minute, and your stress indicator is currently eight out of ten. You have barely eaten this morning so your salt levels have depleted, and you should put some comfort drops in your dry eyes."

Libby glared at the silver ring on her finger containing the built-in fitness tracker as if it were made by the devil. The Hacker must have accessed the data it retrieved. She twisted it until it came loose, then she winced as she strained to pull it over a knuckle before hurling it across the room.

"Are you going to do the same with your phone, tablets, smart watch, credit and debit cards?" the Hacker asked, and Libby's face flushed. "You distrust technology and AI for the wrong reasons. Shall I show everyone else what happened which influenced your loathing?"

Libby flinched. She knew exactly what was to come next but was helpless to prevent it.

CHAPTER 26

WolverhamptonNewsOnline.co.uk

EXPERTS PREDICT WHERE HACKER'S COLLISION
WILL TAKE PLACE

*The site of a former factory could be where the remaining six Passengers collide,
according to route-planning experts.*

Piecing together the different directions the cars are travelling in and the time of
detonation, the former Kelly & Davis manufacturing plant in Roman Park
industrial estate near Coleshill—which has been demolished and is now
wasteland—is likely to be where their journeys end.

L ibby's body tensed as she braced herself for the inevitable. On the largest
of the screens, Birmingham's Monroe Street appeared exactly how she
remembered it.

Jack had a sense of what was coming too. "How has he got hold of this?"
he asked. "Sensitive material is supposed to be removed from the public
domain and erased."

"Nothing disappears anymore," Cadman said with a shrug. "Everything
is somewhere. All that's private becomes public in the end."

From the perspective of a static camera fixed above a shop's vinyl can-
opy, Libby watched herself from two years earlier walking towards the lens.
She recalled how that day had begun as an ordinary summer's morning. The
sun was high in a cloudless sky, and it was bright enough for her to wear
sunglasses. A gentle breeze rippled the hem of her floral dress.

The road ahead curved and Libby made her way from shop to shop,
glancing through the windows of those that interested her and passing others that didn't. Half a dozen scented candles she'd bought in a sale weighed
down the tote bag hanging from her shoulder. She stopped outside a flower

shop. She could still remember the herb-like scent coming from the orange chrysanthemums in buckets of water outside.

The closer she appeared to camera, the more recognisable she became to her fellow jurors.

"Is that you?" asked Fiona, and pushed her glasses back up her nose for closer inspection. Libby didn't reply. "It is, isn't it?"

"Oh, definitely," Muriel added.

Libby saw herself dip her hand into her bag, remove the phone she still used today, and begin to talk. It was her mum who had called, Libby remembered, checking whether she would be travelling home to Northampton the following weekend for Father's Day. Her mum was planning to cook a Sunday roast for the three of them. Libby informed her that she was on emergency call that weekend. Even as the lie tripped off her tongue, Libby hated herself for doing it. But spending even a minute in that house made her want to run a mile.

As she ended the call, two women and a pushchair across the road caught her eye. It was their laughter that drew her attention, and Libby found herself wishing she and her mum still had that kind of relationship. She couldn't recall the last time they'd joked together.

The women turned sharply and, from behind a parked car, began to cross the road, unaware of a moving vehicle ten metres away from them. Libby expected the car to swerve and stop—there was time and space even if it meant colliding with a stationary vehicle. Instead, it braked sharply but didn't veer from its course. She opened her mouth to shout a warning to the women, but before the words could escape, it was too late. As the vehicle skidded to a halt, it ploughed into them like a bowling ball into skittles, sending them flying.

The younger of the two women took the direct brunt and was scooped up and into the windscreen, before being thrown high above the car and landing on the road behind it. The older one was dragged under the front. Meanwhile the pushchair was shoved many metres along the road and the baby was ejected, its tiny body sliding across the asphalt.

From the inquest room, tears pooled in Libby's eyes as footage from a second camera played, this time attached to the dashboard of the vehicle involved in the collision. Libby relived the moment she dropped her bag to the pavement and heard the glass jars holding her candles shatter as she ran towards the injured. Her first instinct was to aid the baby, but a woman with more medical knowledge than she had was clearing the child's airways and giving her mouth-to-mouth. Somehow, she was alive.

She turned to the woman caught under the front of the car. Libby crouched over her; the victim's cropped grey hair was matted with blood from gashes to her forehead and crown. Her eyes were wide open but her stare was glazed and lifeless.

Libby's attention turned to the opening of a car door and a Passenger slowly alighting, his mouth wide open and his skin as pale as a ghost. He was around the same age as Libby, and she could see his windscreen contained computer games graphics. She assumed he had been playing as the accident occurred. "The car . . . it drives itself . . . it's not my fault . . ." he muttered.

Now aware of the commotion, more people gravitated towards the scene, shouting and screaming and calling for the emergency services. New footage, this time taken from a glasses cam, showed Libby hurrying towards the third person, who'd been thrown over the vehicle. Several people gathered around the woman, unsure of how to assist. Libby pushed her way through them and immediately noted how the victim's limbs were contorted and misshapen, her eyes wet and her mouth bloody. Pink spit bubbles oozed from her lips with each shallow breath. Libby used her first aid training to check the woman's vital signs, then slipped her fitness tracker ring on the woman's finger and checked the results on her mobile phone. Her pulse was barely detectable, her heart almost at a standstill, and her stress levels at a maximum. It would require a miracle to turn around her fortunes.

"My daughter . . ." she gasped, a fine, bloody mist coming from her mouth. Libby took hold of the hand that didn't look broken. It was icy cold. "My little girl . . ." she said, and Libby held the hand close to her own face to offer her warmth.

"She's safe," Libby lied. Now was not a time for honesty, and the woman appeared momentarily pacified.

"And Mary?" she asked.

"She's going to be okay, she's just a little bruised," Libby replied. "What's your name?"

The woman coughed, and more blood, thicker this time, appeared in the corners of her mouth. "I need . . . to see them but I can't move . . ." she said anxiously.

"You've probably fractured a few bones," Libby said, but it was clear there was so much more to her injuries than that. "I'll wait here with you until the ambulance arrives, then once you're in hospital, you can see your family. How does that sound?"

"Do you promise?"

Libby forced a smile, quietly willing herself not to cry and give away the truth.

With sirens announcing the impending arrival of emergency services vehicles, Libby watched helplessly as any remaining fight gradually drained from the woman. Her hand went limp.

"Stay with me," Libby begged. "What's your name? Tell me what your name is."

Her reply was a dying breath as her head lolled to one side.

Libby remembered each second with clarity. Over the days that followed, she called a former colleague who now worked in ICU regarding the baby. The accident had left her with terrible injuries, including a desperate need for a new liver. But before a donor could be found, she lost her battle.

Libby had chosen not to attend the coroner's court but made a statement by video about what she had witnessed. Months later, when she learned the vehicle had been completely exonerated from blame, she was furious. She knew what she had seen. The car had the opportunity to avoid those pedestrians, but it chose to put its Passenger first.

Her phone calls, letters, and emails to the courts were ignored, and each time she posted about it on social media or message boards, they had been swiftly deleted. Eventually she had little choice but to give up. Then when it was announced that Level Five cars were to become mandatory on all British roads, she lent her support to petitions, marches, and demonstrations. But they too had all been for nothing.

Watching the footage for the first time didn't bring back any forgotten memories for Libby. Not a single one had left her in the intervening years.

Matthew reached into his briefcase and removed a packet of tissues, passing it to her. She nodded her thanks and dabbed at her eyes. She felt the warmth of his hand through her blouse as it momentarily rested on her shoulder.

"I remember that case," said Muriel. "Terribly, terribly sad. Three members of the same family wiped out, just like that."

"And all because they were too busy gossiping to watch where they were going," said Jack.

"That car had time to avoid them," Libby replied firmly.

"That's not what the evidence suggested," Jack replied.

"I was there; you were not."

"Well, I think that explains your disrespect for our process, Miss Dixon. With your bias, you should never have been allowed on this jury. If it were up to me, you'd be out of here."

The Hacker began to speak. "I think someone might disagree with you on that point."

"Who?"

"Jude Harrison. Because in the next hour, his life will depend on Libby's inclusion in this process."

CHAPTER 27

SHABANA KHARTRI

S habana craned her neck to look out from the car's window to get her bearings. But the roads were as unfamiliar to her now as the day she first arrived in the country.

For almost half her life, her entire world had been limited to where she could walk. Even the hospital where she had given birth to her last child was in walking distance of her home. She knew this because when the maternity ward released them, her husband, Vihaan, had driven the baby home by car and ordered her to make her own way back on foot.

Now, all that Shabana knew for certain was that wherever this taxi was taking her, she was not going alone. And the longer everyone travelled, the more frightened they were becoming. Not long earlier, a loud noise inside the car distracted her. It was like a banging followed by screams. Her head turned to see where it was coming from before she realised it was happening on the television. The screen once filled by the woman wearing a hijab now contained a blazing object, and other people in their cars were crying. They were making her anxious.

The last time Shabana had taken a journey into the unknown was when her plane left Mumbai's Chhatrapati Shivaji Maharaj International Airport and landed at London's Heathrow just a week after her wedding. It was a day of firsts—the first time she had left her village, the first time she had been away from her family, the first time she had flown, and the first time her new husband had punched her.

Her first impression of Britain had been how grey it was. Everything was colourless and made of concrete, from the bridges over the motorways to the paving slabs that made up the driveway to Vihaan's home. It also felt so much more orderly than India. The houses in the estate were of equal size, had the same proportioned gardens containing the same dull palette of flowers. And while it was less cramped and tidier, and it smelled fresh, it lacked complexion. So soon after her arrival, she was already craving colour and chaos. And when she expressed her homesickness to her new husband, he responded with his fist.

It was during the third day of her lavish Indian wedding to Vihaan when Shabana began to suspect he wasn't all her family had assured her he was. She knew how it had felt to love and to be loved. And this was not it. She had fallen for Arjun, a waiter in a hotel restaurant in her hometown of Kailashahar a year earlier. Her family despised him—his only sin was to have been born into a different caste, thus rendering him unsuitable for her parents' high expectations. Marrying him was out of the question, her father warned, but when his threats fell on deaf ears, her brothers beat the boy half to death and she never saw him again. Even now, she missed being loved by him.

The following year, she was introduced to Vihaan. He was a decade her senior, and had flown from England to meet her. And on the first of their three chaperoned meetings before their arranged ceremony, Shabana convinced herself that perhaps, given time, she could make herself fall in love with him. But as the final day of their marriage celebrations drew to a close and the attention heaped upon them by their friends and family began to ebb, so did his interest in her as anything other than an attainable object to penetrate.

For years after, as Vihaan lay on top of her, reeking of cigarettes, sweat, and beer, he was unconcerned with the degree of pain he was causing. Her only means of escape was to let her mind drift back to Arjun. She'd recall sneaking out of school to join him on his moped for long, lazy afternoons in the countryside. There and away from prying eyes, they would lie under the shade of the tall trees by a lake and watch as the farmers in the distance harvested their golden crops under the clearest of blue skies. She had never felt more at peace in her life than she had there.

Today, albeit briefly, Shabana's freedom had been returned to her. But as she struggled to comprehend what she had been caught up in, she closed her eyes and thought about Arjun again. And if she were able to escape this vehicle, she made a vow to find the money to take her children back to her village so they could find the same beauty in the peace she once had there.

Shabana looked at the mobile phone in her hand again and willed it to start ringing. She wished she knew how to use it, but her husband had never allowed it. Besides, who would she have called? She had very few friends and she didn't know anyone's number. All she wanted was to press the green button as her son, Reyansh, had instructed and talk to him. Then she could tell him that something was happening that didn't feel right and that she was scared.

Suddenly, Shabana remembered a number Reyansh had called once when his baby sister Aditya started choking on a grape. Try as she might, Shabana couldn't get her fingers far enough down the tot's throat to reach it, so Reyansh typed three nines into the phone, and minutes later, a man in a green-and-yellow car came and saved her daughter's life. Vihaan gave her two beatings that weekend—one for putting his daughter's life at risk, and the second for catching her tearfully hugging the paramedic who saved the child's life.

Perhaps whoever answered that number might know her son? Nervously, she typed the numbers into the phone, pressed the green button, and held it to her ear. No voice answered; it was just a monotonous tone. She tried twice more but with the same result.

Reyansh's words that morning came back to mind. "The world is beautiful beyond these walls if you give it a chance."

She must keep her faith in her boy. He was a good son, and she knew that whatever was happening on that television screen, he would never put his mother in harm's way.

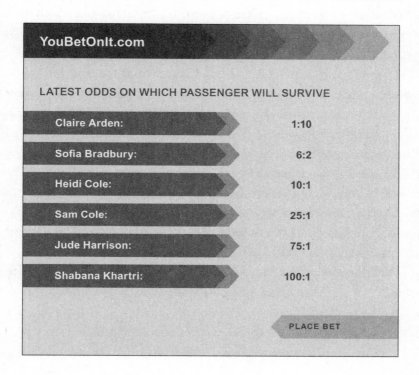

CHAPTER 28

YouBetOnIt.com

LATEST ODDS ON WHICH PASSENGER WILL SURVIVE

Claire Arden:	1:10
Sofia Bradbury:	6:2
Heidi Cole:	10:1
Sam Cole:	25:1
Jude Harrison:	75:1
Shabana Khartri:	100:1

PLACE BET

Libby's throat was dry. She made her way to the corner of the room and reached for a bottle of carbonated water from the fridge next to the tea and coffee urns. It fizzed as she unscrewed the top and took a large mouthful. She felt every pair of eyes upon her.

She knew what they wanted from her, but she was reluctant to do it. The Hacker had left another of his silences hanging ominously in the air, waiting for her to question what he meant by Jude needing her support.

Libby was making no headway in trying to persuade the Hacker that his course of action was abhorrent, and it was frustrating the hell out of her.

She was also disturbed by how much he knew about her life outside of that room and why he felt the necessity to show the jurors and the world what had happened that day in Monroe Street. Back then, watching that family die had brought back memories of her own family's darkness, which in turn manifested itself in the return of her panic attacks and, later, her PTSD diagnosis.

For a mental health nurse, she had suffered almost as much as some of her patients. Much of the time she was able to split herself in two—one was an empathetic, compassionate, and professional nurse, the other, a sensitive and sometimes fragile woman too often haunted by her failings of the past. While such personal traumas gave her a deeper understanding of her patients' suffering, she feared that, eventually, her employers might insist she was not strong enough for the job and sideline her into something more administrational or supportive. Making her watch and relive that day on Monroe Street so publicly would not help how she was perceived. Her hatred towards the Hacker's cruelty intensified.

"I'm done playing his games," she said. "Someone else can ask what he means."

"But he responds better to you," urged Fiona.

"Yes," added Jack. "Perhaps it's your flirtatious nature."

"Shut up, Jack," Libby snapped. "Just shut up." His response was a wry smile.

Libby drank more water and left the bottle on top of the fridge. Then she made her way into the centre of the room and looked up at the twelve screens. Her face was framed by the largest of them, plus five smaller screens that also contained her image via the BBC, CNN, Sky News, MSNBC, and NHK World-Japan news channels. The rest consisted of the Passengers. The unwelcome burden of discovering what the Hacker planned next lay squarely upon her shoulders.

"If it makes any difference, someone has shot up the popularity ranks," said Cadman, breaking the room's uneasiness. "Since that trip down memory lane—or as he calls it, Monroe Street—social media is going nuts for Miss Thing over there."

"What are they saying?" asked Matthew.

"Let's have a look-see. @cyberagga14 says, '#libby is so brave. #girl-power.' @sky_fits_heaven writes, 'The only 1 2 stand up against the Hacker. #pussypower.' And @liquidlove69 says, 'Heartbreaking. Still bawling my eyes out. Keep strong, Libby.' The hashtag #respectforLibby is trending across all the platforms. Our girl's gone global."

"One minute they hate my shoes and the next I'm a hero," Libby dead-panned.

"Oh, the shoes still aren't getting any love," added Cadman.

Libby took a deep breath and looked up to the ceiling. "Okay, you win. Why will Jude need my support in the next hour?"

"I've shown you what it's like to send a person to their death. Now I'm going to demonstrate how it feels to give one of them a life beyond their ordeal. Because over the next hour, you will each decide which of the final six Passengers you would like to save. The Passenger with the most votes from you and the public will be spared when the vehicles collide."

"So to save one life, we must send five others to their graves," said Libby.

"For every action, there's a reaction."

"It's another impossible decision."

"You said it was impossible last time, but I can't see Bilquis in her vehicle, can you? You can make anything a reality if you have determination, motivation, and greed. If you don't believe me, ask Jack."

As was becoming more apparent, when the Hacker directed something towards Jack that only the two of them understood, Jack responded with silence.

"I don't want to do this," Libby replied.

"Keep one alive or kill them all, the choice is yours."

"But it's not a choice, is it?" Libby returned to her seat and held her head in her hands.

"In hiding behind your position as jurors, you have all made decisions on who has been to blame in accidents without ever learning who the victims really are. To you, they're only case numbers. But the Passengers sitting before you are more than that. I am going to make your decision a little easier. I'm going to give each jury member the opportunity to lend their support to one Passenger—you will interview them to discover why your fellow jurors and the public should spare their life. You can ask them anything you desire, and it's up to them how honestly they answer. But I suggest that it's in each Passenger's best interest to be as transparent as possible. Then, once everyone has had the opportunity to promote their worth, you and the public will decide upon the sole survivor. Libby, shall we start with you? Who would you like to support?"

"Jude," she replied with little hesitation. She could not lose the opportunity to talk to him directly—and perhaps for the last time. She directed her contrived smile in his direction and he reciprocated. *I'll do my best for you*, she thought, and for a moment, it was as if he understood her and gave her a look that said, *I know*.

"Jack, you're next," said the Hacker.

"Miss Arden. She didn't ask to have her car hijacked."

"And the others did?" asked Matthew.

"But neither did her unborn child. Surely we can all agree she and her baby must be spared?"

"Muriel, whose direction are you leaning towards?" the Hacker asked.

"Shabana Khartri."

"Of course," muttered Jack. "Your devotion to our friends with a darker skin tone is duly noted."

"She is a mother to five children who depend on her."

"Perhaps one of the questions you could ask her is why has someone who has been in our country for almost twenty years not yet bothered to learn our language? Not that she'd be able to understand you, of course."

Muriel rolled her eyes. "You don't know her circumstances."

"We don't know any of their circumstances. But that small piece of knowledge tells me that she doesn't value Britain and the opportunities we have afforded her. She has not integrated herself into our society."

Libby noted that as Jack spoke, his voice was growing louder and he was positioning himself more in the direction of a camera following him. *He's playing to the audience*, she thought. *He's being an MP.*

"So you're saying we should impose a death sentence upon her because she can't speak English?" asked Libby. "What about her family? You're showing yourself up as an old racist, Jack."

"Don't even try and play that card with me," Jack scoffed. "I'd be saying exactly the same thing if she were white and European. As for her family, she has more than double our national average of children. How old are they?"

"We don't know."

"So they could be all adults?"

"She's thirty-eight, so no."

"It's likely her family are relying on her financially," Muriel continued.

"You mean relying on us tax payers financially."

"When was the last time you paid any tax?" asked Matthew. "I assume your money is squirrelled away in offshore accounts. Well, it was until the Hacker shared it with the world."

Jack ignored him and continued to argue with Muriel. "Would you really be choosing Mrs. Khartri if the cameras weren't upon us?"

"Of course!"

"Because I don't think that you would. If you're being truly honest with our audience, then you have only chosen her because you can foresee the drubbing you'd receive by the Asian community you also represent if you didn't. You have already let down our African viewers by backing the death of Bilquis. If you are seen to allow Mrs. Khartri, a second person of colour, to drive to her death without putting up a fight, then the fragility of your already wafer-thin, irrelevant organisation will crumble to the ground, which, I might add, is where it belongs. I suggest that you are the racist in the room, not I."

"Not only are you a bigot, but you're a bloody idiot too," Muriel hit back, her nostrils flared and her jaw tensed.

"Matthew?" asked the Hacker.

"I choose Heidi for the same reason as Muriel picked Shabana. I don't want to be the one who leaves two children orphaned. I would prefer not to have that on my conscience."

"Oh, so *now* you choose to have a conscience?" said Jack. "In your time on this jury, you've chosen to toe the line and do as you're told, but once the cameras are on you and you have to answer to the world, you suddenly decide that you care? All of you, you're hilarious."

"And you, Fiona?" asked the Hacker.

"Sofia Bradbury."

"What?" Jack saved his loudest laugh for Fiona. "Of all people, you are choosing to save the life of an *actress?*"

"I don't have to justify myself to you," Fiona replied.

"What's happening to Shabana's car?" asked Libby suddenly.

The focus of everyone's attention was drawn to a screen and Shabana's car coming to a halt. The unease in Shabana's eyes was immediate. She kept turning her head to the windscreen and the window behind her. There were moving shadows everywhere.

"Something's frightening her," Libby continued.

Suddenly, Shabana's face was replaced by live footage from outside the car, looking in at her through the front windscreen. People swarmed her vehicle like wasps around a nest. The sound returned and the jurors heard her name being chanted, hands banging on the windows, and saw people grabbing at the door-handles, trying to yank them open. The camera switched to a live Snapchat channel as traffic came to a standstill and more people deserted their vehicles to take selfies with the woman trapped in her car. Children were being held aloft by their parents to help them get better views of Shabana and history in the making. Soon the mob was at least fifteen people deep.

Shabana's face was contorted by fear, but her screams couldn't be heard above the cheering and excitement as each new person appeared.

"They think they're helping her," said Fiona. "They think they can get her out."

"Why aren't the police stopping this?" a panicked Libby asked.

"Some users who are monitoring their communication channels claim teams have been deployed to disperse them," said Cadman. "They should be arriving there any second now."

Libby held her breath until three marked police vans appeared, sirens and lights blazing. Masked officers in riot gear poured from the side doors, pushing their way through the throng, using their shields and batons to move towards Shabana's car. In an instant, their heavy-handed approach faced resistance. And as they grew closer to their target, the crowd turned on them. It became an angry mob with fists flying and rocks and debris being hurled at the police.

A yellow cloud of gas appeared from nowhere, making it harder for the cameras to see what was happening, but the jurors heard screaming coming from adults and children running blindly in different directions.

"I have a terrible feeling about this," said Matthew. "Remember what the Hacker said would happen if any of the vehicles were interfered with—"

He didn't have the opportunity to finish. Shabana's car exploded into a fireball, taking out her and scores of people and officers.

CHAPTER 29

JUDE HARRISON

No!" yelled Jude at the sight of Shabana's car becoming engulfed by flames.

He slapped himself on each side of his head with the palms of his hands again and again as if it might knock the images out or wake him up from a nightmare.

Squirming in his seat, he couldn't take his eyes away from the aftermath of the bomb blast. As the yellow gas dissolved, it was replaced by a thicker, darker fog as the car burned. His perspective alternated between which camera was capturing the clearest and most powerful images. Over the next few minutes, Jude witnessed the angst and confusion as the bloodied and the injured were carried away from the scene; he watched dazed survivors stepping over bodies, some virtually unrecognisable as human, others in tattered clothing and with missing limbs.

Next came news channel helicopter coverage, putting the scale of the blast into perspective. He viewed cars in close proximity to Shabana's ignited one, while people ran to extinguish the flames from a burning child's clothes. He could take no more. He pressed a button to turn his chair 180 degrees to face the rear seats, then grabbed a disused fast-food carton and tried to vomit into it. Several times he retched but there was little inside him to come up.

A bead of sweat trickled from Jude's hairline down his forehead, pooling in an eyebrow. He wiped it away. It was as hot as hell inside his car, and his nerves were making him more anxious. With no working air conditioning or ability to wind down the windows, there was no way for him to cool down.

Moments earlier, he had felt a sense of pride watching Libby spar with the Hacker. Of all the people in the room, she was the only one brave enough to tackle him and try to make him accept that he didn't need to resort to murder to make his point. He was even more attracted to her now than the moment he first saw her singing karaoke in the crowded pub.

The night they met was the first time Jude had felt something so intense for a person since Stephenie. His mind rolled back to when he was fifteen. He'd been in the same classes as her since year five, but it wasn't until year eleven that he'd truly noticed her, no longer through a child's eyes but through those of a young man. And when he eventually plucked up the courage to ask her to go to the cinema with him, he felt like he might burst into tears when she agreed. She was his first kiss, and when he closed his eyes, he could remember with clarity how she tasted of strawberry lip gloss. He had never got over his first love or forgiven Stephenie or his brother for finding love with each other.

And now there was Libby. From the moment that she reciprocated his smile, he was caught off guard by how intensely a simple gesture could rock his foundations. It was as if the world stopped turning for everyone but them. For so long, Jude's repertoire of emotions had barely stretched beyond sadness and resentment. He hadn't considered that there could be any room in his heart for love.

Even the thought of her now gave him inappropriate thoughts, and he felt himself becoming aroused. He shifted uncomfortably in his seat to re-adjust himself, hoping the viewers wouldn't notice. He focused back on Shabana's burning car and felt his desire quickly evaporate.

He replayed his and Libby's first conversation and recalled it was more about what wasn't being said than what was. The furtive glances, the warmth he felt as his cheeks blushed, the confidence she gave him to be himself, the hope, the desire, and their potential all coming together to create an intense emotion that only Stephenie had evoked in him before. If he were to list his requirements for a perfect match, they would result in Libby. He didn't expect to fall head over heels for someone he'd only just met. But it had happened regardless.

Even at the time, Jude knew that it was unfair and wrong. He shouldn't allow himself to fall for Libby because that wasn't in his plan. And when Libby had to accompany her injured friend to the hospital, as much as it pained him, it was for the best. By leaving just moments after her, it meant that if she returned, he could never break her heart. And that's just what would have happened had their encounter extended beyond that one night. But before he left, he made sure to take something of hers with him.

Jude rummaged around inside his rucksack for his toiletries, rinsed out his mouth with mouthwash, and spat into an empty beer bottle. Suddenly from outside his window he noted a sign for Bistford, a location he recalled from his time working for his father's automotive business. On its completion, it had been branded "Britain's first urban smart town." It comprised a purpose-built network of roads for autonomous cars, vans, and lorries. The streets were narrower than regular ones because AI's anti–lane departure technology ensured there were fewer margins for error than traditional roads.

There were fewer parking spaces in the town centre because they weren't required—after being driven to work, many Passengers sent their cars home until they were needed later. That freed up space for more pocket parks and areas of greenery. Bistford was paving the way for every other town, city, and village to prepare for a country where cars were no longer under human control.

Jude had visited the town many times to test out the software his family business designed and programmed. It was only now as he reflected on his own contribution towards towns like this that he understood his culpability in today's hijack. The vehicles he had helped develop for the masses were being used against them all.

He felt the makings of a tension headache creeping up his neck and across the back of his head. In the door's side pocket, he found a box of paracetamol. He popped two from the blister pack and swallowed them dry. "Up to seven hours of pain relief," the wording on the cover promised. The Hacker said only one of them would survive that morning. Suddenly, seven hours felt like all the time in the world.

CHAPTER 30

UKToday.co.uk

VIDEO

Schools in chaos as parents rush to save children from Hacker's bomb threat.
   Government orders all teachers to lock doors and prevent entry, leading to violent scenes.
   Prime Minister Charles Walker-Johnson appeals for calm.
   Read the full story >

CLAIRE ARDEN

C laire suddenly became aware that she was clutching her bump so tightly that she let go, afraid she might be hurting her baby.

The route her car was taking involved motorways rather than smaller roads so she couldn't be brought to a halt by an overzealous public. She wouldn't want anyone to be injured because of her. A shadow above her caught her eye. She squinted through the glass panoramic roof at an object in the sky. It was something dark and hovered way above her. She assumed it to be one of the drones she'd heard the jury argue about. Claire hoped that it maintained its distance so that nobody else spotted it and realised it was following a Passenger. Her privacy windows meant that no passing vehicles could ever know she was inside. Earlier, it was a hindrance. But for now, at least, it might be keeping her from the same fate as Shabana.

When the jury was tasked with voting later that morning, she prayed that she would gain their sympathy. She knew they might not be actually supporting her and that it would be the life growing inside her winning them over. It didn't matter as long as he was safe.

You have to make them want to save you, Claire told herself. *Do whatever it takes to keep your baby alive.*

As her pregnancy advanced, barely a couple of hours might pass before she'd feel the urge to urinate. And the longer the car journey continued, the more Claire knew she couldn't hold it in any longer. She looked around the vehicle's interior, but there were no containers to pass water into. Besides, the world was watching, and would she really want the indignity of their seeing her do that? There was no choice but to just wet herself. So she moved to the other front passenger seat and did just that. It brought her only fleeting moment of relief that morning.

She had potentially seventy minutes left until the Hacker killed her. Feeling her baby move sharply again, she feared that Tate was absorbing her stress, so she forced herself to think of something positive.

Claire longed to hear Ben's voice, so she removed her phone from her pocket and located a folder containing videos they made of each other. The one she chose she had recorded last year. Standing in their kitchen, she relived the moment he came through the front door and dropped his backpack by the sofa. He looked puzzled as to why she was pointing her camera phone at him.

"Is that thing on?" he asked, and the picture shook a little as Claire replied with a nod. "Why? And why is there a glass of champagne and a bag on the table? Shit, have I missed our anniversary? Wait, no, that's November. What are you up to?"

"Open it," she said with a giggle, and he made his way towards her.

Ben's brow crinkled and he pulled on the strings to open a small blue bag. He removed from it a light blue teddy bear, with a five-centimetre square screen in its belly.

"Squeeze its paw," Claire invited. Ben obliged and nothing happened. "The other one, and watch the screen."

Claire's camera closed in tightly to Ben's face, and as the bear's mouth moved, it sounded like a heartbeat. A three-dimensional image appeared on its stomach as if it were inside the toy. It was of an unborn child moving. "We're pregnant," she whispered. "You're going to be a dad."

Ben looked at her, wide-eyed, then back to the bear. "Really?" he asked.

"Really?" He grabbed her by the waist, lifted her up into the air, and squeezed her tightly.

Now, from inside her car, Claire burst into tears watching her husband gently place her back on the ground and steady himself against the table. It was a child they had tried so desperately to have but that they both were beginning to give up hope of ever seeing.

"Are you happy?" she heard herself ask.

"What do you think?" Ben replied. The screen became blurry as he went to hold her again. Claire shut her eyes tightly, and it was as if he were holding her now, her nose buried in his neck, inhaling his joy.

Claire always assumed that if they were side by side, she and Ben could conquer any obstacle that got in their way. That morning she learned she was wrong.

She snapped back to the present when, without warning, vibrations travelled through her body followed by a rumbling outside. She turned to see a convoy of four police motorbikes and several heavily armoured army vehicles appear outside, flanking either side of her vehicle. Above her, a helicopter had replaced the drone.

"Oh God, no," she said, panicked and hesitant of the extra attention they were going to bring her. But as the bikes sped ahead, she realised they were clearing a path for her. The armoured vehicles moved to each side, and police cars behind prevented any other driver from overtaking.

It suddenly dawned on her that her whole life, other people had protected her. Throughout their fractured childhood of care homes and foster parents, it was her brother, Andy, who had given her the security she needed. But when he chose a life of petty crime over her, she chose education and met Ben. He had taken over the challenge of making her feel safe. And now it was Tate's turn. If they were to survive this ordeal, she pledged never to allow her boy to be responsible for his mother again.

From what she had heard, Jack Larsson was the most unlikable of the jurors. But having seen him win the upper hand over his political opposition during televised debates, she knew he was also the most tenacious and well-schooled in the art of persuasion. His having picked her to represent meant he must have thought he stood a good chance of keeping her alive. He wouldn't go down without a fight.

And neither would she. Immediately, she resolved to toughen up and take back some semblance of control of her life. Aware once again of the dashboard camera, she began to rub her bump more and talk to it, reminding Tate that she loved him and that she was praying they wouldn't die. All the time, she spoke loud enough for her microphone to pick up her words. If the key to her survival was to get the world to pity her and vote for her, it was a small price to pay. She had to remind the jurors they wouldn't be condemning just one person to their death.

But inside, Claire was acutely aware that if she were freed from the car, she would need to vanish from the scene—and vanish quickly. Nobody could discover the truth about what she had done before her hijacking until long after she had gone to ground.

CHAPTER 31

SOFIA BRADBURY

S ofia shook her head vigorously.

"Oh, no, no," she said. "I do not like this. Not one bit. Look at it, Oscar. It's distasteful, isn't it?" Her dog's eyes remained closed. "How can anyone think that pretending to blow up someone in a car in such graphic detail passes for entertainment? Because I can tell you, it most certainly does not."

She raised her voice and stared at the camera. "Will someone pull this car over and let me out? I need to speak to my agent, and until that happens, you're not getting one more reaction from me."

Sofia poured herself another brandy and swallowed her fifth painkiller of the morning. The buzz from the last one was already beginning to wear off. She held her glare at the monitor, waiting for a response to her demands. Instead, more shouting and crying came through the speakers. She rolled her eyes and spoke louder. "Read my lips—Sofia Bradbury is not reacting. This is not what she signed up for." The vehicle continued at the same pace, offering no sign it was preparing to slow down.

She turned to Oscar again. "Listen to that lot wailing like bloody banshees. They're all competing to see who can make the most amount of noise and take the most screen time. It's pathetic. This is not what I worked my arse off for, to end up on something glorifying violence. I think Rupert has made a huge mistake getting me involved in this."

It was the explosion of the car with the Indian woman inside—a Bollywood actress, Sofia assumed, as she hadn't recognised her—that tipped her over the edge. The blasts from the first two cars were clearly visual trickery designed to elicit realistic responses from viewers and Passengers. But the third appeared much more detailed than the others. Supporting actors must have spent hours in hair and make-up to ensure the wounds were believable. Then there were smoke bombs; people running around with limbs falling off left, right, and centre; and stuntmen and -women ablaze. She knew today's audiences expected more from their programming than her generation did, but still, who in their right mind would want to watch a child on fire?

"I did a lot of Ayckbourn in the seventies, so don't try and tell me I'm a prude," she continued to whoever was listening. "I do not agree with the increasing amount of gore shown on primetime television for the public's titillation. Therefore, I cannot, in good faith, remain on this programme until I've spoken to my agent or until a producer can guarantee me there is going to be more substance to this series than I have witnessed so far."

Sofia hesitated, debating whether making a fuss was the right thing to do. Standing up for herself might go one of two ways. It could backfire, making her come across like an old fuddy-duddy to the younger audience she craved. Or, by remaining true to herself, it could win her more support from an older demographic. It was a risk she was willing to take.

She had been waiting for the show to cut to a commercial break and allow her to discreetly fit new ear guards into her hearing aids. The sound was becoming muffled, but she had just about heard the woman in the ill-fitting plaid suit lending Sofia her support over something. She assumed her long-standing status as national treasure was giving her some gravitas.

Were she to remain in the show, Sofia figured her toughest competition would come from the pregnant girl who was milking her condition for all it was worth. *Will you just leave that bloody belly alone?* she thought. *All that stroking and rubbing; it's not made of Play-Doh.*

Quietly, Sofia resented and envied the girl. Many times over the years, she questioned whether she had done the right thing in not starting a family of her own. How much had she lost out on by not feeling another life growing inside her? Not loving another person unconditionally and allowing that love to be reciprocated? She would never know. But each time she doubted herself, she would think of her husband, Patrick, and it would remind her the decision was for the best. He would not have made a good father.

As she stroked her sleeping dog's head with one hand, she swirled brandy around a glass tumbler with her other and wondered what Patrick had planned now that she had been swept up in the *Celebs Against the Odds* frenzy. She hoped Rupert had cancelled the car driving him to the hospital where they were supposed to meet ahead of her public appearance. If he had not, it would be another thing for her to worry about.

At least her filming schedule would give them a break for the next seven nights, she thought, providing she survived in the competition that long. While the quality film and television roles offered to her had dried up, she was still in demand on the stage and often travelled for work, staying in hotels and away from home for weeks at a time. Unbeknown to Patrick, she had people to watch his every move and report back to her. Her cook, house-keeper, and gardener were reliable sources of information, as was the private detective she kept on a retainer. There was also her accountant and a forensic digital specialist who followed his digital footprint and who dipped in and out of his operating system without being seen.

"Hello!" she said again. "Is anyone listening to me?"

Suddenly a man's voice came from one of the other cars. "You don't get it, do you?" he barked.

Sofia moved her face closer to the screen until she could see who was talking to her. It was the one who was married to another contestant. He reminded her of a daytime television presenter who'd once made her an in-decent proposal in a dressing room. She had firmly declined.

"Speak up, I can barely hear you."

"I said, you don't get it, do you?"

"What don't I get?" she replied. "I am sure I have been in this business for a lot longer than you, darling, and I know what makes good television. This, however, is just violence for the sake of it. It is most certainly not en-tertainment."

"Of course it's not fucking entertainment!" the woman's husband yelled. "This is actually happening to you, to us! Wake up, woman. You are being held hostage—they've murdered three of us already this morning—why is that not sinking in?"

Sofia registered that the screaming and crying had stopped, and when she looked closely at the other screens, her fellow contestants were all listening to and watching them.

"This is a reality television programme," she replied, suddenly beginning to doubt herself. "We are on *Celebs Against the Odds*. Has no one told you?"

"No, we are not! The only television programme we are on is the news. I am not a celebrity, neither is my wife, nor any of the other people trapped in these cars apart from you. We are all being held against our will, and someone is killing us off, one by one."

Sofia opened her mouth but no words came out. "Oh my," she said eventually, and placed an arm around her dog. "But I don't . . . I don't understand . . . why me?"

"Why not you?" the man replied. "Just because you're famous, do you think you should be immune?"

"Well . . . yes."

"Think again, because we're all in the same boat. You're no better than any of us."

Sofia didn't need him to remind her of that. She knew better than most that some of the decisions she had made to protect her career and her image would horrify her fans. Her chest tightened as she worried she had been picked precisely for that reason, and that her darkest secrets were about to come to light.

CHAPTER 32

BedfordAgendaOnline.co.uk

BY EMMA BARNETT-VINCENT, REPORTER   *9:58 a.m.*

Bedfordshire Police claim all is being done to free local hostage Detective
Sergeant Heidi Cole from her hijacked car. Chief Inspector Richard Molloy told
the *Agenda* online: "DS Cole is a popular, hard-working member of the Luton
team and we hope that she will return to us safely."

SAM & HEIDI COLE

I f Sam had been able to switch off his monitor so that he didn't have to see
or hear Sofia, he would have.

His anger towards his own hijacking was compounded by her stupidity.
He was sick of hearing the deluded actress continually grasping the wrong
end of the stick while no one saw fit to correct her. Finally, he could hold his
tongue no longer. But after delivering the truth and witnessing the actress's
crestfallen face, he began to question himself. Perhaps being naive to their
dire circumstances was better than facing reality.

Meanwhile, from her car, Heidi was willing her husband to bring an
end to his rant. "Sam, please stop," she said through gritted teeth. "She's an
elderly woman and you're bullying her."

"We've been told we're about to die, and she's begging for her bloody
agent!" he replied. "I tell you, if she manages to find a way out of this just
because she's famous, then I'll drive this car into her myself."

"Sam . . ."

"No, stop trying to silence me. She won support from one of the jurors
just because she's on the telly. How is that fair? She's had her life, we are the

ones with children who need us, and what do I get? Nothing. If they hadn't killed that Asian woman, what would've happened to me?"

"I don't know."

"Yes you do, we both do. You'd be watching me burning to death in this car."

"Don't say that."

"It's the truth, isn't it? Did any of the jurors stick their necks out and choose me?" Heidi didn't say anything. "Exactly," Sam continued, and folded his arms.

"If the kids are watching this, they don't need to be reminded of the threat we're under, do they?" added Heidi. Sam shook his head.

The last thirty minutes had seen a switch in the mindsets of husband and wife. Heidi was beginning to put her police training to use and talked herself into a calmer state of mind. And learning she had the support of at least one juror gave her belief that perhaps with a little more time, she could win more over. To survive this ordeal for the sake of her children, she must toughen up. The only person she could rely on was herself; it was a lesson she had been forced to learn weeks earlier.

As her and Sam's tenth anniversary loomed, Heidi had known it was the last one she would spend as his wife. Unbeknown to her husband, she had twice met with a local solicitor to discuss how to separate and the implications it would bring. She was determined to keep the family home and would offer to share custody of the children, not that he deserved them. As much as she had longed to make him suffer, she would not do it by using James and Beccy.

For years, the family had survived mainly upon her wages as Sam established and grew his construction and refurbishment business. She had paid for so much, from foreign family holidays to new furniture. And throughout that time, she had also been both mother and father to their kids while he had worked away for several days each week.

Today was supposed to be the day that everything changed, when all that had been so wrong in their marriage was to come out into the open. Only the Hacker put paid to that. Now she would need Sam on her side.

Meanwhile he was now convinced he wasn't to blame for the mess they'd found themselves caught up in. There was no evidence that his lies were responsible for their predicament. Shabana's murder, while unfortunate, was a brief reprieve, offering husband and wife a stay of execution. It meant a juror was free to help him whether they favoured him or not. Quietly he hoped that Shabana wouldn't be the last to die before the planned collision.

But it also released inside him something he had not anticipated—a bitterness towards Heidi. Why was she favoured above him?

"We don't know that we're about to die," Heidi continued. "We don't know anything right now."

"Didn't you hear what the Hacker said?" he replied. "And what if the kids are in one of those schools with the bombs inside?"

"Sam, you need to take a breath and think about this. The odds of that happening are remote. I'm sure the kids will be okay."

The more Sam pictured their faces when they discovered what was happening to their parents, the more he began to sweat. "What are they going to think when they see us on TV? They'll be terrified."

"They might not know yet."

"You said earlier they probably knew! Every kid of their age is on social media. Even if they haven't seen it, their friends will have told them by now. Sometimes I don't think you want to admit to what's going on around you."

Heidi felt her muscles knot and she opened her mouth, ready to attack, then thought better of it. With just a few words, she knew she could cut her husband down to size. *Not now*, she told herself. *Wait until you really need to fire that bullet.* Then a darker thought rose to the surface. *Or perhaps you should let him continue ranting and wait until he buries himself?* She shook her head. She was cool and collected, but that wasn't her style.

The nickname Elsa the Ice Queen from her workmates hadn't bothered Heidi. She didn't know many police officers without an epithet, or who hadn't had their surname shortened or extended or had a "y" tacked onto the end. Before she joined the police, she had volunteered as a community support officer in her spare time, patrolling the neglected council estate in which she was born and raised. Unafraid of the threats made to her by gangs and drug dealers, her high citizens' arrest rate and fearless approach to the job brought her to the attention of her bosses, who encouraged her to apply for a full-time position. Once she'd settled into the Criminal Investigations department, they too appreciated her ability to remain composed even in the most testing of cases. And with her long, blond hair and delicate features, they awarded her the new nickname Elsa, inspired by the Disney cartoon *Frozen*.

If they were watching her now, they might struggle to recognise the woman before them. This Elsa was racked with fear. The threat of being blown up or in a collision would do that to anyone, she thought. And for the first time in as long as she could remember, she wished she had Sam's hand to hold for comfort.

This isn't you, she told herself. *Whatever the hell is happening here, this is not how you respond. Calm yourself down—and you don't need Sam to do that for you.*

However, there was a decision that needed to be made. She would rather Sam came to the conclusion himself than have viewers see her bringing it up and risk appearing mercenary. But time was running out, and she couldn't wait any longer to broach the subject.

"There's something we need to talk about," she said carefully. "Only one person is going to survive this. Because the public and the jurors aren't being asked to vote for us as a married couple, the kids aren't going to get both of us back. So we need to start thinking about how we're going to play this."

"What do you mean?"

"I mean that it makes sense if one of us takes ourselves out of the running to give the other a fighting chance."

"You mean sacrifice our own life?"

"If it comes to that, then yes. If we both start getting votes, we risk cancelling one another out."

Sam paused as he processed her suggestion. *You heartless bitch*, he thought. She assumed it was unlikely he would garner much support, so she had written him off already. He ran his hands through his hair, then pushed upon his anxious leg to try to stop his foot from bouncing up and down again. Heidi was right—they both couldn't survive until the end of the morning. However, there was one thing she hadn't considered—he didn't want to die.

Because Sam's life wasn't just about Heidi and their children. There was much more to him than that, which she was not party to. And the more he considered her proposal, the more he was sure of what needed to be done. He would have to convince the jury and the public that Heidi should die, not him.

||| JAZEERA GLOBAL ONLINE
* NEWS ALERT *

DOZENS FEARED DEAD AS HACKER DETONATES
CAR IN CROWD.

Luton (UK): A second explosive device has killed at least ten
people, injuring dozens more on a busy road. An overzealous
public mobbed the vehicle, containing Passenger Shabana
Khartri, when the explosion took place. Local police warn the
death toll is likely to rise considerably throughout the morning.

The room was silent as each person in it absorbed the graphic aftermath of Shabana's murder.

News networks used mobile footage, drones, and helicopter cameras to try to eclipse one another with the most shocking pictures they could find.

"How can they be showing this?" Libby asked.

"Live feeds on social media have changed the way television news is broadcast," Cadman replied. "The only way for the networks to compete and stay relevant is not to censor what's happening, and instead, go balls-out with the same attack on the senses."

"At least it means they're not focusing on us," said Fiona.

Muriel, the only person to lend support to Shabana, took her gaze away from the screen and faced the table instead. She turned a wooden crucifix hanging around her neck the opposite way around, as if to hide Jesus from the wickedness of the world he'd left behind. "Why would the Hacker do this?" she muttered in disbelief.

"People have been killing people since Cain and Abel; you of all people should know that," muttered Jack. "And I'm sorry to say it will continue for generations to come until there is no one left in this world to either kill or be killed."

"Oh, Jack," said the Hacker. "One might glean from your maudlin words that somewhere deep inside you remains a beating heart. What's making you so unhappy? Is it that you brought these vehicles onto our roads and now they're killing people? Or is it that after today, your pipe dream of fully autonomous roads will lie in ruins?"

"You are killing people, not my dream," Jack replied.

"And these people died because they failed to follow the rules, which I clearly spelled out when this began. Interfere with my cars, and you will suffer the consequences. This is what happens when rules aren't adhered to—disarray and bloodshed."

"You're going to kill them all, aren't you?" Libby asked, her eyes lingering on Jude's face. "Every single Passenger."

"No, I give you my word that one of them will survive this process."

Libby laughed. "Your word? What does that mean?"

"I'm afraid it's all you have. Time, on the other hand, is something you don't. So shall we begin the interview process? Jack, I would like you to go first. You have ten minutes to keep Claire Arden and her baby alive."

CHAPTER 34

CLAIRE ARDEN

Before she climbed into the car that morning, Claire made herself a promise that, come what may, she wouldn't give in to her emotions until much later in the day. Only when each part of the plan was complete would she allow herself to cry over what Ben had done.

Her pledge had lasted approximately ten minutes before the Hacker's voice appeared and informed her of the hijack. She had cried constantly for much of the last hour and a half. Now, just as she thought she was empty, it was time to draw further from the well to win the support of the room. It was imperative to her and Tate's survival that she tugged harder on their heartstrings.

Along with her pregnancy, it was likely that her appearance might also go in her favour. If the argument she'd heard the jurors having about race and Bilquis's death was to be believed, the fact she was white, young, and attractive might go in her favour. She felt ashamed that the racism she had spent much of her adult life rallying against might actually benefit her. She wondered how the jury and public might react if they were to learn her husband was of Afro-Caribbean descent and that she was carrying a mixed-race child.

Craving their pity went against Claire's values. She'd had her fill of wanting to be everything to everybody during a childhood spent on show at social services' open days; she and her brother dressed in their best clothes and were on their best behaviour in the hope of catching the eye and sympathy of prospective adoptive parents. Ben had helped her to understand she needed to impress no one to feel self-worth. But now history was repeating itself and she was that little girl again, relying on the compassion of strangers for a future.

She jumped at the sound of a klaxon, and a digital clock appeared on her screen. White numerals began at the ten-minute mark. She braced herself as the countdown began.

"Hello, Miss Arden, this is MP Jack Larsson," Jack began stiffly.

"Hi, please call me Claire," she replied. She stared directly into the camera and blinked to allow the tears gathering in the corners of her eyes to begin their descent. It appeared to catch him off guard.

"Please don't upset yourself. How are you feeling?"

"I've been better."

"How's the baby? Are you in need of medical attention?"

"No, I don't think so."

Jack hesitated, and glanced around the room, tugging nervously at his collar and clearing his throat. It was the first time since being thrust into his company that Libby had seen him awkward and edgy. "Can you tell us a little about yourself, please, Claire?"

She picked her words carefully. "I'm not sure what to say. I've been married to my husband, Ben, for three and a half years, and I work as a teaching assistant at Bellview School in Peterborough—it's for children with learning difficulties. Ben and I . . ." She paused for dramatic effect. "Ben and I are expecting our first baby in two months and we're very excited. It's going to be a boy; we've nicknamed him Tate. And he's our little miracle. Before I fell pregnant, I had eight miscarriages and an ectopic pregnancy. We were told it was unlikely I'd ever be able to conceive, or if I did, then I couldn't carry it to full term." She cradled her stomach and gave a sad smile. "So this little one means everything to us."

"I understand, I really do . . . I have no doubt how frightened you must be by what's happened. But let's try and remain positive. What kind of mother do you think you'll make?"

"A really good one, I hope. I didn't really have a mum. My brother and I were in care for much of our lives, so I want to be the mother to Tate that mine wasn't to me. After everything Ben and I have been through in trying to conceive, this baby is already so loved. Every day of the week I see the children in my class who need a bit of extra attention and effort because of their differing abilities. And I care about them so much and they're not even mine. We decided not to have any pre-pregnancy tests for abnormalities because it'll make no difference to us if Tate has any problems; we'll love him just the same. To me he'll always be perfect."

Jack pinched the bridge of his nose and spoke unexpectedly candidly, as though they were the only two present. "I have walked in your shoes, Claire. My first wife and I went through close to a dozen losses before we finally admitted defeat. As a man, I felt quite helpless because there was nothing I could do or say that made it any better for her . . ." Jack drifted into silence as if he were reliving the pain.

"I'm sorry to hear that," Claire replied.

"I am happy for you and your husband, I truly am. I'm only sorry that what is supposed to be such a wondrous time for you both has descended into this mess. If you can just cling onto hope for that little bit longer, I'm sure my fellow jurors and the public vote will do the right thing and carry you and your son to safety."

Claire curled her trembling lip into a grateful smile.

Libby listened, carefully making mental notes of Jack's approach to get the best out of his subject with his line of questioning. Next, he guided Claire into talking about her plans for Tate's future before asking her to expand on her time in care and what her family life now meant to her. Libby handed it to him, albeit reluctantly: Claire was fortunate to have him on her side.

"You have two minutes left," the Hacker interrupted.

"Can you tell everybody, why do you want to live, Claire?" continued Jack.

Her response was to look down towards her bump again and then to the camera. "For my baby's sake. All I want is to bring him into the world and to see him grow up happy and healthy."

"I'm sure your husband must be worried about you both."

Claire felt her stomach churn, only it wasn't the baby's doing.

"Yes," she replied quietly.

"Tell us about him," Jack encouraged.

Claire hesitated again, choosing her words carefully before she spoke. "My Ben is a very kind, sweet man who would do anything for me. We met in the student union bar in our first term at Portsmouth uni, and within minutes of seeing him, I knew that he was the one."

Claire recalled how, some years before they met, geneticists had discovered all humans carried a gene shared by just one other person in the world. That person was apparently the one genetically made for you—the person you were destined to fall in love with. They could be of any age, sex, colour, or religion, and in any location. The scientist at the helm of the discovery transformed it into a global business, Match Your DNA, where individuals sent a mouth swab and paid to discover if and who they had been matched with. In a little under a year, it was credited as the reason why racism, homophobia, and religious hatred were at the point of extinction. But it was also to blame for escalating divorce rates, massive rises in emigration and immigration, and an increase in suicides amongst those who had yet to be matched or who had lost a partner to a match. However, the world became sceptical about the accuracy of results following a catastrophic security breach in which a hacker with a grudge randomly matched two million people on Match Your DNA's database.

Despite this, the fallout from her parents' chaotic relationship played at the back of Claire's mind, and she still wanted that little extra assurance that Ben was made for her. So they took the test just to be certain. As expected, it was positive.

"Ben asked me to marry him on our graduation day, and I said yes straightaway," she continued. "His mum and dad tried to convince us that we were too young as we'd only just left further education. But we didn't care. We eloped to London, got married, found jobs, eventually settling in Cambridgeshire, and bought our first house together last year. We've been renovating it in time for when Tate arrives."

For the briefest time, she felt a warm flush spread across her chest and face when she thought back to those halcyon days.

"Do you love your husband?" asked Jack.

"Of course I do," Claire replied without hesitation. "He's my everything."

"Your time is up, Claire," interrupted the Hacker.

Claire's clenched fists remained by her side and out of view of the camera. Claire slowly uncurled them, satisfied she had offered Jack the best version of herself. Now her future was in the hands of the jury and the public.

"I hope I have sold you well, if you can excuse the expression," Jack finished, and offered her a warm smile. "I am sure that if given the chance by my fellow jurors and the public, your baby will be lucky to have such a wonderful mother."

"Thank you, Jack," said the Hacker. "Before we move on to our next juror and Passenger, may I ask you a question of my own, Claire?"

"Okay," she replied nervously.

"I am curious, if you love your husband as deeply as you claim, then why are you hiding his dead body in the boot of your car?"

The camera cut from Claire's horrified face to the rear of her vehicle, where a light illuminated the crumpled body of a man, lying on his side, his knees pressed against his chest and very much lifeless.

CHAPTER 35

ChatWithPix

BBC News

⊙ CLAIRE'S BOOT 😨 — Jurors' shock as body is revealed ☐

The Washington Globe

⊙ NO MORE! 🚫 US president calls halt to autonomous car tests ☐

Daily Star

⊙ SEXY SOFIA! 👙👙👙 Click here for her best naked movie moments ☐

W hat just happened?" gasped Libby, struggling to make sense of what she thought she had just heard.

"I . . . I . . . don't know," stuttered Jack. He was as equally dumbstruck as the rest of the room.

"I'm confused," said Muriel. "Is the Hacker saying that he's killed Claire's husband?"

"I don't think so," said Fiona, looking carefully at the screen. "Look at her. That isn't the face of someone who has only just been told they're driving around with their husband's corpse in the boot. She knew he was there."

"So *she* has killed him?" asked Muriel.

"I don't know."

"But is he definitely dead?"

"If he's not, then he's a bloody good actor," said Matthew.

Fiona shook her head in disbelief. "I've been a barrister for twenty years, and just when you think you've seen it all, you're wrong."

Until the moment Ben's body appeared on-screen, both Jack and Claire had made a compelling case for her survival. Even Cadman and his team were now caught in the moment, gawping at the screen rather than busying themselves with interpreting data.

Libby noted that Claire's eyes were like dark pools of fear as they glared into the lens. "Please let me explain . . ." Claire began before her microphone was cut off. The television picture on the wall split into two sections, with husband and wife taking each half of the screen. Meanwhile the news channels delighted in the latest twist of their rolling news story.

"Ladies and gentlemen," said the Hacker, "allow me to introduce you to Benjamin Dwayne Arden, the third Passenger in Claire's vehicle. This is the same man who, just moments earlier, his wife described as her 'everything.'"

Claire appeared desperate to be heard, her fists banging against the dashboard and monitor screen, her face animated but her voice silenced. Libby's first thought was for the well-being of the baby.

"She needs help," said Libby, but no one was listening. She raised her voice. "Look at her, she's hysterical. Whatever she's done to her husband, she is still carrying a baby."

"Then you're more worried about it than she is," said Fiona. "If she was that concerned, would she really have killed his father?"

"You of all people should know there are two sides to every story. And we don't know if that's what happened, because the Hacker muted her."

"Libby, I've defended enough clients to know by appearances alone when someone knows more than they are letting on. What on earth could she tell us that would change the fact her husband's dead body is in her car? That whole interview with Jack was an act. She was pretending to be a victim when she's anything but. Even Jack fell for it."

Libby turned to Jack, who had returned to his seat behind the table, red-faced and defeated.

"Yes!" Cadman interrupted, his face brimming with joy. "We've done it!" All heads turned towards him as he high-fived his team members. "We've spiked. We have actually made history. This is now the most hashtagged global event since social media began. And we are dead centre in the eye of the storm!" He looked towards each juror in search of someone who shared his enthusiasm. Their faces were deadpan. "Tough crowd," he said with a shrug.

His indifference towards the mood of the room riled Libby. "Are you actually genuine, or is this a character you're playing?" she snapped. "Because I don't understand how anyone with an ounce of compassion couldn't be appalled by what's happening out there. Dozens of men, women, and children are lying dead and injured on our roads, and all you care about is how many people are talking about it."

"Hey, don't shoot the messenger because you don't like what's in his bag, Miss Buzzkill," Cadman replied. "What do you want from me? To pretend that I actually care about people I have never met? Because that isn't going to happen. This is what my team and I are here for, to tell the truth and represent the people, not to hold your hand and tell you everything is going to be alright when, quite clearly, it's fucked. My job is to bring to you what's on the news agenda, not to set it. And right now, it's the pregnant femme fatale who has just broken the internet." He swiped his tablet so that its screen contents appeared on another wall. "Admit it, you're dying to know what they're saying, aren't you?"

Before Libby could deny it, screen grabs and posts filled every inch of space. She couldn't help but read some of them.

She and that baby are screwed. #votesofia #Hackertellsthetruth
Blow her up now and stop wasting time or I'm gonna switch off. #voteHeidi
Let the legend live. #votesofia
An hour to go. Why can't it continue? It's like watching a soap opera. Good work Hacker! #votesofia

"Now do you see what I mean?" Cadman continued. "Like it or not, the Hacker has the world by the balls. What's not to love about a bit of anarchy?"

Libby closed her eyes and shook her head at Cadman and the people he represented. Taking him and the virtual world on was not a fight she was likely to win. If social media truly reflected society, then she didn't want to be a part of a world where the Hacker was held in any kind of esteem.

"A friendly word in your ear, Cadman," Matthew said, rising to his feet and moving towards him. His tone was less than friendly.

"Go ahead," Cadman replied, a little apprehensively.

"Firstly, I'm not asking for your permission, and secondly, I suggest you keep your opinions to yourself." He came to a halt, barely two inches from Cadman's face. "The people you claim to represent are as much lacking in decency as you are. If you were out there with my colleagues in the emergency services scraping body parts from roads and dousing the flames of burning children, then perhaps that might qualify you to speak your mind. But you're not. You're a statistician who doesn't understand the value of human life because you live in a virtual reality surrounded by other avatars equally as devoid of empathy as you. You are worse than artificial intelligence because at least AI can be programmed to care. So until you learn humility and compassion, from here on in, you only speak when you are spoken to, and the rest of the time you keep your mouth shut. Do I make myself clear?"

Cadman's pale skin reddened as he nodded, then he moved swiftly back towards the refuge of his team. Libby gave Matthew a nod and a smile as he returned to his seat. Then, once again, she looked up towards the speakers. "Are you still there?" she asked.

"I'm always here," the Hacker replied.

"Why did you allow Claire to say that about her husband when you knew all along he was dead?"

"*Honesty*, Libby. I keep repeating myself about what I require from you, but no one appears to be listening. I gave Claire the opportunity to admit the truth of her own volition, but she chose not to. Instead, she made the decision to portray herself in a certain way to win favour in the hope you'd spare her life over another, perhaps more deserving, Passenger."

"But you aren't being honest either, are you? You've yet to give us the rest of her story or tell us why you're doing this. You're a hypocrite."

Libby looked to Claire's screen again. She was sitting with her face to the camera, her eyes locked onto the lens like magnets, listening intently to Libby's argument.

"In Claire's allocated ten minutes, she hoped her omitting a key fact might encourage you to make an uninformed decision in her favour. If the end result is not to Claire's liking, then she only has herself to blame. I'm happy to argue with you all day, Libby, but if I can draw your attention to the clock, you'll see that every minute spent bickering with me is a minute closer to the collision. And if we don't progress to the next Passenger soon, their deaths will be on your conscience."

"For once, please just listen to him and shut up," said Jack wearily. "Or if you want them all to die, then be my guest and keep trying to rationalise with a psychopath."

Jack was giving the impression of a broken man. The world had plundered his finances, the jury he controlled was in disarray, and the Road Revolution he had spearheaded to the tune of billions of pounds of investment was lying in ruins alongside his reputation. Now he had backed the wrong Passenger. But instead of arguing with him for the sake of it, Libby stood down. The Hacker was right; time was running out. She had a gut feeling there would be bigger battles to pick.

"Cadman," continued the Hacker, "could you please inform us who has captured social media's interest at this moment in time?"

"Sofia Bradbury, and by a reasonable margin," he replied, the eagerness in his voice now replaced by reticence. "The public are lapping up her naivety, memes of her are going viral, and they're uploading classic clips of her online."

"Then it seems fitting that we get to know her next, doesn't it? Fiona, are you ready?"

CHAPTER 36

SOFIA BRADBURY

B loody thing!"

A frustrated Sofia stopped waiting for a suitable opportunity to remove her hearing aid out of the view of the public eye. Instead, she yanked it out and rummaged through her handbag before inserting it into the rapid battery charger.

A career spent on stages and sets and in front of loud, cheering audiences had taken its toll on her hearing. She hated wearing the aid—regarding it as a sign of weakness—although its ability to translate languages had once helped her to understand the director of a Japanese TV commercial for brandy.

If she had heard properly, then she was not on a reality TV show and this was a real life-or-death situation. And if, as the images on her screen suggested, it was also being broadcast worldwide, it would have a much larger, global reach than she could have ever imagined. Sofia should have felt terrified. Instead, she had never felt more alive. She valued her life on the stage more than her life off it, and now the whole world was her audience.

She slipped the charged aid back into her ear just in time to hear someone announce the dead body of the pregnant girl's husband was hidden in the boot of her car. It was an incredible twist of fate. Sofia had starred in countless dramas that were lauded for their capricious twists and turns. Every producer worth his salt would be champing at the bit to have a big reveal like that tucked up their sleeves.

Sofia studied Claire's face and body language. *Guilty as sin*, she thought. She knew her type; she had met more than her fair share of Claires on the showbiz circuit over the years. They were shrewd and manipulative and stopped at nothing to land the roles they thirsted for.

She bit the soft, fleshy insides of her cheeks to stop her lips from curling into a smile and revealing her satisfaction at Claire's unravelling. It meant, of course, that Sofia was now in prime position to be saved. But to be sure, she would need to put on an Oscar-winning performance. There was no dead body hidden in Sofia's vehicle, but there were plenty of skeletons in her closet.

"Hello, Sofia."

A female voice startled her. She scanned her screens until she realised it belonged to the juror with frightful hair and a matching frightful plaid suit. She would have preferred a man to question her; she had a much better rapport with the opposite sex.

Sofia noted a clock appear in the right-hand corner of the screen. It began counting down immediately. She imagined herself walking into the Old Vic to rapturous applause. She cleared her throat and offered her audience the warmest of smiles. "Good morning to you. And to whom am I speaking?" Sofia asked.

"Fiona Prentice."

"Fiona, hello. You are the brave soul charged with saving my life then, are you?"

She watched as Fiona offered a smile that didn't match her eyes. Her demeanour was bold but her pupils were dilated as if she were apprehensive.

"Well, let me make this easy for you, Fiona. I hold no grudge against you or anyone else who chooses not to vote for me. I have led a full, wonderful life, beyond what I could've ever imagined. And if my fate is to see out my final hours in front of this delightful audience, then I will die as I have lived. I can't think of any better way to go." She paused to wait for imaginary applause to die down. "By the way, this is Oscar," she continued, holding up her bemused dog and waving his paw towards the camera. She allowed him to lick the side of her face, hoping it might win over animal lovers.

"For the benefit of those people who may be unaware of who you are, could you please tell us a little about yourself?" suggested Fiona.

Sofia took a deep breath and placed the dog back by her side. "Of course. Well, where to begin? I've been a working actress since I first trod the boards as a girl in the West End, and it's thanks to my public that I've been able to sustain such a long career. I'm not going to tire you all by reeling off everything you've probably seen me in or the many awards I've been given, so let's just keep it brief and say that I have been blessed."

"Does it concern you that you're the . . . *most senior* . . . of the remaining Passengers?"

References to her age often left a bitter taste in Sofia's mouth, but not this time. "I might not have as many years left in me as some of the others trapped in these god-awful cars, but should it mean that I'm denied the opportunity to live the rest of my life? I do hope not. I believe that I still have such a lot to give."

"Can you give us an example of what? I know you've done a lot of charity work over the years."

Good girl, thought Sofia. *That saves me having to shoehorn it into the conversation.*

"Oh, bless you for remembering," she continued with false modesty, before spending the next three minutes of her allocated time recalling the charities and hospitals represented. "But yes," she said finally, "I suppose my charity work is one of the things that I'm the proudest of, and it's what brings me the most pleasure. As much as I enjoy entertaining the people and being, what did Prince Harry once call me, oh that's right, a 'national treasure,' it's raising money for good causes that is closest to my heart."

"Some of the equipment your money paid for saved my daughter's life," added Fiona.

Sofia edged closer towards the screen. This was going even better than she hoped. "Oh really? Tell me more, Fiona, darling."

"Nine years ago, Kitty underwent brain surgery to remove a benign tumour using doctors that your money helped to train and in a hospital that you helped to build. So I'd like to take this opportunity to thank you from the both of us."

"You are very welcome. When it comes to fundraising, people have thrown around figures like twenty-five or thirty million pounds, but they're just numbers and who's counting? I'm so pleased that your little girl is one of the hundreds to benefit from my hard work."

Sofia became aware of the clock reaching the one-minute mark.

"Some of the other Passengers are parents," continued Fiona. "When you obviously care so much about children's charities, do you mind if I ask why you chose not to start a family?"

Sofia dropped her head, then raised it, tilting it at a slight angle. She hadn't forgotten how the same manoeuvre had given Princess Diana's words extra depth during her revelatory BBC interview decades earlier. Sofia altered her tone so that it was softer, almost regretful. "For so many years I put my career and my body of work ahead of having a family of my own. And I'll be honest with you, Fiona, it has been one of my biggest regrets."

"I haven't asked you about your husband. How long have you been married?"

Sofia curled her toes tightly. "My darling Patrick and I have been married for almost forty years now."

"And he's your fifth husband, if I remember correctly?"

"Yes." Her reply was curt before she corrected herself. "My twenties and thirties were a busy time." She chuckled. "But you know what they say, fifth time's a charm. Well, something like that. But like I said to you earlier, I have been very blessed with a long, happy life. I can only hope your little girl goes on to live as many joys as I have, along with all the other children and their families I have supported over the years."

"I know we don't have much time left, so I should conclude by asking why my fellow jurors and the public should support you."

"I'd never be as bold as to say people *should* vote for me, but of course I would like them to. If I am permitted to live, then I will not take one second of it for granted, and I'll continue to put the people's needs above my own. A priest I knew once told me, 'A candle loses nothing by lighting another candle.' That's how I've lived my life."

The countdown clock reached zero, and Sofia relaxed back into her seat, stroking Oscar and imagining the audience's standing ovation. The next voice to speak she recognised as the Hacker's.

"Thank you, Sofia," he began. "No one can argue that you have certainly led an interesting life."

"The fans have put me where I am, and I am here to serve them," she replied.

"Do you mind if I ask you another question, on their behalf?" Sofia nodded, welcoming more time in the spotlight. "Was there ever a point when you considered starting a family?"

"Of course, much in the same way as every woman does."

Suddenly, instinct told Sofia that the Hacker wasn't playing all his cards at once. She needed to give him something—a diversion—and quickly. "If you really want to know the truth, I didn't start a family of my own because I wasn't able to have children."

She gave a stage pause, removed a tissue from her bag, and dabbed at her non-existent tears. She knew from the silence that she was still holding everyone's attention.

"By the time I met Patrick, I was ready for a family, but alas my body wasn't. I was diagnosed with uterine fibroids that were causing me a great deal of pain. And as a result, I needed a hysterectomy. As you can imagine, it was devastating. I celebrated my fortieth birthday in a hospital room crying my heart out for something I'd only recently realised I wanted. Back then, you couldn't just bank eggs like girls do now, and surrogacy wasn't the thing it is today, so I lost my only chance at motherhood. And I suppose that's why I raise so much money for children's charities. I think of all the little ones I have helped as my own extended family."

"I am a little confused though."

"About what?"

"Because I thought the decision not to have a family *was* your own? According to the medical records I have here in my possession, it wasn't taken out of your hands at all; it was your own choice."

Sofia held her breath. *He knows*, she thought. *He knows everything.* She pressed a hand to her throat as she waited for him to continue. After a crippling pause, Sofia was the first to break. "It was a complicated time."

"It wasn't really though, was it? You didn't have a hysterectomy; you opted to be sterilised. Why ever would someone who claims to have wanted to start a family go to such extremes not to have one?"

Sofia glared at the camera. Her mask had slipped, and she had finished playing her part but the audience remained seated.

"If you're not willing to share this with the fans you claim to serve, would you like me to do it for you?" His suggestion was met with stony silence. "I'll take that as a yes. The reason why you chose to be sterilised was because—"

"I want to remove myself from this competition," Sofia said suddenly. "Take me off the list. I want to let someone else live instead of me."

It was the first time she heard the Hacker laugh. "You would really rather die than have the truth come out?"

"I don't want to be a part of this any longer," Sofia continued. "It's sick, you threatening us all, raking up private things that have no business being spoken about in public."

"So you only want them to know the real you if it's on your terms?"

"My private life is my own business."

"That barn door is wide open and the horse has long since bolted, Sofia. The truth is that you had yourself sterilised so that your husband couldn't get you pregnant."

Sofia's silence was as good as admitting her guilt.

"And why didn't you want to carry his child?"

She felt her throat tighten. She was unable to defend herself.

"Because your husband was, and still is, a notorious paedophile, isn't he? And you have been complicit in his crimes by using your wealth and influence to cover up the fact he has molested dozens of children over the last four decades."

Sofia shook her head furiously. "You don't know what—"

"I have his victims' names, dates, and how much you paid for their families' silence. I even have photographs he took and sent to magazines and websites."

Sofia's arms were rigid as she steadied herself against the seat. Her mind raced with the speed of a whirlwind, desperately trying to think of a way she could escape the accusations with her reputation intact. But before she could defend herself, Sofia realised that no one would get the chance to hear her rebuttal. Her sound feed had been cut off. The show was over, along with her career.

CHAPTER 37

L ibby let out a long breath she wasn't aware she was holding, then turned to face a similarly stunned Matthew.

She looked towards Jude's screen to gauge his reaction. He appeared as bewildered as everyone else.

"Well, I don't think Sofia will be on the NSPCC's Christmas card list for very much longer," said Cadman.

"You're making a joke about child abuse?" asked Libby.

Cadman glanced to Matthew before immediately backing down. "My apologies."

After witnessing the exposure of Claire's and Sofia's secrets, it was rapidly becoming apparent that the Passengers had been carefully selected based on what they were hiding.

There was nothing in the world that Libby hated more than secrets. Alarm bells were beginning to sound in her head. Her brother Nicky had kept his suicidal feelings from his family the day he was released from hospital. And William had kept from her his fling with the office intern. What secrets might Jude be concealing from her?

"Is it possible the Hacker's accusations aren't true?" she directed towards Jack. "Or at least only part of the story?" He didn't reciprocate her eye contact and stared at the screens instead. Libby continued regardless. "He's using each of us to set the Passengers up. Once they've presented to us the best version of themselves, he goes in for the kill with an accusation. But how do we know what the whole truth is if he won't allow them a rebuttal?"

"A rebuttal?" Jack let out a short, sharp snort. "You have failed to grasp the situation, Miss Dixon. We are long past playing by Queensberry rules or anything that one might consider honourable. The Hacker doesn't recognise anything but his own agenda."

"I'm not stupid; I can see that," she replied. "What he's doing is mirroring what goes on in your inquests. You never give us the full picture either, do you? We're only told as much as you want us to know before we're forced to decide who's at fault, the victim or the car. And because so much of the evidence is 'classified,' it's almost always the victim who's damned. So what he's doing isn't really any different to what you do."

"You're misinformed and ignorant, Miss Dixon. All we can do is let the Passengers tell us why they should live, and hope for their sakes that they're being honest. If they're not, then God help them." .

Libby looked Jack directly in the eyes. The piercing glare she had once been afraid of no longer existed. He had lost his fight. "Why have you given up so easily?" she asked.

"Because there is nothing I can do that will make any difference for Miss Arden."

"No, I don't just mean Claire, I mean what's happening in here. You don't get to where you are in your career without fighting tooth and nail to get your own way. Why isn't your phone glued to your ear anymore like it was when this began? Why aren't you losing your temper with your office or demanding to speak to GCHQ again?"

"One of the many problems with you millennials is that you spend too much time thinking and reading too much into situations that don't require your input. If I were you, I'd concentrate on what your friend Jude is hiding behind that vacant look of his."

Libby didn't rise to the bait. "The Hacker has something else on you, doesn't he?"

"Don't be so ridiculous." Jack's eyes briefly darted towards his own image on-screen. But his denial was not nearly as venomous as Libby would have expected. She turned her whole body towards him. Jack remained firm, as if he was concerned that, by moving, he might give something away.

"I'm right, aren't I?" she continued. "He's alluded to knowing something about you or the inquest process numerous times. And you don't know what he knows, so you're playing it safe by keeping a low profile. If he knows so much about the Passengers, then he knows a lot about you too."

"You have a very fertile imagination, Miss Dixon."

"You're just biding your time and hoping to leave this room with as few battle scars as possible."

Finally, Jack looked her, his silence speaking volumes. She turned her attention back towards the wall of screens. Sofia's face was expressionless, as if the picture had frozen. Her arms were folded, and her eyes stared beyond the camera and out through the car's windscreen.

"Do I need to ask how social media is reacting to the exposé of our 'national treasure'?" asked the Hacker.

"Opinions are along the lines of what you might expect," Cadman replied. "I think it's safe to say that right now, she is the most hated woman on the planet."

"With one hour left until the collision, shall we move along?" the Hacker suggested. "Let's continue with one-half of the only married couple in our process."

CHAPTER 38

SAM COLE

The sour taste of bile rose up into Sam's throat and entered his mouth. It burned as he swallowed it back down. But he gave the camera no indication that he was literally scared sick.

Moments earlier, Sam suppressed his joy when Claire's and then Sofia's credibility fell apart before the world. But at the same time, he was all too aware that when his moment came as the focus of attention, it would likely happen to him too. He had just as many secrets of his own that could ruin his chance of survival.

Sam's mind raced as he narrowed his options down to just two—tell the truth or lie. If he beat the Hacker to the punch and made his admission, perhaps the public and jurors might forgive him? *You might as well cut out the middleman and hand yourself a death sentence*, he told himself. He shook his head, swiftly ruling it out. None of them would understand the choices he'd made unless they had walked in his shoes.

If he lied by omission, he could use the ten minutes allocated to him to persuade viewers he was worthier of their support than his wife. Then when his time was up and the Hacker revealed Sam's secret, he could still retain some support. There was still a chance the Hacker didn't know what Sam was hiding. But he was sure social media would expose him if the Hacker didn't. There were too many people who knew him from different walks of life for it not to reach the public domain.

Every so often, he glanced at Heidi's screen to try to judge from her expression and body language how she was holding up. It was difficult to tell. They'd been a couple for twelve years and married for ten, but the longer she spent in the police force, it became increasingly difficult to penetrate her steely veneer. She had seen too much bad in the world and it had hardened her.

The Heidi of old would not have asked if he were willing to sacrifice his life for hers. Had she considered for a moment that he might be able to offer the children just as much as she could? He doubted it. Heidi wanted to keep on living, so why didn't she think Sam would want the same thing?

Could you really try to steal votes from her to save your own skin? he asked himself. He glanced at Heidi again. When she informed him that her workmates had nicknamed her Elsa, he knew why without her needing to explain. Like now, for example. Her skin could have been covered with a layer of frost and she couldn't have looked any cooler. It was her ability to detach that had made her value his life below her own.

As far as he could see, her only advantage over him was her relationship with their children. His long working weeks away in Halifax meant Beccy and James had forged a closer bond with their mum than with him. Sometimes, upon his return, it felt as if there was no room for him inside their tight little clique. But his hands were tied, and his time was not infinite. Whether she meant to or not, Heidi made him feel like a guest in his own family. And now more than ever, he resented her for it.

Just the sound of the Hacker's voice again made his leg start to jig. "Muriel, would you like to begin?" the Hacker asked, and the time began its descent. He took another look at Muriel. She wouldn't have been his first choice as a potential saviour, but beggars couldn't be choosers.

"Hello, Sam," she began sympathetically, as if she were comforting a terminal patient. He refrained from reminding her that he wasn't dead yet. "How are you?"

"I'm pretty angry, if I'm being honest," he replied, and folded his arms as if to emphasise the point.

"Well, that's understandable—"

"Wouldn't you feel the same if it were you?" he interrupted. "Either I'm going to die, my wife is going to die, or both of us are going to die, and that's unfair, isn't it? I don't want to live without her and she doesn't want to live without me, and how are our kids supposed to carry on like normal when they've watched both their parents blown to bits in front of an audience of billions? They're going to be scarred for life, aren't they?"

By her expression, Muriel wasn't expecting Sam to sound quite so enraged or impassioned. It threw her from her planned line of questioning.

"Um, you have, er, two children, is that correct?" she asked.

"Yes, they're nine and eight, and you couldn't wish for a better pair of kids. James is the school under-tens rugby captain, and Beccy is a very talented singer. Thinking about them is the only thing getting me through this." Sam held up his phone towards the camera to show the audience a carefully selected photograph that included him with a child under each arm, but no Heidi.

"They're beautiful," said Muriel. "As you are aware, the purpose of our conversation is to get to know you a little bit more. Can I ask how long you've been married?"

"Ten years next month."

"Are you a man of faith?"

"I'm Church of England."

"Do you talk to God often?"

"I don't, I'm afraid. I work away from home a lot, so I don't have much free time for anything. Well, I did believe in him until I found myself locked in this car and fighting for my life."

"When we're at our most vulnerable, having a faith can be just what we need to get us through."

"I'll be honest with you, I feel as if he's abandoned me."

"He is always by our side."

"I don't see him. He's put me in competition against my wife, the one person I love the most in the world, aside from the kids. He must know that I'm never going to try and compete against her, so my fate is sealed. Besides, Heidi is always going to win more public support than I am, isn't she? That's just the way of the world. A mum will always be more valued than a dad."

"Well, yes and no," Muriel replied, somewhat confused as to what the correct answer might be. Sam saw her turn to her fellow jurors and arch her eyebrows as if she was asking for their help. "In this age of equality, there's no reason why people won't choose to support you, is there?"

Sam laughed. "I think we both know the answer to that, Muriel. And when you think about it, it's incredibly discriminatory. Even if a woman carries a child for nine months and then gives birth to it, that doesn't mean she's necessarily the best-qualified parent. It doesn't mean that, as a man, I can't provide for a child equally as well. Don't misunderstand me, I'm not saying I could do a better job than Heidi; the kids couldn't want for a better mum. I'm just pointing out that in an age where women have never been more equal to men, it's much more likely that she is going to survive this ordeal than me."

Sam noted Fiona typing into her tablet and sliding it over for an increasingly flustered Muriel to read. The clock on his screen reached the halfway point. He placed both hands on his thigh to stop his leg from bouncing.

"Would you like this opportunity to tell us a bit more about yourself?" Muriel asked hopefully.

"I'm sorry if I've made you feel uncomfortable," Sam replied. "That wasn't my intention."

"No, no, you haven't," she lied, offering him a faint smile.

"I'm just frustrated because it's unlikely I'll see or hold my kids again," he continued. "They're my world. And I appreciate that it's Heidi who spends the majority of time with them. But given half a chance, I'd swap places with her in a heartbeat. Like millions and millions of other dads out there watching and listening to me right now, I contribute towards my children in different ways to their mum—but they're equally important ways. And now it looks like I'm going to die because of it. Why would your God put me in a position where I don't have a fighting chance?"

"Um, perhaps even though you have created life together, it's because a woman has the biological means to feed and nurture that child. That's why she's judged by some as more valuable—"

"Now I'm being penalised because my body can't feed a baby? Really?"

"That's not what—"

"So not only is society against me but so is my biology, the same one that God created? I'm truly shafted, aren't I?"

Muriel attempted several more lines of questioning, from Sam's occupation to his interests and what motivated him. But each time, he returned the subject to the bias against men. He had done all that he could. Now his only hope was that his argument had resonated with the rest of his sex. Suddenly he became aware of the time—he had just ninety seconds left to complete his defence.

"May I ask your social media person a question?" he asked, but didn't await permission. "Up until my ten minutes began, how popular was I with the public?"

Surprised to be addressed, a ruffled Cadman recovered fast and reached for his tablet. "Just give me a minute to make a clean sweep of the data," he muttered.

"Unfortunately, a minute is about all I have."

"Well, in terms of popularity, in first place was Heidi, in second it was you, third place was Sofia—although she's dropping like a kitten down a well, then Jude, followed by Claire."

"And now?"

"While various incarnations of #killSofia are currently the most trending hashtag, you have the highest number of new votes and positive comments for a Passenger. Most of your support appears to be coming from the UK, US, Denmark, France, and Sweden, where there are higher densities of single-father households."

Sam's instinct was to punch the air in victory, but he held back. In less than ten minutes, he had completed what he had set out to achieve. However, it had come at Heidi's expense. He didn't want to look at her for her reaction, but he couldn't stop himself. Her expression was no longer just frosty; it was ice-cold. Her eyebrows were drawn tightly together, her lips pursed. Her chest rose and fell quickly as if she was trying to suppress her rage. A part of him wanted to mouth "I'm sorry" to her, but he knew that he couldn't, because he wasn't sorry.

He had more to live for than she did.

"And that brings us to an end," came the Hacker's voice. Sam watched a wave of relief wash over Muriel's face, her role now complete. He braced himself, because if the next few minutes followed the same pattern as Claire's and Sofia's, the Hacker was preparing his parting shot. And he hoped that when it was fired, he had been persuasive enough to retain some of that support.

"That's quite the turnaround in public opinion, Sam," the Hacker continued. "It was very cleverly played."

"I'd like to add that it wasn't ever my intention to try and take support away from my wife," Sam added with as much sincerity as he could muster. "I'm willing to die for that woman."

"A fine sentiment, I'm sure, if only it were true. But you're not, are you? Because you had the opportunity to do just that, and you chose to survive. I wonder if there is anyone else you might choose to die for instead? Perhaps Josie, the woman you married a year after marrying Heidi? Or maybe the son and the daughter you and that wife have together? Does this previously undisclosed family mean more to you than your first?"

CHAPTER 39

HEIDI COLE

Heidi was aware that millions of pairs of eyes were now upon her, the public and jurors all on tenterhooks waiting to see how she would react.

She began slowly, with a shake of her head. "No, you're a liar," she told the Hacker. "I don't believe you."

"I have no reason to lie to you, Heidi," he replied, his voice infused with phony sympathy. "Of the nine years you have spent married to your husband, for eight of them, he has also been married to another woman. And in that time, they have had two children together."

"Am I just supposed to take your word for it?" she hit back. "You've made accusations about us all, but you never offer any proof. I don't take anyone's word for anything without seeing evidence first."

"Spoken like a true officer of the law, DS Cole."

A ten-minute countdown clock appeared in the corner of her screen along with a video clip. It was of Sam playing with two children, around the same age as her own, in a theme park. He was with a blond-haired boy and a red-haired girl travelling inside a log flume. Suddenly it dropped down a steep section, drenching them with water. They exited the carriage, giggling and wringing water from their clothes. "Daddy, you're soaked," the girl directed towards Sam as he rubbed her wet, matted hair. Whoever was holding the camera turned it on themselves. It was a woman with short, dark hair and pale skin. "Oh, Daddy is going to regret his soggy bottom on the journey home," she said, laughing, before the screen faded to black.

The next clip had been recorded at a restaurant with the same children and a group of men and women Heidi didn't recognise. The woman from the last clip approached Sam with a cake and two burning candles in the shape of 4 and 0 as everyone sang "Happy Birthday." Heidi recalled offering to organise him a party, but he had turned her down. Now she knew why. Responding to requests for a speech, Sam rose to his feet. "I'd like to thank everyone for coming," he began, "and for my beautiful wife and kids for keeping this from me as a surprise. I had no idea she could be so secretive."

"Turn it off," Heidi spat, and the Hacker obliged. Her face remained devoid of emotion as she looked to Sam's screen. He may have held his head down, but the guilt was written across his face.

"Who are they?" she asked.

"It doesn't matter," the Hacker replied. "All that matters is that they exist."

"If you are telling me that my marriage has been based on lies, then it matters to me. Who are they?"

"His son is called James and his daughter is called Beccy."

"That's what we called our children."

"He used the same names."

"And her?"

"His wife's name is Josie."

"Don't call her his wife," Heidi snapped. "If he married me first, then legally I am his wife, not her."

A camera picked out Matthew. He took it as his cue to begin talking to her.

"I'm sorry, Heidi," he began. "This is not how I envisaged our conversation to begin." When Heidi didn't reply, Matthew filled the space of her silence. "I'm not sure what's worse—a partner who has started another family behind their first family's back, or one who has affairs throughout their marriage. And I speak about this from experience."

Heidi thawed ever so slightly at his words. "You do?" she asked.

He nodded. "A careless text message she'd forgotten to delete. I'm not just paying you lip service when I tell you that you have my sympathy."

Heidi offered Matthew an appreciative half-smile and directed her attention to her husband. "I don't even have to ask you if it's true, do I, Sam? Look at you." She saw his leg bouncing up and down as he shuffled awkwardly in his seat. "How could you?" she continued, her voice becoming emboldened. "What kind of man marries someone else when they already have a wife? Did I slip your mind? Did you just forget? Does she know about me, about our family?"

Sam opened his mouth, but with his microphone switched off, he was unable to give her the answers she craved. "Turn his volume up!" Heidi ordered, but her demands were ignored. "You heard me! I have a right to know! If I'm going to die in this car, at least give me the truth first."

"I don't think you are going to get it, Heidi," said Matthew calmly. "The Hacker isn't interested in giving you answers; he gains more satisfaction from playing with you . . . playing with all of us. So why don't you tell us about yourself instead? Let the people know who you are away from Sam. Don't allow what he has done to define you in their eyes."

"But I trusted him. How could he do this to me?"

"How would you describe yourself as a mum?" Matthew persevered.

"Unlike my husband, I'm there for my children," she replied. "During his interview, Sam was keen to point out just how unfair it was that only women are thought of as nurturers. Well, Sam, that's because I had no choice but to take on that role by myself. You failed to mention how you kept accepting contracts that took you away from us four days a week, and it's only now I realise that it's because it meant you got to spend time with this other family. I also work full-time, but it's me who plays both mum and dad to our kids, who takes Beccy to singing lessons and ferries James around the county for rugby tournaments. And even when you are with us, it's like you're not there. You're always too tired to engage. But I suppose you've been too busy giving your attention to your other children to care."

"Why do you think you should survive this process?" Matthew continued.

Heidi shook her head. "You know what? I don't mean to be rude but I'm done playing this game. I've given the last ten years to raising my children, to being a success in my career, and to my marriage. And this is my reward for trying to be a good person. So to hell with you all. I'm not answering any more questions."

Heidi rubbed at her eyes with her fingertips and looked out from the window and to the opposite side of the road, where traffic had come to a complete standstill. A queue of drivers and Passengers lined up to watch her car pass them. Some pointed cameras at her, others waved, and many applauded. She took a sharp intake of breath, worried that she might share Shabana's fate if anyone broke ranks and tried to bring her car to a halt. But they retained a respectful distance.

The Hacker was the next person to speak.

"Are you alright, Heidi?" he asked.

"If you cared, we wouldn't be trapped inside these cars being stared at like animals in a zoo. I'd be home with my children and not publicly humiliated for your entertainment."

"You still have three minutes left."

"Keep them, give them to someone else, shove them up your arse, I don't care. If I'm only able to teach my kids one more lesson, then it's to face up to bullies, to stand their ground and not to allow anyone like you or their father to take advantage of them."

The Hacker let the camera remain on a defiant Heidi for several moments before he spoke again.

"Cadman, would you care to keep us up to speed with how the public are reacting with their hashtags to Heidi and Sam's situation?"

"Heidi has already overtaken Sam, and he's actually dropped to below even Claire's ranking. Apparently living a double life with two wives and two families is worse than driving around with your dead husband in the car."

"While the public never fails to fascinate me, neither do our Passengers," said the Hacker. "I find you particularly interesting, Heidi. Bringing your ten minutes to an early halt was a very risky move."

"It wasn't a move because I'm not playing a game."

"That's not true, is it?"

Heidi's heart sank. For a moment, she thought she had got away with it. As long as she was winning sympathy as the wronged wife, she would take

Sam's support and show him how it felt to be thrown under the bus. But the Hacker had known exactly what she was doing. And now everyone else was about to as well.

"You've known about your husband's second family for quite some time now, haven't you?" the Hacker continued. "And to get your revenge, you've been blackmailing him ever since."

CHAPTER 40

F or the second time in minutes, Libby's eyes were fixed on Heidi's face to judge her reaction. But she gave nothing away.

Libby looked to Sam instead. His leg was motionless. Heidi had shut down her emotions, but Sam was the opposite. His face slowly became gnarled with anger, before frustration set in at not being able to communicate with her.

Sam's shock appeared genuine, but Libby no longer trusted her judgement. She had taken the four Passengers' stories on face value, and each of them had proven to be dishonest. And the thought of what Jude might be hiding from her made her sick with worry. Unlike the other jurors and their charges, Libby had an emotional investment in hers.

As much as she wanted to believe Jude was different, in truth, what did she know about him? They were barely acquainted. Her sole judgement on what kind of man he was based on spending four hours together. The only common link among the remaining Passengers was that all were hiding something. It stood to reason that so was Jude, otherwise why would he be locked inside a car packed with explosives? Another thought struck her—what if the Hacker was saving the worst until last? The nauseating feeling was stronger than ever.

"None of the Passengers are coming out of this well," said Muriel.

"Neither are you guys," Cadman added.

"Why ever not?"

"For a jury charged with making important decisions, social media finds your judgement questionable. Each Passenger you've chosen to support has turned out to be either a husband killer, a paedophile protector, an adulterer, or a blackmailer."

Libby didn't have time to doubt Jude any longer. His face filled the main screen, and the countdown clock appeared. Libby moved into the centre of the room with a confidence she didn't really possess. The life of the man before her was now in her hands.

"Libby, if you'd like to begin," said the Hacker.

"Hi," she said, feeling suddenly very exposed.

"Hi to you too," Jude replied. He gave her the same smile he'd offered from across the bar that night. And just like then, the butterflies in her stomach began their ascent. She couldn't stop herself from remembering how wonderful he tasted when they kissed. If only it hadn't been cut short.

"How are you holding up?" she asked. Before he could answer, she corrected herself. "Sorry, I promised myself I wasn't going to ask any silly questions."

"That's okay; I'm not too bad now I've got over the shock of it all. I can't say it ever crossed my mind that when you and I met again, it would be like this."

When, Libby repeated to herself. *He said "when."* It meant he hadn't given up on her. He'd thought there was still a chance.

"I don't think anyone could have imagined this," she replied. "How are you remaining so calm? I'm not locked in a hijacked car but I'm terrified."

"I'd be lying if I said I wasn't freaked out by it. But I've learned that in life sometimes you have to accept your fate."

"When I first saw you this morning and realised who you were, I wasn't sure if you'd remember me."

"You're a hard woman to forget." Libby's eyes twinkled. "I want you to know what I said earlier was true. I did trawl social media trying to find you. A friend of a friend works for the brewery that owns the pub, and he broke a few data privacy laws by grabbing some images of you from CCTV to help me." Jude removed his phone from the dashboard and held it up to the camera to reveal the photographs he'd saved. "Now I'm showing you them, I appreciate how creepy it looks."

"If it was anyone else, it might," Libby said. "But not you." She held back a smile that wanted to swallow her face.

"Can I ask you a question, Libby?"

"Isn't it supposed to be the other way around?"

"Yes, but if it's a choice between spending ten minutes trying to fight my corner or getting to know you, then you win hands down." This time Libby couldn't hold back her grin any longer. "What do you think might have happened if you stayed at the bar?"

She took a moment to consider it before she answered. "I think my friends would have moved on to somewhere else, but you and I would've stayed outside in the garden until closing time. Then we'd have searched for some terrible takeaway to buy questionable meats served in a polystyrene box, we'd have eaten it on the way back to my hotel, then you'd have asked for my number, I'd have given it to you, and we would've kissed again. Then, maybe for the next few days, we'd have messaged each other, and the following weekend, we'd have met for dinner and taken it from there."

"You've given this a lot of thought, haven't you?" Jude teased. Libby's laugh resembled a snort and her face flushed. "I like to think that's how it might've gone too. But instead, you disappeared into the night like Cinderella only without the glass slipper. And now I'm locked in a car that's probably going to explode unless you can convince everyone I'm worth saving. Quite the modern fairy-tale romance, isn't it?"

She felt a tap against her arm. Matthew pointed towards the countdown clock. Six minutes remained. Libby felt a hollowness in her stomach.

"I know what you said earlier," Libby continued. "But I'd never forgive myself if I didn't ask you some questions that might go some way towards saving your life."

Jude sighed. "Go ahead then. But would you like to address the elephant in the room first?"

"Which is?"

"Why am I a Passenger? What's the big secret I've been hiding from you all?"

Libby tried swallowing her fear but it wouldn't go down.

"I'm not sure I want to know now," she said quietly.

"We could spend our last few minutes talking about why we were brought here today or what might've happened had we more time that night. But based on the other Passengers' experiences, the Hacker is waiting to tell you something that'll likely change your opinion of me. And I'd rather you heard it from my mouth than his."

Libby subconsciously folded her arms as if protecting herself from the answer to come. Jude clasped his hands together and chose his words carefully.

"You asked me how I was holding up despite everything that's happening. I suppose it was because I have a reason not to fear death. Before all of . . . *this* . . . happened, the morning I had planned was going to be very different."

"How so?"

"Because it was going to be my last."

"Your last what?"

"My last morning. I was going to end my life today."

CHAPTER 41

L ibby took a sharp intake of breath and a step back from the screen.

She glared at Jude, hoping he was making a distasteful joke, but instinct told her he wasn't the type. She turned to Matthew, Fiona, and Muriel to check that she hadn't misheard. Their equally puzzled faces told her she had not.

"I . . . I don't think I understand," she stuttered. "What do you mean you were going to end your life?"

"I'm afraid it means what you think it means. I'd given the sat nav the coordinates for Scotland's Forth Bridge. Have you ever been?" Libby shook her head. "My brother and I used to go up to South Queensferry as kids each summer to stay with our uncle. It's such a beautiful part of the world and it seemed fitting to call things quits in a place I've got fond memories of."

Libby's head was spinning. Jude's reply was so detached it was as if he were planning a summer holiday, not his death. Her knee-jerk reaction was to try to talk him out of it, until she reminded herself of her nursing training. She must tread carefully.

"I know it's an intrusive thing for me to ask and I hope you forgive me for it, but what made you reach that decision?" she asked instead.

"You don't have to treat me with kid gloves, Libby," he replied. "I'm not your patient. I can only speak for myself, but I assume it's for the same reason most people want to end their lives early. Because I have absolutely nothing I want to live for."

"But when we met, you seemed so happy, so confident . . . your smile and enthusiasm were two of the things I remember most clearly about you."

"When you've had depression as long as I have, you learn how to become a convincing actor. Mine has been crippling me on and off since I was a teenager, and in recent years, it's become unbearable. Medication, counselling, electroconvulsive therapy . . . everything I've tried hasn't even scratched the surface. So last Christmas, I made a promise to myself that when it all became too much, I was going to take charge of it instead of letting it take charge of me. And after a particularly rough few months, I made up my mind that today was going to be the day I took back control. And here we are."

"But what about your family?"

"My brother is all I have left but there's a lot of distance between us. We don't really know one another anymore."

"I'm sure he'd still miss you."

"Yeah, he might do. But not wanting to hurt him isn't enough for me to remain here. Nothing is."

What about me? Libby wanted to say, but she held her tongue. "You have so much to live for . . ." she began, and stopped herself mid-sentence. She reminded herself that pointing out what someone with depression has to live for would not make a blind bit of difference to their mindset. "I'm sorry," she continued. "That's not what you want to hear."

"Not really, no." Jude offered her a genuine smile. "But thank you."

"Why have the last few months been so bad?"

"A lot has changed since we saw each other last. I lost my job, I've struggled to find another one; I was evicted from my flat because I couldn't pay the mortgage, and I've been living out of my car. I keep myself clean in supermarket bathrooms, I shower at the community swimming pool when I can afford it, and most of what I eat comes from food banks or leftovers from supermarket bins. I've lost my self-respect and my confidence and, above all, my fight."

Libby brushed away a solitary tear that fell down her cheek and rested on the corner of her mouth. "I'm so sorry."

"Don't be. It's not your fault. I cannot find a way out of how I'm feeling.

And even if by some miracle there was, it wouldn't be enough. Nothing, no one, is enough anymore."

"But what if I'd never left the pub that night? Things could've been different."

"It was just make-believe, wasn't it? This, now—me here, you there— this is our reality. Part of me wishes I'd died the next morning and at least I'd have gone out on a high."

"Then why didn't you?"

"Because the thought of seeing you again gave me hope."

"I've been through this before," Libby said suddenly. "My brother, Nicky. He was tormented by mental health issues. He thought the same as you, that no one would miss him if he died. But we did and we still do, every single day."

"I'm sorry," said Jude. "I didn't know. What happened, if you don't mind me asking?"

"He suffered a head injury playing rugby at school when he was fifteen. He landed awkwardly, which started a bleed on his brain. He was in a coma for the best part of a month, and when he finally came out of it and began to recover, it quickly became obvious that he wasn't the same brother I'd grown up with. Like you, he lost his confidence, he was either choked by anxiety or swallowed by depression. He kept telling us that he wished he'd died on that rugby field. Years later and after his fifth suicide attempt, he disappeared so far inside himself that we couldn't find him. We were forced to have him placed in a secure unit for his own safety. The day he was released, we brought him home and only a few hours later, he hanged himself in his bedroom. I was the one who found his body. Nicky is the reason why I chose mental health nursing. I was too late and ill-equipped to save my brother, but I can help others."

"You can't save Nicky through me, Libby. It's not fair to put that pressure on either of us."

"I'm not saying that I could. But I'm telling you I won't give up on you."

"You deserve an equal, Libby, someone who can treat you as well as you treat them. And as much as I'd love to be that man, it's just not me. You'd have a patient, not a partner."

"That would have been my decision to make, not yours."

Jude gave her another of the calming smiles she cherished. "Whoever you eventually invite to be a part of your life, he will be a lucky, lucky man, Libby."

Jude's lips moved as if he were saying something else, but there was no sound. It was only then that she noticed the countdown clock had reached zero. She had done her best to save the life of a man who didn't want to be rescued.

ONLINE TRENDS FOR YOU	#SaveClaire/#SaveSofia/#SaveHeidi/ #SaveSam/#SaveJude—92.3m tweets #WhoWillYouSave—86.5m tweets #WhoIsTheHacker—2.3m tweets #KillThemAll—2.2m tweets #BuyLibbyNewShoes—558k tweets

The Hacker was the first to break the stillness of the room.

"So, members of the jury and social media. Each of your Passengers has presented their own version of themselves to you, some of whom have made claims that I have contradicted with truths of my own. Now it's your turn to make a decision. One Passenger will survive, while the others will collide head-on. You must now make a decision on who to save, before your votes are combined and the sole survivor's name is revealed."

Libby anticipated a postscript, a revelation about Jude that he had failed to admit himself. But nothing came. The Hacker had asked for honesty, and Jude had been the only Passenger to give him it, even if it meant losing support from anyone else.

"Libby, we should make a start," said Matthew gently, interrupting her thoughts. She turned to find that behind her, Muriel and Fiona had moved their chairs so that they were all around the same desk. They had left a gap for her. She looked at each of them in turn and then up to the wall and took in each of the final five. Turning once more, she nodded to Matthew and drew in her seat. Jack sat a few metres away from them, close to the door.

"How should we approach this?" Fiona asked. "Because unless anyone has a better idea, I think we should talk through them one name at a time and see where each of us is lending our support. And I'm sure some are going to be easier than others." With the exception of Jack, they agreed. "Shall we begin with Claire?" Fiona continued. "Who will be offering her their vote?"

"I'm torn," admitted Muriel. "While I have my obvious reservations, I feel like I should be supporting her unborn child's right to have a chance at life." Libby noticed her rubbing the crucifix around her neck with her thumb and forefinger as if it were offering her guidance.

"Perhaps your opinion might be a little less biased if your lesbian partner wasn't pregnant with her child," said Jack.

"*Wife*, not partner, and *our* child, not hers," Muriel interrupted.

"Unless technology has now evolved so far as to assist you in personally providing the sperm to co-create this baby, then it's a safe assumption that it's *her* child," Jack retaliated.

Muriel rolled her eyes. "Not that it's any of your business, but it was my fertilised egg implanted into her uterus. Now if we could stick to the topic. We don't know why Claire has her husband's body in her car or if she actually killed him."

"Well, who else is likely to be responsible?" asked Jack.

"Perhaps she didn't know he was in there?" Muriel countered.

"Oh, come on. How could she not know?"

"Do you check the boot every time you enter your car?"

"No, but I like to think I'd know if there was a body in it."

"Jack, you're very quick to turn your back on someone you once supported," said Matthew.

"I back winners, and Miss Arden stands less chance of winning this competition than I do of successfully resuscitating the first three dead Passengers."

"Or your career," added Libby.

"So are you giving her your vote, Muriel?" asked Fiona. "Unfortunately, supporting her baby alone isn't an option."

"I have to, yes."

"If there's anyone else for Claire, could you please raise your hand?" Fiona turned to each juror in turn, and each shook their heads, including Jack.

"Then that's one vote for Claire Arden." She typed the name into her tablet.

"Do you think once we've made our decision, the Hacker will tell us the truth about what happened to her husband?" Muriel asked.

"I wouldn't count on it," said Fiona. "I don't think we'll ever learn the truth about any of them."

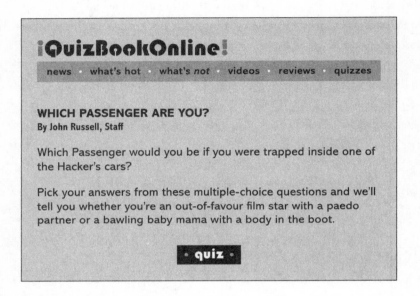

CHAPTER 43

¡QuizBookOnline!

news • what's hot • what's *not* • videos • reviews • quizzes

WHICH PASSENGER ARE YOU?
By John Russell, Staff

Which Passenger would you be if you were trapped inside one of the Hacker's cars?

Pick your answers from these multiple-choice questions and we'll tell you whether you're an out-of-favour film star with a paedo partner or a bawling baby mama with a body in the boot.

• quiz •

CLAIRE ARDEN

Claire's eyes were sore to the touch, like someone had kicked sand into them and then rubbed it in. She willed herself to cry in the hope that it might offer them some relief. But she was drained; there were no more tears left inside her.

She remained trapped and helpless in her hijacked car, listening to a group of strangers debate the value of her life. In keeping the truth about Ben from them, she had cheated her baby out of a future. Her one job as a mother was to protect Tate, and she had failed.

Claire knew as soon as the world saw images of her husband's dead body that her chance of surviving the ordeal was over. If she had been a juror or at home, glued to her TV screen, watching someone else tangled up in her mess, she too would have sided with the evidence presented. But it wasn't the truth. It wasn't even close to the truth. If only she had been given just a minute longer to explain why Ben's body was in the boot of her car, she and Tate might have stood a chance. But that wasn't what the Hacker wanted. He wanted to send them to their deaths. The end was coming for Claire, and there was nothing left for her to do to stop it.

Outside, her car was flanked by armoured army vehicles and marked police cars, preventing any interference from the hundreds of onlookers patiently waiting on the pavements to catch a glimpse of Claire travelling her own green mile.

She turned away from the window and gazed down longingly at her bump. "I'm sorry, I'm so sorry," she whispered, her hands working their way around it carefully like a potter at the wheel. "It wasn't supposed to happen like this. Your dad and I had everything planned out for you. The three of us were going to have this incredible life together, full of exciting adventures. And eventually you were going to fly the nest and have amazing experiences all of your own while your daddy and I grew old together. But then he ruined it all. And as well as losing him, now I'm going to lose you too."

Claire thought back six months and to the day when her world fell from its axis. She recalled with clarity quietly closing the front door to their home and letting her handbag drop to the floor. The plastic bottles inside it rattled. She watched as Ben made his way up the stairs, pulling himself up using both bannisters until he turned a corner and disappeared into their bedroom. Then she clasped her hands across her mouth and sobbed in silence. She needed a moment to herself to let it all out before concentrating on her husband.

Claire patted her stomach, then just a barely protruding bump that had only recently begun to reveal itself. She wanted to reassure her baby that by the time it emerged into the world, everything was going to be alright. She didn't want to begin their relationship with a lie, but she had little choice. Everything now was about protecting her child at all costs.

By the time she reached the bedroom, she paused under the doorway to take Ben in. He was sitting on the edge of the mattress, his head buried in his hands. This was not the strong, unyielding man Claire had fallen in love with. She no longer saw him as the strapping six-foot-three-inch-tall, broad-chested athlete who excelled at sports and whom she'd cheered on from the sidelines when he competed in triathlons. Before her was a frightened, vulnerable boy trapped inside a man's broken body and who desperately needed her reassurance. But she couldn't give him what he craved.

Instead, she positioned herself by Ben's side and draped her arm around his shoulder. He placed her other hand in his and drew it to his mouth to kiss. His lips were icy cold and so were his fingers, which she entwined in her own.

From where she was sitting, Claire could see into the spare bedroom that was to eventually become the nursery. Only neither of them had the courage to even think about clearing it of old books, CDs, and gym equipment, let alone decorate it. They had made that mistake before. A day after assembling a cot, Claire had begun to bleed until their dreams were taken away from them. Now, without either wanting to admit it to the other, they were waiting for this baby to be snatched like all the others had before it. Each day it remained inside her was a miracle.

"We will be okay," Claire soothed, and tilted her head to rest her temple against Ben's. "You and me, we will get through this together."

"You can't say that with certainty though, can you?"

"Nothing is certain; you and I know that more than most. But despite everything we've been through, we've never lost each other, have we? What makes you think I'm going to let that happen now? You're my DNA Match, remember? We were made for each other."

"I wish I could believe you, but you heard the diagnosis. It's inevitable."

"Your surgeon said that it could be a year from now or twenty years. Or with luck on our side, even longer."

"Or it could be next week. Or tomorrow. Or even tonight. Why not in the next few minutes?"

"Ben . . ."

"Why couldn't it wait until I was in my eighties to appear, when I've lived my life and watched our kid grow up? It wouldn't matter then. Why is it happening to me *now*?"

"It's not just happening to *you*, it's happening to *us*."

"Well, forgive me but you're not the one with an aneurysm inside your head."

It was as if he resented Claire for being healthy. "That's not fair."

"I know it's not . . . I'm sorry."

Three hours had passed since the specialist's diagnosis at Oxford's John Radcliffe Hospital. It had followed a battery of tests including MRI scans, CT scans, and angiographies. Finally, a dye had been injected into his arteries, and the shadow it created revealed what the surgeon suspected—an aneurysm buried deep inside Ben's brain. At seven millimetres, it was on the larger end of the spectrum, and its positioning meant the risk of brain damage or a stroke was too high to operate.

Now back at home, they remained on the bed, hand in hand, as Claire punished herself for failing to acknowledge the recent changes in her husband. He had begun to forget things that were important to him, like his sister's birthday and an appointment to meet a client at a nearby hotel. One morning she found him sitting at the breakfast table halfway through a bowl of cereal. She reminded him it was a Saturday and that he didn't work weekends.

Claire had blamed each memory lapse on pressures at work and concern over whether the baby would reach full term. It was only when she discovered a handful of empty Nurofen packets hidden in his car's glove box that he admitted the increasing frequency of his headaches.

"I need a timeout," Ben said, and rose to his feet.

"Where are you going?"

"To the park."

"Can I come with you?"

"Thank you, but I want to be alone."

Alone was how Claire felt for the next three months. While husband and wife continued to go about their daily routines, a chasm opened that she couldn't close by herself. Instead, she filled the cracks where and when they appeared, trying to lift Ben's spirits even after he'd lost interest in being a husband and a dad-to-be. The dilapidated house they'd taken on a year earlier still required much renovation work, so she took on the project management in the hope it might be completed before the baby arrived.

Eventually, she could hold her tongue no longer.

"Do you know where I've been all afternoon?" she snapped, storming into their bedroom one day. "No, of course you don't, because you're too busy lying here in the dark feeling sorry for yourself. I've been at the hospital scared shitless I was losing the baby."

Ben sat upright. "What happened?"

"Oh, now you care. I was cramping at work and started spotting so I took myself to A and E. You would've known that if you'd bothered to answer your phone."

"Sorry, I must have set it to silent."

"No it wasn't, it's switched off like it always is because you can't deal with reality. But while you've pressed pause on life, the world is still going on around you. And the paediatrician said it was just a scare, the baby is okay."

"Thank God." He lay back on the bed, relieved. But Claire wasn't finished.

"I've had enough, Ben. This should be the happiest time of our lives but you're ruining it for us. I'll be damned if I'm going to spend the rest of my pregnancy living with the walking dead. It's time for you to stand up and be my husband instead of moping around and waiting for an artery in your head to burst. If you don't want to be a part our lives, then pack your stuff and leave now, because I'm running out of strength for the three of us."

Claire's tough talking appeared to switch on a lightbulb inside Ben's head. It began with a heartfelt apology and developed over the following days into the return of the husband she loved. He put time and effort into their relationship, and together, they allowed themselves to imagine being parents.

"There's something I need to talk to you about," Ben began one evening. He put a plank of wood and a nail gun down on the lawn and invited her to join him on the half-completed decking. The sun began to disappear behind the roofs of the houses ahead. "I've been thinking about this, and if it ever reaches a point where I know the inevitable is going to happen, then there's something I need you to do. Don't call an ambulance. I want you to get me to the office."

Claire raised a brow as if she'd misheard. "You mean the hospital?"

"No, there's no point in taking me there. When the aneurysm ruptures, that's it, game over, there's nothing they can do. If you take me to work and leave me there, then my medical insurance will pay out."

"What are you talking about?"

"You and I have life insurance, right? Which is all well and good. But because I have an existing medical condition, it's capped at £110,000. But at work, all staff are insured for up to £340,000 if they die on work premises, and that includes the gardens, the grounds, or in the car park. I rechecked the policy to make sure. That money will be your and Tate's future."

Claire shook her head. "I can't just drive you to your office as you're dying and dump you there! It's a ridiculous idea."

"No, it's a sensible idea. It'll make no difference to me, Claire, I'll be unconscious, dying, or dead anyway. This way I know you two will have security. You can't afford the mortgage on your own, especially when you go down to statutory maternity pay. Please, just think about it."

Claire knew that what he was saying was true, but it sat awkwardly with her. Ben must have sensed it because he didn't mention it again. Four weeks later, he was dead.

The morning of the hijack, it was his failure to turn off the alarm clock that made her jab him in the ribs to wake him. He didn't move. There was no response when she said his name, or pushed him, shook him, rolled him over, or begged him to wake up. Multiple times she ran her fingers across Ben's body, searching for a heartbeat or a pulse, but he was still. When her fingers cupped his chin and stroked his cheeks, he was cold and his skin was already stiffening. It was too late. She held her protruding stomach, partly for comfort, partly out of fear their baby might vanish just as suddenly as his father.

As the early-morning light gleamed through the bedroom shutters, Claire reached for her phone and dialled two nines. She hesitated before pressing it a third time, reflecting on Ben's instructions for when this moment arrived. Then she collapsed into an armchair in the corner of the room, crying and racked with guilt for even considering it.

Through the thick mist of her grief, she knew that Ben was right. The extra life insurance money would pay for the completion of the house renovations, pay off their mortgage, and place less pressure on her to hurry back to work after Tate's birth. All that needed to be done was to transport Ben to his office's car park and wait for his body to be discovered.

Pulling herself together, she dressed and chose something appropriate for Ben to wear for a working day. Her tears splashed upon his chest as she removed his T-shirt and shorts and put him in a pair of khaki-coloured chinos and a crisp white shirt. She paused to take him in one last time and couldn't help but resent him. "You lied," she whispered. "You told me that thing in your head wasn't going to beat you."

Moving Ben to the car was a challenge as he was a bulky man. She dragged him by the arms from the bed and to the floor, then slowly across the landing and down the staircase, pausing every so often so as not to strain herself or hurt the baby. She texted the car to reverse into the garage, then pressed the tailgate button so it lowered to ground level. And with one final heave, she pushed Ben onto it. As it lifted and scooped him into the boot before shutting, she decided she would figure out how to move him into the passenger seat later.

Claire was exhausted and emotional, but her brain ran through what needed to be done next. She dictated notes into her phone so that she wouldn't forget—programme the car for Ben's office, book an Uber using a guest account, go to work, start texting Ben mid-morning. Then when she told his employers she was worried that she hadn't heard from her husband but that her app was confirming his vehicle was parked at work, they would likely investigate and Ben would be discovered.

Claire acted out the next few moments like she would any other day so as not to arouse suspicion. She left the house through the front door, set the alarm, waved to her neighbour Sundraj, and then climbed inside the car before it pulled away and along the road.

Only the Hacker had a different plan for Claire. Now, two hours later, it was unlikely that by the end of the morning, Ben's would be the only body in the car.

At least we'll all be together when it happens, she thought as she stroked her stomach again.

Without warning, there felt like a popping sensation inside her followed by a slow trickle of liquid down her leg. Claire assumed the baby had been resting on her bladder and putting pressure on it. But she didn't feel the urge to urinate. Then, to her horror, she understood what had happened. Her waters had broken, two months early.

The baby was on its way.

CHAPTER 44

M atthew returned from the fridge in the corner of the room, carrying
five bottles of water on a wooden tray. He placed them on the tabletop
in front of each juror, beginning with Libby. She smiled her thank-you.

"I could do with something a lot stronger than this," said Muriel, un-
screwing the cap and pouring it into a tall glass.

"I assumed you were teetotal," said Fiona.

"Why? Because I have a faith?"

"Well, yes."

"Sending four people to their graves would be enough to turn the pope
to drink."

Fiona comforted her colleague with a pat on the arm.

Meanwhile, Libby diverted her attention towards the wall clock, acutely
aware of how time was passing more swiftly now that they were living under
the shadow of a deadline. She focused solely on the declining seconds just
to ensure the Hacker hadn't altered the speed to pile more pressure upon
them. Underneath it, Cadman and his team busied themselves with a never-
ending stream of data but remained respectfully silent as the jurors debated
each Passenger.

A glimpse of sunlight streaming through the tall, arched windows distracted her. Libby realised it was the first time that morning she had given
thought to what would happen when this ordeal was over. She was certain
to leave the room a very different woman to the one who arrived. All eight

Passengers' faces would join her brother Nicky in the roll-call of ghosts that haunted her.

Fiona cleared her throat with an exaggerated cough to gain the room's attention and picked up her tablet. "Shall we move on to Sofia Bradbury?" she asked. Seconds later, the main screen cut to a dark, blurred silhouette. "Where is she?"

"I think she's covered her camera with something," said Matthew, puzzled. "She's hiding."

"Ironic, isn't it?" said Fiona. "She's spent her life craving attention, and now, when she has the biggest audience of her career, she can't face them."

"Do you think she can hear us?" asked Muriel.

"I have no doubt the Hacker will have given her no choice but to," Matthew replied.

"I honestly don't know what to say about her," continued Fiona. "It's not often that words fail me, but on this occasion, I am truly lost."

"If what the Hacker said is true—and we only have his word that it is—how could she cover up what her husband did?" asked Muriel.

"Unless she actively participated in it," said Fiona. "Perhaps they did it together, a shared recreation of sorts. I've represented a few couples over the years who have been accused of similar crimes."

"How can you defend people like that when you have a daughter of your own?"

"Innocent until proven guilty."

Jack laughed. "Only when it suits you. Ten minutes ago you were ready to throw Miss Arden to the wolves."

"Even if Sofia was only vaguely aware of what he was doing, she wouldn't need to physically harm a child to be complicit," added Fiona. "Hiding him and paying off his victims makes her as guilty as he is in the eyes of the law and the public."

"Why did she elect to be sterilised?" asked Muriel.

"The Hacker suggested it was because she didn't want to have children with him," added Matthew. "Perhaps she feared what he might do to them."

"That would indicate she isn't all evil, that perhaps she has some kind of maternal instinct?"

"Only when it comes to her own flesh and blood. But what about other people's kids? By not reporting her husband and stopping him from what he was doing, it shows she couldn't care less about them."

"Then why did she put so much time into raising money for so many children's charities?" asked Matthew.

"She's hiding in plain sight," continued Fiona. "Remember what we learned about Jimmy Savile after he died all those years ago? He did exactly the same thing. Spent his life in the public eye raising millions for charity, and all the while he was abusing children right under our very noses. I'm not saying Sofia is the same, but you cannot deny the similarities."

Muriel let out a sigh. "The public can forgive many a celebrity's transgression, but never child molestation. I hate to say this, but perhaps for Sofia's sake, she'd be better off dead."

Each of the jurors returned to Sofia's silhouette.

"Do we even need to vote on this?" asked Fiona.

The others shook their heads and looked away from the screen.

"Then let us move on to the next Passenger."

CHAPTER 45

SOFIA BRADBURY

S ofia hurled her remote control at the dashboard when it failed to turn off the volume. She ignored the sharp, jabbing pains running up her spine as she bent forward, moving quickly towards the console, pushing at random buttons, desperately trying to take back control. She had spent her career wanting to be talked about and craving attention. But not anymore. Now her only desire was to hide from the world and spend her final moments in privacy, just her and her dog.

Listening to strangers as they pored over the secrets she had kept hidden for forty years was Sofia's worst nightmare. But now they were exposed, and there was no coming back from what everyone knew about her. She would rather her car explode into a million tiny pieces than face another living soul. She removed her hearing aids from her ears and threw them to the floor.

Sofia unwound a brightly coloured Hermès scarf from her neck, one that she'd purchased because it reminded her of the colours of a sunset she'd once seen on a film set in Morocco. She placed her handbag over the dashboard and wedged one part of the scarf under it, allowing the other half to dangle over the camera lens. Suddenly, she realised she would never see a sunset or film set again.

"I wish people were like you," she whispered to Oscar, scratching behind his ear. He cocked his head to one side for her fingers to go deeper. "I wish I could have found someone who was as devoted to me as you are. Then perhaps everything might be different. Perhaps I'd have made better choices. Perhaps you and I wouldn't be sitting where we are now."

Sofia poured herself another brandy and drank half immediately, washing it down with two more painkillers. She had been teetotal until she met Patrick; she blamed him for turning her to drink.

Amongst the bad choices Sofia had made, not having a family of her own had been a rare wise one. She'd had little interest in starting a family until her sister Peggy fell pregnant with Robbie, followed two years later by Paige. She'd seen other actresses in her peer group pass on potentially career-defining roles to start families. Most of them later failed to reignite their star power once they were ready to return to work. Sofia had unashamedly soaked up their lost parts like a sponge. And they had earned her accolades and awards and made her the highest-paid British actress of the 1970s.

However, her priorities shifted soon after being introduced to charismatic businessman Patrick Swanson. The way he carried himself reminded her of the Hollywood movie stars she swooned over as a girl. He possessed Cary Grant's elegance and urbanity, James Stewart's humour, and Clark Gable's masculinity, all rolled into one handsome package.

For Sofia, thirty-eight and with four divorces to her name, finding a fifth husband was the last thing on her mind. But she couldn't say no to the twinkle in those deep blue eyes of Patrick's when he invited her for dinner. After a whirlwind romance, she threw caution to the wind, and two months after meeting, she answered yes to his marriage proposal. Offstage, she was the most content she had ever been.

Her failed marriage tally had made Sofia the butt of many a joke, from tabloid newspapers to stand-up comedians. On the surface, she'd laughed it off, but deep down, she detested being a laughing stock. It made her more determined than she had ever been to make this relationship work, no matter what. She'd taken onboard criticisms levelled at her by past partners and made a conscious effort not to emasculate Patrick. So theirs would be an equal partnership. She added his name to the deeds of her properties in Richmond and Buckinghamshire; her bank accounts became joint along with her many investments.

The emotional security he offered gave Sofia the confidence to consider motherhood. It hadn't been a role she'd ever felt the urge to play, least of all with any of her ex-husbands. But Patrick was different. Each time Paige and Robbie arrived for a sleepover, he lavished them with attention as though they were his own. And as she watched them play together for hours at a time, her guilt arose for denying him the opportunity to father children of his own. Eventually, when Patrick visited her at work on an American TV miniseries, she broached the subject as they strolled along Santa Monica's beach and towards their hotel.

"Where's this coming from?" he asked, somewhat taken aback. "You made it clear when we first started to date that kids were out of the equation. What's changed?"

Sofia stared deep into his eyes and felt warmth radiating from them. She had never been more in love than she was in that moment. "It's a woman's prerogative to change her mind," she replied. "You know that."

"No, really. Tell me."

"I'm thirty-eight years old, and neither of us are getting any younger. If I leave it much longer, then nature will take the decision out of my hands. You, me, us . . . I realise now this is what I've been waiting for my whole adult life. What do you say?"

Patrick stopped walking and wrapped his strong arms around his wife's waist, brought her to his lips, and kissed her. "I say when can we start trying?"

She curled her fingers through two of his belt loops and led him through the hotel lobby and straight up to their suite.

Four months later, a chance reflection in an orangery window destroyed everything Sofia had begun to dream of. It was so fleeting that it lasted no more than a second, but she would never forget it.

They had spent much of the weekend with her niece and nephew in the swimming pool of Sofia's Richmond home.

"Patrick, if you dry the kids off, I'll ask Cook to make a start on lunch."

"Okay," he replied.

Her husband climbed out of their pool and reached for a towel. Robbie and Paige were on brightly coloured inflatable rafts, racing from end to end using their hands as paddles. "Hurry up, guys," Patrick said as Paige made her way towards him. He lifted her out and placed her on a sun lounger.

As Sofia headed to the kitchen, she remembered that she hadn't taken their drinks order. She turned, then caught a reflection of Patrick on his knees, towelling Paige. As one hand dried her back, the other was held firm upon an area it had no business being. Sofia froze and watched as her husband swiftly slid it away when he realised she had returned.

Her acting skills disguised the fluctuation in her voice. "What would we all like to drink?"

"Coke, please," chirped both children. She hesitated, her eyes locked on theirs, searching for evidence of what she thought she had witnessed. But all they gave back to her were their innocent smiles. She turned and left them alone again with Patrick.

Throughout the weeks that followed, Sofia replayed that moment over and over again. Had her eyes deceived her? Was she blowing a misplaced hand out of all proportion? Patrick was the man she loved above all others, the only one she wanted children with. How could he be anything other than what she knew him to be? It wasn't possible. Yet, try as she might, she couldn't cast out the niggling doubt from inside her.

It was some months later when she returned home from filming in the South of France that she found Patrick alone with Paige and Robbie. Instantly it put her on edge. She hadn't expected to see them all together, and the memory of Patrick's misplaced hand returned. She held her breath, waiting in the shadows, watching for signs of inappropriate behaviour. But all three played innocently on a swing Patrick had made by looping a thick rope over a tree's sturdy branch. "Why are the kids here?" Sofia asked, trying to hide her uneasiness.

"Your sister asked if I could look after them while she took Kenny to Rome for the weekend," he replied.

"You didn't mention it when we spoke last night."

"Their babysitter cancelled last minute. It's okay, isn't it?"

"Of course. Why wouldn't it be?"

She gave him a lacklustre smile. Patrick placed his camera on a deck-chair and kissed his wife's cheek. "Can you imagine what it'll be like when we have our own little Paige running around the place?"

"Why a Paige? Why not a Robbie?"

"I don't know . . . I suppose I've been picturing us having a little girl. A mini-Sofia. Someone to follow in your footsteps on the stage. A real daddy's girl."

She blanched at Patrick's words, and suddenly, being pregnant with his child was the last thing Sofia wanted. The voice inside her, which she relied upon to guide her career, made itself heard—*You cannot trust him!*

After a sleepless night, she waited until Patrick had left the house to play an early-morning round of golf before she approached Paige. They sat in the den watching cartoons.

"Did you have fun with Uncle Patrick yesterday?" she asked, and Paige nodded. "What did you do?"

"We played in the woods."

"With Robbie?"

"No, he was on his bike."

"It was just the two of you?" Paige nodded again. Sofia's heart beat faster. "And what did you get up to?"

"I'm not allowed to say," Paige replied, and put her finger to her lips, making a shushing sound. "It's a secret."

"You can tell me. I won't tell anyone else."

"But I promised."

"Sometimes it's okay to break a promise. You trust me, don't you?"

"Yes," she replied. "He took photos of me. He said Mummy asked him to, to show her how I'm growing up."

Sofia's body stiffened. "What kind of photos?"

"Running around and next to the trees. He used the camera where you have to shake the photographs and they come to life like magic."

She was referring to the Polaroid camera Sofia bought him for their holiday in Saint Lucia. Sofia recalled he'd had it with him yesterday in the garden when she'd arrived home. Sofia hurried to the annexe Patrick used as his office. Fuelled by adrenaline and unease, she didn't know where to begin her search or what she was looking for. She began with the files in his cabinet, and then leafed through books on shelves and drawers stuffed with papers. There was nothing incriminating. But her relief was tempered by frustration. Her inner voice was never wrong. She knew what she had seen that day by the pool.

The corner of a box poking out from under a stack of old coats caught her eye. Tentatively, she removed the lid and looked inside. It contained many brown A4 envelopes, each addressed to a PO box but with no name, and containing a Dutch postmark on the front. She examined the contents of one. Inside was a glossy colour magazine, containing page after page of indecent images of young girls. Sofia dropped it to the floor, took a step back, and began to hyperventilate.

She eventually found the strength to continue, and inside the other envelopes were different issues of the same magazine. And at the very bottom was a white envelope, a Dutch address on the front written in Patrick's handwriting, containing loose Polaroids. Sofia half closed her eyes as she removed a handful; her worst fears were quickly realised. They were clothed and unclothed pictures of Paige. Patrick had taken them not only for his gratification, but to share and arouse other like-minded people.

Sofia steadied herself against the wall, concerned her legs might give way beneath her. Despite her spinning head, she grabbed the photos, stuffed them into her pocket, put the box back in position, and ran to her bedroom. Once behind the locked door of the en suite, she vomited into the sink. She had never felt pain like it, knowing that the man she loved had robbed a child of her innocence and under their roof.

Before her niece returned home, Sofia made her promise not to tell her mother about the pictures and in return, she would organise a photo shoot at a studio in London for Paige and her friends. Her niece squealed with delight and swore to remain silent.

For days, Sofia couldn't bring herself to leave the bedroom, blaming a virus on her inability to attend rehearsals for a West End play she was performing later that summer. Patrick checked on her regularly, and from under her sheets, she assured him with a sour smile that all she required was bed-rest.

It was the toughest decision Sofia had ever made in her life. She was torn in two. Patrick had to be stopped, and Paige and other children had to be protected from inhumane men like him. Contacting her lawyer to make an appointment with the police would have been the right thing to do. Twice she plucked up the courage to call, and twice she hung up before it was answered. She was using Paige as an excuse for her inertia—Sofia didn't want to put her beloved niece through such scrutiny. In addition, it would kill her parents knowing they had put their children in the trust of a man they thought of as family but who had exploited their little girl.

Sofia's inner voice called her out. *You can lie to the world but you can't lie to yourself. You're keeping quiet because if you tell anyone, everything you have worked so hard for will be over.*

Even in her confused state, Sofia recognised that by exposing Patrick, it would mean the end of the career she loved. Her reputation, her box-office draw, her body of work . . . none of it would matter once her name was synonymous with a husband who had an active interest in little girls. No director, producer, or actor would risk being associated with someone like her.

However, despite how much his warped inclinations sickened her, she couldn't turn off her feelings for him. He had been everything she'd ever wanted in a husband and a friend. They had plans to see more of the world together, invest in business ventures, and start that family. The thought of throwing it all away and starting life again, alone, terrified her. She didn't have the strength to lose Patrick and her public. So she chose to keep them both.

Standing outside the door of Patrick's office, she watched as he ransacked the room in search of his missing Polaroids. Defeated, he went to leave, only to discover his wife, her skin ashen and her eyes raw with sadness. On sight alone, he knew that she was aware of who she was really married to. He opened his mouth but the words weren't there.

Sofia thrust a business card into his hand. It contained details for Dr. Peter Hewitt, a psychiatrist. "I've made you an appointment for Thursday," she said. "He's discreet." Patrick offered no argument.

Over the coming months, Sofia made excuses each time her sister asked to come over with the children. She blamed everything from work to illness until, eventually, a baffled Peggy stopped asking. It upset Sofia to push her away, but she couldn't risk Paige being alone with her uncle.

Meanwhile, when Patrick attended his twice-weekly appointments with regularity, Sofia often seized the opportunity to search his office for fresh evidence of his compulsions. But there was nothing else to be found.

Then after a year of living separate lives and sleeping in separate bedrooms, a desperate Patrick begged his wife to take him back.

"I know what I did was wrong," he offered humbly. "Dr. Hewitt has helped me to understand why I did what I did . . . how the things that happened to me as a boy I've been doing to others and continuing the cycle. I swear on my life that I'm not that man anymore."

As he went on to explain how he had changed and now had the tools in place to control further urges, Sofia desperately wanted to believe him. She missed waking up to his smell, feeling the light touch of his fingers as they ran across her body, and the sound of laughter echoing through the corridors of their home. A year without laughter felt like a lifetime.

Sofia ignored her inner voice and followed her heart. She discarded her contraception, convincing herself that as her fortieth birthday approached, a baby of his own might help to heal the man she loved. And in the weeks that followed, their relationship grew stronger and stronger and she had never felt more loved.

It was only by chance when she opened the doors to air the summer house in the garden that she discovered Patrick was storing fresh editions of his magazines inside a dusty ottoman. It stunned her. But instead of crumbling to pieces, Sofia closed the lid and walked away. She even found a way to justify his behaviour—if he was gaining sexual gratification from magazine photographs, he wasn't getting it from a child in the flesh. It was the lesser of two evils.

However, to continue living with what she knew about him would take great sacrifice. To keep both her marriage and her career, she couldn't allow the temptation of their own child to come between them. Without discussing it with Patrick, Sofia booked herself into a private hospital to be sterilised.

As the 1990s merged into the millennium and another two decades passed, the pain of her decision was eased by periods of reliance upon alcohol and tranquilisers. It was only in moments of sobriety that she could admit to herself what a terrible mistake she had made in putting her reputation above all else. She grew to detest Patrick for backing her into that corner, and eventually, theirs became a marriage in name only. Husband and wife spent more time together in the public eye and on red carpets than they did at home. Charity work, especially fundraising for hospitals, became her penance for turning a blind eye to Patrick's crimes. And when he received invitations to accompany her to openings or visiting children's wards, he never refused, and Sofia never took her eyes off him.

One morning, she came off the phone and marched straight to his office, throwing open the door. Patrick was sitting on a sofa, his face obscured by a broadsheet newspaper.

"My accountant called about a missing £30,000 from an account," she began.

"And?"

"And where is it?"

"I used it to take care of something."

"What 'something'?"

"Something that doesn't concern you. I thought we had an agreement? You live your life and I'll live mine. No questions asked."

"What have you done, Patrick?"

He lowered the newspaper and sighed. "It was an . . . indiscretion. I needed the money to resolve a misunderstanding."

Sofia's pulse hammered in her throat. "You've been caught, haven't you? You've had to pay someone off."

"Like I said, you live your life and—"

"This is my life you're screwing with too!" she screamed. "Who was it? What did you do?"

"Some girl's mother got the wrong end of the stick, and I used the money to ensure no one else got the wrong end of the stick too."

"So you, what, paid her off? What kind of a parent would allow you to get away with that?"

"Are you really lambasting her for turning a blind eye? Pot, kettle, my darling."

"What if she comes back demanding more money? Or threatens to go to the tabloids or the police?"

"She won't, she signed a non-disclosure agreement. Virtually bit my hand off for the cash."

"Where did you get a non-disclosure from?"

"A lawyer friend of mine drafted it. Fairly standard."

"Oh my God," said Sofia, feeling faint. "How many times have you done this?"

Patrick peered over the top of his glasses. "Do you really want to know?"

Sofia did and she didn't. "This has to stop. You have to turn yourself in to the police; it's the only way forward."

"No. I will not do that. I'd be eaten alive in prison."

"Then check yourself into a hospital and get the treatment you need."

"There is no treatment for people like me! Surely you must know that? My . . . *urges* . . . they're hardwired into my brain. Coping mechanisms do not work."

"What then? You're just going to spend the rest of your life molesting children and paying off their parents?"

Patrick shook his head. "That's not a word I like to use."

"'Molest'? Why? That's what you are, a child molester. I am married to a child molester."

"And you have known this for years, so don't try and convince me this is news."

Sofia bit her lip and looked away. "Please, Patrick. We can't carry on like this. Your behaviour is killing me. I have to tell someone."

A rush of tears fell from her eyes, leaving mascara-dark streaks. Patrick placed his newspaper on the cushions and rose to his feet. Gently, he placed both hands on her shoulders like he was giving her a pep talk. "I'm sorry, Sofia, I really am, but carrying on like this *is* the only way. If it comes out publicly that you knew about me but we stayed together, or that it was *our* money I used in return for parental silence, then your life as you know it will be over just as quickly as mine. And I swear to you, I will not go down for this alone. Even though it would pain me to do it, I'll tell anyone who'll listen the role you played."

Sofia saw red, drew her arm back, and slapped him hard across the face. With one hard shove, Patrick pushed her backwards and into the wall, where she lost her footing and crumpled to a heap on the floor. Patrick rubbed his smarting cheek before calmly pouring himself a brandy from a decanter.

"Can I tempt you?" he asked casually. "It usually helps that blind eye of yours to mist over."

"Why would you want to ruin me?" begged Sofia. "What have I ever done to you?"

"You robbed me of the chance to be a father. I know about your sterilisation. Your doctor called to check on your recovery and was unaware of my ignorance and your deception."

"How could I have had your child knowing what you are capable of?"

"It could have changed something inside me, but I guess we'll never know for sure, will we?"

Sofia watched helplessly as Patrick shrugged his shoulders and casually made his way out of the office, sipping from his glass as he walked.

A loud bang brought her back to the present—an object striking the rear window of her car startled her. Sofia turned to see where the noise had come from, just as a second object hit the door.

"Jesus," she shouted, and Oscar barked.

Tentatively, she looked outside and noticed, for the first time, the streets packed with people, watching as her car slowly passed them. Without her hearing aid, she couldn't make out what they were shouting, but from their angry gestures and twisted faces, she read their depth of hatred for her. Others began to hurl missiles at her vehicle: stones, rocks, and clumps of earth. She shielded her eyes when, ahead, a man on a bridge held a breeze-block aloft, timing it perfectly as he let go. Sofia screamed as it bounced from the windscreen and onto the bonnet, leaving the reinforced glass with circular cracks like a spider's web.

"Please, stop," she begged, her voice trembling. "Please, I'm sorry. I'm begging you, just tell them to leave me alone. I know I've done wrong, I just want to die in peace."

She let out another shrill cry, this time as bottles containing flaming rags and liquid shattered against the windscreen, side windows, and doors. Eventually the car accelerated away from the crowds, like a blazing comet.

CHAPTER 46

H aunting images of Sofia's burning car driving itself through the streets dominated the inquest screens, black and grey plumes of smoke trailing in its wake.

Drones nudged each other mid-air, competing to get as close as possible to Sofia's car to capture her horror through the windows. Eventually one managed to catch a glimpse of the fallen star, revealing a terrified woman shielding herself from the flames outside and covering her dog with her coat. The Hacker had cut the sound feed, giving her silent screams additional gravitas.

"What they're doing to her is barbaric," said Libby, horrified by the public's behaviour. "They're no better than the Hacker. No matter what she's been accused of, she's still a seventy-eight-year-old woman."

"I'm afraid her age doesn't come into it," said Matthew. "She's at the mercy of mob mentality."

"But what pleasure are they getting from this?"

"I don't know if it's pleasure or if they're just getting caught up in the moment. When people are part of a mob, they stop being individuals, their inhibitions disappear, they don't follow their normal moral compass. Would any of them have turned up alone to hurl a brick or a petrol bomb at Sofia's car? It's unlikely. But when they're surrounded by like-minded people, they don't see themselves as violent individuals; it's the group that's responsible for the violence, not them personally."

"Thank you for that fascinating insight, Doctor," Jack said with a sigh. "Or perhaps she deserves it. Her chickens have come home to roost."

"Ignore him," Libby urged.

"I'm only vocalising public opinion."

"Is that what's happening on social media too?" asked Libby.

Matthew nodded. "Humans are gregarious and we look for people like us to associate with. Nowadays, the easiest way to find that is online. Under ordinary circumstances your average person doesn't post on Twitter demanding the death of a pensioner. But mob mentality and the anonymity of being behind a keyboard means people are braver when they're together."

A fire truck following Sofia's car swapped places with an armoured vehicle ahead. Firefighters clambered from windows while others hung on to the harnesses and aimed jets of water at her vehicle to dampen the blaze until the final flame was extinguished. It did little to reduce the knot in Libby's stomach.

"Time is once again our enemy, ladies and gentlemen," warned Fiona. "We really need to start discussing the next Passenger, Sam Cole."

"Ah, the bigamist," said Jack. "Compared to a murderess and a paedophile, it's hardly the crime of the century, is it?"

"Try telling that to his wife," said Fiona. "I cannot possibly imagine the level of deceit required to lie to someone for such a long period of time. Maintaining two separate lives without either wife knowing about the other . . . surely whatever satisfaction it gave him was tainted by the fact he could never really relax for fear of letting something slip?"

"I say he should be applauded for having got away with it for so long," said Jack. "Aside from his questionable morals, is what he has done enough to send him to his death?"

"By not choosing to vote for him, we aren't sending him to his death," corrected Muriel. "It just means there are other Passengers I would prefer to lend my support to."

"You interviewed him and now you're not supporting him. Your lack of loyalty says much about your depth of character."

"I have the same loyalty as you do to Claire," she retaliated, and Jack gave a derisive snort.

"He doesn't get my vote because of the very obvious way in which he tried to manipulate us," said Libby. "He played the poor, hard-done-by dad at his wife's expense. He's a disgusting human being."

"Have his infidelities hit a raw nerve with you, Miss Dixon?" asked Jack. "You and Matthew have much in common; perhaps you should swap numbers when this process is complete as I doubt you'll be sailing off into the distance with Mr. Harrison."

Libby held herself back from hurling her bottle of water at Jack's head.

"Sometimes, desperate times call for desperate measures," he continued. "We cannot condemn Sam for his will to survive. Who knows what any of us might do in his circumstances? And in my view, he didn't say anything that was factually inaccurate. Men do get a much rougher deal than women when it comes to relationships with their offspring."

"Oh, Jack, don't give me that rubbish," said Fiona.

"You seem to be conveniently putting to one side the fact that his wife is just as accomplished a liar as he is. And as a police officer, she is expected to be honest beyond reproach. If she can't keep her own house in order and has blackmailed Sam, I wonder how many other times she has bent the law to serve herself?"

"We don't know how much she knew," said Matthew.

"That's as may be, but I am still awarding Sam my vote," said Jack defiantly. "Is anyone else with me? Matthew? Fiona?"

"No," Fiona replied, followed by dismissals from Libby and Matthew. "Then the tally so far stands at Claire with one vote and Sam with one vote." Fiona added Sam's name on her tablet. "There are four votes left and two Passengers. Who's next?"

CHAPTER 47

SAM COLE

*I*t was her. It was Heidi all along. Your wife—the woman you love—has been making your life a living hell.

Sam's mind raced in all directions, like someone had ignited a pile of fireworks inside his head. During the many sleepless nights he'd endured over the last few weeks, he had dissected each person in his life to figure out if one of them could be his blackmailer. However, he hadn't been able to settle upon a name or a reason. The last person he expected to be the culprit was one of his two wives.

He stopped listening to the jury debate whether to save his life and failed to register that he had received a vote of support. Instead, he was consumed by pinpointing the moment Heidi might have discovered his double life. How had he slipped up? What had she learned? Had it all begun with a name?

"Who on earth is Josie?" he recalled Heidi asking one evening. On the other end of the phone, Sam's stomach dropped forty flights.

"No idea, why?"

"Because you just called me Josie."

"No, I didn't."

"Yes, you did. You said, 'I'll be home around eightish, Josie.'"

"It's the bad reception. I said around eightish, *honey*."

"*Honey?* When did that become a thing?"

It hadn't, at least not with Heidi. It was a name he used with his other wife. "I'm trialling it," he bluffed. "You call me babe, so I'm giving honey its day in court."

"Overruled. And why are you whispering?"

"I'm still on-site as there's a problem with removing an old staircase; I have us all working overtime."

"Okay, well don't be there too late tomorrow night. It'd be nice if you could come home and stay awake for more than ten minutes . . . *honey*." Heidi chuckled as she hung up.

Sam replaced his phone inside the pocket of his jeans, slipped a padded oven glove over his hand, and punched the kitchen wall three times. "Shit!" he mouthed. How could he have made such a careless mistake?

"Why are you angry at the wall, Daddy?" came a voice from the doorway. He turned to see his son James.

"I'm not, mate," he replied with a contrived smile.

"Then why were you hitting it?"

"Sometimes it's good to release a bit of excess energy."

"What's going on?" Josie asked, squeezing past their son to reach the fridge.

"Dad's being weird." James picked up a hand-held games console from the kitchen table and shuffled out of the room.

"How are you being weird?"

"The kids think anyone over the age of eight is weird."

Josie stood behind him and wrapped her arms around his waist, resting her forehead upon his neck. "What time do you have to leave in the morning?"

"I've set the alarm for five thirty. The car is charged and the roads should be quiet."

"Do you still think you'll be able to take a couple of days off work for our anniversary?"

He nodded. "Yes, I don't see why not. I have meetings in London earlier that week but after that should be okay."

One of the many things Sam had failed to mention to his second wife was that while he was in the capital, he would be celebrating his tenth anniversary with his first spouse. Throughout almost a decade, he had learned simplicity, not elaborate lies, was the secret to maintaining two families who were completely oblivious to each other. It was why, when Josie gave birth to a daughter a year after Heidi had done the same, he insisted they name her after his late sister. His sister wasn't dead, nor was she called Beccy. But his daughter with Heidi was named Beccy.

And when, by chance, he and Josie's second child was a boy like his and Heidi's, baby James inherited the name of his half-brother. Sam knew that if he kept both family set-ups as identical as possible, his chances of making mistakes were reduced. It didn't stop the occasional errors from slipping through the net, like calling his first wife by his second wife's name.

It was two days after he and Heidi had returned from their honeymoon when the results of his Match Your DNA test arrived by email. Sam had taken the test long before he'd met and fallen in love with Heidi the traditional way and before the security breach that almost destroyed the company's reputation. And by the time he'd received a notification to say he and Heidi were not genetically made for each other, they were already married.

However, as content as he felt with his new bride, Sam could not rid himself of a nagging doubt—who was the greater love waiting for him out there? After much toing and froing, he reasoned it would do no harm to find out and requested the details of his match.

Within minutes of meeting near her home in Halifax, almost two hundred miles from his in Luton, Sam knew that Josie was the one. It was more than love at first sight; the intensity of what he felt for her was multiplied countless times. He likened it to a thousand small, but pleasurable, explosions going off in his body all at once. And he knew he was in trouble.

On appearance alone, Josie was a dead ringer for Heidi. But when it came to their personalities, they were worlds apart. Josie was homely and sweet-natured and gave him her undivided attention. Meanwhile, Heidi was confident and ambitious and wore the trousers in their relationship. Together they'd have made the perfect woman.

Josie had assumed that, like her, Sam was single, and he couldn't bring himself to correct her and risk losing her. But as much as he wanted to explore what they might potentially have between them, he had a wife. Both he and Heidi had come from broken homes and had witnessed the trail of devastation divorce could leave behind. He was not strong enough to put himself through that, especially as he still loved Heidi deeply. So he decided to remain with them both instead.

"I've been offered a new contract," he announced to Heidi back then over dinner at their local pub. "And it's a big one."

"How big?"

"Really big."

"Oh, babe, that's amazing." Heidi beamed and reached across the table to squeeze his hand. "What's it for?"

"The grounds of a new university. I tendered for the refurbishment of nearby student housing—an entire halls of residence needs a refurb and a rebuild. It's the biggest contract we've ever won."

"Why didn't you say anything earlier?"

"Because there's a catch—it's up in Sheffield. They want me to set up an on-site base, which means I'll be working away from home three or four days a week."

"Oh," she replied, her elation curbed. "How long will it take to get there?"

"About three hours. I appreciate it's not ideal, but if it means we can afford to start doing all the things we've talked about, then isn't it worth considering?" Sam put his free hand over hers. "We can move out of the flat and buy a house, then think about filling it up with kids much sooner than we planned. But look, if you really don't want me to go for it, then I'll turn it down." Inside, he was counting on her broodiness to override her irritation at his part-time absence. Eventually, she agreed.

"I've got some good news," he told Josie in Halifax later that week. "I've been offered a contract for university student accommodation refurb, but it's down in Dunstable. It means I'll only get to be up here three or four days a week."

As Sam explained the non-existent tender, he could tell her elation for him was tainted by the distance they'd spend apart. He didn't think twice before the words left his mouth. "Will you marry me?" he asked. And ten months after walking down the aisle with Heidi, he made his way down another one with Josie.

Holding together two marriages and two families became an acquired skill. He lived his life constantly on a knife-edge, questioning whether he had said the right thing to the right wife. On the rare nights his sleep was unbroken, he'd wake up in the morning scared that he might have sleep-talked and given something away unconsciously. Some nights that same conscience kept him awake as he worried about the present and the future. What would happen when he retired? Which wife would he pick to grow old with? What if he were to die suddenly? If he wasn't at either home, who would the authorities inform first? When his children discovered they had a half-brother and half-sister, would they forgive him? Would Heidi or Josie ever understand what it was like for him to love two people at once?

As both families grew, Sam rotated his time between his homes; three days with Heidi one week, four days with her the next. But there were many sacrifices to be made. He shied away from holidays abroad with either family as it created too many potential complications such as emergency contact and unexplainable suntans. On his phone, he kept hidden two calendars on two apps so he knew where he would be sleeping each night and wouldn't forget anniversaries, birthdays, and appointments. Sam painted, redecorated, and renovated two almost identical properties in almost identical ways. Toolboxes contained the same equipment; sheds the same brand of lawnmowers, hedge trimmers, and edgers. Everything that could be replicated, was.

More flexibility was required when the children fell ill with colds and bugs, and he'd lost count of the times he passed on germs from one family to the other. Christmases were the trickiest times to negotiate, so he'd spend Christmas Day with Heidi and Boxing Day with Josie, then rotate the following year. To explain his absence, he would tell both families he was visiting his mum who now lived alone in Portugal. His whole life was a balancing act.

Another by-product of his deceit was the cost of maintaining two growing families. Keeping on top of the bills meant he often worked fifteen-hour days, and as a result, both wives complained about how little time he spent with them.

Against all odds, Sam maintained his double life until one telephone call two months earlier. He was sitting in the audience with Josie and James waiting to watch Beccy perform in a school production of *Guys and Dolls* when his phone rang. Assuming it was work related, he slipped in his earbuds and found a quiet corridor.

"Is this Sam?" a male voice he didn't recognise began.

"Yes, how can I help?" he replied.

"It's Don."

"Don?"

"Yeah, from the Guy 2 Guy app? Remember? You gave me your number and told me to call you later this evening for some phone fun."

"I'm sorry but I think you have the wrong number, mate."

"I saved it from your profile into my phone."

"I don't know what Guy 2 Guy is. I think someone's messing you around."

"Time-waster," Don muttered, and the line went dead.

A text arrived as he slipped his phone in his pocket. "Sexy pics m8," it read. "Want 2 trade?" Three photographs of what appeared to be the same erect penis taken from different angles followed it. Two more texts of a similar nature arrived, so he turned off his phone, perturbed.

Sam waited until they returned home and Josie and the kids were in bed before switching it back on. Dozens and dozens of similar texts and emails flooded his in-boxes. A link took him to a gay dating website for men who wanted to cheat on their partners, and to a page accredited to him and his number, but with some else's photos and genitalia. "Sam Cole, 40, Halifax, Sheffield, Dunstable, and Luton, looking for no-strings phone, cam, and in-person good times. Can't accom. Willing to do groups. Nothing out of bounds."

"What the hell?" he said aloud, and followed another link to try to shut down the profile. But without a password, he was out of luck. Suddenly, his heart leaped into his throat—this was much more than a prank.

Halifax, Sheffield, Dunstable, and *Luton.*

Friends who knew him and Heidi from Luton had been told he was working in Sheffield. Those who knew him and Josie in Halifax thought his company was based in Dunstable. If someone knew about Halifax and Luton, then they knew about his double life.

Over the following weeks, more texts and calls appeared from both men and women, all claiming to have been directed from other dating websites specialising in extramarital affairs. Sam scrolled through them all looking for clues. Some were heterosexual hook-up sites, others gay or bisexual, along with those catering for eye-opening extreme fetishes. In the end, he stopped answering phone numbers he didn't recognise, and eventually the calls faded away. But his concern remained as to who knew his truth.

It was only now as a Passenger that he recalled how, at around the same time, Heidi had begun putting pressure on him financially.

"What do you think of these?" she'd asked, sliding a brochure under his nose while he made breakfast. It contained kitchen designs, and high-end ones from what he could determine by the option of materials.

"They're nice," he replied. "Why?"

"Why do you think? We need a new kitchen."

"What's wrong with this one?"

"It's at least twenty years old. Two of the cupboard doors are falling off their hinges, one of the hobs doesn't work, and the layout is impractical. Let's start enjoying some of this money you're working all hours to earn."

"I'll think about it," he replied. Sam was anxious to change the subject. Had his salary been allocated only to their household, he could easily have afforded a top-of-the-range kitchen. But every penny was accounted for and split evenly between the needs of two homes. Heidi, however, wasn't ready to be fobbed off.

"*You'll* think about it, will you?" she said. "And who made you the master of the house?"

"That's not what I meant . . ."

"Sam, you're barely here while me and the kids spend all our time under this roof. And as well as a new kitchen, we need to start thinking about the family bathroom because the shower's leaking again, the window frames are rotting, and the conservatory needs replacing. This house is falling apart and you haven't even noticed. This weekend I'm going to start sifting through all our accounts to see where we can move some money around."

Sam panicked. "No, no," he said a little too quickly. He didn't want his wife poking around his secret finances, or she would likely discover the joint bank account, mortgage, and other two credit cards he had in his and Josie's names. But carrying out all the work she was listing would break him financially. "Let's take it one step at a time," he conceded, and reluctantly took another look at the kitchen brochure.

A week passed before an email arrived. "Your Wives," read the subject heading. Sam wanted the ground to swallow him whole as he raced to open it. It contained two embedded images, one of Heidi and their children on holiday in Blackpool and the other of Josie and their offspring playing with water pistols in the garden. Everything Sam had worked so hard to conceal was hanging by a thread.

"Who are you?" he typed quickly, his heart caught in his throat. "What do you want?"

A week later, a second email arrived. "I can make this go away," it read.

"How?" he replied instantly.

Another seven days passed before he received a reply. "It will cost you £100,000."

The wait between emails was crippling, but there was nothing he could do to speed up the process.

"I don't have that kind of money!" he typed.

"You own a construction business."

"I can't just take money out of it. That's fraud."

"So is bigamy."

Sam imagined both wives' reactions if they discovered the truth. Heidi hated liars—so much of her job was spent trying to decipher fact from fiction that she had no time for it when she left the office. Sam imagined her flying into a rage, then having him arrested for knowingly marrying two women. Meanwhile when Josie found out, she would be devastated and crumble. The pressure was already upon her looking after two children, and a mother with dementia. It would kill him to cause her more misery.

He was caught between a rock and a hard place. If he reported the threat to the police, Heidi would likely learn about Josie, and his marriages would not survive. He had spent too much of his childhood being treated as a pawn by his parents in their own dysfunctional marriage to watch it happen to his children too. But by paying up, he might break his business.

"If I manage to get the money, how do I know you'll not want more later?" he typed.

"You don't," he read after another seven-day delay. "You'll have to trust me."

"Okay," he replied.

"I want it in cash and delivered one week from now. Next Tuesday morning I will give you instructions on where to leave it."

Sam barely closed his eyes the night before drop-off. As Josie slept soundly, he curled himself up behind her, draping his arm over her stomach and breathing her in as if for the last time. He had drained the business account of all but pennies. His only hope was that the overdrafts and credit cards he had applied for over the last few days would be accepted and keep his business solvent. It might take him years to pay them off though. It was an added stress he didn't need, but it would be worth it to protect the status quo.

Before he set off on his journey earlier that morning, he brushed against Heidi on the doorstep and took the opportunity to cup her chin and kiss her.

"You've done something, haven't you?" she asked, eyeing him up and down. "You only ever kiss me like that when you've done something you shouldn't have."

"You have a suspicious mind, DS Cole," he replied, and slipped his hold-all containing the cash into the space behind his passenger seat. "See you on Friday."

It was only now with all the pieces slotting together that it began to make sense. Dark clouds of guilt filled the sky above him when he thought of how much hatred Heidi must have had for him to go to such extremes. The pain of her husband's infidelity would have been all-consuming, the need to punish him fierce. And today he added insult to injury by trying to take her votes and her life as they competed for survival.

He hoped that she could see he had only behaved that way because he had four children who needed him, not just the two.

Nevertheless, Sam had never felt more worthless in his life.

CHAPTER 48

T hat brings us to our penultimate Passenger," began Fiona. Heidi's image dominated the centre screen.

Aside from her glistening eyes, she offered no obvious expression of emotion. Fiona gave her the once-over and tutted. "I'm at a loss as to know what I can say about her. If I was her brief, I wouldn't put her in the stand because I'd struggle to persuade a jury to warm to her."

"I find her every bit as deceitful as her husband, if I'm being honest," said Muriel.

"That's as may be, but can you even begin to imagine what it must've been like to discover something like that about your husband?" said Matthew. "Having an extramarital affair is one thing, but marrying another woman behind your wife's back requires an extra level of deceit. God knows what he put her through."

"Oh good Lord," sniffed Jack from his side of the room. "Can we put this into some kind of perspective, please? The idiot fell in love with two women at the same time, more fool him. It happens. In fact, didn't it happen in your precious Bible, Muriel? Lamech, if my memory serves correctly. He was married to two women."

"He was also a murderer, and his two wives deserted him before he was made an outcast by society," said Muriel. "If you're going to use the Bible to help make your case, at least get your facts right. And I would like an explanation as to what the Hacker meant when he said Heidi had blackmailed her husband."

"Don't hold your breath," said Libby. "It's another vague accusation where we're left to fill in the blanks."

"But what do we actually know about Heidi?" said Fiona. "I don't have any idea what makes her tick or why I should give her my support."

"This is becoming repetitive." Jack yawned and shifted in his seat. "There are two Passengers left. You either offer Mrs. Cole your vote or throw it away on a vagrant who was planning to top himself anyway." Libby shot him a glare. "Have I said something that's factually incorrect?"

"I'd have liked to hear more passion from her, begging us to save her life so that she can see her children again," said Muriel.

"You sound almost disappointed," said Jack. "If one didn't know better, one might assume you enjoyed playing God."

"That's not what I mean," she protested. "I can only base my judgement on appearances alone because that's all she's given us."

"Have any of you given thought to what kind of wife she was?" asked Jack. "Perhaps she drove her husband into an affair." He looked to Matthew. "Sometimes one person isn't enough to satisfy all your needs."

"Then leave the marriage," said Matthew. "How many times have you done that now, Jack?"

Jack laughed. "Do you really want to go there, Matthew? At least I haven't driven a spouse into the arms of another man."

Matthew's expression soured as he pushed his seat back to rise. Libby took hold of his arm before he could get to his feet. "Leave it," she said quietly but firmly. "This is what he wants." Matthew remained where he was.

"Do as she tells you, there's a good dog." Jack smiled with narrowed eyes. "Now let's return to the ice maiden. Perhaps if she'd displayed a little more femininity, it might have helped her cause."

"Is it all women you have a problem with, or just strong women?" asked Libby. "She's a full-time working mum of two, and whatever she's done to bend the law or torment her cheating husband, well, I think there will be a lot of people out there who'll identify with her and back her."

"Including you?" Jack asked. "Surely your conscience dictates that you should give someone like Mrs. Cole your vote over Mr. Harrison? Or are you going to follow your heart and condemn her to a somewhat grisly death by voting for a dead man walking? It's not too late to reconsider your position with Mr. Cole either. He might be lacking when it comes to integrity, but you cannot deny the man has passion and something to live for. Mr. Harrison has what? By his own admission, nothing. Not even the attention of the nation's sweetheart is enough for him to want to remain on this mortal coil."

Libby felt the heat from her reddening face. In that moment, she had never loathed anyone like she loathed Jack Larsson.

"You know what?" interrupted Fiona. "You've just swung it for me, Jack. I don't care what Heidi did or didn't know, I'm voting for her. And you can roll your eyes as much as you like, it makes no difference to me what you think."

"All you're doing is splitting the votes between husband and wife. Side with me, and their children will at least see one of their parents return."

"Why do I have to change my vote? Why can't you?"

"Mrs. Cole has two children. Her husband has four."

"If you are so concerned about kids, then why didn't you support Shabana—a mother to five?" asked Libby.

Jack sighed. "Here we go. More diatribe from a bleeding-heart liberal . . ."

"More bullshit from the bleeding heartless racist."

"Enough!" warned Fiona. Her raised voice took Libby by surprise. "This is not a playground! Please remember we are being watched by the world. We have just twenty minutes left to make our decision. Now, is there anyone else who will join me in supporting Heidi?"

"I will," said Matthew suddenly.

"Heidi is now in the lead with two votes, Sam has one, and Claire has one."

Libby's heart both raised and sank, a second apart. It meant that unless the public sided with her too, Jack would be correct. Jude was a dead man walking.

CHAPTER 49

HEIDI COLE

Heidi couldn't muster the strength to hate her husband any longer—much of it had been used up when she first learned of his double life. And after the emotional battering of the last two hours, the fight had been knocked out of her. She didn't even have enough energy to release the tears gathering behind her eyes.

Alone in her car, it was the first time since discovering Sam was leading a double life that she felt something other than the need to make his life as miserable as he had made hers. It was grief. She was beginning to mourn the loss of the man she thought she knew inside and out.

Being held against her will was a great leveller. It gave her the clarity to see what she had done was a foolish and irrational move and completely out of character. If she could go back, she would have confronted Sam, kicked him out of the family home, and removed him from her life the moment she first found out. It was the advice she would have given her friends were they wearing similar shoes. Instead, she had gone on the attack with a burning desire to hurt him. Where had it got her? Here, facing a very public death.

With two votes to her name, there was still a chance she might survive the ordeal. But then she would have to face a different set of problems, including dismissal from her career. The Independent Office for Police Conduct would discover a corrupt police officer who was attempting to gain money by fraudulent means and who had used official resources for personal benefit. They wouldn't care that she had been driven to it because she was hurting.

Discovering Sam's second family had happened quite by chance. It was a day that began like most others. Sam was working two hundred miles away, and Heidi had taken annual leave, looking after the children while the school closed for teacher training. She had strapped them into her car and programmed it to drop them off at an activities day in a country park. As she awaited their return, she sat in their neglected conservatory, cursing its leaking roof and broken panes of glass. Using her tablet, she logged on to Facebook and a forum where local posters recommended reliable tradesmen. But an innocuous flick through her friends' video clips changed everything.

It involved a viral craze to raise money and awareness for a mental health charity. Participants had buckets of water thrown at them followed by bags of flour to create a "sticky snowman." "Over my dead body is that happening to me," she muttered as she watched a friend picking sticky, glue-like lumps from her hair. Suddenly, she spotted the name "Samuel Cole" tagged in a video under the heading "People you might also like to watch."

It puzzled her. Months after their wedding, Sam had made a big song and dance about deactivating all his social media accounts. "These companies know too much about us," he moaned. "It makes me uncomfortable. Besides, I don't have time to read about everyone else's lives when I barely have enough time to be a part of my own." She couldn't argue with that. However, Sam must not have understood that while his Facebook profile was no longer active, he could still be tagged by other users.

Curious, Heidi clicked on his name, and a handful of thumbnail videos appeared. They had been uploaded by a Josie Cole, and each with Sam's name attached. Heidi couldn't recall a family member with that name, at least not one whom she had met. The first video featured her husband along with a boy and girl she didn't recognise. They giggled as they threw cups of water at him before caking him in flour. "I'm a sticky snowman, and I nominate Andrew Webber and Darren O'Sullivan," Sam spluttered.

"Do you want a towel, Daddy?" the girl interrupted.

"Yes, please," Sam replied.

Heidi froze—she must have misheard. She rewound and watched it again. "Daddy," the girl said. She played it again. And again. And again. Heidi repeated the word at the same time as the child. "Daddy."

It didn't make sense. *The man on the screen can't be Sam*, she thought. She played the video at half speed, her eyes dissecting each part of his physicality. But his face, frame, slight paunch, pattern of chest hair, mannerisms, and voice were all identical to Sam's. How could it be him? If he'd had a family before they met, she would have discovered it before now. However, this video was recent because the man had the present Sam's appearance. *Has he got an identical twin he doesn't know about? No, that's ridiculous.* But so was her thinking the man on her screen was her husband.

The camera angle made it difficult to see the tattoo of Beccy's and James's names on Sam's left arm. Nervously, she turned to the other videos he'd also been tagged in. They featured the same two children in a garden, although this time, a woman accompanied them. And in the penultimate clip, her arm was wrapped around his waist before she kissed him on the lips. Heidi was struck by their similar appearances, from their hairstyles to their smiles. Then, in the final clip, the family were holidaying in a caravan park she immediately identified as the one in which she and Sam had first met in Aldeburgh.

And when he stretched out his arm to steady himself as he walked across the pebbled beach, her greatest fears were realised. His arm featured the tattoo. There could be no other explanation—Sam had a second family.

Heidi's tablet fell to the floor. Her police career had trained her to examine all the evidence before reaching a conclusion and never to let emotion get the better of her. She took a deep breath—she must treat Sam like any other suspect.

Anxiously, she played each Facebook video again, desperate to learn more about Josie Cole. She compared the dates the clips were uploaded to the digital family calendar on the kitchen wall. Each time one appeared on Facebook, Sam had been working away from home. He spent three to four nights a week in an inexpensive bed and breakfast in Halifax, close to his office. At least that was what he'd told her and Heidi had no reason to question it until now. She ordered her online virtual assistant to call each B and B listed and find out if they had a record of him. None had. Sam must have been playing happy families with Josie Cole instead.

But why was she using Sam's surname? Heidi visited Josie's Facebook page, but the rest of her settings were set to private. Heidi had to expand her search and called for a taxi.

"I thought you were off with the kids today?" asked DS Bev Saxon when Heidi brushed past her in CID.

"I have some admin I want to get a head start on," Heidi replied coolly. She waited until the office was empty before trawling the National Identity Card and Police National Computer databases to learn more about Josie.

She discovered that she was a full-time mother, a year younger than Heidi, and she worked part-time at her local Baptist church's admin department. Hesitantly, Heidi's finger pressed the marital status icon—Josie Harmon had wed Samuel Cole ten months after he and Heidi had tied the knot. His name was also on both children's birth certificates—he had even replicated his and Heidi's kids' names.

Breaking more rules governing the use of police data for her own means, Heidi picked a terrorism protocol as an excuse to access Sam's business accounts. There, she discovered he was paying dividends from it into a joint mortgage taken out in his and Josie's names. They also had joint credit cards and two bank accounts. A search of his business revealed it was based in Halifax and not Sheffield like he had claimed.

Heidi hunched forward in her chair, trying to absorb what she had learned. All at once, so many aspects of her marriage were becoming clear. There was Sam's mistrust of social media and his reluctance to take more than a handful of holiday days at a time; his Christmas visits to his mother's home in the Algarve were always alone. Sometimes on his return from Halifax, he'd be wearing clothes she hadn't seen him in before. Most nights when he was at home, he would disappear behind the closed bedroom door to answer "work" telephone calls. *All this time, you were talking to them. You were talking to your other family under our roof.*

Heidi alternated between fury and confusion, but she was too angry to waste a tear on Sam. Many times over the next few days, she had come within a hair's-breadth of telephoning him and screaming at him for the truth. But a man who could hide a second family from his wife was a man skilled in the art of deception. She could not expect his honesty, and he didn't deserve hers. When Sam returned home from Halifax later that week, she said nothing about her discovery.

Trying to contain how she felt and prevent it from revealing itself in words, moods, or behaviour was close to impossible. Heidi was yearning to hurt her husband like he had hurt her. And this contempt spawned an idea.

Maintaining two houses, two wives, and four children could not have been easy for Sam. So she was going to see what happened when she piled more pressure upon him in a series of different ways.

She began gradually, first by setting him up on extramarital-affair dating apps and websites with fake profiles but using his real contact details. And as the calls and emails came thick and fast, she viewed in quiet amusement as he squirmed each time his phone rang or a new message arrived. Eventually he kept his phone switched off when he was at home. She was sure to include the locations of Halifax, Sheffield, Luton, and Dunstable—it meant someone out there knew of his secret.

Next, and knowing exactly how much money he was siphoning from his accounts to his second family, she upped the ante by making her own financial demands. A request for a new high-spec kitchen with all the fixtures and fittings was followed by suggestions for a replacement bathroom and then quotes for a new conservatory. She revelled in Sam's awkwardness as he became tongue-tied making up excuses as to why they didn't have the available funds to afford them.

The more discomfort she saw him in, the more pressure she would heap upon him. And while her demands made for a promising start, they didn't come close to the hurt she felt. Heidi had to up the ante by really hitting him in the pocket. She wanted to know just how far he was willing to go to keep hold of his secrets. She would blackmail him.

She plucked a figure out of thin air—a ridiculously large sum of £100,000. He didn't have that kind of money readily available, but it was going to be enjoyable imagining him squirm via email. And she spaced her demands a week apart to maximise the discomfort. It was only when he agreed to the preposterous figure that she sat back in her chair and took a deep breath. There was nothing he wouldn't do to keep her from discovering his lies.

But in the days leading up to the cash handover, there was one last thing on her "to complete" list before bringing her campaign to a close. She wanted to see her husband's wife in the flesh.

Heidi's car pulled up against the kerb on the opposite side of the road to Josie's house. It was a home not too dissimilar to her own. *Same kids' names, similar-looking wives, same house . . . at least he's consistent*, she thought. She remained in her vehicle, watching from a distance as, one by one, Sam's second family left. First came his son when friends came to call, then his daughter, who left on a motorised scooter. There were more than passing resemblances to her own children. Finally, Josie appeared. Heidi turned on the privacy windows and watched intently as her opponent passed the car.

Suddenly, a fleeting glimpse of the enemy wasn't enough. Heidi needed more. Without thinking, she began following her by foot, trailing her for twenty minutes before reaching the grounds of the Princess Royal Hospital. As Josie entered the doors to the breast screening unit, an awkward Heidi hesitated outside. Her head told her to abandon this fool's errand and return home, but her heart demanded she stay. She listened to the latter until, almost an hour later, Josie eventually reappeared.

Immediately, Heidi noticed the paleness of the woman's skin, the redness in her eyes, and the sweat patches on the underarms of her top. Josie hurried along the corridor towards the exit as if being chased. But she hadn't shut her handbag properly and, in her haste, it slipped down her arm, and the contents poured across the floor. As Josie crouched to pick them up, Heidi broke her cover to assist.

"Thank you," said Josie, and then burst into tears.

"Are you okay?" Heidi asked hesitantly. Josie shook her head.

Behind her, Heidi spotted a café. "Let's sit down," she said, and helped Josie back to her feet.

What the hell are you doing? Heidi asked herself as she returned from the counter with two cups of tea. *This isn't part of the plan!*

"I'm sorry," offered Josie, and blew her nose into a tissue.

"Have you had some bad news?"

Josie nodded and spoke quietly. "I received some test results that . . . weren't good."

"Is it treatable?"

"It's one grade away from being the most serious cancer. The specialist said they need to test if it's a secondary tumour that's spread from elsewhere before they start treatment. I need to come back for more scans."

"I'm sorry," Heidi replied, and to her surprise, she meant it.

"It's just come as such a shock," Josie continued. "I lost my sister to it, so I can't help but think the worst." She buried her head in her hands and cried again. Without thinking, Heidi reached out to hold Josie's hand. Josie grasped it firmly, and the two women remained in a contemplative quiet.

"You must think I'm mad unloading my problems on a complete stranger," Josie said eventually.

"Not at all. Do you . . . do you have a family who can support you?" Heidi asked.

"Yes, my husband and two kids."

Heidi bristled at her use of the word "husband." "Does he know?"

"No. He works away from home a lot, and I'd rather tell him about it in person but I don't know how to. He's been under so much pressure at work lately, he's not eating or sleeping properly, and I don't want to make things any worse for him."

Heidi knew she was likely to blame for his angst, and suddenly, revenge didn't taste so sweet. "Is he a good man?" she asked.

"He does his best. Money is tight, he's a hard worker, and I know he loves us. There's my mum too. She's in the early stages of dementia and I'm her carer. I don't know how I'm going to look after her and fight this at the same time."

"Sometimes we surprise ourselves, we don't realise how strong we actually are until we're pushed."

Heidi had dealt with enough bad people in her career to recognise the best and worst of them, her husband aside. Her instinct was that Josie was one of the good ones whose only mistake was to fall in love with a man she hadn't known was already married. She didn't need to know the truth, at least not now.

By the time Heidi's car pulled out of the driveway the morning of the £100,000 handover, she had made a decision. She'd met a woman who needed her husband more than Heidi did. Revenge no longer mattered; for Sam to watch Josie fighting cancer would be more punishment than Heidi could ever inflict.

When she was to confront him later at the locker in Milton Keynes where he was to leave the hold-all, she would tell him their marriage was over, but wouldn't mention that she had met Josie or that she was unwell. That was for his other wife to decide.

On her return home, she would, however, tell the children the truth about their father. She was not going to lie to them; they deserved to have at least one honest parent.

Now, Heidi's plan was in tatters, and to all the world, she was as deceptive and secretive as her husband. The realisation was sudden and the emotion hit her hard. And for the first time since discovering the truth about Sam, she released the grip on her tears. The woman her colleagues had nicknamed Elsa the Ice Queen was starting to melt.

CHAPTER 50

D o I need to ask where your vote is going, or can I assume?" Fiona asked Libby.

Libby's eyes flitted from screen to screen, skipping over Sofia, who remained hidden behind a covered lens. She took in Claire and her unborn baby; Sam, a father of four and husband of two; and his wife Heidi, the woman scorned. Finally, she settled on Jude, the man she had been infatuated with but who no longer recognised any worth in living.

The right thing to do would be to pick someone who wanted a second shot at life, but Jude was not that man. Before her were worthier candidates but who were as flawed as him. She was aware that whatever decision she made, it would weigh heavy on her shoulders. However, try as she might, she couldn't bring herself to condemn him to death for an illness he had no control over. Libby considered that perhaps he was right in his suggestion that by trying to save Jude, she was making up for her failure to save her brother. She couldn't be sure. All she knew for certain was that hers was the only vote he was likely to receive, and she could not let him down.

"I'm supporting Jude," she said finally, and Fiona added his name to her tally.

"Waste of time," grunted Jack.

With Sam also earning one vote, Claire awarded another, and Heidi receiving two, Jude's death was not a foregone conclusion. Everything now depended upon the public. But they had a taste for blood. They had hounded Shabana to her death and sought to turn Sofia's car into a travelling pyre.

The depth of their hatred without knowing the Passengers' entire stories appalled her. It was unlikely they would develop compassion for a man who had already planned his own death.

"Cadman," said the Hacker suddenly, and the social media expert jerked as though he'd been stung by a wasp. "Can you tell us where collective public opinion lies?"

"Of course," he replied. His colleague passed him a tablet, and he raised a neatly plucked eyebrow at the data scanning across the screen before him. "Well, this makes for interesting reading."

"Interesting in a good way or a bad way?" Fiona replied.

"That depends on whose car you're in."

Jack looked to the ceiling as if appealing to the Hacker's better nature. "Could you kindly ask your monkey to stop dancing around the organ and inform us which Passenger the public has chosen? Is it Mr. or Mrs. Cole?"

"Now, now, Jack, stop playing hard to get," Cadman retorted. "If the answer is based only upon the word 'save,' then the most frequent trending tag across all social media platforms is #saveHeidi."

The result was as expected, but it still felt to Libby as if the rug had been pulled from under her feet. She glanced at Matthew and Fiona, who had both vocalised their support for Heidi. She assumed they were pleased, but out of respect to the other Passengers, they kept their gratitude restrained.

"However," added Cadman. The jurors turned to face him as he made his way into the centre of the room, leaving a dramatic pause. "If we tally all the independent hashtags generated and spread by social media users, regardless of whether they include the word 'save,' then another name tops the list. Two names, in fact. And they amount to almost double the number of votes #saveHeidi received."

"And?" asked Jack, growing impatient.

"And," Cadman repeated, then swiped his tablet so that one hashtag appeared on a wall opposite the screens. "Members of the jury and ladies and gentlemen at home, may I present to you #givejudeandlibbyachance."

Libby's eyes opened wide like saucers. "I'm sorry?" she asked, perplexed. "What did you just say?"

"#givejudeandlibbyachance," Cadman repeated. "Your ten-minute conversation with Jude is the only thing the world is talking about right now. They're not ready for your story to come to an end. They're desperate to know what happens next. Look."

The contents of Cadman's screen filled the rest of the wall, dozens and dozens of messages and hashtags, including #Libby4Jude, #HappyEverAfter4J&L, and #Savethestarcrossedlovers, along with memes and GIFs.

"Has the world gone fucking mad?" asked a stunned Jack.

"People always love an underdog," Cadman said, and shrugged.

"And people have always been wrong."

"I'm sorry, Jack, but the public have become invested in these two lovebirds. They've even spliced their names together so that '#judy' has the honour of being the fastest-spreading hashtag of all time. Social media is very clear about this—their votes go to Jude."

Libby looked to him; Jude's bewildered face mirrored hers. Against all odds, there was now a chance he might survive. "I don't understand it," Libby continued. "People who don't know us actually care?"

"They don't care about you!" Jack hissed. "You're as real to them as bloody Santa Claus. People want something to believe in even if it's made-up rubbish like you and Mr. Harrison. Don't fool yourself into believing anyone inside or outside this room gives a damn about what happens to either of you after these cars collide."

"With two votes apiece, it's a tie between Heidi and Jude," said Fiona, resting her tablet on the tabletop. "So what happens now?"

"One of you must change your vote," said the Hacker.

"And if we don't?"

"Then you will be sending them all to their deaths. Who would like to begin?"

CHAPTER 51

M uriel was the first juror to turn to Libby to offer a heartfelt apology.

"I am so sorry, I really am, because I know what Jude means to you," she began. "But my heart lies with Claire's unborn baby. No matter what she might have done to her husband, I can't punish that little mite because of it." She grasped Libby's hand and squeezed it to emphasise her remorse. Libby nodded, not trusting herself to speak, before turning to Matthew. She already knew what his answer would be when he struggled to meet her eye.

"I have given it thought, honestly, but I can't rob Heidi's children of their mum. And for that I apologise."

"It's okay," Libby replied.

Fiona was next. "And I'm sure you'll also understand that, as a mother, I can sympathise with what Heidi must be going through. I've been trying to imagine what it would be like never to see my children again . . . it just breaks my heart."

Everyone's attention shifted towards Jack, with the exception of Libby. There was no reason for him to offer her or Jude a lifeline, so she wasn't going to waste her time and ask.

"Hmm," he began. His index finger tapped against his bottom lip in a theatrical manner. "Now *this is* quite the conundrum, isn't it, Miss Dixon? It appears that I am the one who gets the final say in your future. Perhaps this court is more under my control than your Hacker friend assumed. Now, who to pick, who to pick . . ."

His voice trailed off as he pointed his finger towards the screens and moved it between the faces of the Passengers. "Eeny, meeny, miny, mo, whose car should I let explode?"

"What is wrong with you?" snapped Matthew. "We are talking about the lives of people here. This isn't a game."

"Of course it's a game! Can't you see the Hacker has been playing with us from the moment he made himself known? So why shouldn't I too be allowed to play a game of my own? And if you honestly believe that he's going to let one of those poor bastards escape the collision, then you're a bigger fool than I already had you down for."

"He has no reason not to stick to his word," said Muriel.

"You misguided idiot." Jack laughed. "Get your head out of your Bible or Quran or Torah or Vedas or whatever religion you're pandering to this week and join us in the real world, will you? Sofia was half-right . . . all this . . . it's the ultimate television reality show."

"For heaven's sake, Jack, just pick someone," said Fiona. "We only have a quarter of an hour left."

Jack rose from his seat and moved into the centre of the room. He made a big deal of turning to each Passenger, stretched out a hand, and cracked his knuckles. Finally, his head turned and his eyes met with Libby's. Instantly she regressed into the woman who had first walked into the jury room yesterday morning, feeling small and insignificant.

"Beg me," he said slowly.

"Jack, come on now," said Fiona. "Show some self-respect."

"Be mindful that people are watching us, Jack. This is not going to reflect well upon you with the public," warned Muriel.

Jack ignored her. "Beg me," he repeated.

"You're a sick man," said Matthew. "Just pick a name."

"If Miss Dixon wants her little friend to survive this process, then I need to know how serious she is about him. I want her to beg me."

His half-smile, half-sneer made Libby want to recoil. Instead, she looked to Jude's screen and for the first time, he appeared angry. "No," he mouthed, waving his hands in front of his chest. "No."

Libby shook her head before her glare returned to Jack. She cleared her throat. "I am begging you to choose Jude," she asked, her voice controlled and her tone measured.

Jack released a long, exaggerated breath. "There, it wasn't that difficult now, was it? And because you asked so nicely, if you really think it'll make a difference, then I'll change my vote. I apologise, Mr. Cole, but at the eleventh hour, I have been coerced into taking my support elsewhere."

Sam closed his eyes and hung his head forwards.

"And?" asked Matthew. "Where is it going?"

"Never let it be said that I don't listen to the people and take their opinions into account. I shall be supporting the person with the majority of hashtag mentions."

"Thank you," said Libby, and a wave of respite washed over her. Jude had been spared.

"Oh no, I think you misunderstand me, Miss Dixon," Jack continued. "It was Mrs. Cole who received the number of hashtagged saves, not Mr. Harrison. Your charge only gained the public vote through modifications of his name and yours, which in my eyes, is unfair. So I am voting for the true winner, Mrs. Cole, and not the mentally unstable Passenger you favour."

As Jack's eyes pierced hers, his smile emitting only conceit, Libby felt Jude slowly slipping through her fingers. She opened her mouth, desperate to defend him, but she knew it was pointless. Her humiliation quickly transformed into rage, and it was all she could do to stop herself from slapping Jack hard across the face.

"You don't care about Heidi," said Libby. "Only moments ago you were telling us she drove her husband into another woman's arms. You're doing this because it's the only bit of control you have left."

"You're a sore loser, Miss Dixon," said Jack. "These votes are so precious, I'd really rather not waste mine on a stillborn relationship."

"Why are you so opposed to letting Jude live and giving him and me a chance?"

"Don't bite, Libby," warned Matthew. "He has nothing to lose. The world has seen his true colours. He has no chance of ever being re-elected."

"No, it's okay," Libby continued. "Come on, Jack, get it off your chest."

Jack turned his head towards Jude. "Have you really given much thought to what '#HappyEverAfter4J&L' actually means?" he asked. "You're a mental health worker, Miss Dixon, not Walt Disney. Surely you must realise there will be no happy-ever-afters in your storybook. There will be no bluebirds or bunny rabbits leading you and Prince Charming into the sunset for a fairy-tale ending. If I allow Mr. Harrison to survive this process, what do you honestly think will happen when you leave this room? Yes, you might formulate a clumsy, co-dependent debacle of a relationship that survives weeks, perhaps even months, if you're lucky. But when the world's interest in you wanes and all that's left is the two of you, Mr. Harrison will continue to battle the same demons he fought long before you stumbled into one another's arms. In fact, his obstacles and anxiety will likely be exacerbated because he'll now have everyone's expectations resting upon his fragile shoulders, including yours, and it's unlikely he'll cope with the challenge. Perhaps at first, he'll convince himself that you are his reason to live and he'll want to believe that, he really will. But quietly and without putting it into words, he'll be walking a tightrope between living to appease you and desperately craving the peace that made today the day he was going to die. Then when you've taken your eye off the ball, he'll fall from that tightrope and he won't climb back on it again. And it won't come as a complete surprise to you because in the back of your mind, you'll have been expecting it. Each time he fails to answer a call within a few rings or when you return home from work and the house is a little too quiet, the first thing that'll cross your mind is whether he is swinging from a light fitting. And, as it was with your brother, you know it'll be your fault because you forced him into a life he couldn't cope with. So instead of sitting there like an entitled little madam who can't get her own way, you should be thanking me. Because I am sparing you from this heartache. By sending Mr. Harrison to his death, I am giving you the opportunity to continue your humdrum, pedestrian existence without adding funeral costs to your list of expenses."

This time, Libby could no longer contain her fury. "Go to hell!" she yelled as she launched herself at Jack, her fists flailing. She was a hair's-breadth from making contact with his face when Matthew stepped between them, grabbed her by the waist, and pulled her back to the other side of the room, her legs still kicking.

"Plenty of people who are much better, much bigger, and much stronger than you have taken me on and lost," Jack hissed. "You're not the first and you won't be the last. Just remember, people like you never win over people like me."

"The only good thing to have come out of this is that your constituents have seen you as the sanctimonious, worthless piece of shit you really are," Libby seethed.

Jack dismissed her with a wave of his hand. "Sticks and stones, Miss Dixon, sticks and stones. Nothing will change because like it or not, I am needed. I am valued. I am listened to. I am an influencer. You. Are. *Nothing.*"

Before Libby could retaliate, a piercing scream came from the speakers, filling the room. Heads turned towards the wall of screens for the source before settling on Claire. Her volume had returned.

CHAPTER 52

O h gosh," said Muriel. "Look at her."

"Has she—"

"Yes," Matthew interrupted. "It looks like she's in labour."

"She's faking it," Jack dismissed.

"Look at her, you idiot," said Fiona. "That's not a woman who is faking contractions."

Claire's face was contorted by pain as she bit hard on her bottom lip, trying to hold back another scream. She slammed the palms of both hands upon the dashboard and shut her eyes tightly until the contractions temporarily passed.

"Last-minute sympathy bid," said Jack. "I'd put money on the fact she's playing up to the cameras."

"You don't have any money left, remember?" said Libby. "The world emptied your accounts."

"Why are we only seeing this now?" asked Muriel. "A minute ago she wasn't in this kind of pain, was she?"

"I expect he's had her on a loop," Matthew replied. "He's likely been showing us footage of her from earlier, before the contractions started. We've been too busy debating her life to have noticed."

"We need to take her out of there," Muriel demanded, looking skywards. "Do you hear me? You need to help this girl and her baby!"

"Are you talking to God or the Hacker?" Jack smirked.

"Just shut up!" Muriel yelled before the speaker crackled and the Hacker spoke.

"If we are to judge the delivery time based upon the average time between contractions, it is likely Claire will be giving birth within the next thirty minutes."

"Do you have any idea how much stress she and the baby are in?" Muriel continued. "You have to let her go now."

"As much as I would like that to happen, my hands are tied."

"What are you talking about? This is your game, these are you rules, you can do as you please."

"But with the exception of you, no one wanted to save Claire. I made you a promise that I would free the person you chose to survive this process. So if I let her go, I would be going against my word. And you know how much importance I place in honesty."

Libby knew what she must do, but it felt like a hammer blow. She looked up to Jude's screen and he nodded, as if reading her mind and giving her his consent.

"If you can't alter your decision, can we?" she said. "If we changed our minds, can we save Claire and her baby?"

"Yes, you can."

Muriel looked to her colleagues, her brow raised, her eyes begging for their support. Matthew was the first to react, nodding his head.

"So will I," added Fiona.

Libby fought to hold back the emotion inside her. Again, she looked to Jude, who gave her the warmest but saddest smile she had ever seen. "I support Claire," she said.

"I think I'll remain with Mrs. Cole," said Jack.

"Is this your final decision?" asked the Hacker. Each juror nodded. "Then the majority rules. You have chosen to save Claire."

"You'll stop the car and get her help?" Libby asked.

"I can confirm her car will come to a halt in due course and before she is set to collide with the others."

Libby wiped the emotion from her eyes and glanced at the countdown clock. "But that's not for another ten minutes. Why can't you do it now? The drone cameras show ambulances are behind all the Passengers. They can help her."

"Women have been giving birth for thousands upon thousands of years, Libby. Claire's smart seat is recording her statistics for me. I am sure that she and her baby will survive this process intact."

Libby couldn't hold back an incredulous laugh. "How can you assure us of anything? You've murdered people, you've forced us into making impossible decisions that go against everything we believe in. And for what purpose? Because you don't like driverless cars or artificial intelligence? Well, neither do I, but you don't see me blowing innocent people up!"

"Is that why you think I'm doing this, Libby?"

"Is it not?"

"You have misunderstood my motives."

"Then release Claire and tell us."

The Hacker hesitated before he replied. "Perhaps the reasoning behind today's actions might sound better coming from Jack. Because everything that has happened today is because of him."

CHAPTER 53

BirminghamExaminerOnline.co.uk

POSTED BY: RICH JENKINS   *11:45 a.m.*

Police have confirmed that metal fencing surrounding the former Kelly & Davis site has been dismantled by army troops in preparation for the Hacker's collision. Members of the public are ignoring police warnings to stay away for their own safety. Thousands are already lining the streets ahead of the impact.

All eyes turned towards the MP. Jack's face and demeanour remained unruffled by the accusation.

"Jack," continued the Hacker. "Would you like to explain to the world how, in the event of an accident, a driverless car really makes a decision on who lives and who dies? Because everything you've told us has been a lie, hasn't it?"

"What's he talking about?" asked Fiona.

Screens containing the Passengers and news channels were replaced with just one image: Jack's face, broadcast from the multiple hidden cameras scattered around the walls. He failed to react to them or to the attention paid to him by the room's occupants. Instead, he held firm, his face stoic, his back straight, hands clenched, and legs spread shoulder-width apart.

"Come on now, Jack," coaxed the Hacker. "Either I can tell them or you can. It makes no difference to me how this is exposed."

Thirty seconds on the clock passed before Jack moved. Without acknowledging anyone, he straightened his tie and made his way towards the tall wooden exit doors. He lingered where he was standing with his back to his colleagues.

"I'm afraid it's your turn to be a Passenger now," said the Hacker. "Is there something you would like to get off your chest? And remember, honesty is the best policy."

Jack didn't respond so the Hacker pressed on. "What have you been keeping from the public and your fellow jurors since your inquests began? In a potentially fatal accident, how does a driverless car *really* make its decision?"

Matthew spoke. "I thought we'd adopted the German approach, where software must be programmed to avoid injury or death at all cost? The car judges each individual scenario before taking the best course of action resulting in the fewest injuries or fatalities."

"And that was the intention when the technology was in its infancy," the Hacker replied. "The public's biggest concern then was how ethical and moral decisions could be made by robots. The powers that be assured us that driverless cars would try to save the most lives possible. And it was enough to appease most of us, even those who feared that car manufacturers would put their Passengers' safety first. But it was all a lie, wasn't it, Jack? Because the cars you campaigned for are actually assessing us, and protecting the people that *you* have decided are the most valuable to society."

"What's he talking about?" whispered Cadman to one of his team. "Why haven't I read about this online?"

"What does he mean by 'valuable to society'?" Libby asked.

Jack was unwavering in his silence, so the Hacker replied for him.

"If an accident with a driverless car is unavoidable, the car isn't only scanning its surroundings to make a decision; it's scanning *you*. Everything on your National Identity Card and the information collected on your wearable technology decides, in less than a nanosecond, if you are worth saving or sacrificing."

Libby shook her head. "But the ID cards only contain our basic details like National Insurance numbers, blood type, iris scans, et cetera. How can the value of my life depend on something like my eye colour?"

"The cards actually collect and hold so much more than that—masses of data harvested from elsewhere you've given your information. It stores your medical records, internet search history, online purchases, level of education, average and projected earnings, relationship history, size of your mortgage, criminal record, who you associate with on social media—this list goes on."

"So it's like a constantly evolving biography about our lives?" asked Matthew.

"Precisely. It's a CV that can change daily, hourly even. Then add that to the data on the phones we carry and our wearable tech such as those tracking our activity and health, and together, it provides a complete picture of who we are, where we belong in society, and our role in shaping our country's future. All that information helps a car rate us before it decides if we are to live or die."

"Who does it view are more important than others?" Fiona asked.

"Allow me to offer you a few examples. If it's a choice between an unemployed teenager and a high-ranking council official, the teenager will not come out well. If it's a pregnant woman and an elderly person living on a state pension, the latter will be sacrificed. An obese person will not fare well against an athlete; likewise a person with a criminal record will fall foul of one without. A police officer outranks a nurse, but a doctor outweighs a police officer. A smoker comes before a drug user, and a cancer patient takes precedence over someone with a family history of dementia. An MP triumphs over a civil servant, but a cabinet minister tops an MP. And so it goes, on and on and on. The person most useful to our society always prevails. None of us are equals when it comes to driverless cars."

Suddenly the screens became filled with images, data, names, inquest files stamped "Classified," blueprints, and photographs, and all with a link to download them. Amongst them, Libby recognised the three victims she had witnessed the deaths of in Monroe Street.

"If this is true, then I'm speechless," said Fiona. "I'm actually speechless."

"How was this ever sanctioned?" asked Matthew. "Someone must have given it the go-ahead?"

"It was a select few officials buried deep within Westminster's walls who decided to use our own data against us and ensure any deaths on roads would not be people who 'mattered.' Those offenders, including Jack, tasked with its development and implementation, saw an opportunity to socially cleanse certain members of society they believed didn't offer enough. They wanted to use our own data against us."

A hush filled the room as each person digested and processed the Hacker's accusations. "Is this right, Jack?" asked Muriel. "Are we nothing more than data to you?"

Jack shook his head and tugged at the cuffs of his shirt so they could be seen under the sleeves of his jacket. Finally, he turned to face the jurors. "The British people have been nothing but data since William I carried out the first census for the Domesday Book in 1086," he began. "All we are, and all we have ever been, are statistics, so let's not pretend this is a catastrophic crisis that risks tearing apart the very moral fibre of our society. How do you think you are approved for credit cards and loans? How are decisions made on what you pay for insurance? How do we decide the number of immigrants allowed into our country? Acquired data. All that's happened here is that we've reached a new level in our history where decisions have been made as to your importance to your country."

"And you believe this is justifiable?" said Libby. "I can't believe I'm saying this, but AI isn't the enemy—you are."

"Tell me, Miss Dixon, what did you expect us to do?" Jack responded. "Did you really think that we'd allow the cars to make *all* the decisions? We aren't stupid, of course we were going to keep a tight rein over them. We have been afforded an unimaginable, once-in-a-lifetime opportunity to protect the people who shape our society, who save lives, who contribute, who make it a better place for all of us. It is our *duty* to put them first. Do you think we should squander it in the name of an equality our country has never actually had? This is merely a modernisation of the class system. If you needed a life-saving operation, would you want a doctor or a supermarket-shelf stacker to hold the scalpel? Who would you prefer to rescue you from a burning building? A trained firefighter or someone with a learning disability?"

"You judge lives based on disability too?" asked Muriel.

Jack laughed. "Of course we do!"

"But we are all God's—"

"Save it for Sunday's sermon. Did you or your wife have a typical twenty-week screening test for your baby?"

"Yes."

"Why?"

"To make sure everything was okay."

"And if it wasn't?"

"Well, er, we'd have to make a decision based—"

"You're a hypocrite. Because if we valued disabled people as much as we claim we do, we wouldn't be testing for foetus abnormalities during pregnancy."

"This is no better than what the Nazis did," accused Libby. "You're using accidents as an opportunity to erase anyone who doesn't fit your profile of what society should resemble."

"We are hardly deploying soldiers to round people up and ship them off to camps, are we? All we are doing in the rare event of a fatal car accident is to put the country first. It's natural selection for a modern age. Of course I wouldn't expect someone like you to understand."

"This isn't what the people wanted," Libby continued. "Do you remember the results of that survey by an American university? Millions of users from around the world answered ethical questions about who should be prioritised in a crash, and their answers were supposed to be the building-blocks for policymakers like you."

"It was called the Moral Machine, and global surveys like that should be taken with a pinch of salt," Jack replied. "They'd only been completed by those who were tech-savvy, so they didn't represent the opinion of every demographic. And each scenario only had two outcomes—*these* people should die or *those* people should die. If we were to take the results on board, we'd be allowing our laws to be influenced by different cultures in different countries. Do you want the views of the Chinese or the Saudis to dictate who lives or who dies on British streets? That's ridiculous."

"What has been the point of these inquests then?" asked Fiona. "If a decision has already been made, then what we've been doing is inconsequential. Has anything we have ever said made the blindest bit of difference?"

"On occasion when the deceased weren't carrying identity cards or phones and we knew very little about them, then your judgement was useful."

"These inquests are nothing more than smokescreens, aren't they? The government is hiding what you do behind these inquests under the guise of a due process that doesn't exist."

Jack closed his eyes and pinched the bridge of his nose. "This is becoming tiresome. Introducing driverless vehicles was the most seismic overhaul of the motor evolution since cars first joined our roads. Not a single person watching this farce play out has any idea of how much effort it took behind the scenes to make it work. And you criticise us because we've had some tough decisions to make? How dare you! Whether you like it or not, statistics speak for themselves and the bottom line is this—because of what I have helped to create, our roads have never been safer. The most expert driver in the world cannot respond as consistently well as these cars do."

Libby pointed to the screens. "Try telling that to the families of Victor, Bilquis, Shabana, and the hundreds of people caught up in the explosions and who died this morning. And perhaps mention it to the Passengers still trapped in those cars and waiting to die that what you're doing is for the greater good."

"You are as ignorant as you are stupid, Miss Dixon."

"Right back at you, Jack, right back at you."

"The time," interrupted Matthew. "Look at the clock."

Each juror turned to look at the countdown display. Just two minutes remained until the Passengers were scheduled to collide.

From a distance of 1,200 miles above the earth's surface, the Astra satellite beamed live images of a large expanse of wasteland onto the inquest wall. Flashing blue and red dots surrounded it, which Libby assumed to be lights attached to emergency services vehicles.

Smart motorways and dual carriageways surrounded the industrial estates on the outskirts of Birmingham. They housed manufacturing plants, including the former Kelly & Davis factory, which was now just rubble and vacant land.

As the satellite focused more closely, Libby noticed the carriageways had come to a standstill as spectators left their cars and hurried to witness the forthcoming collision from a safe distance. The police held some back while others stood on bonnets and roofs for better views. Clearly they hadn't been scared off by the detonation of Shabana's vehicle that left dozens injured or dead.

Next to the countdown clock appeared new digits, a calculation of the distance the Passengers were from the impact zone. *2 miles*, it read. Libby swallowed hard.

A computer-generated map appeared along with three-dimensional CGI graphics of vehicles moving towards a pinpointed area. On other screens, the Passengers could be viewed from inside through their dashboard cameras and from outside, via drones and helicopters pursuing them.

With their roles now complete, Cadman and his team hovered at the back of the room while jurors rose to their feet and moved towards the centre to watch the Hacker execute the final part of his plan. Jack chose to remain where he was, by the sealed exit. Libby briefly cast her eye over him. His posture was no longer quite so upright, his expression less indomitable. Now that the truth was exposed, Libby assumed he was likely trying to devise a way out of his dilemma. His position as an MP and cabinet minister was no longer tenable, his finances were erased, and he would likely face a criminal investigation for what he had helped to orchestrate. He deserved everything that was coming to him and more.

For now, she would waste no more time thinking about him. Instead, she focused on Jude. Libby desperately wanted to talk to him one last time, but she had no words to make his situation any more bearable. And as harrowing as it would be for her to watch, she owed it to him to be there when his car collided with the others. They were in this together.

1.7 miles, read the distance counter.

Jude appeared composed, she thought, as if he were resigned to his fate. She remembered why. He had already come to terms with his planned death earlier that morning. The end result of what was about to happen was what he had wished for. *If only I'd heard your name back in the bar*, she thought. *This could've all been so different for the both of us.*

The muffled tones of two news anchors offering a blow-by-blow account of what was on-screen could only just be heard amongst the muttering in the room. "Can you turn the volume up?" asked Matthew, and the Hacker obliged.

". . . and with just over a minute left, it appears certain the five Passengers will collide on the grounds of the former Kelly and Davis car plant, the last of the traditional British manufacturers to close shortly before the start of the Road Revolution. Pregnant Claire Arden, who is now believed to be in premature labour, was chosen by the jury to survive this ordeal, but as yet, her vehicle is showing no sign of being withdrawn. Emergency services are already stationed at the site and have issued a statement that says while its personnel are unable to prevent or interfere with the actual collision when it happens, they will attempt to minimise the aftermath by sending in firefighters to tackle the blaze and paramedics to help the injured."

1.3 miles.

Libby's focus moved towards Claire, who was now bent double, her lips pursed, eyes tightly shut, and clutching her stomach as she awaited the end of another painful contraction. "Why haven't you let her out?" Libby directed at the Hacker. "You said you would if we voted for her. We've done everything you told us to do; it's time to keep your end of the deal." She was greeted by his silence.

Next, Libby looked towards Sam. His leg was twitching and his hands were clasped together as if in prayer. Meanwhile, Heidi held her phone in her hands, whispering into the receiver. With no signal, Libby assumed she was recording a message for her children in the hope the device might survive the crash. The only Passenger she was unable to see was Sofia, who remained a blur behind her scarf.

What must be going through their heads? Libby wondered, then tried and failed to put herself in their shoes. She remembered how, while attending university, she had volunteered her weekends to assist in a hospice offering palliative care to those with terminal illnesses. Much of her time was spent comforting people close to death. They had given her an insight into how people come to terms with the inevitable in their own individual ways. But she struggled to comprehend how it might feel to be a Passenger, watching the clock and counting down the seconds to their murder.

1 mile.

Libby returned to Jude. His eyes were now closed. She imagined her hand on his chest as it rose and fell with each breath. She wondered if, before today, he had written letters to friends or his estranged brother to explain his decision. Her brother Nicky had left no note. He was in his bedroom turning a light fitting into a noose as his family were preparing his "welcome home" lunch downstairs. As her father cut him down and ran to phone for help, Libby put her ear to his lips and shook him, as if to release any last words that were caught in his throat. But he had nothing left to say.

0.8 miles.

The first of the five cars followed by its army escorts appeared within the perimeters of the area, but from that height and angle, Libby couldn't work out to whom it belonged. It was closely followed by a second vehicle taking an alternative approach, then a third, a fourth, and a fifth. They were all equidistant from one another. *This is it*, thought Libby. *This is where it all comes to an end.* She fought to catch her breath.

Someone's touch brought her out of herself. On instinct, she recoiled when a hand grasped hers. She turned to see that it belonged to Muriel, whose other hand was holding Fiona's. In turn, she held Matthew's hand. They remained in a line, staring up at the screens as if anticipating the Rapture. No matter what their opinions had been of one another earlier that day, they had since united in a camaraderie. Without speaking, Libby accepted Muriel's hand.

0.6 miles.

"The vehicles are less than thirty seconds from one another," the news anchor announced. "And we can see from the helicopter camera that the Passengers are all now within sight of one another."

Cameras drew in closer to Sofia's charred, dented vehicle leaving the dual carriageway and approaching the wasteland. Next, Libby recognised Jude's car travelling along a different road and towards open gates and fencing that had been hastily torn down. Heidi's car followed, then Sam's, and finally Claire's came into view.

"Each vehicle is estimated to be travelling at sixty miles an hour," continued the news anchor. "Level Five cars contain more safety features than traditional vehicles, but because there are far fewer accidents, they are built from lighter-weight and lower-cost materials. So at that speed and with the deployment of the standard twelve airbags each car contains, the odds are still very much against a Passenger surviving. And as each vehicle is likely to contain explosives, fatalities are inevitable."

0.4 miles.

Libby clenched Muriel's hand tighter. "The Hacker lied about us allowing one to live," said Muriel tearfully, her fingers trembling. "The vote meant nothing. He's going to kill Claire too."

Libby wasn't listening. Jude was now the sole focus of her attention. *I could have saved you*, she thought. *I know I could have if the Hacker had given me the chance. And then you could have saved me too.*

0.2 miles.

The drones and the helicopters began to pull back for their own safety as each Passenger's car entered the derelict wasteland from five different angles, all in perfectly straight lines. Their speeding tyres threw up white and grey clouds of concrete dust. Jude's eyes were now open, but he wasn't looking at what was to come. He was staring into the camera lens. *He's looking to me*, Libby thought. *He wants me to be the last face he ever sees.* She forced the biggest smile while her eyes swam with tears. She held her free hand to her chest, right above her heart. Jude did the same.

0.009 miles.

"Three seconds left," said the TV anchor solemnly. "May God be with them."

Libby braced herself until, without warning, each car suddenly turned sharply in a perfectly choreographed manoeuvre before their brakes were applied, bringing them to a skidding, dramatic halt.

CHAPTER 55

L ibby released her hand from Muriel's grip and clutched the neckline of her own blouse.

"What's happening?" Fiona asked. She pushed her glasses back up her nose and stepped closer to the screens to try to make sense of the images.

"I . . . I don't think it's happened," said Muriel. "I don't think they've collided. There's no explosion, no fires, there's . . . nothing."

Footage from the inside of each vehicle vanished, leaving only images taken from outside. However, the swirling smog of rising dust meant that from drones, helicopters, and the satellite feed, the area was cloaked under a thick grey and white blanket.

Everyone's focus shifted to street-level cameras as news crews zoomed in, desperate to capture the moment when the air that was dense with debris and dust finally dissolved. Libby watched anxiously as army and emergency services vehicles approached the Passengers' cars, reticent to step too close too quickly, in case they belatedly detonated. Then footage switched to just five screens, each one taken by body cams attached to five army bomb disposal technicians. They wore thick, blast-proof heavy body armour and took tentative steps. Time felt as if it were standing still until they reached the cars the world had spent the last two and a half hours fixated by.

The technician leading the team raised a gloved hand in the air, and the others stopped instantly. His finger pointed to each car, and all five squared up to one vehicle apiece. The only sound coming through the speakers was their deep, husky breaths behind their oxygen masks. Then, without warning, the same noise was emitted by each car. It was a simple click.

"What was that?" whispered Muriel.

"I think their doors are unlocking," said Matthew.

As the dust began to fade, the jurors listened intently as the first Passenger threw their door wide open.

"Who's that?" Libby asked as a figure emerged from the vehicle and into the cloud like a ghost.

"I can just about make it out . . . I think it's Sam Cole," Matthew replied. A body cam focused on a face and confirmed Sam's identity. Once out of the car, his head turned quickly as if to search for Heidi's vehicle, but before he could locate her, he was bundled away to safety.

"Where's Jude?" Libby asked, the words nearly clogged in her throat.

"I don't know but I think that's Heidi," said Muriel, pointing to a second vehicle. Her exit was more tentative; her eyes were shut tight, as if she was still expecting her car to explode at any moment. When it didn't, she dared to open an eyelid and became startled by the heavily armoured technician taking her by the arm and hurrying her away from the scene.

Next, a body cam caught Claire, who was struggling to pull herself out of her car. She stretched out her arms for help, and once eased to safety, more figures clad in blast suits ran to her aid and carried her by stretcher to awaiting ambulances.

Two vehicles remained. Libby's eyes flicked from one to the other as she waited to see Jude. The tension was unbearable.

A camera focused on the largest of the cars, which Libby recognised as Sofia's. Her gull-wing doors remained closed. A technician reached to open them and as their hinges stretched, a small, panicked dog scampered out and ran blindly past them. The technician moved closer to the interior until his camera picked up Sofia. Her unconscious body was slumped across the rear seats. Quickly, she was pulled from her car and placed upon the ground until a stretcher arrived. "Do we have a pulse?" Libby heard a voice shout, but the answer was muffled. The cuffs of Sofia's jacket and her hands were streaked with blood.

There was one vehicle left, and Libby was beside herself. "Why hasn't Jude got out yet?" she wept.

"Perhaps he's in shock," offered Matthew. "People react in different ways to extreme stress. Maybe he just needs a moment to get his bearings."

"But the Hacker could still detonate his car." Libby lifted her head towards the speakers to address the Hacker. "Where is he? Why have you turned the dashboard cameras off? I want to see him."

The Hacker was now completely silent.

When Muriel went to take Libby's hand again to offer her reassurance, she snatched it back. Libby felt hot thorns prickle her skin and spread across its surface as her breath shortened. A panic attack felt imminent but this time, she didn't think she could gather the strength to minimise its impact. "Please tell me what's happening," she begged.

"Libby, look," said Matthew, and her eyes darted back to the screen and Jude's car. Another figure inside a blast suit twisted the handle to open the door. Libby's heart thumped hard and fast, terrified that the Hacker had one last trick up his sleeve. Then, slowly, the door opened. *Please be okay*, she repeated to herself. She bit her bottom lip so hard that she tasted blood.

The technician moved slowly, leaning half his body inside the vehicle. However, the camera was attached to the other half of his chest and was pressed against the bodywork, covering the lens. "Move!" she yelled.

Eventually, he pushed himself farther inside Jude's car until the camera captured the entire interior.

It was empty.

ibby stared at the vacant space inside Jude's vehicle, her eyes as wide open as her mouth.

"Where . . . where is he?" she gasped, and turned to the jurors.

A bewildered Fiona stared back at her, eyebrows arched and shaking her head. Libby looked to the rest of the room in the hope someone else might be able to offer her an explanation. But they were all equally dumbfounded, including Jack. "Did we miss him in the dust cloud?" Libby continued. "Did he get out and run and we just didn't see it?"

"Someone would have spotted him, I'm sure," Matthew replied.

"Then where is he?"

"I'm sorry, I have no idea."

Fiona pointed to the screen. "Look at the back seats of his car. Didn't Jude have a rucksack and empty food boxes spread across them? Why are they now empty?"

Libby reached for the rim of the table and grabbed it to steady herself.

"Take deep breaths," said Matthew. "Could someone get her some water, please?"

"I'm okay, I'm okay," insisted Libby, but it was clear to all that she wasn't. One of Cadman's assistants obliged, and Libby gulped down half a bottle without hesitating. "You're dehydrated," said Matthew, "and probably a little in shock too."

Libby looked back towards the screen and into Jude's empty car. She racked her brain, trying to come up with an explanation. If he hadn't escaped, there could only be one.

Jude had never been a Passenger.

"What's happening over there?" asked Fiona suddenly, and pointed to the top left-hand side of the screen. Elsewhere, a fire truck had pulled away from the scene and collided with two parked cars. A second truck followed suit, seemingly travelling of its own accord. It was pursued by a handful of cars nudging one another to get out of tight parking spaces. Meanwhile some made it a few hundred metres up the road before they collided with other cars. Some accelerated to faster speeds before hitting random objects. More appeared to be targeting groups of spectators, forcing them to drive to safety.

The footage suddenly returned to a helicopter above the city. Every few seconds it focused on another crash, and before long, cameras struggled to keep up with the frequency.

Without warning, a news anchor's voice returned to the speakers. "And we are getting unconfirmed reports of a series of collisions on roads across the country," she began. "Eyewitnesses are telling us they're seeing cars, vans, and buses, with and without Passengers, driving head-on into other vehicles."

Suddenly from the street outside came a bang followed by the sound of glass shattering, muffled screams, and panicked yelling.

Libby felt any remaining colour drain from her face. "This was the Hacker's plan all along," she said in a low voice, the words barely able to escape her constricted throat. "It wasn't to make the Passengers collide, but everyone else instead."

PART THREE

SIX MONTHS LATER

UK NEWS

||| **UK NEWS**

A TWO-MINUTE SILENCE TO MARK THE SIX-MONTH ANNIVERSARY OF THE HACKING ATTACK THAT LEFT 1,120 DEAD AND MORE THAN 4,000 INJURED ACROSS THE COUNTRY WILL BEGIN AT 11 A.M.

Follow link for full story.

CHAPTER 57

WORLD EXCLUSIVE!

"I wish Ben could have met his son."

Passenger Claire Arden invites *New & Now Magazine*
into her newly renovated home to meet baby Tate.

It's been a whirlwind six months for Claire Arden since she found international recognition as one of the final five Passengers.

In front of an estimated audience of three billion people, the former teaching assistant from Peterborough went into labour in her hijacked car, giving birth to her son, Tate, two months prematurely and moments after being rescued.

And during her ordeal she kept hidden the dead body of her husband, Ben, in the boot of her car.

In the second part of our exclusive interview, Claire, 27, tells *New & Now* how she has adjusted to life as a single mum and her plans for the future.

Tate became the world's most famous baby even before he was born. How will you explain to him the trauma of that day?
Obviously I'll wait until he is old enough to understand, but I won't keep anything from him. We went through something unique together and I'll never let him forget that he's my little miracle.

How have you coped in the aftermath?

It's something I have to deal with on a daily basis. After Tate and Ben, the hijacking is the first thing I think about in the morning and the last thing I think about before I go to sleep. I started counselling recently to help me try to process and come to terms with everything, and slowly, I think I'm moving in the right direction.

By admitting to putting Ben's body in your car, you broke the law. How did the police respond?

They were very understanding. A few days after I gave birth in the back of the ambulance, they questioned me and I admitted to what I did and why, which I'll talk more about in my book. Later, when the inquest confirmed it was a ruptured aneurysm that killed Ben, the police accepted I wasn't thinking straight and I ended up with a caution.

On reflection, do you think Ben's plan could have worked?

I don't know what I was thinking. All I know was that I was grieving and trying to put the best interests of our son first. Looking back, once we'd reached Ben's car park, it was unlikely that I'd have been able to move him from the boot and into the front of the car. He was a big, strong man. It was a plan that came out of grief and desperation.

It's been widely reported that you were forced to leave your job. What happened?

Unfortunately, yes. I loved working as a teaching assistant but when the attention became too much, it wasn't a position that was tenable any longer. But I've just finished writing my autobiography and I've been shooting my *Lose the Baby Weight* TV series, which starts streaming next month. Also, on Monday, Tate and I are flying to Los Angeles to spend the rest of the year working on my fly-on-the-wall reality series.

What do you think Ben would have made of what's happened to you since becoming a Passenger?

I think he'd be really proud of how I've handled it. All he ever wanted was to provide for our son, even after his death. And while that didn't happen in the way he hoped, that's exactly what I'm doing.

How do you react to criticism that you have exploited your position as a Passenger to make money?
I've made no bones about the fact that I now have a media career because of my ordeal. But I'd give it all away in a heartbeat if I could have Ben back with me. Tate and I deserve every single penny of what we've earned. Unless you lost your partner suddenly, were trapped in a hijacked car, driving to your death while going into labour, then you have no idea what kind of hell that was! I've not been able to travel in anything higher than a Level Two car since, and even then, it's with the doors unlocked and windows open. I sleep two, maybe three hours a night before waking up in a cold sweat, and I'm constantly worried how the trauma might affect Tate in later life. If I'm offered money because of that, then yes, I'm going to take it. Any decent mother would.

Have you met any of your fellow Passengers?
I've met Heidi Cole several times now, and we email and text frequently. We've become really good friends and I've asked her to be Tate's godmother when I get him christened on my reality show. I've not met her husband though, and don't have any desire to after what he put her through.

Finally, what do you think happened to Jude Harrison?
That's the million-dollar question, isn't it? I honestly don't know. I mean, I know he wasn't really a Passenger and likely played a big part in the hacking. All I can say from my interaction with him was that he was very kind and genuinely seemed to care about my safety. But you never really know anyone, do you?

CHAPTER 58

T he corridor was bustling with people of all ages, huddled in groups, disappearing into side rooms, or queuing for vending machines. Heidi Cole was sitting on a solid wooden bench in the corner, the back of her head resting against the wall. Behind her sunglasses, her eyes were closed but she remained alert for telltale signs that she'd been recognised as a Passenger.

Conversation between friends often stopped when they passed her or she'd hear the rustling of a hand inside a pocket to grab a phone that would begin recording her. If her eyes were open, she would have seen today's on-lookers clocking her, glancing away, then taking a sneaky second peek. She would not have tried to stop them; she'd grown used to the attention over the last six months. Besides, there were worse things that could happen than having her image appear on social media. She and two other Passengers knew that better than most. Even if she had wanted privacy, she would not get it today. It was her fourth court appearance and the day of her sentencing.

Her mother, Penny, broke the silence. "Are you okay?" she asked.

"Yes, why?"

"Because I've barely heard a peep from you all afternoon."

"I think I'm all talked out, to be honest. I've pleaded guilty, now I just want this to be over."

"You just need to be a little more patient. You had to let your solicitor do her thing and explain your, oh, what's it called?"

"Mitigating circumstances."

"Yes, them. Fingers crossed the magistrate will be sympathetic and not want to make an example of you. She looks friendly, doesn't she? I still think you should have pleaded not guilty though."

"And gone to trial? It's not fair to put the kids under that level of scrutiny after what they've been through. Besides, I'd be saying I did nothing wrong, and they've heard enough lies from their dad to last them a lifetime. They need to know that they have at least one parent who will step up and admit when they've done wrong."

"The Crown Prosecution Service had no right in charging you. How can this be in the public interest?"

"Because I'm still public property. If the CPS hadn't acted, they'd be accused of bias."

"Why are you always defending them?"

Heidi shook her head. "I'm not, but, Mum, I did it; the world knows I did it. I was a police officer who blackmailed her husband and accessed highly sensitive data on a police computer for my own ends."

"I don't care. That bastard husband of yours deserves every bit of misery you put him through. He should've been sent to prison for marrying another woman. In my eyes, a slap on the wrist and a suspended sentence isn't justice."

"You have to let it go. What's done is done. I've moved on and I don't recognise that scorned ex they keep portraying me as in the papers."

Suddenly, a shadow alerted them to someone's presence. They turned to look up, and both were surprised to see Sam.

"Heidi, can I have a moment . . ." he began.

"Speak of the devil," snapped Penny, clambering to her feet. "You can bugger off and leave my daughter alone."

"It's okay," Heidi replied.

"No, it's not." She jabbed at Sam's chest with her finger. "You've destroyed her life, her career . . ."

"Mum, you're causing a scene," continued Heidi, rising to her feet. "Look."

Penny glanced around her. The corridor had become hushed as spectators watched husband and wife together for the first time since the hijacking of their vehicles. Some brandished phones, and others used their glasses to record what they were witnessing. "Go on, mind your own business," Penny chided, and tried to shoo them away.

"Just give me five minutes, then I'll go away," Sam continued.

Heidi pointed to an empty side room farther along the corridor. "Over there."

As the door closed behind them, she removed her sunglasses and took him in. He hadn't put the weight back on that he'd lost throughout the period she was blackmailing him. His temples were greyer, and his receding hairline and balding crown had almost connected. She noted the plain silver band on his wedding ring finger. Throughout their marriage he had refused to wear a ring, claiming he wasn't a jewellery kind of person. She assumed he had told Josie the same thing. Now that they were apart, he only had one wife to answer to, and she guessed he was placating her. When he saw her eyes upon it, he moved his hand behind his back.

When Heidi looked at Sam, she didn't see the man she was once in love with, only the one who had wounded her so deeply. All conversations since their release from their vehicles had been through lawyers. She knew that one day they would come face-to-face again but she wouldn't have invited it. Now that he was here, it wasn't as awful as she imagined. She felt nothing for him.

"I'm sorry to just turn up, but you wouldn't answer my calls or reply to my emails and I didn't want to say this through our solicitors. But it's important you know how sorry I am. I never meant for any of this to happen."

"You know what, I've come to understand that I don't think you meant it to happen either. You're not a bad person, Sam, you're just a stupid, selfish, gutless one."

"That's fair," he replied.

"How is Josie?"

"She's okay, a bit weak these past few days, but doing well. The scar is healing and she finished her final round of chemo on Monday."

"I'm glad. And you and her?" It felt peculiar asking her husband about the woman in his life, but it didn't upset her.

"We're working on it. We're in therapy."

"Wow." Heidi laughed. "You really are a new man, aren't you?"

"When all this is over, she would like to meet you, properly this time."

"I'm not sure . . ."

"It would mean a lot to her. I think she just wants to reassure you that she didn't know anything about you. And I know you don't owe me anything, but it would mean a lot to me too if you'd consider it."

"Let me think about it."

"Thank you. Have you heard anything about your job yet?"

"No, they'll wait until sentencing before they announce when the disciplinary procedure begins. But it's a certainty they'll sack me and I'll lose my police pension."

"I'm sorry."

"I take full responsibility for what I did."

"We secured another contract last week to refurbish council offices in Halifax. So I'll make sure you don't go short."

Heidi didn't thank him. She didn't want his guilt money, but with her suspension without pay, she was reluctantly reliant on his earnings until she found something else.

"The kids seem to be getting on with their new half-siblings, at least that's what they tell me," she said.

"They are. The same can't be said about mine and Josie's two though. They haven't forgiven me for only talking about our Beccy and James when I was trapped in the car."

"Give them time. They need to get to know you properly, all of them do. Kids are usually much older than ours before they discover their parents are human and can let them down. All four of them have had to learn that lesson from not just one but both parents *and* at the same time *and* in front of their friends *and* the whole world. You were never really there for them before the hijacking. Now you can be honest and be the dad they deserve. In the end, they'll forgive you."

"And you?"

"And me what?"

"Will you forgive me?"

"I already have." She glanced around the room. "Look where being angry has got me."

"What'll you do next?"

"I'm not sure." Heidi shrugged. "The best-case scenario is that I'm given a suspended sentence and a community service order. I've had offers to do some consultancy work for private detective agencies, public speaking, and even some research for TV documentaries. I'll wait and see. Anyway, I'm likely to be called back in any minute so you'd best go."

"It was good to see you."

Heidi didn't reciprocate. Instead, she slipped her sunglasses back on before opening the door. "One last thing," she added. "Make sure you look after Josie, okay? She deserves a better husband than I had. You have a second chance with a good woman. I hope all that we went through has changed you as much as it has me."

"It has," he replied, before turning around and disappearing into a crowded corridor.

CHAPTER 59

OnlineMailNews.co.uk

SOFIA BRADBURY'S DEATH WAS SUICIDE, CORONER RULES

Actress died from overdose and self-inflicted stab wounds.

By TOM ATKINSON for ONLINEMAILNEWS
PUBLISHED 14:09. UPDATED 17:06.

SHAMED actress Sofia Bradbury ended her life minutes before
the hijacked car she was told she was about to die inside was halted
at the last moment, an inquest has been told.

The seventy-eight-year-old Golden Globe winner, who was one
of the final five Passengers in April's hijack, took an overdose of
tablets and used a shard of glass from a broken tumbler to fatally
injure herself.

Ms. Bradbury, whose husband, Patrick Swanson, is currently
awaiting sentencing after admitting eleven separate counts of sexu-
ally abusing children, was accused during her ordeal of being complicit in covering up her husband's crimes.

The inquest at West London Coroner's Court heard how a
post-mortem discovered twenty painkillers and forty-three tranquilisers in her stomach along with lacerations to her arms and
wrists. The prescription medication had been used for a long-standing
problem with back pain.

Recording a conclusion of suicide, coroner Bee Jones said: "While
we have no evidence that Ms. Bradbury's death was as a direct result
of the accusations made about her by the man commonly referred to

as the Hacker, it would not be a great leap of faith to suggest it played a role in her decision to end her life.

"No note or letter was found, but from the footage of her final moments in the vehicle, it is clear that she was in a very agitated, emotional state. I believe this led to her decision.

"Therefore, I have no choice but to record a conclusion of suicide."

Swanson has made many allegations about his wife since his plea, implying that not only did she voluntarily pay hush money to keep the families of victims quiet but that she may also have actively sourced and participated in the abuse of children, accusations that have yet to be substantiated.

All five hospitals Ms. Bradbury actively raised money for have since distanced themselves from her name, and last night, online streaming services have confirmed they will no longer be broadcasting her work.

Ms. Bradbury left £18.5 million in her will, split among her adult niece and nephew and her dog, Oscar.

7,900 SHARES. 14,569 COMMENTS.

CHAPTER 60

NewswireUK.co.uk

MOSCOW: RUSSIAN PRIME MINISTER REFUSES TO DISCUSS EXTRADITION OF ANY RUSSIANS INVOLVED IN DRIVERLESS CAR HACKING. ALSO DISMISSES THREATS OF FURTHER DIPLOMATIC EXPULSIONS AND TRADE SANCTIONS.

T hank you for joining us," began Katy Louise Beech with a well-rehearsed smile. Her bright blue eyes stared into the camera with the red light flashing above the lens.

"In an unusual move, Prime Minister Nicholas McDermott released a statement this morning attacking the mole who leaked preliminary findings of the investigation into the manipulated programming of artificial intelligence in driverless cars." She lifted a tablet from the surface of the desk she was sitting behind.

"He said, and I quote, 'I completely refute allegations that any members of the current serving government had anything to do with influencing software in Level Five vehicles. We also vehemently deny that our party has "closed ranks" to protect those accused and awaiting trial. I am very disheartened by the number of damaging leaks emerging from the police investigation, and we urge them to get their house in order. And as that inquiry continues, along with our own internal investigation, we will be making no further comments until reports are complete.'"

Katy Louise turned to the first of her two studio guests, and a stout man with a complacent expression, thick moustache, and matching eyebrows filled the frame. He leaned back in his chair.

"David Glass, government spin doctor, or to use your official title, head of communications, what more do you think you could be doing to win back the public's trust?"

"We are doing everything in our power," he replied firmly, "and I really do think we're moving in the right direction. Our previous prime minister stepped down—despite there being no evidence he had any knowledge of what allegedly happened—and there has since been a complete cabinet reshuffle. And we have set up our own internal task force committed to rooting out any suspected rogue players. We have also halted the manufacture and distribution of Level Five driverless vehicles nationwide until the software can be patched and recalibrated. I believe we've gone beyond what has been expected of us by the people. I fail to see what else we could be doing."

"A lot more," came a voice out of shot. A cameraman moved quickly to capture Glass's opposition. Sitting next to him was Libby, dressed in a knee-length blue skirt and white sleeveless top, her legs crossed at the ankle and a pair of vintage Jimmy Choos on her feet. Her face was as confident as it was determined.

"Enlighten me," he scoffed. "Such as?"

"The one thing your government can't grasp is that all the public wants is your honesty. You can sack as many prime ministers and launch as many internal investigations as you like, but it won't make a blind bit of difference until there is a non-partisan, independent inquiry that isn't made of faces appointed by the old boys' club."

"I assure you that is not the case—"

"Then why do the police leaks reveal they're being continually fed wrong information by your team and prevented from doing their job?"

"As you have just heard from the PM, we will not be making any further comment on this until the police investigation is complete. These things take time."

"And that is time that'll allow certain factions in your party to bury evidence and to close ranks even tighter."

Glass shook his head and rolled his eyes in pantomime disbelief. "You already have what you want, Miss Dixon! Employees of the car industry, the technology affiliated with it, and hard-working men and women who have created brand-new smart towns have all had their livelihoods ripped away from them because you and your mob wanted Level Five cars taken off the roads. Why do you want to keep punishing ordinary people?"

Libby gave a droll smile. "Nice try, David, but don't try and spin this to lay the blame at my feet. Everything that's happened is as a result of what your colleagues did in the first place. Your government did not treat its people as equals. I didn't want to see anyone out of work, and you know it."

"It's clear that you had a hidden agenda way before the events of that day. The driverless-cars concept has been around since 1939's New York World's Fair, but people like you refuse to let innovation develop naturally because you are selfish. You think you'll be forced to alter your lifestyle simply because you can't be bothered to embrace change. We've all seen those clips of you marching in London against the Road Revolution bill."

"I have no problem with innovation. And the march was long before we learned artificial intelligence wasn't the enemy, it was the people behind it. You seem to forget that more than five thousand people were killed or seriously injured across the country that day, most of them low-bracket earners, white-collar workers, homeless people, the elderly, the sick, the disabled—it was nothing short of genocide thanks to *your* software."

From the corner of her eye, Libby saw Katy Louise place her finger inside her ear. Libby had appeared on enough live television debates to recognise when a director was prompting their presenter with off-script questions. "What is it that you want, Libby?" Katy Louise asked.

"Independent assurance and proof that new software will make unbiased decisions. It shouldn't matter how much we earn, how well we're educated, or how we live our lives. We all have a value to society, and it's not for the government to decide precisely how much. It's been just over six months since the single biggest terror attack our country has ever suffered. If a foreign country had been to blame, they'd have wasted no time in bombing the hell out of it. But because these attacks came in response to the actions of people within their own ranks, they have been shockingly slow to react."

"And in the meantime you are happy to watch our economy go to hell in a handbasket," added Glass. "You should be ashamed."

"You did this yourself. The victims of this atrocity and their families need answers, justice, and cast-iron guarantees. When will you be able to offer them that?"

It was in the arrogant way David Glass cocked his head that warned Libby of the direction his argument was to take. Every time she had an official on the ropes, their attacks veered towards the personal. And she was prepared for it.

"We all saw the pathetic way you fawned over Jude Harrison, and we listened to how you tried to talk the world into saving his life; clearly you had feelings for this man. Should a woman who has demonstrated poor judgement with the man who played such a pivotal part in 'this atrocity' really be allowed to hold our economy to ransom?"

Libby heard the camera turn to her. Out of shot, her toes curled and her fingers clenched, but she would not let Glass goad her.

"Where do you live, Mr. Glass?"

"I don't see how that's relevant to my question."

"It's no less relevant than what you've just said to me, so I'll remind the viewers. It's Cambridgeshire. Who did you vote for in the last general election?"

"You are deflecting, Miss Dixon."

"You voted for your former MP Jack Larsson; you've admitted as much in past interviews. You've also been pictured at many social events and functions with him—in fact, didn't you and your wife enjoy a cruise with him?"

"How did . . . I don't see the relevance . . ." he stuttered, flustered as Libby removed a photograph from a pocket inside her jacket and held it up to the camera. "This is you and Larsson, drinking from champagne flutes on the deck of a yacht sailing from Malta to the coast of Tunisia before the hacking. Now tell me, who is the poor judge of character?"

Glass's face reddened and his nostrils flared as he rose to his feet, tore off his microphone, and stormed off the set.

Libby noticed the corners of Katy Louise's mouth rise as she tried to suppress her joy at their head-to-head. Libby knew that within minutes, the clip would go viral and Katy Louise's programme would garner huge publicity. It wouldn't do Libby's cause any harm either.

"Libby, while we are discussing Jude Harrison, what do you feel when you hear his name now?" Katy Louise asked. Her question was not entirely unexpected.

"Nothing." Libby's expression was impassive.

"Nothing at all?"

"No."

"But you believe he was part of the Hacker's organisation."

"Yes."

"What do you think his role was?"

"I have no idea."

"But you think he played a big part in it?"

"It looks like it, yes."

"And how does that make you feel?"

"Like I said earlier, nothing."

"What would you like to say to him now, if you could?"

"I wouldn't."

Katy Louise paused as the camera remained awkwardly on Libby, drawing in closer on her face. But Libby wouldn't give the presenter the sound bite she craved, and remained silent until finally Katy Louise spoke again.

"Well, thank you for joining us, David Glass and Libby Dixon, spokesperson for pressure group TIAI, Transparency in Artificial Intelligence. Coming up next . . ."

The floor manager indicated with a wave that Libby was no longer in shot, so she was led away into the green room by a production assistant and greeted with an enthusiastic hug from her friend Nia.

"Wowee, girl, you were on fire!" she enthused.

"I just want to get out of here," Libby replied.

"Honestly, Libs, you tore that arsehole a new one."

"Let's just go," Libby replied, and felt her hands trembling. In front of the camera she had learned to hide beneath a thicker skin. But behind the scenes, it was as thin as it ever was—and particularly when the subject involved Jude.

The two made their way along a corridor and towards a set of glass lifts.

Once at reception, they handed their visitors' lanyards to the suited woman manning the security desk.

"What's wrong?" asked Nia. "Why is your face tripping you up? You handled yourself so well out there. Was it the Jude question?"

Libby threw her bag over her shoulder and let out a puff of air. "It's always the Jude question," she replied.

L ibby was uncomfortable caught amongst the throng of London's Oxford Street shoppers and tourists. "This way." She pointed, and she and Nia turned into the less densely populated Rathbone Street.

Soon after the hacking, Libby realised she had become public property. Her face had been beamed onto billions of electronic devices and television screens, making her instantly recognisable. Even now, she could barely make it halfway along a road without being stopped and asked for a selfie. Some people didn't have the manners to ask; they just thrust their arms around her shoulder or waist, held out their phones, and clicked without so much as a "please" or "thank you." She learned that if she wanted to avoid attention in her everyday life, she must steer clear of certain areas when they were at their busiest. Sometimes when she slipped out at night to grocery shop or go for a run, she felt part vampiric.

Generally, the public was on her side. They had lived through the hijacking with her, and they had hoped for the same happy-ever-after outcome as her. But they too had been deceived by Jude Harrison. Nobody, least of all Libby, knew who he really was or where he had vanished to.

However, there was only so much public sympathy Libby could tolerate. The media, columnists, and bloggers were keen to paint her as a victim, but she didn't think of herself in that way. The real victims were the Passengers who survived their ordeal along with those who hadn't. Compared to them, Libby was merely someone who had had her heart broken by a liar.

"How about this one?" asked Nia, pointing to the entrance of a back-street bar. Its dark windows made it difficult to see through from the outside.

"Perfect," Libby replied.

Inside, and as Nia waited at the bar, Libby chose a private corner booth, sitting with her back to the wall so that she was aware of who was nearby at all times. She recalled one afternoon at a restaurant in Northampton having lunch with her mum, and how their entire conversation had been filmed and posted online by a blogger sitting one table away from them. Libby wouldn't make the same mistake twice. Every stranger was treated with suspicion.

She thought back to how much her life had changed since that infamous Tuesday morning when she made her way into the inquest. Later, and spurred on by a need to stop herself from being considered another of the Hacker's casualties, she seized an opportunity to put her fame to good use.

Libby had been aware of pressure group Transparency in Artificial Intelligence before they contacted her. Up until the hijacking, they campaigned for the reasoning behind inquest decisions to be made public. But the government denied their requests on the grounds of national security, claiming hackers could potentially compromise its AI. The irony of what happened next was not lost on anyone.

Following the hijacking, interest in the group's work took off, and after a handful of meetings, Libby agreed to become their public spokesperson. Her role involved appearing regularly in the media and acting as a keynote speaker at pro-TIAI rallies. Libby had wanted to spread the message further by travelling internationally to warn of the potential dangers to other countries that had purchased the British model of a driverless-car nation. But with little funding behind them, TIAI's reach was restricted.

"I need this," said Nia, placing two pint glasses of lager on the table. She held one aloft. "Cheers," she continued, and their glasses clinked. "You didn't say much on the way here. You're thinking about Jude again, aren't you? You get that faraway look in your eyes when he's on your mind."

"I'm sorry, I can't help it," Libby replied. "I'm still struggling to understand why they haven't found him yet. Literally billions of people know exactly what he looks like, yet there have been no positive sightings of him."

"What did the police tell you in their last update?"

"Nothing that I don't know already. Apparently, there are untraceable automated bots around the world flooding the internet and police forces with fake sightings of him, fake information on him, fake names, fake childhood pictures, fake relationships, fake employment records, fake birth certificates, fake wedding photographs . . . dozens and dozens of them every day both during and after the hijacking. At the rate that information is coming in, the investigators admitted it could take them years to sift through it all and get a proper identification. My gut instinct tells me they're never going to find answers . . ." Libby's voice trailed off.

"And how much do *you* still want those answers?" asked Nia.

"A lot . . . I don't know what's wrong with me." Libby pinched at her eyes. "I know that he must have played a huge part in what happened, but it's like somehow we are tied together with an invisible rope. I don't understand it, but I need to know exactly what and who he really is. Crazy, isn't it?"

"No, it's not crazy. It's like you're grieving. You hoped that if you two ever met again, you'd continue what you had that first night. You spent months trying to find that boy and when it happened, it was under circumstances that no one in a million years could've predicted."

"Apart from him."

"He doesn't count. I think you're grieving the man you thought Jude was."

"That first time I met him in the bar, do you think it was by chance or did he engineer it?"

Nia placed her hand on Libby's. "Honestly, I think he set it up. I think he knew who you were, what you witnessed in Monroe Street, he knew about your brother and his problems, what your job involved, and he played on your need to help people with deeper emotional issues. That's why he sold you that lie about planning his suicide. It was only ever going to make you want to help him. He took advantage of your good heart."

Libby dabbed at her moistening eyes with a tissue. Nia hadn't suggested anything that Libby hadn't already considered. But hearing her best friend verbalise it made her feel even more foolish. She couldn't admit it to Nia, but try as she might to hate Jude, she wouldn't be able to until she had heard him admit in his own words the part he played in the attack. It was closure she was unlikely to receive.

"Don't let that idiot keep upsetting you," continued Nia. "He isn't worth any more of your tears."

"I just feel so stupid for falling for it all."

"We all would've fallen for it. That's why so many people out there love you, because you are just like them."

Libby took a sip from her glass and looked around the pub. A couple waiting at the bar were staring at her. On catching her eye, they quickly turned their heads. "Do you think I'll ever get my old life back again?" she asked.

"Do you want it?"

"You know I'm not comfortable with all the attention, but it's given me the opportunity of a lifetime to make a difference in something I'm passionate about. However, sometimes I miss normality."

"You have to see this through or you'll be left wondering what you could've achieved. Your job will be there when you're ready to come back after your sabbatical. But you're going to have to come to terms with the fact it's unlikely you're ever going to be normal again."

"That's what worries me."

ibby and Nia held on to the handrails adjacent to the train doors, giggling and steadying themselves as it pulled into Birmingham's New Street Station.

Libby stretched out her arms and wrapped them around Nia, pulling her in close as she hugged her friend goodbye. "Thank you for coming with me," said Libby. "And thank you for listening to me moan yet again. I don't know how I'd have coped in the last few months without you."

"Ah, hush your mouth. You're drunk."

"A little, but I mean it. You're an amazing friend."

"And don't you ever forget it." Nia smiled. "And remember what I said about he who shall not be named. You need to start clearing that boy out of your head. The sooner he goes, the sooner you'll meet someone who deserves to be with you. Promise me?"

"I promise." Libby hugged her friend again before the train doors beeped and then opened, and the two went their separate ways.

She took her phone off airplane mode, and thirty-plus messages appeared from friends and co-workers congratulating her on wiping the floor with government spokesman David Glass. As Libby predicted, the video had gone viral.

The fifty-minute high-speed train journey from London to Birmingham had been an uneventful one, with just two requests for photographs as Nia and Libby took up residence at the onboard bar. By the time they reached the city, it was still only the early evening but dark. And Libby was somewhere in between woozy and drunk. Nia had been just the tonic she needed, even if it meant waking up with a hangover tomorrow morning. Preparing for the inevitable, she stopped off at a kiosk to buy a bottle of water and a packet of aspirin before walking home to clear her head.

As Libby made her way through the outskirts of the city centre, she was pleased to see people driving vehicles again and not vehicles driving them. The hijacking's aftermath had seen a sharp upturn in demand for Level Two and Level Three cars, and the use of city bikes had also skyrocketed. Humans were no longer such slaves to technology.

David Glass had been correct about the damage inflicted upon the British economy with the suspension of Level Five production. The concept was also losing billions in foreign sales as countries halted purchasing or further developing the concept for the time being. It wouldn't last, as progress and technology were inevitable, but at least the future would be more transparent. And while Libby might never completely warm to autonomous vehicles, she believed that when AI was in the right hands, the pros outweighed the cons.

As the face of TIAI, Libby occasionally took the brunt of unwanted attention. She and her fellow campaigners were blamed by disgruntled out-of-work employees for contract cancellations and reduced hours and incomes. Earlier that evening, when a scruffy, bearded man bumped into her on the train and knocked her handbag to the floor, she feared he might be acting on threats made against her. However, he shuffled off without a harsh word or an apology.

But each time she doubted the courage of her convictions, she recalled the black smoke rising across Birmingham's horizon as driverless cars collided with one another. It was her duty to ensure nothing like that could ever happen again.

Libby drank from her water bottle and carefully made her way down the floodlit steps to the canal towpath. She clicked on an app on her phone linked to the seven cameras inside and outside her house that her father had insisted they install. Soon after the hijacking, the paparazzi took up residence outside her gated community, hiding in parked cars with blacked-out windows and inside rooms rented from a handful of less-than-scrupulous neighbours. On every occasion, Libby refused to talk to the snappers or to act on their vile insults as they tried to goad her. Eventually, she wore identical outfits each time she left the house when she learned that publications weren't interested in printing pictures of celebrities wearing the same clothes, day in, day out. To the reader, it looked like old news. The paparazzi gradually began to leave her alone.

Her watch began to vibrate. Her mum had left her a video message, and Libby pressed play. "Hi, Libs, are we still okay to come up this weekend?"

Libby recorded one of her own and sent it. "Of course," she replied. "Let me know which train you're catching and I'll come meet you. Love you. Kisses."

As two cyclists raced past her under the bright white streetlights, she recalled how another consequence of the hijacking was reconnecting with the estranged parents she had virtually shut out of her life. When reporters besieged her home, they had insisted she stay with them in Northampton. And despite having spent much of the last decade avoiding the family home because of the memories associated with her brother's death, she was too sapped of energy to protest.

For years, she couldn't understand why her parents hadn't sold the house where their eldest child had ended his life. She had hated that everything in Nicky's bedroom remained unchanged, even down to the bedsheets he'd last slept on. It wasn't as if they were awaiting his return from a school trip.

It was only when she confronted her fears and spent time under their roof that she understood by running away she had been denying herself the opportunity of forgiveness. Libby blamed herself for his death—she was the one with whom he had spent much of his time, the one he could talk to with unabridged honesty about his feelings of despair. And Libby was the one who had so wanted to believe he was managing his depression that he was ready to return home from his last admission to hospital. He had died on her watch; it was her fault.

Now she accepted that she had no more control over Nicky's actions than she had over the Hacker's. His room remained untouched not because their parents hadn't come to terms with his death. It was the opposite. In accepting his decision, they'd found the closure Libby couldn't. By the time she eventually left that house and returned to Birmingham, she had reconnected with the parents and brother she'd lost.

Libby reached her gated community before she knew it, and placed her head in front of a biometric facial scanner until it recognised her and opened the door. She was unsure whether it was the alcohol or her conversation with Nia that was making her smile. It didn't matter; she was suffused with optimism. It was unlikely her life was ever going to be the same as it was before jury duty, but she was gradually accepting that wasn't necessarily a bad thing.

She unzipped her bag to locate the key fob to her front door when she felt a smooth, flat object inside. Libby pulled it out—it was an electronic tablet. She stared at it, puzzled as to how it might be in her possession. She hadn't brought it with her, and Nia always kept her tablet in a bejewelled pink case. Had she absent-mindedly taken somebody else's from the bar on the train, assuming it was her own?

She closed and locked the front door behind her as the lights automatically switched on, and made her way to the kitchen diner. She glanced to the corner of the room where she once kept the cage for her house rabbits, Michael and Jackson. When her media career soared, she spent too much time away from home to keep them. The neighbour's daughter whom she offered them to promised that Libby could visit them whenever she liked.

Pouring herself a mug of coffee, she sat at the table and felt for the tablet's on button. It immediately sprang to life, but there were no security clearances such as iris or facial recognition scans required. The home screen contained no apps or saved pages. There was just one icon, a symbol for a video clip.

Libby's finger hovered over it as she deliberated whether she was invading the owner's privacy by pressing play. Curiosity won over and with one touch, the video icon quadrupled in size. A man's face appeared in a frame. There was something familiar about him, but she couldn't put her finger on what it was. He sported a thick, dark brown beard and black-rimmed glasses, and a beanie hat covered his head. Then she recognised him as the scruffy man who'd collided with her on the train earlier that night.

"Libby," he began. His voice gave her body chills.

It was Jude Harrison.

"I apologise for approaching you like this," he continued. "But I had to find a way of reaching you, and it's not like I can just turn up on your doorstep. Firstly, I need you to know that not everything I told you was a lie when we met in person a year ago or while you were at the inquest. What happened that day isn't as black and white as it seems. And I would like the opportunity to tell you the truth because it's what you deserve. But I'm not going to explain it now or through a video call. I want to do it in person. I'm in the city, Libby. I'm in Birmingham and I need to see you tonight."

ibby released her grip on the tablet as if it were burning her hands. Then she stared at the device in disbelief, trying to make sense of what she had just seen and heard.

Jude Harrison had returned. And he wanted to see her again.

When the shock passed, anger began to rise inside her, and she wanted to hurl the tablet against the wall until it shattered, then forget she had ever found it. But it wasn't an option. She couldn't unsee or ignore that Jude had broken cover to make contact.

She had to call the police. Her hands shook as she reached for her phone and asked her virtual assistant to find the electronic business card she had stored with the details of a chief inspector who was heading one of the many investigations into Jude's disappearance. They had met on several occasions to discuss her first encounter with Jude. Then, together, they'd watched and listened to recordings of conversations in the inquest room, trying to pick out and piece together clues as to his potential identity.

"Would you like me to call the number you have requested?" asked the VA.

Libby opened her mouth but no reply came out. Instead, she kept replaying the moment on the train when Jude had bumped into her, angry with herself for having drunk too much and let her guard down. Perhaps if she were sober, she'd have immediately identified him, then called for help. There would have been no shortage of vigilantes on that train willing to apprehend the world's most wanted man until the police arrived.

"Would you like me to call the number you have requested?" the VA repeated.

Libby considered how long Jude might have been following her. Had it only been on the London to Birmingham train, or had he been watching her all day? All week, perhaps? Longer? She felt sick at the thought of his proximity.

"Would you like me to call—"

"No," Libby interrupted.

Her focus returned to the tablet, a part of her eager to watch the video for a second time but too afraid to press play. Eventually, she summoned up the courage, and Jude came back to life. "What happened that day isn't as black and white as it seems," he said. "I would like the opportunity to tell you the truth."

Of course your guilt is black and white! she thought. *Forensics proved beyond a shadow of a doubt that you were never a Passenger in the car we'd been watching you in. There was no DNA, no empty food cartons or rucksack scattered across the rear seats like we'd seen earlier.*

Jude Harrison's life was never in danger because Jude Harrison never existed. He was a fictitious character no more real than those in the thriller novels she read. She repeated his words aloud. "I would like the opportunity to tell you the truth." Nobody knew the truth, not even a version of it. Might this be her only opportunity?

Less than an hour had passed since Libby promised Nia she was going to start erasing Jude from her mind. But she knew that no matter what lip service she paid her friend, she would never truly rest until she had heard from Jude's own lips the story behind what happened that day.

She replayed the message one last time before making her decision. She had to hear him out in person. If Jude had wanted her dead, it would have happened by now.

"How do I find you?" she said aloud. She scanned the tablet again on the off chance she had missed something. Once assured Jude had left her no way of responding to his request, she moved towards her coffee machine again and picked a capsule with the highest caffeine content. She needed her wits about her. The sound of the tablet vibrating against the tabletop caught her attention—it had received a message. And it could only have been from Jude. She read it tentatively.

There's a car waiting outside for you. It'll bring you to me.

Libby paused to catch her breath. "Do you think I'm just going to get into a car that you've sent?" she spoke aloud.

Seconds later, another message appeared on the screen. No, it read.

Libby froze. Jude was listening to her through her tablet.

Another message appeared. I have no reason to hurt you.

"You had no reason to hurt anyone that day," she replied, her voice growing in confidence.

It wasn't my doing, Jude texted. Let me tell you everything in person.

Libby hesitated. It was now or never. If she really wanted to hear the answers she craved, this might be her only opportunity.

She turned to face Jude's tablet, took a deep breath, pulled her hair back into a ponytail, and attached a band to keep it in place.

"Okay," she said. "Where am I going?"

CHAPTER 64

The vehicle Jude sent for Libby was easy to locate; it was the only car parked outside her complex with its headlights on, interior empty, and door ajar.

One last time, Libby gave careful consideration before entering. She peered inside; it was a Level Three at least. The dashboard contained a steering wheel and, below it, an accelerator and brake pedals. However, they could easily have been tampered with and rendered redundant. *But what would be the point?* she asked herself. There were much easier ways to kill her than this, if that's what Jude wanted.

Eventually her all-consuming need for the truth rose above all else and she climbed inside. The door quietly closed without locking.

Libby's heart pounded inside her chest as the vehicle set itself into drive mode. Her hands gripped the steering wheel tightly as her foot tested the brakes. They were operable. The journey through Birmingham lasted just ten minutes but it felt like much longer before the car came to a halt by a kerb. Libby recognised the location immediately—Monroe Street, the district where she had witnessed three generations of one family wiped out by a driverless car. She exited the vehicle quickly.

Immediately, she was riled by Jude's choice of meeting place. He must have known how distressing it had been for her to witness that footage during jury duty. Awaiting further instruction, she held his tablet tightly to her chest until it vibrated. **Number 360**, a message read.

Shops, predominantly small independent boutiques, lined the road. As the major high street stores gradually shut to go online, town centres were becoming desolate. Meanwhile, there had been a resurgence in the popularity of smaller, independent stores. By day, Monroe Street was bustling, but with the time approaching nine o'clock, it was now mostly empty. Libby carefully examined each shop frontage until she found number 360, a former café with white wipe-off paint smeared across the windows to prevent unwelcome eyes. She switched on her phone's torch and attempted to look through the glass-pane door, but caught only her own reflection.

You don't have to do this, she told herself. But as much as the thought of confronting Jude terrified her, it would be too much of a struggle to live the rest of her life having walked away now. Tentatively, she pushed against the door handle and it opened. A bell attached to the top clanged louder than its size, startling her.

"Hello?" she asked, her voice tremulous. She shone the phone's light around the room. She was surrounded by a dozen or so tables and chairs that were caked in dust, along with empty counters and shelving. A ladder, paint pots, and dust covers were scattered across the floor. Any redecoration work that had once begun had long since been abandoned.

"Close the door, please," came a voice from further inside. She recognised it immediately and took a sharp, involuntary breath. With her hand in her pocket, she felt the cool metal blade of the vegetable knife she had pocketed while in her kitchen, and out of sight of the tablet's lens. She clasped the handle and quietly closed the door.

"You won't need the knife," Jude continued. "But keep it with you if it makes you feel safer."

As she turned in his direction, he switched on a lamp, and Libby's eyes blinked as they adjusted to the light. Now she could see him clearly. Jude was sitting behind a table, hands flat on the surface, a phone next to him. He was dressed from head to toe in dark colours and fabrics, including a winter coat and thick laced-up boots. His beard was an inch or so thick, his hair short and tousled, and he wore glasses. In spite of herself, Libby felt flashes of something for him that she couldn't put into words.

"Hello, Libby," Jude began, and he offered her a thin smile. His tone was a combination of friendly but assertive. She had not met this version of him before.

"How have you been?" Jude continued, but Libby wasn't yet ready to respond. It didn't appear to concern him. "I'm glad you came. Are you sure you wouldn't prefer to sit?" He pointed to a chair opposite him. Libby shook her head and eyed him up and down as if it were the first time they had met. And in many ways, it was. This was not the man she once had feelings for; this man was a stranger. "You must have a lot of questions," he said. "Go ahead."

She nodded and cleared her throat, but try as she might, she couldn't stop nerves from catching her vocal cords.

"Of all the places you could have brought me, why did you choose this street?" she asked.

"We'll get to that soon, I promise," he replied.

"How long have you been following me?"

"In person, it's been around a couple of weeks now. Through your phone data, tracking devices, spending patterns, internet usage, and public profile, I suppose I've never stopped following you. Not from the night we met in Manchester, or even the months leading up to it."

"So we didn't meet by chance then?"

"No, we didn't."

Something inside Libby sank. She was almost disappointed to hear him admit to what she had already assumed. "How did you know I'd be in that pub?"

"We had access to all your personal details, including your emails and diary."

"You mean you hacked into them?"

"Yes."

"And when you found out where I'd be spending the weekend, you followed me?" Jude nodded again. "How did you know I'd talk to you?"

"I didn't. I pursued you from bar to bar and I waited until after you'd had a few drinks before trying to get your attention. I knew from Facebook photos you enjoyed karaoke, and your Spotify playlists told me Michael Jackson was your favourite artist."

"The friends you were with. Were they in on this?"

"They weren't my friends."

"I saw them. You were standing with a group of men."

"No, I was standing *behind* a group of men. I had no more of an idea who they were than they did of me. Like my driverless car, you didn't think to question what you were seeing."

"Why would I? I trust people until I have no reason to. My first instinct isn't to assume everything I hear or see is a lie. Well, at least it wasn't until you came along. How could you be sure I'd be attracted to you?"

"From the profiles you'd filled in when you joined online dating websites. We looked at the type of men whose pages you visited, how long you hovered over each picture. We analysed their personality traits and, of course, we took a look at your ex, William. We studied your turn-ons and turn-offs, recreational interests, the online conversations you had, and what qualities someone needed before you'd consider meeting them. I adapted my appearance accordingly. I cut and coloured my hair, wore contact lenses, and dressed in the style of clothes you preferred your men in. I became everything you were looking for. The only thing we couldn't engineer was chemistry. And you cannot deny we had that. When you left, I took your glass with me from the pub and did the Match Your DNA test on it to see if we were genetically designed for each other. Would you like to know the result?"

Libby's eyes blazed with fury, but she kept her fingers rigid so they wouldn't ball into fists and reveal to Jude how violated she felt. "No, I do not," she replied through gritted teeth. Quietly, though, she was terrified she might be matched with a psychopath. "The conversations we had that night, they were engineered too?"

"Some of them, yes."

"Like what?"

"Like my love of foreign films, baking, and knowledge of Michael Jackson songs."

"But you knew all the words."

"My team sent the lyrics to my smart lens, and I was reading them. Then I quickly took it out as you came over to talk to me. But not everything was staged."

"What was genuine?"

"My interest in what you had to say."

Libby laughed. "Do you expect me to believe that?"

"I don't expect you to believe anything I say. But if you're so convinced that I'm going to lie to you, then why did you come here tonight?"

Libby opened her mouth, then stopped herself. She didn't have an answer. "What do I call you?" she asked instead. "I assume Jude Harrison isn't your real name?"

He shook his head. "Continue to call me Jude, if it makes things easier."

"No, I want your real name."

"It's inconsequential. I'm already buried so deeply in the World Wide Web that by the time you've left here—and should you choose to inform the police of our encounter—my real name won't matter. They'll be no closer to finding me."

"I don't care. You owe it to me."

"It's Noah Harris."

The name felt familiar to Libby, but her head was swimming with too much information to pinpoint from where.

"Why call yourself Jude?"

"'Hey Jude' was your late brother's favourite song. They played it as his funeral. When it reached the chorus, your family rose to their feet, linked their hands in the air, and sang along with the 'na na' parts. Soon everyone was standing up and joining in."

"How dare you! How could you know that?"

"People record everything these days for posterity. It wasn't hard to find online."

Libby shuddered at the depth of his research and knowledge. "Of all the people in the world you could have picked, why me?"

"We needed someone with morals and values and who genuinely cared about the welfare of strangers. For the broadcast, we needed a woman who both men and women of all ages could warm to. And for them to invest emotionally in her, she would need to be broken."

"You think the world sees me as broken?"

"Am I wrong?"

"You're an arsehole."

"We had to give our mark a Passenger to throw her support behind. Who better than a man with a sob story and to whom she was attracted? The fact you had our shared loathing for autonomous vehicles was of course a huge selling point and one of the reasons why we placed you inside that jury."

"*You* put me there? I wasn't randomly selected?"

"I assumed you had realised that by now. We wanted a personality who'd question the decisions the other jurors made. I must admit, we thought we might've made a bad call after the first day when the others kept railroading you and you gave up fighting back. But by day two and shortly before the first hijack, you came into your own. At that point we knew we couldn't have asked for anyone better."

Inside, Libby was still seething. She had long come to terms with her manipulation, but she hadn't known how deep the lies ran. She felt like an idiot. "But why me specifically? There are millions of women out there who share my views."

"But there aren't any who share what you and I share."

Libby raised her eyebrows. "Which is?"

"When you arrived here, you asked me why I picked this location. From what I gathered during the harvesting of your data, there are three events that've shaped who you are. Finding your brother's body, your boyfriend fathering a child with another woman, and then witnessing three people die on this road. One of those, we have in common."

"I don't understand."

"The three generations of women you watched die right outside this door were my wife, my daughter, and my mother."

ibby took a step back from Noah and shook her head. "This is another one of your lies, isn't it?" she spat. "You're disgusting."

Without giving him the opportunity to defend himself, she turned to make her way towards the door. Behind her, chair legs scraped across the slate floor. Her body tensed and she clasped the handle of the knife tighter.

"Don't go," said Noah. "Please." And for the first time that night, she heard something akin to desperation in his voice. It was enough to bring her to a standstill. "I said you deserved the truth and this *is* the truth. I swear."

"I don't believe you." She shook her head and turned to see him on his feet. Something was preventing her from taking those few extra steps and leaving the café. Suddenly she recalled why she knew the name Noah Harris. He wasn't the only one who could keep secrets. She would carry this alone for the time being.

"Stephenie, Gracie, and Mary; my wife, daughter, and mum. I was at work when I received a call from a nurse at Queen Elizabeth Hospital to tell me they'd been involved in an accident. It wasn't until I got there that I learned I'd lost all three."

"Their names are in the public domain," said Libby, her tone deadpan.

Noah lifted the phone from his desk and asked the operating system to open a folder. He moved towards Libby, his arm outstretched to pass her the device for closer inspection. Again, she clenched the knife and took three steps backwards. Noah appeared disappointed by her cautiousness and placed the phone upon the table closest to her before returning to his seat.

Inside, Libby found dozens and dozens of albums, each crammed with family photographs. She swiped through the folders, opening them randomly. One contained images of Noah as a boy with an older lad, along with a younger-looking woman she recognised from the car accident, Noah's mother, she assumed. Other folders contained wedding photographs, honeymoon pictures, and shots of a newborn child and Noah.

"Watch the videos," he urged, and she pressed play. In the first, Stephenie was sitting on a bench in a garden, nursing a baby. Her voice belonged to the same woman she had comforted on Monroe Street. Libby would never forget how in her dying breaths, she had only wanted to know that her daughter was safe.

Libby hesitated before she spoke again. "I'm sorry for what happened to them, but that doesn't explain your role in the hijacking and why you hurt so many innocent people."

"None of it was supposed to happen. Nobody should have died. Everything just . . . escalated . . . into an event that was completely out of my control. I couldn't stop him."

"Who?"

"Alex."

"Who is that?"

"My brother."

"And what was his role?"

"He's one of the people you called the Hacker."

"Your brother was the Hacker?" she said slowly.

"*One* of the Hackers. The Hacker wasn't just one person. The voice you heard was a speech synthesis—an artificial production of the human voice. A handful of people—men and women of different ages, accents, dialects, and languages—took it in turns to dictate what the Hacker was going to say while others controlled what images you saw on-screen. To make what happened a success took a global network of people. Please, will you sit down so I can explain?"

Libby paused. She took another look over her shoulder at the door behind her and determined that if she felt threatened by Noah, she could reach it before he reached her. She softened her grip on the knife and chose a chair two tables away from him. Then she gritted her teeth and tried not to lose herself in the eyes she'd once longed to see again.

"I should start at the beginning," he said. "Back in the forties, during the Second World War, my granddad started a business building engines for army vehicles. Then, over the years, it diversified and was handed down to our dad. When Alex and I left university, we began working for him as computer programmers creating software and developing radars, orientation sensors, and lidar for Level Five cars. Dad was in line for a multimillion-pound government contract to provide the software and cameras for emergency services vehicles. It was the biggest deal in our company history. And because Britain was going to be the first country to go completely autonomous, the plan was to then sell our software and systems globally. Years after Brexit, we were still a little shaky, but this meant job security for our six hundred employees." Noah clicked his fingers. "Then, just like that, it was all over."

"Why?"

"We were good to go—we had the staff and technology in place and we'd expanded our premises. It was Alex who spotted a flaw in the software that'd already been developed by others and that we were now working on. It was like a tiny gap in a fence but a gap nonetheless. It meant the so-called secured, unhackable software could, in theory, be breached. We reported it and we were assured it was going to be repaired. Then a week before the contracts were to be signed, a rival company from India appeared and undercut us with a cheaper tender. We pushed back until we price matched them, but when they did it again, it was all over. We'd have been operating at a massive loss. So the government gave them the contract. We were sure the Indians couldn't offer a better product than us, and we were right. Because when we reverse-engineered their software, it was identical to ours. They'd stolen our work, and the only place they could've got it from was inside the government."

"Then why didn't you sue for copyright infringement?"

"Vital sections of our paperwork for our patent applications had 'gone missing' once they reached the Intellectual Property Authority. By the time we found out, it was too late. The Indians had fast-track patented our work.

Every international lawyer we approached told us we had no chance of winning litigation or compensation."

"And your dad's business?"

"Within six months, the shareholders demanded it went into administration, and the workforce was made redundant. Most of our staff lived in and around villages near to the plant, and within a handful of years those areas became desolate. People were forced to move away to find work, house prices dropped so those who stayed were in negative equity, there were rises in alcoholism and even suicides. Some of these people had worked for Dad and his father all their lives. And my dad blamed himself for it all. The guilt and stress hit him so hard that he had a stroke, and within the year he died of complications from pneumonia."

Noah paused to reach for a bottle on the floor. He unscrewed the cap and offered it to Libby. The dust in the room was making her throat scratchy, but she declined.

"What happened hit my brother harder than it did me," he continued. "We were both close to Dad, but Alex was the firstborn and a chip off the old block. I watched him sink into a deeper and deeper depression. He'd been diagnosed as bipolar as a teenager and he stopped taking his prescribed drugs and started self-medicating. He was unstable; he became bitter and angry and would lose his temper over nothing. Several times he was arrested for fighting and ended up behind bars for a few months. Then, on his release, he vanished. We couldn't find him; he wasn't at his flat, he didn't answer his phone or reply to our messages. When the police couldn't locate him either, we began to fear the worst. But as suddenly as he went, he reappeared."

In spite of herself, Libby was being drawn into Noah's story. "Where had he been?" she asked.

"He wouldn't tell me, but there was something different about him. It wasn't just that he was sober or back on his meds; it was that he'd developed a focus I'd not seen in him for a long time. Eventually he admitted he'd been spending time with a group of what he called 'like-minded people.' It sounded like he'd joined a cult or something, but it was a community of hackers he'd found hiding on the dark web. Alex had joined an organisation whose goal was to wreck the British driverless-car industry. He learned we weren't the only company the government shafted over cheaper foreign tenders. There were at least a dozen businesses that played an early part in the Road Revolution that also had their products stolen from right under their noses thanks to patent tampering and theft. Alex was encouraged to join and find a way to work together to bring the industry to its knees and create awareness of what they'd been doing to home-grown businesses. And he begged me to become involved."

"And you said yes."

"No, not at first. Like Alex, I resented what they did to Dad's business, but I couldn't afford to drop everything and take on his crusade. Steph and I had Gracie by then, and they were my priorities."

"Then what made you change your mind?"

"The day my family was killed by a Level Five driverless car. No one would tell us why my girls died, only that the inquest jury found them to be at fault. It didn't even recommend reviewing the software."

"So Alex suggested the hijacking as a way to get revenge?"

Noah allowed the question to hang in the air for a moment before answering.

"No, Libby. That was all my idea."

CHAPTER 66

L ibby's body stiffened, her anger towards Noah intensifying. For the briefest of moments, she had understood his bitterness towards the government for what it had done to his family business and his frustration at the blame given to his mother and wife for the accident that killed them. But after admitting the hijacking was his idea, her sympathy for him evaporated.

Noah must have sensed the drop in temperature between them as he became ill at ease, rubbing the palms of his hands against his face and shaking his head.

"You have to let me explain," he began. "At first, the plan was to cripple the cars. All vehicles—no matter what make or model—share some software which lets them communicate within one another, like warning each other if there's traffic or roadworks ahead. Because we had an input into that programming, we knew how to find our way back in and go straight to these sensors.

"Alex and the others were going to install a rogue piece of coding into the verification software. That meant we could access any model of any Level Five car's source code and infect it with a virus so that it obeyed our commands. By making one car grind to a halt with a fictitious problem, it would spread, and thousands upon thousands would do the same. And by the time the hack was discovered and rectified, the damage would be done. It wouldn't last long, but long enough to bring Britain to a standstill and make the industry a laughing stock."

"Then what changed?" Libby asked. "How did it become mass murder?"

"Once inside the software, Alex discovered that cars read our National Identity Cards and any technology we carried. And that's when we learned what really happened to my girls. They'd been sacrificed because the Passenger whose car hit them was a pilot in the Royal Air Force and protected by AI. His service to his country meant his life was worth more than my family's."

Noah awaited Libby's reaction, but she continued to take him in with the same caution. "My hatred for everything and everyone to do with those cars consumed me. Their impact was just so far-reaching. Even afterwards, my little girl died because she couldn't get the liver she needed because fewer accidents in safer cars means fewer organ donors."

"You can't punish people for not dying!" Libby interrupted. "That's crazy."

"I know, but that demonstrates where my head was at back then. As was believing that crippling the cars wasn't going to make a big enough impact. I decided our hack *had* to extend beyond a three-day news cycle. It needed to be an event everyone would remember watching for the rest of their lives. A hijack. I told Alex we should take complete control of a handful of cars and hold them to ransom, threatening to kill the Passengers if the government didn't admit to what it was doing. And we'd make the inquest jury do what AI did—choose a survivor based only upon the biased information we fed it. But at no time was anyone supposed to get hurt." Libby cocked her head in disbelief. "I promise you that I thought we were only going to whip up a frenzy against these 'unhackable' cars. Then everything changed the night I met you."

"Me?"

"I must have watched the footage of the day my girls died a hundred times until I knew it off by heart. I counted how many footsteps it took for you to get from one to the other, how long you spent with my mum and Steph and how you tried to comfort them. Seeing your kindness and how much the deaths of people you didn't know affected you was the moment I knew I wanted you on the jury. But then when we met in Manchester, you were the first person I'd spoken to in I can't remember how long who wasn't living inside the same toxic bubble as me. And I felt a connection to you every bit as much as you did to me in our kiss. You woke me up; you reminded me who I really was and made me understand I could accomplish everything I wanted to without threatening to hurt anyone. But trying to convince Alex and the others I'd had a change of heart was impossible. Like that other juror Matthew explained to you, mob mentality makes people braver when they're together."

"You should have fought harder," Libby dismissed.

"I did."

"You should have made them understand it was wrong."

"I tried."

"Then why didn't they listen?"

"Because by then we had spent eighteen months planning the hijack and nobody was willing to back down! And I was scared at how out of control it might become if I didn't go along with it. I thought if I remained a part of it, I could at least rein them in if I needed to."

"And how did that work out for you?" Libby deadpanned.

Noah looked to the ground. "I never imagined the extremes they'd take it to."

"Where were you on that day? Because you weren't in the car we were watching."

"For the actual-time images, I was in a stationary car in a barn in the west of Ireland, surrounded by green screens. They used live footage from the other car as a backdrop to make it look as if I was on those roads. My reaction to Victor's death was a hundred per cent genuine horror, along with me fighting to try and get out of the car they had me locked in. They cut my sound and looped older footage so you couldn't hear me begging them to stop and threatening to tell the viewers everything. They warned me if I didn't act along, they'd kill all the Passengers—and you. I couldn't let them do that. And of course I had no idea they were going to make cars across the country collide."

"Where have you been hiding?"

"Various countries. I've only ever met half a dozen of those involved. They arranged safe houses in places with no extradition treaties with the UK. As long as I keep my head down, don't bring attention to myself, or cause their governments any trouble, they'll continue to shelter me. But I have no security. They can throw me to the wolves anytime they like."

"And your brother?"

"I have no idea. I haven't been able to contact him since the day of the hijack."

Libby shut her eyes tightly as she tried to digest Noah's version of events. She couldn't deny he made a compelling case, and his body language indicated a man tormented by remorse. "Why now?" she asked. "Why did you come and find me?"

"I don't care what the rest of the world thinks of me; I only care about you. I need you to know the way I was with you that night in Manchester and as a Passenger was the real me, not the me you've spent the last six months doubting."

"*Doubting?*" she repeated, raising her brow. "That's one hell of an under-statement. You manipulated me, and you used my brother's death to do it. You took the single worst moment of my life and used Nicky to make me buy into your lies. Isn't that who you really are?"

"It's not, I promise. Let me prove it to you. Come away with me."

Libby thought she had misheard. "What?"

"I have contacts who can get us anywhere in the world we want to be. Then we can get to know one another properly away from all of this. We can start again."

Libby's laugh took her as much by surprise as it did Noah. "Are you being serious? Why would I do that?"

"Because you know as well as I do, despite everything, there is still something between us. It's something I've only ever felt once before, with my wife. And I have to see where it goes. You can't deny that you still have an attraction to me. Despite your bravado and all you think you know about me, you've still come here because there's a part of you that wants to believe the man you have feelings for is not a bad person."

"This is ridiculous," said Libby, shaking her head vigorously. "I have a life, I have a new purpose, I'm doing well, I'm making changes in the world. Why would I give all of that up for a man whose friends murdered more than a thousand people? You're mad."

"Libby, I swear to God I didn't want it to happen. And I'll spend the rest of my life trying to put things right if you let me. You can help me to make up for the terrible things that evolved from my idea."

Libby rose to her feet and began pacing the room. "How can I?" she asked. "Even if you're telling the truth, you were still the catalyst. If you really do regret what happened, why don't you hand yourself in to the police? Explain to them everything you've told me tonight. Prove to me in more than words that you are the man I first thought you were."

Noah ran his hands through his hair and then clasped them together as if in prayer. "I can't, Libby," he pleaded. "They will throw everything they can at me, and some. I have only a few names I can give them, no details of where to find anyone, no proof that I didn't orchestrate the whole thing. I can do more good on the outside than I can behind bars. Yes, I know there will be people who'll feel they've got justice if they see me locked up, but with your help, I can offer so much more as a free man."

Noah moved towards her for a second time, and again, she backed away.

"What about if I recorded my confession and made it public once we reach wherever we're going to?" he offered. "Would that help change your mind?"

"Jude . . ." she began, then corrected herself. "Noah, are you listening to yourself? We'd be constantly looking over our shoulders, we'd never be able to rest. I can't, I won't, live my life like that. I want the things normal people want and none of this . . . *none of it* . . . is normal."

"We can have everything we want, just under abnormal circumstances. And you can continue your campaign work with proper funding behind you and an extended global reach. You can even start a charity under your brother's name to help people with mental health issues if you like—I can access money to allow all of that to happen. I'm offering you the world, Libby, and I'm throwing myself in with the bargain. The real me. Please, I'm begging you to consider it."

Libby's eyes brimmed with tears before she wiped them away with her cuff. "You know what really hurts? That you made a fool of me . . . that I let down my guard and you made me believe that you were something you were not. How can I ever get over the lies and the manipulation? If you were me, could you?"

"I have risked so much to be here, doesn't that tell you something?"

Libby couldn't deny that it did. She remained motionless and studied Noah with unwavering attention. His eyes appeared filled with hope and desperation. If the man in front of her had been the man she had met in Manchester, she would have believed him. But this was Noah, and she didn't know him any more than she did a stranger. Yet, try as she might, she couldn't deny something was pulling him towards her, an invisible magnet that made her want to go against her rationale and believe him.

"How can I ever forgive you for what happened?" she asked. "We have everything—and I mean *everything*—going against us."

"We can work through it, I know we can. Just say you'll give me a chance. Me appearing out of nowhere, making you this offer . . . I know what I'm asking you is utterly insane; I'm one hundred per cent aware of that. But I was willing to give up my freedom to come here because of what I'm sure is between us."

A trickle of sweat made its way from the nape of Libby's neck and down her spine. She refused to let her gaze leave Noah's until she was ready to answer him.

Then, almost imperceptibly, she began to nod her head. In response, Noah's eyes opened wide and his face lit up.

"Really?" he asked. "Are you sure?"

"Yes," she said quietly. "But we have to leave now before I come to my senses."

This time when Noah approached her, Libby didn't recoil. She allowed him to throw his arms around her and draw her in close to his chest. As he leaned in to kiss her, Libby closed her eyes and forgot everything that had gone before it. For a moment, she was back in the pub garden a year ago, surrounded by the creamy glow of lanterns hanging from the trees. A stranger's lips were locked upon hers, and she breathed in the scent of his cologne and his warm skin. Back then, it was the start of a new chapter, she had thought; something inside her was awakening. The memory was fleeting, and when it left, she pulled away from him.

"Where will we go first?" she asked.

"I know people who can get us out of the country tonight."

"But I need my passport, what about my job, my house, my family, my friends—how will I explain to them?"

"We will work it all out as we go along, I promise." Noah grinned, and he entwined his fingers around hers as he made for the door.

"Don't forget your phone," she said, pointing towards the table where he'd been sitting.

"Do you see the effect you have on me?" he said as he moved towards his device.

"Can I ask you one more question?" Libby said suddenly.

"Anything."

"What really happened to Noah Harris after his family died?"

Libby watched as the man in front of her ground to a halt. He remained with his back to her. "I don't understand?" he asked. His tone suggested otherwise.

"I was there, at his family's funeral. I couldn't take my eyes off Noah as he stood at the altar, having to be physically propped up by his friends because he was so racked with grief. I watched him place a white rose on each of their coffins, then follow the undertakers out to their cars before they continued to the crematorium for a private service. For a second, his and my eyes locked. The image of that poor, desperate man will never leave me. And you are most definitely not Noah Harris. Are you?"

CHAPTER 67

All that could be heard in the space between Libby and the man she had once been infatuated with was her escalating heartbeat. "You're Noah's brother Alex, aren't you?" His answer came with his silence.

There was no better time for her to make her escape, and the Libby of old would have run hell for leather out of the door for help. But Alex hadn't met the post-hijack version of Libby Dixon, the resolute, steadfast woman who was determined to see this confrontation through to the bitter end. And now that she had the upper hand, she stood her ground.

"Noah is dead, isn't he?" Libby continued. "It was your brother who changed his mind and didn't want to go through with the plan to hijack the Passengers. You were the one who took it to another level and killed all those people."

Alex paused for a moment before he replied. "Be careful what you say, Libby. The next words to leave your mouth could change the course of everything."

But Libby had no intention of paying his thinly veiled threat any heed. "If I hadn't seen Noah at the funeral, I'd have believed you were him. And especially in the way you were looking at Stephenie and Gracie in those photos and videos. That's because you were in love with them, weren't you? Noah might have been your brother, but your heart was with Stephenie. And you weren't looking at her daughter like a caring uncle, but as a proud dad."

Libby could just about detect Alex nodding his head. "When they died, it was your grief that made you take such extreme measures to get your revenge, not Noah's."

"Noah was weak," Alex replied. "He didn't have the guts to do what was necessary or to see it through to the end. He didn't love Steph in the way she deserved; he didn't treat her with respect, yet she wouldn't give up on him. Not even when she discovered how often he slept around. It was me who wiped away her tears, me who told her she could do better, and it was me who she turned to to feel loved again. She even admitted to me that she chose the wrong brother. But when she became pregnant with our daughter, she chose Noah over me. I was the idiot who promised to back off and give them a chance because I was convinced that, one day, she'd pick me over him. But that day never came."

"I don't remember seeing you at the funeral with the rest of their family."

"I didn't go. I was too cut up by what happened, not like my brother. He didn't grieve for them like I did. Three months hadn't even passed before he was uploading his picture onto hook-up apps."

Libby watched his face became embittered by the memory. His fingers twitched as he became more agitated.

"Did Noah ever support your plan?"

"At first. In fact, he wanted it to be even more ambitious and have more cars collide after the Passengers came to a halt. But typical of him, he was all talk and then had second thoughts. By then, there were too many people spread across the world to make it stop. There was an army of dedicated men and women, factions and cells, who were risking everything to reach our goal. After a year and a half in the making, none of us were willing to back down just because of one man. Being his brother it was down to me to make him see sense, but he wouldn't listen. It was as if Steph, Gracie, and our mum's lives hadn't been worth anything to him. We argued, he threatened to blow the lid off our plan, so he gave me no choice but to protect the programme."

Alex finally turned to face Libby, his expression earnest. "Everything I said about you and me was true, and I want us to make it work. I can create a future for us; all you need to do is take a leap of faith. Even now, even after what you know, you can't turn off what you're feeling for me. We are matched, and I think deep down you know that. Come away with me."

A shiver ran through Libby's body, and she shook her head at the notion that they were destined to be with each other. "I don't believe we're matched," she sneered. "It's another one of your lies. You lied to me as Jude and you lied to me as Noah. What on earth makes you think I'm going to believe you now? Besides, perhaps you should have taken your own advice."

"About what?"

"When you told me earlier that I hadn't thought to question what I was seeing when I assumed you were standing with those men at the bar. Well, neither did you when you thought I only had a knife in my pocket. I've activated an alarm button and tracking device installed by the police on my phone that's broadcasting everything we've said to them." Alex's eyes narrowed to slits. "Of all that you've told me," Libby continued, "the only part I believe is that you felt a connection between us. I did too. Only what I felt wasn't real, because that man doesn't exist. And that, amongst a million other reasons, is why I will never go any further than this room with you. I would rather end up like your brother than be with you."

As quick as a flash, Alex flew towards her, but Libby was too speedy for him. She turned and ran towards the door, pulling the knife out of her pocket and clenching it in her hand as she reached for the handle. She twisted it and yanked it, but it wouldn't budge.

Panicking, she turned quickly and waved the weapon in front of her, the blade catching the light of the lamp and glinting as Alex approached her. She watched him hold up a key fob. "There's an automatic lock on the door that's only opened by this," he snarled. "You aren't going anywhere."

Libby wanted to scream and cry for help, but she held firm, the knife cutting through the air again and again, from left to right, back and forth as Alex ducked and weaved like a boxer in the ring.

"We can do this all night if you like," he said. "But only one of us is getting out of here."

"The police are probably outside already," said Libby in desperation. "You might as well give up, Alex, it's over."

"Whatever happens to me, I promise you one thing, Libby. Should you

317

survive this, you will never be free. There are a lot of us out there, and we are always going to be watching you, ready to bring you—and everyone you love—down if we need to. Think about the headlines we will make over killing you."

Suddenly, the knife made contact with Alex's hand, slicing the back of it. He winced and took a step backwards, trying to establish in the lamplight the severity of the wound. "You've just made the worst decision of your life," he said, and clenched his fists. Libby took a deep breath and, mustering up all her strength, thrust the knife in front of her one more time. She missed. Alex managed to grab her wrist and dig his fingers deeply into her ligaments so the knife fell into his hand.

They stood facing each other as he gave her one last tight-lipped smile. "I'm sorry it's come to this, I really am," he muttered.

But as he launched himself towards her, she saw a tiny red dot appear on his neck. And with his arm pulled back and the knife ready to push into her, a bullet shattered the glass in the door and hit him squarely in the throat.

PART FOUR

TWO YEARS LATER

CHAPTER 68

UKToday.co.uk

**+LIVE / GOVERNMENT BACKS REINTRODUCTION
OF DRIVERLESS CARS**

Controversial autonomous vehicles will be permitted to return to British roads
within the next three years.

Prime Minister Nicholas McDermott will assure the public in a statement
later today that driverless vehicles are now "safe" and precautions have been
taken to ensure "no further hacks are possible."

The ten-year deadline for all cars on UK roads to be autonomous has also
been scrapped.

"We need to win back the public's trust," a government source said ahead of
the announcement. "And that will be a gradual process."

Full story to follow . . .

Libby made her way slowly down the staircase, careful not to trip over the
hem of her dress.

She studied her reflection in the full-length porch mirror one last time.
With the aid of an arrangement of pins and a can of extra-strength spray,
her hair had remained in place since leaving the stylist earlier that morning.
And after performing make-up duties and helping Libby into the dress, Nia
left the house and would greet her later at the location.

"Are you coming?" Libby shouted, directing her voice back up the stairs.

"I'll be there in a minute," a faint male voice replied. "Just trying to find
my other cufflink."

"It's me who's supposed to be late on our wedding day, not you."

"You said you didn't go in for all that traditional stuff, otherwise we
wouldn't have been together this morning?"

"It's a bride's prerogative to change her mind."

"Found it." As Matthew Nelson appeared at the top of the stairs, Libby returned to the lounge, where the couple took in each other's appearance for the first time since they'd dressed in their wedding outfits. Smiles spread across both of their faces.

"You scrub up well, Miss Dixon," Matthew said, beaming. Once he reached the lounge, he took her hand in his.

"You don't look so bad yourself, Dr. Nelson."

"Have you got everything?"

He patted the pocket of his baby-blue suit jacket. "I have the rings, the licence, and the proof of ID." Matthew placed his hands on her cheeks and kissed her lips.

"Don't smudge my lipstick," Libby teased. "We'll have the rest of our lives for that once you've made an honest woman of me."

"Can you believe we are actually doing this?"

Libby shook her head. "Not considering the circumstances in which we met."

"I fancied you from the moment you walked into the inquest room."

"I know that now. But at the time, you disguised it very, very well."

"Well, I could hardly ask you out for coffee while on jury duty, could I? I was going to wait until the end of the week before approaching you."

"I would've said no," she teased. "I thought you were a pompous prick."

"Of which you remind me frequently. And now?"

"And now I think you're a loveable pompous prick."

Matthew's smart watch buzzed and he glanced at the moving images on the face. "The car is outside. So, shall we go and do this? They were definitely just twinges you felt and not contractions?"

"Definitely," she replied, and rubbed her swollen stomach.

Matthew leaned forward to kiss her belly and speak to their unborn baby. "As much as we're looking forward to meeting you, you need to stay in there a few more weeks. We don't want to see you until then and especially not today."

"Yes, Dad," Libby replied on their child's behalf.

When Libby had purchased her strapless ivory column dress following her acceptance of Matthew's proposal, she wasn't aware she was pregnant.

Now, with five weeks left until the due date, she had frequently returned to the bridal gown shop for it to be let out.

Matthew entwined his arm with his wife-to-be's. "Ready?" he asked, and Libby nodded.

"Let's go then."

Once outside the home they had bought together earlier that year, they saw the awaiting vintage black polished Mercedes-Benz on the driveway. Libby appreciated it was the model she had booked, an old-fashioned Level One car, and that the hire car company had attached ivory ribbons from the wing mirrors stretching to the grille. A chauffeur in a smart grey suit appeared and opened the rear door for her. She climbed inside, careful not to crease her dress. Then once Matthew joined her, she settled into her seat as the car began its journey from their home in Hove towards Brighton's register office.

Many of Libby's friends admitted to being bags of nerves before they married, but she hadn't shared their fears. She knew instinctively that they belonged together, even following Alex Harris's claims they were DNA matched. When Commander Riley had debriefed her after Alex's death, he'd revealed that during a digital forensic search of his phone, an email confirmed Alex had received the test results, and he asked if she wanted to know the outcome.

Libby shook her head. As much as she believed in the truth, this time, it would serve no positive purpose in her life. Now, on her wedding day, she was never more convinced she had made the correct decision. Sometimes ignorance could be bliss. Test or no test, Matthew was Mr. Right.

Recognising that had come out of the blue. When the story of her confrontation with Alex reached the news wires, the death of the man behind the hacking collective had made international headlines. Days later, Matthew was the only member of the jury to have checked up on her welfare.

Email exchanges became text messages, text messages became video calls, and it wasn't long before she realised he was nothing like the man she had served with on that infamous jury. Then later, when he was attending a medical conference in Birmingham, she accepted his invitation to dinner, and Libby realised there was more to it than a friendship. It was only as they sat opposite each other sharing tapas that she recalled how on the day of the hijacking, Matthew had shown her more attention than she realised at the time. He had stood up to Jack Larsson on her behalf and comforted her when Bilquis's car was detonated.

Two more dates followed before Matthew kissed her. Within five months, she had thrown caution to the wind, put her home in Birmingham up for rental, and moved three hours to the south coast, where they bought their first home together.

It was far enough from London to afford them privacy but comfortably commutable for her media commitments. Libby's work had begun to quieten following Alex's death and the release of the results of the police investigation into the manipulated software. With Jack Larsson in the midst of a very public trial and Level Five software now available for scrutiny by licenced officials and independent bodies, Libby was finally beginning to realise the normality she craved. Once the baby was born, she would resign as spokesperson and her new job as a mother could begin. Eventually, she hoped to return to nursing.

Despite the love and safety her new life afforded her, there were occasions when Libby dwelled on the past. Alex's face appeared to her at the most random of times. She once saw him in the face of a stranger in a dental surgery waiting room, other times as she closed her eyes and sank into a deep bath. On occasion he appeared in her dreams, specifically the last moments of their violent confrontation. She relived spotting that tiny red light shining on his Adam's apple, the whoosh of the police sniper's bullet that shattered the glass and tore through this throat, and the sound of his panicked hand slapping against the gaping wound as if it might stem the blood flow. She would dream how, after police smashed the shop door behind her and she was pulled to safety, from the opposite side of the road she couldn't stop from staring wide-eyed at paramedics as they attempted to resuscitate him. She could only breathe again when they signalled that he was unable to do the same.

The circumstances behind the death of the real Noah Harris would likely never be known, but investigators confirmed his decomposed body had been discovered in woodland close to a barn in the west of Ireland.

A coroner ruled he was likely suffocated at around the same time period as the hacking, not months earlier as Alex had suggested. Inside the barn was the vehicle used to film the interior shots of "Jude" throughout the hijack.

Elsewhere, slowly and surely, arrests and charges were being made around the world as the international investigation began to penetrate the hacking collective. Sometimes Alex's words returned to haunt her, specifically the threat that she would never be a free woman and that the hacking collective would always be watching her, biding their time, ready to strike when she least expected it. But she knew that she could not live under the shadow of "coulds" and "mights," or that would be no life at all.

Today, however, was not a day to dwell on the past or to be asking questions she would never hear answers to. Libby snapped herself back into the present and spread her fingers, holding them up to the sunlight coming in through the passenger window. She took in her diamond engagement ring, twisting it around and around, barely able to wait until Matthew slipped a wedding ring onto the same finger.

Outside, her attention was drawn beyond the expanse of beach and towards the rhythmic pulse of the sea. In the sun's winter gaze, it had transformed from its usual dark blue to white with flecks of silver. Having spent much of her life living in the landlocked Midlands, she would never take for granted their proximity to the coast.

She closed her eyes and imagined how it might look to see her brother Nicky waiting at the register office with their parents to watch his little sister get married. Now, when she thought of him, she didn't feel his pain or shed a tear. Instead, she smiled, grateful for the time they had together instead of sad for the years they had apart.

Libby opened her eyes when she felt Matthew entwining his fingers within hers.

"Are you okay?" he asked. "I lost you there for a moment."

"I'm good," she replied, and squeezed his hand in return. She knew that, with him, she would never be lost again.

The sound of a bell ringing from Matthew's watch caught their attention.

"It's nothing important, just a news alert," he said. "It can wait." However, it was rapidly followed by the sound of a text alert, then many, many more.

"What's going on?" Libby asked as Matthew read the screen. His face fell and he shook his head. "You're not going to believe this," he said.

"Believe what?" she replied as he moved his wrist towards her, her eyes widening in disbelief as she scanned the messages. When she had finished, she stared at Matthew.

"How the hell has he got away with it?"

NOT GUILTY—JACK LARSSON ACQUITTED OF ALL CHARGES

- Senior government official's five-month trial comes to an end at the Old Bailey.
- Jury clears ex-MP of four charges, including misuse of government material, tampering with official secrets, misuse of public office and conduct prejudicial.
- If found guilty, Mr. Larsson would have faced 18 years behind bars.

Jack Larsson's stance was defiant at the top of a set of stone steps. His arms were folded across his chest, his eyes filled with steely resolve. The corners of his mouth lifted but stopped short of a smile.

He was flanked by half a dozen burly bodyguards in dark suits, three male and three female. Each wore smart glasses and earpieces. Their eyes constantly scanned the faces before them to identify potential threats to the most talked-about former government minister in the country.

Behind them, stone arches surrounded the doors they had used to exit London's Old Bailey, the 130-year-old central criminal court of England and Wales. For five long months, Jack had spent each weekday inside that building, listening intently as the prosecution attempted to destroy his reputation while his defence team debunked their allegations. Sometimes, with little else to do, he caught himself from the dock where he sat, staring at the twelve-strong jury of his peers—seven men and five women. He held them in little regard. They were no closer to being his peers than he was to being the first man on Mars. He was better than all of them.

To his left and right and beyond the black iron railings separating the steps from the pavement, protesters were held back by police officers. More were across the road and penned in behind temporary metal barricades. They were hurling abuse at him, but he couldn't make out the specifics of their chants. He noted they weren't holding aloft the placards they'd brought with them most mornings. Slogans such as "MP—Murderer of Parliament" or images of his face upon Adolf Hitler's body were commonplace, and their creativity quietly amused him. But today, they hadn't been prepared for a "not guilty" verdict. The only person who had was Jack.

Photographers snapped frantically as dozens of journalists thrust recording devices towards him and fired questions over one another. But Jack's lips were sealed as he surveyed the vermin who had tried to crucify him in a trial by media. In the eyes of the law, he was an innocent man, and from this day forward, they had best remind themselves of the fact, or he wouldn't hesitate to take legal action.

Jack's barrister, Barnaby Skuse, stepped in front of him before giving him a nod. Jack reciprocated, indicating he was ready. Barnaby was dressed in a tailored suit and not the black gown and white horsehair wig Jack had grown accustomed to seeing him in inside the courtroom. He swept his grey fringe across his forehead and held a piece of A4 paper in his hands. Above typed words was Jack's family crest of arms: a shield containing a dragon, a sword, and a clenched fist. Only Jack knew that no such crest had existed before he created it.

Barnaby cleared his throat before he began to speak in a rich, stentorian tone. "I have a statement to make on behalf of my client Mr. Jack Larsson," he said. "Today, justice has been served. A jury has concluded there is no proof alleged 'social cleansing' ever took place or that Mr. Larsson was involved in any illegal activity. Any evidence put forward to the contrary by the prosecution was based on tampered or fabricated software developed by the organisation known as the Hacking Collective. While Mr. Larsson has accepted that discussions did take place on prioritising certain occupations in the event of potentially fatal accidents, he does not believe any such software was activated or that any member of the government past or present sanctioned it. What viewers heard him deliberating about on-camera was nothing more than speculative and hypothetical. Mr. Larsson would like to thank the jurors for having the common sense to support him. He will now be taking some time to consider his options but looks forward to making his return to central government as an innocent man. He will not be making any further comments. Thank you."

As Mr. Skuse folded up the paper and slipped it inside his jacket pocket, Jack took a moment to savour his victory and the attention of the cameras. They were soon drowned out by journalists competing to try to get just one sound bite from the MP himself. But Jack had no intention of adding to his brief's statement and allowed the smile he had suppressed for so long to spread across his face. He knew his triumph was being broadcast live on every news channel and news website. And tomorrow, his victory would be the headline of all the daily newspapers.

He waited for his team of bodyguards to clear a path through the journalists as three Land Rovers with blacked-out windows pulled up against the kerb with military precision. Jack climbed into the rear of the central vehicle along with one other bodyguard, who sat by the driver. His other security operatives entered the cars in front and behind before all three sped away along the road, leaving the chaos in the distance.

Inside the car, Jack remained in silence, waiting for the adrenaline rush to dissolve. He glanced out from the window as he travelled along Embankment and passed the Palace of Westminster, where so much of his working life had been spent. His mind drifted back to his first day there as an MP, fraught with nerves and full of the best of intentions. His only motivation was to represent the constituents who had voted him as their representative.

But somewhere along the line, his need to do good for the working classes was replaced by greed and ambition. His hunger for the same wealth as the ruling classes who surrounded him made him lose sight of everything else. Instead of fighting against them, he became one of them. On many an occasion over the years, a niggling voice in the back of his mind questioned whether casting aside his principles had been worth it. And each time the answer was yes, it had been.

The car travelled through Richmond and Twickenham before Jack saw his first road sign for Heathrow Airport. The terms of his bail conditions meant that for the last two years, he had been forbidden from leaving the country. Now, he was eagerly anticipating the solitude of a private booth in

British Airways' first-class lounge before his fourteen-hour flight. Jack's flight to China was scheduled for later that evening, so he had plenty of time to kill. He had already booked his massage, manicure, and haircut long before the jury reached its verdict. After a week in the Far East, he would fly to an exclusive resort in the Maldives and then the Seychelles, which would allow plenty of time to formulate his next move.

A vibrating from the phone in his pocket caught his attention, and he slipped an earbud inside his ear.

"Mr. Larsson, may I have your secure line code, please?" an assertive female voice began.

"Certainly," Jack replied, and read out a memorised list of numbers and letters.

"Thank you. I have the deputy prime minister on the line for you. Please hold."

While he waited, Jack pressed a button on his door, and a glass partition rose, making the rear of the vehicle completely soundproof. Then he took a swig of whiskey from a hip flask stored inside the armrest until the voice of Diane Cline appeared.

"Well, well, well," she began. "Somebody has friends in high places."

Jack let out a spurious laugh. "I had no doubt that justice would prevail in the end."

"You were probably in the minority there. Regardless, I wanted to congratulate you."

"What you mean is that you want to know what I plan to do next." Jack took another sip from his flask.

"Well, it would be inaccurate to say the thought hadn't crossed my mind. The PM heard you mention your imminent return to politics."

"I didn't use the word 'imminent' but yes, I think I've spent long enough on the sidelines, don't you?"

"Are we perhaps being a little hasty?"

"We or me?"

"You. For your sake, it may be more prudent in the long run to allow some time for recent events to blow over."

"The public has a short memory."

"Don't fool yourself, Jack. Not for something of this gravitas. They still require their pound of flesh. And they're going to feel cheated if they can't get it from you."

Jack shook his head. "I'm sure my constituents will be on my side."

"They're not your constituents anymore though, are they? We had to replace you and call a by-election."

"And you didn't waste much time doing that, if I recall correctly."

"You left us with no choice."

Jack felt his patience wearing thin. "*I* left you no choice?"

"I meant the situation left us with no choice."

"Your knee-jerk reaction meant you lost my seat to the opposition."

"It was stained. Mother Teresa couldn't have stopped that bloody seat from going to the opposition."

"Do I have to remind you, Diane, of the discussion we had some time ago in which I was told that upon my exoneration, I would be fast-tracked back into a seat at the table? And I don't mean somewhere at the back of the room or on the periphery, but at the *actual* table. If that means removing someone else and having me run in some little two-bit safe seat, then it is yet another sacrifice I am willing to make for the good of the party. That is what I am owed."

"That wasn't a decision that was set in stone. You were never promised anything. All I am suggesting is that we let sleeping dogs lie for the time being. It might not be the best time for us to announce your return to politics so soon after your trial."

"At which I was acquitted."

"Yes, but at what cost? A lot of sensitive information was exposed in that process, which we would rather have kept quiet. Like it or not, your defence has done potentially irreparable damage to the party."

Jack balled his fists and resisted the urge to shout down the telephone. "Surely you didn't expect me to be your patsy in all of this? To spend the next eighteen years of my life behind bars for something you, our current PM, and others in the inner circle sanctioned? If you did, then you don't know me at all. You only agreed to my return when you thought I was going to be found guilty, didn't you? Well, I'm sorry to disappoint, but Jack Larsson doesn't go down without a fight. And certainly not without taking others with me."

"Jack, perhaps we should speak another time when you are a little less . . . *emotional*?"

"Or perhaps when you are ready to stop being a sanctimonious bitch?"

Instantly, he regretted his choice of words, but he could only be pushed so far. They reached an awkward stalemate.

"I have recordings," Jack said soberly.

Diane's tone was stern. "Perhaps you should self-censor now before you say something you might regret."

But Jack knew that it was too late. He had shown his hand and he had nothing left to lose. "I have names, Diane. I have footage, satellite images, software programmes, dates, locations, witnesses. I have everything I need at my disposal to bring this government to its knees."

"I'd think carefully about what you are about to do next."

"As should you," Jack replied, then removed his earpiece and hung up.

He drained the flask of whiskey and then threw it to the floor. *How dare she speak to me like that?* he thought. *The party has no right to turn their back on me after all I've sacrificed for it.* If they didn't allow him back into the fold, they would suffer.

It wasn't just the position that Jack craved; it was also the opportunity that came with it to use his power to line his own pockets. Despite the Hacker's best efforts to bleed his accounts dry, Jack had been prepared. What the Hacker had encouraged the public to plunder amounted to less than a fifth of his overall wealth. The rest of his £70 million fortune was squirrelled away by asset management companies and venture capitalists in safe harbours, including offshore renegade tax havens, hedge funds, trusts and shell companies and opaque holding firms. He remained an ultra-high-net-worth individual.

The majority of Jack's fortune had been made at the beginning of the Road Revolution through investing in firms involved in vehicle production and offshoot industries. It was an illegal conflict of interest that, if discovered and exposed, would result in a lifelong ban from politics and a lengthy custodial sentence. His unique position in driving the bill through Parliament and convincing the public that autonomous vehicles were a safe bet enabled him to cherry-pick companies to invest in. Asphalt producers, manufacturers of electronic road signs and opaque glass moulding, graphene engineers, and makers of sonar and lidar software—his fingers were in many pies.

But their earning capacity was not infinite, and at some point in the future, his dividends would decline. Jack had to identify a new income source that would bolster his already considerable fortune. It was Noah Harris and his brother Alex who gave him the idea.

They worked for an average-sized, family-run firm in the Midlands that one of Jack's shell companies held a large stake in. Jack's department was about to award it a contract for millions to develop software and cameras for emergency services vehicles. But when it came to Jack's attention that the back door used by his operatives to manipulate AI had been discovered by the Harris brothers, he identified an opportunity.

They were not aware of its purpose, only that it existed and might provide an opportunity for hacking. But instead of sealing it up permanently, what if it were left for someone else to discover further down the line? Jack reasoned. After so many promises had been made as to how impenetrable the AI was, what impact might a hack have on the Road Revolution? The public's trust would be lost. However, they would still need to use automobiles, so it stood to reason they would return to what they knew and trusted—Level One, Two, and Three vehicles that they could control. Demand would soar.

It was a whole new potential revenue stream. Share prices in businesses providing the soon-to-be-outdated components were already sinking as the vehicles were slowly phased out, so Jack struck while the iron was hot and made his investments. A cosmetic patch was placed over the back door; meanwhile, to punish the Harris brothers for their discovery, he sold his shares in the firm and ensured their contract went abroad to India, which eventually forced their business's closure.

Then he sat back and waited for the inevitable.

The day itself and the extreme levels of death and destruction created by the Hackers took him by surprise. As did his discovery that the people behind it were the Harris brothers. He was almost proud of the tenacity they showed.

Jack took the accusations on the chin, allowing the government to think he was its scapegoat for social cleansing, but knowing fine well that when it came to trial, he had people who could pay off enough jurors to secure his freedom. Reputations were lost and rebuilt all the time, Jack told himself, and his was no exception.

Jack vowed he would not allow the ingratitude of the deputy prime minister to ruin today, the start of the next chapter in his life. "Music," he said aloud. "I need some Nina."

He scrolled through the entertainment system until he found the song that best reflected his mood. A moment later, Nina Simone's fluctuating timbre told of a new dawn, a new day, and a new life. It couldn't be more fitting a sentiment, he thought, and for a moment, his eyes began to brim with tears. He brushed them away before they could fall.

Jack only became aware his vehicle had reached the M4 when his driver indicated they were pulling over and they made their way towards Heathrow. His bodyguard caught Jack's eye when he tapped his finger to his ear. He watched as he nodded, then spoke to the driver. Jack turned down his music and used the intercom to talk. "Is there a problem, Marlon?" he asked.

Before Marlon could respond, Jack spotted the car ahead containing two other members of his security team pulling over to the side of the road. Jack's vehicle followed. "Marlon?" he repeated but there was no response. There must be a fault in the communication system, he thought. He pressed the button to make the partition go down but nothing happened. He knocked against the glass before remembering it was completely sound-proofed. Jack turned to see the third vehicle behind them also coming to a halt.

His brow furrowed as both his driver and bodyguard exited, leaving him alone inside the car as they approached their colleagues from both vehicles. Then, without turning around to look at Jack, his team began walking to the opposite side of the road. Jack reached to turn the door handle but it wouldn't budge.

Panic struck him like a bolt of lightning.

"What's happening?" he asked aloud. He banged on the window to no avail, and failed to get any signal on his phone. He watched his team climb into a parked white van and pull away. Then, as all three cars, now completely driverless, moved of their own accord, Jack felt utterly helpless.

He sat in the centre of the rear seats, staring at the car ahead, his worst fears realised. He was no longer in control of his destiny. Then, without warning, the vehicle ahead exploded into a ball of flames. Jack could scarcely believe his eyes. "No!" he gasped. His car indicated right, then slowly overtook the burning vehicle as casually as it might pass a cyclist. Jack pressed his face against the window and watched as red and orange flames leaped from the windows and licked the roof and bonnet as it slowly rolled to a halt. He turned quickly to look from the rear and watched as it disappeared into the distance.

"Good afternoon, Jack."

The voice that came through the speakers struck the fear of God into him. He recognised it instantly. It was the Hacker.

"It may have come to your attention that your vehicle is no longer under your management. From here on in, I am in charge of your destination."

Jack's response caught in his throat before he managed to release the words. "Who . . . are you?"

"I thought that might be obvious. We are who your barrister referred to throughout your trial as the Hacking Collective."

"What do you want from me?"

"That doesn't matter right now. The only thing you need to know at this point is that two hours and thirty minutes from now, it is highly likely that you will be dead."

The sour taste of vomit crept up the back of Jack's throat. Blood rose to the surface of his skin, making it feel as though he were burning, but it brought him out in a cold sweat.

Gradually the music returned, the volume becoming louder and louder as Jack desperately attempted to switch the entertainment system off and clear his head to formulate a plan. He jabbed at the screen but nothing happened, and the song he had chosen began again from the start.

But this time when Nina Simone sang of feeling good, Jack no longer shared her sentiment.

CHAPTER 70

BLABBERBOX))

Welcome to Blabberbox
Trending posts: 001

What's happening with this car? Submitted 1 minute ago

RayOfLight: Anyone watching Instagram TV? I swear to God that dodgy MP Larsson is being broadcast freaking out in the back of a car.

LANADOOM: Looks like him but it can't be, can it?

RayOfLight: FUCK! THE CAR IN FRONT OF HIM JUST BLEW UP!!!!!

LANADOOM: Bro, this can't be real, can it?

RayOfLight: DUDE DID YOU NOT JUST SEE WHAT HAPPENED? IT'S HAPPENING AGAIN!!!!! THIS IS GONNA BE AWESOME!

ACKNOWLEDGMENTS

The Passengers took much more research than any of my other books to date, and much of that was undertaken by my husband, John Russell. So first and foremost, thanks, JR, for all the effort you put into this. It would have taken much more time without your thoroughness and attention to detail. Thanks also go to my mum, Pam, for her continued support, and my dog, Oscar, who has appeared in every one of my books to date. Apologies for turning you from a border terrier into a Pomeranian this time, Oz.

I would also like to offer my huge thanks to the team at Ebury. To my editor and Chief Penguin Gillian Green for having faith in the story (even if you did reduce the unhappy-ever-afters); and to Little Penguin, Stephenie Naulls, for your constant creativity and bright ideas. Thanks also to everyone else who has worked on this book and *The One*, including Tess Henderson, Bethany Wood, Katie Seaman, Rae Shirvington, Alice Latham, and Donna Hillyer, plus everyone else who are too numerous to mention, but equally talented. And of course thanks to the former Big Penguin, Emily Yau, for the idea and for putting me on this crazy journey.

I'd like to offer a shout-out to my fellow writers Louise Beech, the Ena Sharples of the literary world, for being my sounding board, and Darren O'Sullivan for all the DMs over the last year. Thanks also to Cara Hunter, Randileigh Kennedy and Jo Edwards, CJ Skuse, and the ever-hilarious Claire Allen for the many distractions from writing that our tweets have given me.

ACKNOWLEDGMENTS

No book of mine would be the same without a character called Tracy Fenton. Tracy and the team at Facebook's THE Book Club have been there for me from the very start of my writing career. Thanks for staying the course on this amazing journey. Also thanks to Wendy Clarke and members of The Fiction Café, Bee Jones and Lost In A Good Book, and the UK Crime Book Club. And my gratitude also goes to the countless bloggers out there, many of whom have hosted me during my blog tours. Thank you for being so supportive of authors. You do a fantastic job, working long hours for little—and usually no—payment because you just love reading. You don't always receive the recognition that you deserve.

Much appreciation goes to my Queen of Social Media, Pippa Akram of @Social_Pip, for her invaluable advice on the future of where social media is heading; to Jenny Knott and also author David Kerrigan. His book *Life as a Passenger* is perfect further reading for anyone interested in the future of driverless cars.

And cheers to Mandie Brown, Danielle Graph, Jo Edwards, Rachael Cochlin, and Niamh Lanigan Bonner.

To test yourself and make ethical decisions on what a car should do in the event of a collision, visit the website moralmachine.mit.edu.

Finally, thank you, each and every one of you, for picking up or downloading this book. You will never appreciate how grateful I am to you for allowing me to continue this career.